D0007624

Blind Switch

To receive a free catalog of Poisoned Pen Press titles, please contact us in one of the following ways:

Phone: 1-800-421-3976
Facsimile: 1-480-949-1707
Email: info@poisonedpenpress.com
Website: www.poisonedpenpress.com

Poisoned Pen Press
6962 E. First Ave. Ste. 103
Scottsdale, AZ 85251

Blind Switch

John McEvoy

Poisoned Pen Press

Copyright © 2004 by John McEvoy

First Edition 2004

10 9 8 7 6 5 4 3 2 1

Library of Congress Catalog Card Number: 2004103309

ISBN: 1-59058-095-8 Hardcover

Poisoned Pen Press
6962 E. First Ave., Ste. 103
Scottsdale, AZ 85251
www.poisonedpenpress.com
info@poisonedpenpress.com

This book is for
My wife Judy,
And our children
Julia, Sarah, and Michael,
And our grandchildren
Madelaine, Colin, Cecilia, and Amara

Acknowledgments

For their heartening interest in and various contributions to this book, I owe thanks to Ann Healy, Christopher Martin, Huseyin Sehitoglu, Dr. Lee Atkinson, Carolynn and Bill Sheridan, Lou Ann and Joe Kellman, Dr. Charles Lipman, Donna Lipman, Frier and Tweedie McCollister, Nipper McCollister, Gwen Macsai, Jim Doherty, Sandy Doherty, Neil Yonover, Dan Sroka, Lew Kreinberg, Tally Rosengren, Rhonda Rosengren, Rene Rosengren, Nancy Kreinberg, Ira Kaplan, Jim Dunleavy, Diane Goldin, and the late Lou DiCastri.

Grateful am I, too, for the invaluable insights and advice provided by Barbara Peters and Robert Rosenwald.

Count no glory in beginnings and ends
Count the glory that I have had such friends
—William Butler Yeats

Chapter 1

Jack Doyle became a fixer of horse races shortly after his fortieth birthday when he realized, with a thumping finality, that Life sure as hell did have his Number and was crunching it.

He'd sparred with this realization for several years, using his old AAU middleweight footwork to evade and dazzle while dancing through a succession of hype-laden, mid-level marketing and advertising jobs and two surprisingly, at least to him, dismal marriages.

A free spirit, full of himself and liberal with usually unwanted advice for others, Doyle had suffered an occasional deep cut here, a bad bruise there, but his pound-for-pound world-class ego had always brought him back into the center of the ring, defiant grin in place, ready for another round. Then they caught him with his guard down.

It was an early April morning in Chicago, clear and clean and sunny in the Loop, and Jack had strolled into the office jaunty as ever, issuing greetings to co-workers as he headed for his desk. It was not there.

Ralph Olegaard, Doyle's immediate superior in marketing at Serafin Ltd., stood looking at the vacated space, hands behind his back. Doyle looked around the large room. His was the only desk missing. A look of delight flashed across his face.

"Hey, Swede," Doyle said, "is this the day? They've finally come to their senses and moved me upstairs to the big time?"

Olegaard said, "They've taken your desk away because they say you don't work here anymore. Why didn't you tell me you were going to quit?"

"I didn't quit," Doyle said.

◇◇◇

After saying a hurried goodbye to Olegaard, Doyle had confronted his Serafin Ltd. Team Leader, Rance Coffey, who assured Doyle that there had been no mistake made.

"We're in the process of doing some right-sizing here. And you were among those chosen for termination.

"You just don't fit in here," Coffey had told Doyle. "I've had mucho bad feedback. Your account management record is pretty strong, but you rub a lot of people the wrong way." Coffey looked pained as he ran a hand through hair that appeared to have been slicked back with W2 motor oil.

"Actually," Coffey continued, "Ralph Olegaard likes you." Coffey chuckled as he scanned the personnel file in front of him. "In one of his reports on you, Olegaard wrote, and I quote, 'It could be said of Mr. Doyle what was first said of George Washington—that he was kind to his inferiors, civil to his equals, and insolent to his superiors.'"

Coffey's smile disappeared as he closed the file folder. "What I've seen more than anything from you, Jack, is insolence. I'm not going to put up with it anymore. Olegaard may like you, but I don't. Case closed."

Doyle felt his face flush as he looked directly at Coffey's shifting eyes. He said, "Maybe I'm just tired of doing more spinning than a presidential press spokesman. Maybe I should never have gotten into this bullshit business in the first place," Doyle added as he departed Coffey's office. He had heard this sort of assessment of his work before, although no traces of it ever had appeared on Doyle's sanitized job resumes.

Still in shock later that day, Doyle went to his health club, Fit City, membership in which was paid for by Serafin Ltd. as a corporate perk. Doyle tried to shake off the hurt he felt in the club's boxing room, a place where had worked off the effects of previous disappointments. His blue eyes narrowed and his sandy hair darkened with sweat as he first rattled the speed bag, then rocked the heavy one.

Out of the corner of his eye, Doyle noticed Moe Kellman come through the door. Kellman was a diminutive man in his mid-sixties who affected a white, electrified-looking haircut like Don King and who worked out daily at Fit City with ferocious dedication. To Doyle, he looked like a tough old dandelion.

Doyle and Kellman were often the only two Fit City members to use the boxing room, which was tucked away in a corner of the basement of this temple of cardiovascular modernism, far removed from the space-age equipment areas populated by glistening yuppies.

Doyle liked Moe Kellman—he was among the very few Fit Cityites Doyle could bring himself to talk to on a regular basis—but he ignored Kellman that afternoon. Moe shrugged off the rebuff and launched his workout, occasionally glancing over as Doyle hammered the heavy bag. Moe could hear Doyle muttering, "The bastards…the bastards." Doyle pounded away until he could lift his arms no more.

◇◇◇

Doyle had never before been fired, though he had dodged a few bullets via anticipatory early departure. "Sorry, friends, I've sold enough gas guzzlers, I'm off to the lite beer league," Doyle would announce in his practiced farewell and landing-on-his-feet style. Footwork—he'd always had it, always would…or so he had believed.

But this dismissal from Serafin Ltd. Doyle found to be a crusher. He spent days reviewing his blotchy career, his sorry marriages. His initial foray into matrimony was made with a fellow public relations major at the University of Illinois. Two years of declining ardor and interest preceded Marla's declaration that "I realize now that I fell in love with the *idea* of you. But I wound up marrying *you*. Big mistake." Now, he confronted this question: was he really the "azzhole" he had been judged to be by his second wife, Erma the German?

"Ven vil you VAKE OP?" He could still hear Erma asking that. They had been wed only a few months, but this statuesque au pair he had rescued from domestic service in a Lake Forest mansion was onto his perceived failings in a hurry. Stormy marital months they were. Only Doyle's clever footwork—he had never struck a woman in his life, and wasn't about to start—saved him from a number of late night Final Solutions when the War Bride of the Nineties advanced. Erma was a big girl with a matching appetite for progress, which she equated with eventually being ensconced in a home the likes of which she used to work in. Doyle had no way of getting her there.

"Honey," he would say to Erma, "I'm doing the best I can. Nobody said it would be easy, even in America. If you can't laugh at the script," he once advised her, "the curtain will come down and smother you."

Sometimes Doyle would issue these pronouncements face to face, other times he would grunt them into the heavy bag as he pounded away in the gym, hoping that somehow such fervently issued truisms would zip through space into Erma's suddenly receptive consciousness. He was very fond of Erma. He was also very sure that he was doomed to disappoint her. Erma proved immune to the reality about their lives he was attempting to convey. Doyle concluded that the problem was the language barrier, the one between him and most women he had known.

Their marriage ended when Erma learned that even the promise of parenthood had been denied her by Doyle.

"God gave me a natural vasectomy when I was sixteen," Doyle confessed to Erma one night. "It was called the mumps."

"Vil you adopt?" she inquired tearfully.

"My life is already second-rate," Doyle replied. "I won't add any more second-hand stuff to it, I just can't."

Erma was gone for good the next day.

◇◇◇

Two weeks after his desk and job had been concurrently removed at Serafin Ltd., Doyle finished a workout at Fit City feeling sharp, in form. He had been spending four hours a day in the gym and had pared six pounds off his already trimmed-down physique. Unfortunately, his limited life savings were undergoing similar diminution while the Chicago job market had not yet opened its arms wide to him.

Moe Kellman, his T-shirt sodden with sweat, entered the locker room as Doyle was toweling off following his steam bath and shower. Doyle grinned at the little man. "How many sit-ups today?" Doyle asked Moe.

"In the seven hundreds, kid. It's the garlic powder pills I started. They've turned me around."

Doyle said, "Turned you around? You've been knocking off sit-ups and pull-ups like a machine since I've known you in here."

Moe blushed. "C'mon, lunch is on me," he said. They went to Dino's Ristorante on Chicago's near north side. As usual, the place was jammed, with a long line of hopefuls at the reception desk. The restaurant was a popular one with the city's movers and shakers, and those who ardently desired to join that category. Dino, the owner, quickly spotted Moe, who was slicing his way through the taller crowd like a Munchkin drum major. He was wearing a beautifully cut Italian silk suit, dark beige, with a tan silk shirt under a glistening white tie. Doyle, in his black sport coat, red and white checkered sport shirt, and tan khakis—he'd pushed his business suits to the back of the closet—followed closely in Kellman's wake.

Maybe that's why Moe wears his hair frizzed up like that, Doyle thought, makes him easier to spot.

After Dino, a stocky, swarthy man had bowed, scraped, fluttered and fawned for a couple of minutes, and Moe ordered the garlic soup, to be followed by shrimp-garlic pasta. Doyle didn't feel all that hungry; he opted for an Italian beef sandwich and a Bushmills Manhattan.

"So," Moe said, "you got yourself bumped out of your job, I hear. What've you got in mind for yourself?"

Doyle sat back in his chair. The Bushmills was in there, doing its job. He felt relaxed, expansive. "No more bullshit jobs, I can guarantee you that," he said. "I need to make some nice money. But I'm all through jollying up to assholes worse than me. Like my Grandpa Mike used to say, 'I'd rather curry horses than curry favor.'"

Moe smiled at this, then turned to signal Dino. Waiters charged forward bearing the steaming food. Dino hovered as Moe swirled a forkful of pasta, departing only when Moe had indicated his approval of the dish.

Doyle was irritated by the fact that Dino had made no attempt to check with him about his meal. "I've had better Italian beef at the state fair in Idaho," Doyle said.

The little man shrugged. "The beef here is dreck," he said. "I would've told you that if you'd have asked. But you don't do much of that, do you?" Moe nodded in agreement with himself. He went back to vacuuming up his meal, noodles and beans and shrimp disappearing beneath his neatly trimmed white mustache as if via conduit.

Doyle looked Moe in the eye. "You're right," he admitted.

"I know I am. If you'd just listen—and I know you're smart enough to at least listen—I've got something for you."

"Name it."

Moe said, "I want you to fix a horse race."

This little fucker takes the cake, Doyle thought. "Which one?" he asked.

What Kellman had in mind was a race at Heartland Downs, the big Chicago track, in late June, during the third week of the thoroughbred meeting there. "My people," Moe said, leaning forward over his empty plates, "want to cash a nice bet on a little horse called City Sarah."

"What do you mean, 'my people'?" Doyle asked. "The nation of Israel? Your family?"

Moe shook his head in disgust. "See, that's what I've heard about you. It's your mouth gets you hung out to dry for what, what are you, thirty-eight, forty years? Why don't you shut it and do some business for yourself for a change," he advised, adding, "There's twenty-five grand in it for you."

Doyle was stunned by this offer. He pondered it as he polished off his second Manhattan. No question, he could use the money. And he definitely needed something brand-new to do, having found himself absolutely unable to muster another charge at the corporate barricades. He realized that, surreal as it might seem to him, Kellman's offer was at least the extension of a helping hand, something that Doyle had, over the years, hardened himself to reject. Since late childhood he had created a persona of iron independence so strong that it might well, at this stage of his life, be threatening to crush him.

In the weeks since his firing, Doyle had found his life deteriorating into a succession of anxious days, fretful nights, pain-drenched dawns. He was starting to drink more, and more often, than he should. And he didn't like that about himself. In the past, Doyle had managed to limit what he called his "Celtic dark periods" to no more than a few days of dipping into booze and the most mournful items in his jazz collection. He'd once played Billie Holiday's version of "Good Morning Heartache" for nine hours straight while holed up in a darkened apartment, emerging hung over but cleansed.

Now, influenced by this latest Serafin Ltd.-administered life jolt, Doyle had begun to identify with the hapless creatures on the "Dogs for Adoption" show, a staple of early morning cable television toward which he frequently found himself channel-surfing. Peering blearily at the screen, Doyle had occasionally been poised to dial 1-800-PUPSAVE, but he never did. Most of the canines on offer, Doyle figured, were cute enough now when young, but would probably grow up to bite his nuts off once they got to know him.

Instead of dialing, Doyle would force himself into sleep, where he frequently hosted the same dream: it featured Doyle confiding in a beautiful blond female psychiatrist who busied herself replenishing his cocktail glass while assuring him that his myriad fine qualities were soon to be universally recognized. With the dream's departure, depression would come to Doyle with a *crack* like ice floes separating.

Depression was something Doyle knew about, going back to the year of his brother's death. Owen Doyle, Jack's only sibling, ten years his senior, was the acknowledged star of the family. Big, good-natured, a natural athlete with a natural penchant for charming and pleasing people, Owen had enlisted in the Marines right out of high school, wanting to toughen up for two years before accepting a college football scholarship. Eight-year-old Jack hated to see Owen go, for he idolized his brother. Nineteen months into his enlistment, Owen died in a Camp Pendleton helicopter training accident, and everything changed in the Doyle family.

Jack's insurance salesman father disappeared into drink, his mother into mournful silence. Nothing Jack ever did, no achievement of his, could ever match their memories of the beloved Owen. Jack became convinced his parents would trade him in a second for a return of their eldest son.

Jack found himself hating Owen, and hating himself for doing so. His grades plummeted as his school discipline problems escalated. He felt his parents didn't give a damn what he did. Finally, a high school phy-ed instructor had channeled Jack's aggression into boxing. The sport was his salvation, providing Doyle with a sense of worth even though he never became much more than an average amateur fighter. As a resident of his emotionally damaged home, Jack had been an island unto himself. Enrolled at the university, escaped from that depressing scene where he'd grown up, he felt emancipated. But, as Jack well knew, the residue of Owen's snuffed-out life would always dust his soul.

Doyle looked across the table at Moe, who was drinking espresso and finishing off a half-order of roasted garlic that Dino had slavishly proffered.

"How would you do something like this?" Doyle asked.

Speaking in a soft voice, Moe said that Doyle would go to work for a horse trainer named Angelo Zocchi, a distant relative of the fawning Dino. Doyle would be on the menial shift at Heartland Downs for trainer Zocchi, walking sweaty horses back and forth after they had gone through their morning exercises, and also, with shovel and pitchfork, cleaning up their lower GI products. That would be the start. Further instructions would follow, Moe said, after Doyle's initial efforts were assessed.

"Eventually, if things work out," Kellman said, "you'll pull off the stiffereeno." Seeing the puzzled look on Doyle's face, he added, "Stiff the horse—so it doesn't win."

"Stiffereeno?" said Doyle. "That sounds like something Sinatra's Rat Pack used to call their boners." He shook his head. Then Doyle found himself laughing at this employment scenario.

"Are you kidding me?" he said to Moe. "I've shoveled marketing and sales and advertising shit most of my adult life. Now you want me to work with horse shit? What are you, an ironist?"

Doyle pushed his plate aside. "Why doesn't this Angelo do this himself? Or have one of his regular employees do it? Why bring me in?"

Kellman looked appreciatively at Doyle. "That's an excellent question, Jack. First off, you looked to me like a prime candidate for a number of reasons, one of which is that you're not the kind of guy anybody will walk all over out there at the racetrack. But the main reason is that Angelo Zocchi has held a trainer's license for over thirty years. We don't want to put him in any jeopardy of losing that license. He's got to be distanced from this thing—on the off chance anything might go wrong."

"Ah, the off-chance remote possibility factor," Doyle said. "In other words, you need a fall guy. Just in case this caper collapses."

"If you play this the way I know you can, nothing'll go wrong," Moe said as he rose to leave. "$25,000, Jack, let's not overlook tax free, when the job is done. Think about it. Let me know. I'll see you at the gym."

Doyle watched the dandelion head bounce through a field of phonies clustered near the restaurant's front door. Moe nodded at some of the waiting people, smiled at others, shook a few hands as he neared the door. "Goodbye, Mr. Kellman, goodbye,

Mr. Kellman" members of the wait staff chorused as the little man departed.

"I've got a little buzz on," Doyle said to himself. He sat at the table for a few minutes, thinking about all that Moe had said. He couldn't help but smile at just the thought of the job he'd been offered.

Doyle found himself strangely pleased that Kellman not only thought him capable of carrying off some kind of racetrack scam, but that he'd recognized Doyle's readiness to do something that would be, for him, so completely different.

As much as he was surprised at the offer, the possibilities involved, so was he somehow flattered. "Thanks, Moe," Jack whispered to himself, grinning. "You've got your man."

Summoning Dino, Doyle put a final Bushmills on Moe Kellman's tab. "In for a penny, in for another round," Doyle said to the now unsmiling Dino.

Chapter 2

To Jack Doyle, the racetrack was a revelation. Like most Americans, his knowledge of thoroughbred racing was minimal, gleaned primarily from an occasional office outing in which an afternoon at the races meant losing his ass betting the so-called "expert" tips provided by a punk clerk from accounting.

Working in the stable area at Heartland Downs was an eye-opener. For one thing, Doyle had never before observed in one place more ugly men and healthy-looking women.

Doyle was surprised at how quickly he adapted to his new routine. It involved rising at 4:30, leaving his north side apartment at 5:00, then driving the twenty-five miles in his leased Honda Accord to arrive by 5:30 at the track's secured lot where he parked amidst the vehicles, most of them dice-dangling Chevy beaters, that had transported the other grooms and hotwalkers. These amigos soon decided that Doyle was a dilettante horse owner who reveled in the menial stable tasks because he wanted to maintain a hands-on approach to his investments. Evidently, there were a few such misguided souls who populated America's backstretches in the mornings when they could have been home sitting on their assets. Doyle did not disabuse his co-workers of their inflated notions of his status.

What Doyle discovered that he liked best was the horses, amazingly powerful but for the most part docile creatures; the clear morning air at trackside, filled with the sounds of these beasts pounding through their exercises; the odor of the horse barns, a combination of liniment, horse manure and hay; and, finally, the upfront hustling of people who were trying to win something directly off their fellow horsemen without any bullshit nineteenth hole conniving or three-martini *mea culpa* lunches buffering the combat zone. Every man's hand against that of every man…and the women, too. I love it, Doyle thought.

Doyle's first meeting with his new boss, Angelo Zocchi, took place on a bright Monday morning. It did not go well. The sixty-year-old Zocchi, a weathered piece of work who had been on the racetrack most of his life, hadn't hired a male gringo in years—"they all drink too much back here," Zocchi contended—but the Word Had Come Down.

Zocchi's first words to Doyle, after he had appraised him with a look of disapproval, were: "Don't fuck up."

Doyle grinned. "People pay thousands of dollars to attend seminars and get such advice," he said. "You've got state-of-the-art leadership skills, Angelo."

Angelo produced a laser-beam look. "They'll tell you what to do when the time comes," he said. "I don't deal in this crap except when I'm told to. They don't need this money they try for—it's a power trip for them, from the old days, just a gig. They try to pull one off every two, maybe three years, and they always find some chooch like you to tool it.

"Just do what you're told," Angelo added, "that's all. Then get out."

Doyle was required to obtain a state license before he could begin working as a groom for Zocchi. On the line of the application that inquired about felony convictions, Doyle wrote in "none," while thinking to himself, *so far.*

◇◇◇

Other than Angelo Zocchi, who seemed to regard him with a mixture of fear and contempt, Doyle's fellow workers were an amiable lot, particularly E. D. Morley and Maggie Howard. Morley was a middle-aged ex-boxer from Chicago's West Side whose real name was St. Charles Robinson. A few years back, St.

Charles Robinson had assumed a new identity upon becoming a Rastafarian.

"I dig the hair and the dope, mon," he explained to Doyle, "and I om picking up the accent very nizaleey."

Maggie Howard was a twenty-six-year-old exercise rider from Sallisaw, Okla., a bouncy little item with tousled black hair and gray eyes whom Doyle had heard described—in racing parlance—as "having great hands" and "a wonderful seat on a horse." Doyle didn't know from the hands, but he could enthusiastically endorse the Howard seat. Payday of Week Two, Doyle invited Maggie to have dinner with him after the races.

"No chance," she responded.

"I like directness," Doyle said, "so maybe you can tell me why."

"Because I think you're a phony, and you're up to something back here. You aren't any groom," Maggie snorted.

"I've got the scars and the alimony receipts to prove it," Doyle said. "Two times a groom." Although disappointed at her response, Doyle still had to admire Maggie's smooth-striding retreat down the shedrow. "That was a joke," he called after her. "Think about it—I mean dinner, sometime." Maggie never broke stride.

◇◇◇

Doyle did not miss a day of work. In Week Three, he was instructed by Angelo Zocchi to begin grooming the "target horse." By this time, Doyle had learned a few things about his new occupation: how to sidestep manure, keep alert at all times while avoiding being stepped on by any of these thousand-pound, frequently fey animals he cared for; how to water and feed them, and pick dirt out of their feet; how to brush, comb and rub-rag them to a Simonize glow. Zocchi was a taskmaster; Doyle, as he had been for most of his life, was very good at tasks whose worth he could recognize.

Doyle's Project—named City Sarah—was a four-year-old black filly with a dazzling burst of speed on the racetrack and the disposition of an eager puppy off of it. Although she was a relatively cheap item in Zocchi's well-stocked public stable—a claiming horse, whose genetic composition confined her to competing on the lower end of racing's class scale—City Sarah was the stable pet. City Sarah eagerly nuzzled greetings to anyone who visited her stall, ate jelly doughnuts whenever they were offered, and developed an obvious affection for Doyle, who had never been held in comparable esteem by anything that weighed a half a ton or by anything that weighed considerably less.

At the end of that week, Doyle was summoned by phone for dinner at Dino's with Moe Kellman. Plans were thereupon unfolded. Angelo Zocchi, Moe said as he dipped breadsticks in a specially prepared garlic paste, was to enter City Sarah in two races she could not possibly win. "Put her in over her head twice for thirty-five grand claiming, she'll be nowhere," Moe assured.

Next, the Real Foray into Fraud: Angelo would run City Sarah back down at her true class level, $25,000 claiming, and she would fail once again, this time courtesy of Doyle's work. With this trio of clinkers dotting her dossier, City Sarah would again be entered for $25,000 claiming—and this time she would win.

The odds, Moe said, would be "exactly what my Group is looking for. We'll bet our money, the horse wins, and that's that. Very simple, Jack," Moe said, waving a breadstick for emphasis.

Doyle had to admit he was by no means clear on this. "So what's the big difference between a twenty-five grand horse and a thirty-five grand horse," he began. "I don't get it."

"It's big," Moe assured him. "Look, racing's got kind of a caste system. It's based on ability, and it's defined by numbers. Did you know there's a big, big difference in talent between even five grand and thirty-five hundred dollar horses?"

"No, I didn't," Doyle said. "I'm not sure I understand a lot of this."

"You don't have to. Look," Moe said, reaching into a bowl of garlic-stuffed olives Dino had placed next to the breadsticks, "you know from German Jews and Polish Jews? Lace-curtain Irish and pig-shit Irish? I don't even have to go into this with you, Jack. Just take my word."

I hope it's as strong as your breath, Doyle thought as Moe reached again for the olives; he was palming them like peanuts. "You haven't told me how I do this thing," Doyle pointed out, adding: "Get one thing straight—I won't hurt this horse. I won't give her any dope or something like that."

Moe's dandelion head went from side to side. "You don't have to. Hopping horse went out with spats. The testing labs have gotten too good. They discover the dope, then throw the book at the trainer. We don't want to put Angelo out of business. He's a good horse trainer, and he's straight, but he owes us. Angelo will tell you what to do."

Doyle considered Moe's description of the Plan. "Won't there be guys who pick up on this? Who'll recognize what's going on?" he asked. "Won't they jump in and bet this horse when your guys do?"

Moe dismissed that possibility with a wave of his hand. "Jack, remember this: brains, discipline and patience are the key to the successful bettor. That explains why there are so few of them. Don't worry about the odds we're going to get," Kellman grinned.

◇◇◇

So, they ran City Sarah twice against $35,000 claimers, and she got her ass kicked, just as Moe Kellman had predicted. Doyle found he didn't like this at all.

For the first in City Sarah's series of three races, Doyle stood at the rail, rooting loudly, as the black filly led the field through a fast half-mile before deflating to finish tenth of twelve. As Doyle led her back to the barn, City Sarah was blowing like a bellows.

"Come on, you little mother," Doyle said to City Sarah, patting her neck as they walked down the sandy path, "you ran your eyeballs out, you did your best. God love you."

As Doyle was preparing the feed tub for City Sarah that evening, E. D. Morley sauntered down the shedrow. He looked admiringly at the still exhausted horse. "She's a hard-trying bitch, ain't she?" Morley said.

Ten days later, another field of $35,000 horses showed their backsides to City Sarah. When an irritated Maggie Howard complained to Doyle about Zocchi's misplacement of the horse in her races—"What's he doing with this nice little horse?" Maggie had asked—Doyle could only mumble a vague reply. He felt terrible. He drove from the track to one of the neighborhood bars near his apartment, and into one of those Tom Waits-nights he was so familiar with, packed with mixed emotions and mixed drinks.

When midnight arrived, Doyle realized he had confessed his entire life-plight to an off-duty waitress named Maureen Hoban at O'Keefe's Olde Ale House. Maureen was only eight months or so out of Cork, Ireland, she said, but was apparently already a veritable Margaret Mead of American bar disappointments. Doyle liked her immensely.

Doyle bought numerous rounds for the two of them. He was amazed at a coincidence uncovered in the course of their lugubrious conversation—Maureen knew his co-worker, E. D. Morley!

"Sure, I met that Rustafartian fraud at the racetrack," she giggled. "I go there on my off-days from work. I love your American harses."

As closing time neared at the Ale House, Doyle was sorrowed to discover that Maureen was the first woman he had ever met who, the more he drank, the worse she looked, with the booze flushing makeup out of her pores in rivulets. But Maureen's shrewd reading of his situation regarding the fixed race, Doyle found, had a beauty of its own.

"You're a fookin' fool if ya don' go after that mooney," Maureen advised. Doyle again recited his various reservations, but Maureen banished these with a wave of her arm.

"Wot am I hearin' now?" his counselor from Cork continued. "You're broke down flat, are ya not? Said ya wouldn't go back to them stiff-necked jobs ya used to do, am I right here?

"Acarse, there's the risk somebody'll grass on you, but the kind of mooney ya're talkin' about, well, chance is sure to be built in, is it not?

"Just you forget now about hurtin' that little harse's feelins', or the tiny off chance of gettin' caught out. No," Maureen concluded, "ya should just thank the God ya've turned your back on that the little Jew man wants to pay ya so much for doin' so little."

This, Doyle decided, was just the pep talk he had needed. He was primed with purpose as he lurched to his car, Maureen in tow. No, she didn't want to go home with Doyle, Maureen said, though she appreciated his insincere offer. All she asked in return for her sterling advice of the evening, she said, was to be notified in advance as to the date of City Sarah's "go" race—so that she might herself make a "wee small wager" into this betting coup. Relieved that he would not have to share the rest of the night with Maureen, whose eye shadow appeared to be loosening in sheets, Doyle promised her he would most assuredly let her know the date of the Big One.

◇◇◇

With her second consecutive dismal failure behind her, City Sarah next was entered at her "winnable" level of $25,000. Another lousy effort here—this one to be effected by Doyle—was the second-to-last brush stroke on Moe Kellman's conniving canvas.

Angelo Zocchi called Doyle to the stable office that morning, then locked the door. "This is what you do today, Doyle—you give that filly extra heavy rations of feed, two hours before race time. An hour before, you start giving her all the water she wants. Don't let anybody see you doing this, don't talk to anybody about it."

Angelo sighed as he sat back in the chair behind his battered desk. "That's the whole package," he said.

Doyle was puzzled. It seemed too easy. "So what will all that do?"

Angelo, not looking at Doyle, got up and moved to unlock the office door.

"Back when you was an AAU boxer or whatever the fuck you were, you ever fight on a real full stomach?"

Realization swept over Doyle, carried on a wave of very unpleasant memory. "Yes, I did," Doyle started to respond, but Angelo was already out the door.

Doyle now understood perfectly. He recalled a steamy summer night in the Eagles Club in Rockford, Ill., maybe 1979, his third bout in an AAU tournament.

Doyle had won his first two bouts easily. Having made weight for the next one, a semi-final event that night, Doyle—hungry, dehydrated, and emboldened by his two earlier successes—walked to a bakery near the Eagles Club, where he bought and quickly consumed two quarts of cold milk and a warm cherry pie. Two hours later, a squat Mexican hard case from Chicago's Pilsen neighborhood had buried a left hook slightly below Doyle's navel, causing him to spew a stream of vomit on the ringside timekeeper's head.

Doyle shook his head. "I see."

◇◇◇

Doyle didn't sleep the night prior to what he had begun to think of as The Stiffereeno. Badly in need of someone to talk to about all this, he tried Moe Kellman's haunts; Moe was not to be found. Doyle then called O'Keefe's Olde Ale House, in quest of the sympathetic Maureen, only to be informed that his confidante from Cork had quit her waitress job there. For the life of him, Doyle could not remember where he had taken Maureen when he'd driven her home from O'Keefe's that drunken night.

"I'm not from Immigration," Doyle had emphasized to O'Keefe, but he had failed to pry loose a phone number or address for Maureen. Unnerved, he paced his apartment floor up to the dawn, then headed for Heartland Downs. "Hell with it, I'll just get it done," Doyle said as he drove.

Doyle followed Angelo Zocchi's instructions to the letter that overcast, humid spring day. At noon, he gave City Sarah her ample, non-raceday sized portion of feed. She finished it right up. Doyle then offered more, which was gratefully received.

"You're like a damn beagle, you'd eat yourself to death," Doyle snarled at City Sarah, bitterly regretting that Midlife Bustout had reduced him to talking to horses.

Doyle gave the filly several buckets of water early that afternoon, and she polished off another one right before he put a halter on her prior to leading her over to the paddock for the third race. When he pulled her out of her stall City Sarah appeared more ready for a nap than for a race. She looked at Doyle with as incredulous an expression as horses can manifest.

City Sarah's race that day was at six furlongs for $25,000 claiming fillies and mares. She got beat more than twenty lengths—as the heavy favorite.

The jockey was furious when he brought City Sarah back to be unsaddled in front of the grandstand, from which cascaded a series of heartfelt boos. In a molten mixture of Spanish and English, he cursed City Sarah, cursed Doyle who had shame-facedly gone onto the track to slip a shank on the halter, and he leveled a hard look at Angelo Zocchi. The jockey was Heartland Downs' perennial leading rider, a tough little number named Willie Arroyo, whose will to win was legendary among Chicago racetrackers. Listening to Arroyo's tirade, Doyle was reminded of Genghis Khan, another real short guy who hated to lose.

After dismounting, Arroyo spat on the ground between Angelo Zocchi's feet.

"Theez goddam 'orse *burp-ed*, she burp-ed I tell you, ina gate," Arroyo said angrily. "She cooe 'ardly move!" he continued disgustedly. "Eet was like rideen a goddam water bed, she was *slooshing* in 'er belly so much."

Arroyo kicked at the ground, then looked accusingly up at the silent trainer. "Steef! You steefed theez one, An-Hello."

The jockey slapped his whip against his right boot. With a sudden sweet smile, he looked up at Zocchi.

"Con I ride 'er back next time?" Arroyo asked.

"Mind your mouth," Zocchi growled. "We'll see."

Chapter 3

Saturday, June 16. The Day.

Moe Kellman had phoned Doyle earlier in the week, to touch base and offer congratulations. "You did real nice," Kellman had said. "I'll see you Saturday night at Dino's. Just keep your mouth nice and shut—I know that's hard for you—and your favorite bank teller will be in for a big surprise."

Before hanging up, Moe asked, "Doyle, you going to bet some for yourself? Our action's mainly going down in Vegas. If you want to play some of your twenty-five grand out there just say so, we'll take care of it." Doyle turned down this offer.

That afternoon at Heartland Downs, an hour before City Sarah's race, Doyle—his adrenaline meter on fast-forward—was pacing in front of the horse's stall when E. D. Morley sauntered up. He was accompanied by none other than Doyle's counselor from Cork, the elusive Maureen. E. D. had on his "going to the races" outfit of white shirt, pressed jeans, and white cowboy hat atop his dreadlocks. Maureen, wearing a bright green pants suit, regarded Doyle from behind a pair of oversized sunglasses.

She gave Doyle a big smile, then a hug. "You're lookin' grand," she said, "and so's your little harse. Don't ya tink so, E. D.?" she inquired of her companion. Morley nodded in agreement, a big grin on his broad, black face.

Doyle said to Maureen, "I tried to call you the other night. Couldn't track you down anywhere."

"Ah, well, I've moved on from O'Keefe's," Maureen answered. "I'd tell you where I'm going to be, but sure I just don't know that now. I'm kind of between apportunities, as you lads put it over here."

"Well, speaking of opportunities," Doyle responded in a low voice, "you might risk an Irish punt or two on City Sarah this afternoon."

Maureen lowered her glasses and raised her eyebrows. "After the miserable way the poor ting's been runnin' here lately?"

"She'll run big today," Doyle vowed. Maureen looked at him, smiling broadly. Morley winked at Doyle and clapped him on the back. "Good luck, mon," he said.

Minutes later, when Maggie Howard stopped to chat, City Sarah was full life, poking her head out of the stall to nuzzle Maggie, then bouncing around behind the webbed barrier.

"Hey, she's a different horse today," Maggie said appreciatively. "She's looking good. You know," Maggie added, "I hardly ever bet, but I think I'll put a few bucks on Sarah today." Maggie handed E. D. a $10 bill. "On the nose, okay? Will you take care of that?"

"Aay, Moggie, we do dat," E. D. said with an accent more exaggerated than usual. Turning to leave with Maureen, E. D. gave Doyle another broad wink.

After they'd departed, Maggie said to Doyle, "Ain't you gonna bet on this pretty little horse?"

"Already have," Doyle said.

◇◇◇

En route to Dino's Ristorante that night, the joyous sounds of Angelo Zocchi's work force still resounded in Doyle's ears as he drove through the Chicago streets. `

"She win for FUN, mon...."

"All by herSELF...."

"City Sarah's BACK!" This from Maggie Howard, who was far more pumped by the filly's return to regular form than by the proceeds of her bet.

City Sarah that afternoon had romped by five lengths, paying $18.60 to win for each $2 bet. Utilizing his trademark "victory leap," jockey Willie Arroyo had dismounted from her in the winner's circle as if coming off a trampoline, vaulting upward from the stirrups before landing lightly aside City Sarah.

"Theez filly run like a little train today," Arroyo grinned at Zocchi. "No slooshing in her belly," he added as he patted City Sarah's neck.

"Nice ride," Zocchi said, abruptly dismissing the jockey. Zocchi looked very relieved. Doyle felt that way.

Leading City Sarah to the test barn, where she would have to supply urine that would be examined by the racing laboratory for illegal substances—this happened to the winners of all races and to beaten favorites, too—Doyle tried to estimate what this victory might have meant to the Kellman "family" coffers. Besides winning at 8-1, City Sarah had keyed a trifecta that—thanks to the arrival in second and third place of a couple of longshots—paid nearly $4,000 for each $2 invested. Doyle soon stopped speculating about what gargantuan amounts of money were involved here, well aware that he would never be told what they were.

◇◇◇

As usual, Dino's Ristorante was jammed, but Doyle found Moe sitting alone at his usual six-person table. He was burrowing through a serving of linguini in garlic and clam sauce from a platter wider than his concise shoulders.

"Very nice work, Jack," Moe smiled as Doyle sat down. "Very nice. Have some dinner, and tell me how it went."

Doyle opened his menu, and the envelope was there, containing the $100 bills—two hundred and fifty of them—as he'd specified. "No dinner tonight, Moe, thanks. I'm not hungry anyway. I feel like having a few pops, but I can't stand drinking in the same room as your asshole buddy Dino. We'll get together," Doyle assured Moe. "I'll see you at the gym."

Before turning to leave, Doyle said, "This a one-time deal, Moe. You know that, right?"

Kellman carefully wiped his hands on a napkin before reaching to shake with Doyle. "Understood, kid, understood. Trust me on this," Moe said, and Doyle departed with a fond look over his shoulder back at Moe's white dandelion head. Doyle was confident he could do just that.

◇◇◇

Twenty-five grand in his pocket, but Doyle could not get off on it. Trying to pinpoint how he felt, Doyle thought long and hard before coming up with "soiled...maybe sullied."

Doyle hit three of his favorite haunts on the near north side, buying drinks for friend and stranger alike. But nothing worked to lessen his sense of deflation and the feeling of disappointment in himself, not even his final stop, at Andy's, the near north jazz spot that was one of Doyle's favorite hangouts. "I needed the money," he said to himself, "but goddamn it I should have figured out another way to get it. This just wasn't *right*, this way."

"Part of the problem," Doyle mumbled, "is that you pulled off something few people have, and you can't even brag about it to anybody."

The harder Doyle tried to celebrate, the worse he felt. On a night that Doyle had made more money than his salesman father had ever made in half a year, he headed home just after 10:30. Doyle had a bit of a buzz on from the drinks, and he knew it, so he was extra careful, parking the Accord with precision in the dank lot beneath his four-plus-one apartment building.

They had been waiting, crouched, on the off side of the car that bordered the parking space marked "Doyle." Jack had locked the door and was starting to turn away from the Accord when he heard—much too late—sounds he knew shouldn't arise.

They were very good. Doyle couldn't even fully pivot before he felt a knee jam into his lower back and a powerful arm encircle his neck, felt the arm then jerk his chin up and back so quick and hard he thought his eyeballs were going to exit the rear of his head.

Quiet instructions were being issued as Doyle struggled. He heard a mixture of them, urgently whispered: "Keep him like that...Not a sound, now...Up with his sleeve..."And when the needle hit midway up his extended right arm, Doyle realized that they were not going to kill him, realized what this was all fucking about. His body already in the sway of whatever they'd shot him up with, Doyle fought to keep awake and alert. This, too, was a losing battle.

Last Doyle felt, the envelope with the twenty-five thousand was being extracted from his jacket and his assailants were gently positioning him, like a salmon on a bed of slivered ice, across the backseat of the Accord.

Last Doyle heard as they slipped away were the little sounds of rubber soles across the concrete garage floor and what, in his narcotic-driven slippage, he bitterly discerned to be voices, one a man's, the other a woman's, in the respective singular accents of...*Kingston*, was it? And...*Cork*?

Chapter 4

The two men parked the car nearly a mile from the southern border of Willowdale Farm, Harvey Rexroth's Kentucky showplace. The trip to the back gate that led to the stallion barn took them less than twelve minutes, even in the dark. They trotted quickly, with purpose, without speaking. They quickly climbed over the white slatted gate and went forward, one on each side of the graveled path, moving silently through the damp grass.

Each man was dressed completely in black, each wore a black nylon mask. The shorter of the two led the way, moving confidently, as if he were very familiar with the site.

Once they had reached the complex that housed Rexroth's stud horses, the most valuable animals on the property, the shorter man motioned to the left and they angled that way. He then gave a signal to stop. The taller man moved alongside. For a few moments they crouched in silence. The only sound was a slight breeze from the west that moved gently through the rhododendron bushes that outlined the stallion barn's walking ring. There was no sign of any night watchman. No surprise there, thought the shorter man, they're right where they should be—nowhere close to here.

After slipping silently through the door of the two-story brick building, they walked softly down the broad middle aisle separating the stallions' stalls. Their stealthy movements on the rubber-padded barn floor did not go unnoticed. The horses were immediately aware of them, aware that strangers had arrived. Some of the horses shifted their feet in their stalls, uneasy about the presence of these visitors at this unusual hour. Two horses poked their noses against the tall metal screens that served as stall doorways.

After he'd counted down the row on the right, the short man whispered, "It's that one." He pointed to the second stall from the far end of the row. They crept toward it, trying not to further arouse the horses' curiosity. "I'll take his head," said the smaller man, "you slip in there." He carefully opened the stall door. "Wait till I get a good hold of him," he hissed.

The small man held the palm of his left hand forward as he reached for the horse's halter. In his hand were peppermint candies. "C'mon babe," he invited, "c'mon babe." The horse, a nine-year-old bay named Uncle Francis, responded suspiciously to this invitation from this stranger, backing away and tossing his head. But as the shorter man kept talking softly, persuasively, soon Uncle Francis moved his nose forward to the man's palm and snuffled up the candies with his lips. Like most horses, he liked peppermints.

"*Git* to it," the short man said sharply to his companion. He continued to feed the horse peppermints, taking a stronger grip on the halter with his free hand. His companion slid along the wall to the rear of the stall. He turned on the hooded flashlight he'd carried from the car.

Poised behind the horse's left rear leg, the taller man raised his right arm high. In his hand was an iron crowbar. With a sudden, devastating motion he brought the crowbar down as hard as he could against the leg of the unsuspecting horse. Under the impact of the powerful blow Uncle Francis' cannon bone cracked like an icy tree branch in winter. The horse screamed in agony as he crashed to the floor of the stall.

Uncle Francis continued to make terrible sounds as he thrashed in the straw bedding, trying to fight his way to his feet. The taller man adeptly dodged the horse's massive body as he moved to the stall door. Uncle Francis somehow got himself upright, lurching on his three good legs as the other dangled like a broken hinge.

The shorter man quickly closed the stall door. The piteous sounds of the stricken horse reverberated throughout in the dark barn; the other stallions, very aware of the terror in their midst, had begun a crescendo of neighing that counterpointed Uncle Francis' cries of pain.

It would not take long for others on Willowdale Farm to become aware of this event. Lights were already being turned on in the farm manager's residence, some three hundred yards up the gravel lane, when the two black-garbed figures trotted briskly in the opposite direction, their grisly mission accomplished.

Two days later, the Saturday edition of Harvey Rexroth's daily newspaper *Horse Racing Journal* carried a front-page story describing the "tragic" death of Uncle Francis, a multiple stakes winner and "promising" stallion who had, for some freak reason, in the middle of the night, apparently lashed out with his left rear leg and kicked the back of his stall so powerfully that his cannon bone shattered.

"There was nothing that could be done to save the horse," owner Rexroth was quoted as saying. "We summoned the best veterinarians around, and they agreed that this gallant runner would have to be put down for humane reasons. This is a tremendous loss to Willowdale, and to the racing and breeding industry, for we were convinced Uncle Francis would sire a succession of youngsters as talented as he was."

Knowledgeable breeding experts responded with skepticism to this claim, for Uncle Francis—following his excellent racing career—had proved to be a disappointment as a sire. Once they'd hit the racetrack and failed to impress, the market value of his young horses had plummeted, as had that of Uncle Francis. He wasn't unique in this sense, for not every good racehorse makes a good sire. But he was evidently unique in paying such a severely painful price for his progenitive inadequacies. Insured for $8,000,000, he was worth far more dead than alive. None of this was mentioned in the *Journal* story.

Reading the story while lying on his motel bed late that Saturday night, on the outskirts of a town one hundred ten miles from Willowdale Farm, the shorter man of the midnight duo cackled with delight.

"This sumbitch Rexroth is crookeder that we'd ever think to be, man," he said appreciatively. He was talking to his partner and roommate. But Jud Repke was asleep and did not hear the words of Ronald Mortvedt.

Chapter 5

Doyle awoke in a mental haze. After battling his way toward consciousness, he realized he was on the old brown couch in the small living room of his furnished apartment. Vaguely, very mistily, he recalled awakening in the backseat of his car in the apartment building's garage, pulling himself up the short flight of stairs to the elevator, later fumbling for long minutes with his front door lock.

As he struggled to recall the happenings of the night before, Doyle was aware of some pounding noises as he looked up at the crack in his ceiling, a fissure in the plaster that meandered like the Mississippi. Some of those sounds, he knew, were reverberating in his head, after-effects of the powerful sedative that had been so rudely administered the night before. Then, he realized, there were other sounds as well, evidently emanating from the other side of his front door. Doyle struggled to his feet, temporarily losing his balance as he did so, then staggered toward the source of the noise.

"Rock fucking bottom," he said to himself, "that's what I've hit."

When he unchained the door, that assessment was immediately confirmed. On the threshold, badges displayed in raised wallets, stood a dark-complexioned man of medium height and a tall, brown-haired woman. The man, whose black hair came to a widow's peak, wore a navy blue blazer, gray slacks, white shirt under a dark red tie. "Mr. Doyle," he said, "my name is Damon Tirabassi. I'm an agent of the Federal Bureau of Investigation. So is Ms. Engel, Karen Engel," he said, nodding to the woman. She, too, had on a navy blue blazer. Her skirt was gray and her white blouse buttoned at the throat. Agent Engel's green eyes appeared to reflect bemusement, if not sympathy, for Doyle's obviously painful condition. She was as pretty as her partner was serious, Doyle noted.

"What time is it?" Doyle blearily managed. "And what do you want?"

"Eleven o'clock of the morning after," Tirabassi answered, adding, "the morning after the night of your race-fixing payoff."

Doyle took a grip on the door. "What the hell are you talking about?" he said, struggling to reconstruct his recent hours. Then it all came back to him like a cascade of mountain water: the footsteps in the garage, the arm around his neck and needle in his arm, the whispered sounds that he was absolutely sure he knew too well.

Maureen and E. D., those dirty bastards, Doyle thought. Heat rushed to his face as a tide of embarrassment swept over him. Goddam, they'd played him for a world-class sap. And what had he fallen into with these FBI agents? He shook his head, attempting to rattle some sensible thoughts into place. Then he motioned the two of them inside and closed the door.

"Mr. Doyle, how about a cup of coffee?" Karen asked, a hint of kindness in her low voice. "Then we can sit down and discuss your situation."

"Why not?" Doyle replied, wondering what kind of situation this might be. Rock fucking *below* bottom, maybe. He thought about calling a lawyer. The problem was, the only lawyer he had ever employed was Dave Rutchik, who had represented him in his two divorce proceedings. Doyle got skinned both times, and after his parting from Erma had fired Rutchik, telling him "I'd rather be represented by a junior bail bondsman than another night school lawyer like you." Doyle dismissed any thought of legal advice for the time being.

The three of them went into the tiny kitchen of Doyle's three-room furnished apartment, decorated in a theme of contemporary haphazard. The apartment had a small bedroom; a living room that contained the couch, armchair, bookshelves, and a desk that fronted the north-facing windows; and the kitchen, whose stove was spotless from not having been used except for boiling water since Doyle had taken up residence. Also unchanged was the large poster of Thelonius Monk left behind by the previous tenant, a local jazz pianist currently working out of town. Doyle was an avid jazz fan, and he also liked the expression on Monk's slyly knowing face.

Tirabassi and Engel sat at the small table as Doyle boiled water, then filled cups with instant coffee. Even this small effort seemed to exhaust him; whatever E. D. and Maureen had doped him up with, its residual effects were strong. Doyle needed a day on the couch, then a night at the gym, maybe including a stint in the sauna, to work all this out of his system.

The agents broke their silence as Karen asked, "Do you have any cream? Or milk?"

Doyle started to rise, but she moved before him to the refrigerator. After peering inside, she said, "Are you culturing specimens for a laboratory?" Doyle remembered the several carryout items he had intended to either reheat or remove, items that continued to lurk on his refrigerator shelves.

"The milk is toward the back," Doyle said. "I don't take it with coffee. I hardly ever use milk," he added weakly. Karen sniffed at the quart carton. "No kidding," she said. "You should throw this out." Without waiting for a reply, she did so.

Doyle put his elbows on the table, resting his head in his hands. Then he said, "When you're all done critiquing my housekeeping, could one of you maybe get around to where you tell me what business you think you have with me?"

Though his head was still pounding, the coffee was working to help clear Doyle's mind. He began to further size up his uninvited visitors.

Tirabassi appeared to be close to Doyle's age and was of similar medium build. His forehead was furrowed with worry lines. He reminded Doyle of Father DiCastri, the assistant pastor at the parish of his boyhood, a man so laden with concern for his fellow man that his rare smiles were widely reported by parishioners whenever they appeared.

The woman, Karen, was another, decidedly different story, in Doyle's grudgingly admiring estimation. With her tall, athletic figure, attractively wide-set eyes, and open expression—one that suggested she was not going to be as quick to judge Jack Doyle as was her partner—Karen sat in pleasant contrast to Tirabassi, who impatiently tapped two fingers of his right hand on the table as he coldly regarded his host.

The woman was the first to speak.

"We're here, Mr. Doyle, as a result of information we received suggesting your involvement in a fixed horse race." She paused, allowing time for that to sink in.

Doyle felt his heart skitter briefly into overdrive, but he looked at Karen without changing expression. He said nothing.

Tirabassi said, "The race in question was at Heartland Downs. It was a race won by a horse you used to work with when you were in the employ of a trainer named Angelo Zocchi."

Doyle cleared his throat. "Yes, I worked for Zocchi. Then I quit working for Zocchi. So what? And what 'fix' are you talking about?"

Tirabassi shrugged. "Maybe 'fix' is overstating it," he said. He leaned toward Doyle, frowning, the intensity of his expression nearly bringing together in a horizontal line Tirabassi's thick, black eyebrows. "But maybe not," he said. "Something went on with that race, something kinky." He shook his head disapprovingly. "And you were part of it, Mr. Doyle."

Doyle said, "Something kinky? What the hell does that mean? I think you're blowing smoke," he added, looking at Karen.

Said Tirabassi, "Let me spell it out for you. The Bureau was alerted to this situation by an extremely reliable source, a man named Scotty Roxborough. He's a bigtime linemaker in Las

Vegas. Roxy sometimes helps us out with information, and sometimes we help him out. He informed us that there was an unusual amount of action on that race at Heartland Downs, most of it going down on that horse you groomed, City Sarah. Roxy said race books all over Vegas were hit with money on that horse."

Tirabassi reached into his suitcoat and extracted a notebook. He began to read from it. "According to Roxy—and this is a guy who knows—the win payoff was suspicious in itself. The horse was listed in the track program and the *Racing Journal* at odds of twenty to one. But she went off at only eight to one. Even more suspicious was the number of bets using the horse in what Roxy called the 'gimmicks'—exactas or trifectas. Roxy said there hadn't been a race like this for several years, since a trifecta race at Gateway Meadows. That one eventually led to the conviction and imprisonment of half a dozen participants."

Karen cut in. "Horse racing, Mr. Doyle, is one of the most closely monitored businesses in the country—both by its own operators and regulators and, in some cases, with help from people like Roxborough. For the most part, the sort of massive attention it gets works well to keep racing clean. As you may know," she smiled, "there's more fraud in banking than horse racing."

"The racing people," Tirabassi interjected, "want to insure that the sport is on the up and up in order to maintain the public's confidence. And the Vegas people want it to be that way so that they don't get taken by crooks putting something over on them. They react very unkindly to that. They watch horse race betting as carefully as they keep track of the off-the-field associations of NFL quarterbacks. And NBA referees, for that matter."

Doyle shifted in his chair, but remained silent. The pounding in his head had settled into a low, steady *thrum*, punctuated by an occasional sharp flash of pain, as if Mongo Santamaria were at work in there. Even the pleasant sound of Karen Engel's voice failed to offset this rhythmic discomfort. He thought, fleetingly but bitterly, of Maureen and E. D.

"We were alerted to all this by the agent in our Chicago office who maintains contact with Roxborough," Karen said. "He checked with his local sources, who confirmed that there was something out of line about that race. The same agent spotted you while reviewing routine surveillance tapes of a man named Moe Kellman. We knew who he was. The restaurant owner, Dino, told us who you were."

"What's 'routine' about a surveillance tape?" Doyle snapped.

Karen ignored the question. "Moe Kellman, as I'm sure you are aware, is one of the Chicago Outfit's major money movers. We know that, even though we've never been able to build a case against him. Kellman oversees the operation of many of the Outfit's legitimate businesses, ones that have been started with money he helped to launder years ago...."

Doyle pondered this information, which was brand-new to him. He'd suspected that Kellman's background was not exactly pristine—after all, the talk of "my people" between a couple of such men of the world as themselves suggested otherwise.

But, Doyle knew, Chicago was full of phonies claiming to be "connected" to the Outfit, or "clouted up" at City Hall, or in the police department; Doyle had met, and seen through, a number of them. He realized now that Kellman's subtle hints over the course of their conversations were, unfortunately for Doyle, the real thing; that the little man actually stood tall in the local criminal hierarchy. This knowledge made Doyle's headache worsen.

"I know Kellman," Doyle admitted. "We work out at the same gym. But so what? There's undoubtedly all kinds of other twisted citizens there morning and night. Keep in mind, the membership roster is heavy with lawyers and securities traders."

Doyle began attempting to retrieve pieces of the conversations he'd had with Kellman over Dino's dining tables. When some of these pieces came back to him, especially discussions of City Sarah's racing schedule, Doyle felt a wave of unease. To his immense relief, he heard Tirabassi say, "We don't have any audio tapes of you and Kellman, or Kellman and any other of his interesting dining companions, for that matter. That's an Outfit hangout, and Dino's is checked for bugs daily by one of their best security men."

Doyle struggled not to grin at this revelation. "So, why are you hassling me?" he said to Tirabassi. He was beginning to feel better on all fronts.

Karen immediately deflated him.

"We've tied you to Kellman," she said, "and we've established that you worked for Zocchi. Not only that, but that you worked on the horse in question, this City Sarah. And we know you left Mr. Zocchi's employment shortly after that race.

"We've been to the track and checked with Zocchi about you. He described you, I'm quoting, as an 'uncooperative' individual whom he was 'not at all sorry to see go.'"

Fuck you too, Zocchi, Doyle thought.

"Did you ask Zocchi about this so-called fix?" Doyle said.

"We interviewed all of the stable personnel," Tirabassi replied. "All but you, that is, since you'd so abruptly quit. Probably with the money you'd made from setting this thing up."

Doyle winced at that statement. To Tirabassi he said, "All you've unloaded on me here seems to add up to a bunch of nothing. You may not know it, but I used to make my living in advertising and sales. I've got a built-in bullshit detector, developed during those days, and it's pulsating…it's *humming*, the more I listen to you two.

"If you had anything solid on me, we wouldn't be having this cozy little coffee klatsch. You'd have served me a warrant at the door and hauled my ass downtown." He got to his feet and stretched his arms expansively, trying to look nonchalant.

The agents exchanged glances. Then Tirabassi said to Doyle, "We've got a Mexican illegal, a busboy from Dino's, who is facing deportation charges. Bye bye Chico, you know what I mean? He's very willing to testify that he overheard parts of a conversation in which you and Kellman talked about a fixed horse race."

Doyle snorted. "For Chrissakes, come back to the real world, man. Dino doesn't keep a busboy down there who knows more than ten words of English. If he did, they might hit up Dino for a huge raise to get them in range of the minimum wage. No, I can't imagine your deportee as some kind of star witness in court.

"I think you two are blue-skying here, as we used to say over at…well, my former place of business."

"Mr. Doyle," Karen responded, "please sit down a minute and consider a few things. One, we can cite you as a 'known associate' of Moe Kellman, and we've got a file on him that's thicker than the Chicago phone book, even though he's never been convicted of anything. Plus, we can tie you to the scene of the reported fixed race. You worked with that horse, you can't deny it.

"Now, these things might not add up to a conviction in your case," she conceded. "But they certainly add up to a package of damning information we could dump on the desk of any legitimate employer you might seek to find work with in the future.

"This is not the kind of background information that'll lead you to a corner office anywhere. Think about it."

"Well, well," said Doyle, "and here I was under the impression that all those old J. Edgar Hoover techniques of threat and implication were things of the past. I thought I'd been hearing all about the 'New FBI.' You're shaking my faith in federal law enforcement.

"I don't get it," Doyle continued, genuinely puzzled. "You tell me all this stuff about a fixed race, involving me, you say, but you admit you don't have a case against me. Still, you make threats about messing me up with future employers. What's the deal here, folks? Out of the immense citizenry of this great nation, why has your little corner of the Federal Bureau of Investigation selected Jack Doyle's life to play with?"

Karen looked over at her partner, who nodded for her to continue.

"Actually, Jack, there's something you could do for us. Something that would serve to wipe your slate clean with us."

Doyle said angrily, "Whatever you're talking about, it's got blackmail written all over it. I know very well how personnel managers react to visits from people like you."

"Let's start thinking of this more as an invitation to cooperate," Karen smiled, "an opportunity to 'give something back,' as the professional athletes say. You put one over in one area of the horse business. Maybe we can't prove it, but you did it. You know it, and we know it. It was unworthy of you, Jack. This is a chance for you to make up for it.

"Just listen to what we have to say. It won't take long. It's not distasteful, or dangerous, but it might actually prove satisfying to a risk-taker like you. And it's in your best interests," Karen added.

"You're serious about this, aren't you?" Doyle said in amazement. "What the hell could I do for the FBI?"

Tirabassi broke his silence. "You ever hear of a man named Harvey Rexroth?"

Chapter 6

Twenty minutes later, Doyle and the two FBI agents sat in a well-worn, high-backed red booth at the rear of Petros' Restaurant, two blocks from Doyle's apartment.

When it appeared that his conversation with Engel and Tirabassi was going to go on for some time, Doyle told them, "Look, this is all very interesting. But I'm not exactly at the top of my game this morning. I need some breakfast."

"I assume you mean 'Not here,'" Karen said, grimacing in the direction of Doyle's refrigerator.

"The only time I eat in is when I have carry out," Doyle said. "Let's go down the street."

Petros' was one of the thousands of Greek-owned restaurants in Chicago, the vast majority of them featuring reasonable prices, decent food, and moderate pretensions. Petros, Doyle informed the agents as they walked south on Clark Street, was a bald-headed import from Mikos who was convinced he looked exactly like the old television detective Kojak, portrayed by Telly Savalas, and loved to be referred to by the actor's first name.

As they entered and walked toward the back booth, Doyle gave his usual greeting to Petros, who was seated at a table with clear sight lines to the cash register and its buxom female operator. "Hello, Smelly—no, Telly," Doyle called out. Petros scowled. "Go sit down, Jeck, I'll tell Gus to start up burning your eggs."

Karen ordered a muffin, Tirabassi just coffee. "Give me the full load, Elaine," Doyle said to the waitress. When it arrived, that proved to be scrambled eggs, hash browns, sausages, and three slices of buttered toast.

Karen shook her head. "Cholesterol concerns aren't exactly on your front page, are they?"

Doyle grinned. "Not a factor, my dear. I come from a long line of Micks that thrived on bacon and eggs until they died in ripe old age. My cholesterol count is almost in a dead heat with my weight, one-sixty. When we'd take our annual physicals at Serafin Ltd., my doctor used to turn pale with envy every time he reported this to me. He'd throw the test results down on his desk and spit out the information."

Tirabassi finished his first cup of coffee. "Do you think we could get back to the matter at hand, Doyle? Or are you going start bragging about your triglyceride count?"

The matter at hand, and particularly the subject of Harvey Rexroth, was not one he was "tremendously familiar with," Doyle admitted. "I know who Rexroth is, some kind of media mogul. He's mentioned in the papers every once in awhile, or there'll be his photo at some fund raiser. Homely-looking sucker, as I recall. But," Doyle asked as he finished his third piece of toast, "where does he come into this picture of yours that's got me in it?"

Over the next hour, interrupted only by the periodic appearances of Elaine the waitress with coffee refills, the two agents combined to provide a summarized oral biography of Harvey Theodore Rexroth, age forty-four, owner of palatial homes in Kentucky, Florida, and Montana and a $12 million condo in New York City where his business was headquartered.

◇◇◇

Harvey Rexroth descended from a family of wealthy Montana ranchers, their presence in the Treasure State tracing back to the turn of the century. Harvey's great-grandfather, Horace, maintained two hundred thousand sheep on thousands of cheaply acquired acres. Horace for years was known in the West as the Mogul of Mutton.

His eldest grandson, Harold, was the first to branch out into business beyond the borders of the wide-open ranges. Sent east for schooling, he was graduated from Harvard, then its Business School, and soon began to diversify his family's holdings, acquiring newspapers all over the West and Southwest. Later, following the Reagan Administration's deregulation of the communications industry, he began adding radio and television stations to the huge media company that became known as RexCom.

Harold was recognized one of the most belligerent, avaricious, and successful figures in that sector of American commerce, "which is saying something," as Karen pointed out. He was hated by his rivals and despised by many of his employees, which was no surprise, since Harold was as niggardly and notional as most of his fellow media barons. Rexroth's workers were for the most part underpaid, yet expected to perform Herculean tasks at an accelerated pace. Harold Rexroth was well known in journalistic circles for his oft-repeated pronouncement that "editors are a dime a dozen, and reporters come cheaper." He was a very popular speaker at national newspaper publisher conventions.

Harold Rexroth choked to death on a piece of lamb chop nine years earlier. This had happened when he was having dinner in a New York restaurant with four RexCom executives, none of whom, they claimed later, was familiar with the Heimlich Maneuver.

Harold's son Harvey Rexroth inherited control of RexCom, whose other family-member minority shareholders he treated like steerage passengers on his great ship of commerce. He was as penurious, conceited, and arrogant "as his daddy," Tirabassi said, "but there is one big difference between Harvey and Harold—Harvey is as twisted as they come. His old man may have been a tyrant and a tightwad, but he was no crookeder than his competitors. You can't say that about Harvey."

"Other than being rich and famous, what crime has Harvey committed?" Doyle asked.

"That's where you come into the picture, Doyle," Tirabassi replied. "Rexroth is involved in thoroughbred racing and breeding in a number of ways. You've had some exposure to the racing part of it. Exposure of a criminal nature," the agent added accusingly. "But before we get to your role, you need to hear some additional background." He nodded to Karen.

"RexCom for the most part is a thriving company," she began. "Harvey, despite his numerous quirks, has been a very able businessman, following in his father's footsteps—with one very major exception.

"About ten years ago, Harvey entered thoroughbred racing as a partner with some of his RexCom executives in a couple of horses. The partnership did well. One of the horses ran in the Kentucky Derby, to which Rexroth reacted in characteristic fashion. He was so excited about the horse's future after it ran second in the Derby that he forced his partners to sell out their interests to him. Since these men worked for him, that was pretty easy to accomplish. Then he changed trainers and began buying horses by the carload. He spent millions to acquire a beautiful breeding farm near Lexington, Kentucky. In other words, he jumped into racing with both hands and a wide-open wallet. There were plenty of Kentuckians eager to welcome Harvey and his money.

"Harvey's racing stable did okay," Karen continued. "Nothing fantastic, no more Derby starters at least to date, but he had a few stakes winners. He also had a number of trainers. He is a very impatient man, and if the horses didn't perform to his expectations, no matter how unrealistic they were, he usually fired the trainer. But he always paid these men well, so he never had trouble finding a successor for any of them. He was far more liberal in his payroll practices regarding racing than in any of his other businesses.

"Four years ago, a newspaper called *Racing Daily* ran a long story detailing what it termed Harvey's revolving door policy regarding trainers." Karen paused to smile at Elaine, who reached across the table to freshen their coffee. "To say that Harvey took offense at this story is putting it very, very mildly. He was enraged. He threatened a lawsuit, until his attorneys pointed out the folly of that. He made angry phone calls to a man named Walter Sandler, whose family had owned *Racing Daily* for over fifty years. Rexroth never received the satisfaction he was seeking.

"It was at that point that Rexroth made what was probably the first serious business error of his career. He was so angry at the *Racing Daily* for the story that he decided to strike back by going into competition with it. He decided to launch his own national racing paper.

"Rexroth spared no expense. He hired away some of the *Racing Daily's* people, brought in big-time talent from other publications. He called his paper *Horse Racing Journal*. By virtue of spending money faster than his horses were running, he got this project off the ground in less than six months. He made all kinds of public pronouncements about how his new product would dominate.

"The problem was that Rexroth let his desire for revenge cloud his business judgment very badly. He completely misread the situation regarding horse racing and its need for daily publications. The old paper, the *Racing Daily*, was already tottering. Its circulation was way, way down from previous years. Horse racing itself was staggering. In contrast to years past, when racing was the only legal means of gambling all over the country, things had changed tremendously. States had developed lotteries, they had casinos, and there was a whole younger generation that had very little interest in racing. As a result, the *Racing Daily* was already on the downward slide."

Karen paused to thank Elaine for refilling her coffee cup. Tirabassi shifted impatiently before Karen continued.

"When Rexroth came in with *Horse Racing Journal*, which was pretty widely recognized as a good product," she said, "he believed he'd blow Walter Sandler's paper off the map. He undoubtedly knew that the shrinking market couldn't support two such papers, and he was very confident that his glittering, new, highly promoted publication would take over the market that was left.

"Rexroth was wrong. What he had failed to take into account was the extraordinary loyalty of the *Racing Daily's* aging fan base. There were thousands fewer of them than in the earlier glory days of racing, but they had read *Racing Daily* all of their horse-playing lives, and most of them decided to stick with what they knew.

"Rexroth was stunned by this negative reaction to his pride and joy. He remained in denial for almost a year. He continued to pour money into his new paper, but it didn't work. He couldn't pry away enough readership from Sandler's paper to make even distantly future profits a possibility. Rexroth soon imposed all kinds of editorial changes, ordered huge cutbacks in staffing, slashed expenses and overtime, but without really improving his bottom line. After an early show of interest, maybe because of the novelty of the paper, readership leveled off. And it was at a level that cost him a bundle. Rexroth is a very stubborn man. He took a huge financial hit.

"But that wasn't what bothered him—the bulk of the Rexroth fortune remained intact. No, apparently what really affected Rexroth was the embarrassment he had suffered in this failed venture. He pretty much retreated from public life, spending most of his time on his farm in Kentucky. He'd only occasionally visit the racetrack to see his horses compete. The disastrous experience with *Horse Racing Journal* left a big scar on his monumental ego, a scar that hasn't healed."

Doyle said, "Okay, I get the picture regarding Rexroth and his financial flop. But so what? He lost a ton of money. What's illegal about that? Where does the FBI—and me, for that matter—come into the picture?"

Tirabassi said, "Doyle, sit back and hear us out. We're getting to the part that has to do with you. In fact, Karen, let me take it from here, okay?" She nodded her assent.

"A couple of years ago," Damon said, "the Bureau—along with several other agencies, I might add—succeeded in cracking a small ring of horse killers. There were six of them, most from the Northeast. What they did was accept contracts on horses from the owners of those horses, if you can believe that. This ring—these people—all were figures in the world of show horses. You know, the equestrian shows. This is kind of a society sport, and it's expensive to be in, but most of the people have money. As it turned out, some didn't have as much as they thought they needed. That's why they hired these killers."

Doyle held up his hand to stop Damon. "Hold on a second. You mean to tell me that people who own horses, and presumably like them, would cold-heartedly have them killed anyway? That's kind of a stretch for me, pal. I've been around the racetrack, remember. I've seen how those animals are cared for and treated—very, very well, is how. What you're describing is hard for me to picture."

"Jack," said Karen, "take our word for it. It's true. In fact, the only way that we finally cracked this ring was when we got a tip on one of its members and turned him with a promise of immunity. He testified about who was working with him, and who they were working for. The list of their employers included some of the biggest names in the show horse world. This was a sensational case."

"Yeah, I remember seeing something about it in the paper," Doyle said. "But refresh my memory—what was the motive for these people to kill their own horses?"

Damon responded, "It was a way for them to recoup their investments. Say a guy has paid a hundred grand for a top hunter/jumper prospect. He has the horse a couple of years, and it turns out to be a loser. Can't win ribbons at any of the major shows, can't win much prize money at the minors. He's got this horse insured for at least a hundred grand, the price he paid, but it turns out he couldn't sell it for more than twenty-five thousand. Rather than eat this loss, he calls in the horse killers. The horse suffers an 'accidental death,' one that is hard to discern—many veterinarians were fooled by the methods used and thought the deaths resulted from natural causes. Or the vets and insurance examiners thought the accident looked strange, but couldn't prove it. In a few cases, a veterinarian was a willing accomplice of the horse killers.

"These guys were very discreet, very clever, very good. It's quite possible that they'd still be operating if there hadn't been a classic 'falling out among thieves' that led to the tip that led to their arrests and convictions. When those cases were finished, believe me, all the agents involved breathed a sigh of relief. Case closed, everybody thought.

"But," Damon said, "it wasn't over. These show horse guys were finished, all right. But they were succeeded by crooks working the thoroughbred side of it, primarily involving thoroughbred breeding stock, stallions and mares. There's huge money involved here, far more than at the show horse level.

"It started in Louisiana, one case three years ago, two the next year. All involved deaths that looked kinky to the insurance investigators, but they had to pay off. These were not major horses, by the way. The best one was insured for two hundred thousand, the others for quite a bit less.

"Then, about eighteen months ago, deaths of this sort began to occur at a major Kentucky farm. It's called Willowdale, and it's owned by Harvey Rexroth."

Doyle looked at the agents with disbelief. "Don't try to tell me that this Rexroth, the guy who inherited a gazillion bucks, is knocking off his own horses for profit? What the hell would his motive be for that?"

"I think you'd have to know Rexroth to understand this," Karen replied. "From the time he was a juvenile delinquent saved from jail by his family's influence, up to this very day, he has continually flaunted the law. He was the kind of kid—we know this from doing deep background on him, back in his hometown—who blew up cats and set fire to dogs. Pulling the wings off flies was too tame for this weirdo. When they packed him off to prep school in the East, he was twice almost expelled for cheating on tests. And for no reason, really. He's got an IQ of one hundred and seventy-five. But he wants to do things *his* way.

"When he was in his last year of prep school, he and two other miscreants were believed to have bullied a freshman fraternity pledge into accepting a dare that led to his death. It involved alcohol, and this poor kid drank nearly a fifth of vodka at the urging of Rexroth and his pals. The kid died. Rexroth was reprimanded—there was no proof he was directly responsible—and that was the end of that.

"In his business life, Rexroth has been similarly bullying and overbearing and cruel—all from behind the protective wall of his big money. We're sure he bought off witnesses in at least one death he caused when driving while drunk. This is a bad, bad man, Jack. He should be wearing a scarlet A on his chest for amoral. And the sad part is that he's gotten away with every rotten, illegal, or near-illegal thing he's ever tried."

"But I still don't get why he'd kill his own horses."

Damon nodded. "It's true he doesn't have do it for the money. But the money, by the way, isn't exactly chump change. One of the Rexroth stallions that died was insured for seven million. He collected. There was another for nearly two million. So we're talking major money.

"Who knows the motives of a man like this? But he's probably doing it for two reasons. He's angry at the failure of these horses to live up to the value he placed on them, and he's found a way to recoup his losses. And, far simpler, because he can. He can get away with it, he believes. So far, he's been correct. He must be laughing his ass off at the people he's deceived and cheated and made fools of."

Doyle said, "Why don't the insurance companies drop him?"

"Believe me, they'd love to," Damon said. "They've even threatened to do so. But if they fail to pay off a claim of Rexroth's without having proof that he's cheated him, or if they refuse to insure any more of his horses, he'll crucify them in his newspaper and chase them right into court seeking damages besides. Despite their suspicions, the insurance people don't have a scrap of proof of any wrongdoing on the part of Rexroth. That's what they are desperate to come up with. So are we. And that's where you come into the picture."

Suddenly, Doyle let out a laugh. The agents were startled, but there was no way he could hold back. The absurdity of the situation hit him like a good left hook. Here he was, less than twelve hours from having been held up and stripped of his gleanings from a gambling coup, and agents of the federal government were trying to enlist his cooperation in bringing down one of the country's richest men. He laughed again before saying to Tirabassi, "Okay, let's have it. Let's have the explanation of how Jack Doyle, unemployed sales rep and retired horse groom, is going to come to the aid of his government."

Karen was the first to respond. "About two months ago," she said, "we had an inquiry, an anonymous inquiry, whether we had made any progress in solving the mystery of the two sudden deaths of the two expensive horses at Rexroth's farm. It was a man who called us, one with a very noticeable accent—we later identified it as a New Zealand accent. Anyway, we had to tell him, quite honestly, that we were stymied. We said we'd welcome any help we could get. He said he'd call back. It was a short conversation, and the call was untraceable.

"A week went by. The man called again. This time, he asked to set up a meeting. He wouldn't give his name yet, but he said he would explain everything when we met with him. The date was two days later, at a forest preserve parking lot on the northwest side of Chicago, not far from O'Hare Airport. Damon and I both went that day, and that's when we met Mr. Bolger."

Damon picked up the narrative. "Bolger, it turns out, is the farm manager at Willowdale, a job he's had for slightly more than a year. He came to this country from England, where he'd worked on some big horse farms. Before that, he'd gotten his start in the horse business in New Zealand. He's a native of New Zealand—a 'Kiwi,' as he put it. He's pretty proud of it, too.

"Bolger said that he was positive something 'wonky,' as he put it, was going on with these horse deaths at Willowdale. He said there'd been two horses die since he'd started work there, both healthy animals who all of a sudden, late at night, keeled over from heart attacks. He didn't believe these were natural heart attacks. Bolger said he didn't know how it was being done, but he was convinced these animals were being murdered for the money they were worth in insurance. He was very emotional about this, and very angry. Obviously, the man cares about horses."

Doyle tapped a finger on the table. "Hold it right here. I've got a question. If Bolger is so put off by this business, why doesn't he just quit his Willowdale job, haul his ass back to Kiwi land?"

"The reason," Karen answered, "is that he wants to stop what he believes are these murders of horses. He told us it only took him a few months before he came to thoroughly dislike Rexroth. He thought about quitting then. Then the first horse died, the second only two months later. Bolger is determined to get to the bottom of this, and he believes that can only be done if he stays on the job at Willowdale.

"We spent a couple of days, Damon and I, talking this through, then the two of us consulting with our superiors, trying to determine how best to utilize this information. The consensus finally arrived at was that we couldn't depend solely on Bolger. After all, two of his predecessors had been dismissed by Rexroth. We tracked both of them down, but neither—one was a guy named McCollister, the other an older man named Doherty—would volunteer any information. It's possible Rexroth either bought them off, or threatened them, in order to insure their silence. Our concern is that Bolger himself might be a target of threats. He sure doesn't seem to be the kind of man who'd buckle under, but you never know. We can't take that kind of chance.

"What was decided, then, was to keep Bolger in place and introduce someone to assist him on-site at Willowdale Farm. Naturally, we wanted to use one of our agents, but we couldn't find one available who had any experience with racehorses, or their breeding. The person we needed had to be convincing enough to be given the job after we had provided him with phony work references, ones good enough to gain him an interview.

We also were to have Bolger introducing his name to Rexroth, saying he'd heard he was a good man and worth hiring."

"It was at that point that you kind of fell into our laps, Doyle," said Tirabassi, permitting himself a small smile.

"This goes beyond mind-boggling," Doyle said, again unable to contain his laughter at what he deemed the absurdity of this scenario.

"I don't know the first thing about a thoroughbred breeding farm," Doyle said forcefully. "Why would you think I'd be able to pass any inspection I'd get?"

"Because," Damon said, "Bolger will be the man doing the main inspecting, as you put it. He can brief you on the basics. Doyle, we know you're a smart guy, and a fairly quick study—you showed that when you worked for Angelo Zocchi. We think you're just the man for this job."

Said Karen, "Think about it, Jack. You can, we might put it, clear your name with us while doing something very useful. Providing you cooperate and work with us on this, you'll never have to worry about any unofficial 'discouraging' we might do in regard to your future employment. In fact, if you keep your end of the bargain, you can expect an endorsement from us.

"This whole project should not, we hope, take more than a couple of months. We want to nail Rexroth before he can do any more damage. You and Bolger, we hope, will be able to lead us to the evidence we need. We don't want this case prolonged. And I'm sure you don't, either," Karen said.

"Let's assume," Doyle said, looking skeptical, "that I somehow pass the employment test. Let's assume I actually get this job at Willowdale. What do I do, when I do? I'm no undercover agent."

"Whatever suspicions Bolger has about Rexroth's crimes," Damon said, "he can't be too obvious about seeking confirmation. Otherwise, Rexroth'll get on to him. And, obviously, Bolger can't be everywhere on a big farm like that. He needs an ally, a confederate, somebody he can point in the right direction. Somebody he can trust."

Karen leaned forward, elbows on the table, looking Jack directly in the eye. "Do you think this is the scenario we would have written? Having to involve somebody, well, like you? But we've been thoroughly frustrated in trying to get Rexroth."

Damon said quietly, "Desperate situations demand desperate measures. I think that's what this amounts to, Mr. Doyle."

Jack said, "Why in hell would Bolger trust somebody he'd never met—somebody like me?"

Karen smiled at Doyle. "Because we told him he could, Jack. We gave him assurances. Now," she added, "you're going to live up to them."

Doyle wasn't laughing now. The sound that came out of him was more a groan. I could probably refuse, he thought, as he looked at the expectant faces of the two FBI agents, and they couldn't really nail me with any charges that would stick. But there's no question they could prevent me from getting any kind of decent job in the future.

Doyle shook his head in wonderment at the watershed moment he'd just reached in his rapidly changing life. "Jesus Christ—Jack Doyle, junior G-Man. I can't believe this is happening." He plunked his coffee cup down on the table, then slid the check onto Damon's placemat.

"How do I start with this thing?"

Chapter 7

"Jack, I feel bad about how it worked out for you. That's why I asked for a meeting today."

Moe Kellman had phoned Doyle the previous night, three nights after Doyle had been robbed and laid low, literally and figuratively. "How did you find out about what happened to me?" Doyle had asked.

"I hear a lot of things, Jack," Moe had replied. "How I hear, that's not important. What I hear is that you got ripped off, that somebody took all you earned from us. I was sorry to hear that, Jack."

The two sat in bright sunshine on this summer day in first-row box seats directly behind home plate at Wrigley Field. These were the best seats Doyle had ever had at a baseball game, and he said so. "Had them for years," Moe shrugged.

Moe Kellman, Doyle had learned, was a man who always had the best seats no matter where he went. His business was fur, luxury level fur, which was still a staple of his "people," be they Outfit higher-ups or the members of the police and judiciary that helped them continue to thrive in an increasingly competitive criminal world. The animal rights, anti-fur movement had failed to make any inroads whatsoever with the stratum of society served by Moe Kellman.

When Doyle had arrived that afternoon, he'd said to Kellman, "I didn't know you liked baseball."

"I don't," Kellman replied. "I'm a Cubs fan. There's a difference."

Doyle looked around at what legions of loyal Chicago Cubs fans referred to with reverence as the "friendly confines." The grass almost shone in the sunlight, a slightly lighter shade of green than the ivy that covered the outfield walls of this compact old ball yard.

Doyle hadn't been at Wrigley Field since a September afternoon two years earlier when he had chaperoned a group of wide-eyed Serafin clients from Salt Lake City to a Cubs-Dodger game. The men in that middle-aged group had almost genuflected at their first sight of this Chicago sports landmark. The women had occupied themselves by ogling the goodly number of good-looking athletes occupying Cubs uniforms. How they played was secondary.

Today, Doyle noticed, although it was a Wednesday afternoon, the Wrigley stands were nearly filled—filled, as usual, by an almost exclusively white crowd of northsiders, suburbanites, and out-of-towners. The many youngsters in the crowd were almost matched in number by the suit-coated businessmen who talked on their cellular phones inning after inning.

Out in the bleachers, halter-topped girls sat with their bare-chested boyfriends, spending as much time applying suntan lotion and ordering from the busy beer vendors as they did watching the action on the field. Behind them, from the rooftops of the old apartment buildings that bordered the ballpark on Waveland and Sheffield Avenues, gatherings of young people monitored the game in progress from amidst clouds of smoke that billowed skyward from barbecue grills.

Don't any of these people work? Doyle wondered.

Aloud, he said to Kellman, "How can you be a Cubs fan? How can anybody? They haven't won a pennant since World War Two."

"Listen," Moe replied, "this is a great place to get a tan. And a great place to relax. There's no pressure to concentrate—these schlubs are hardly ever involved in games that mean anything, so you've got a nice, comfortable absence of tension.

"And from a financial standpoint," Moe said, "you got to love this operation."

He took a drink of his beer, then carefully dried his impeccably trimmed white mustache with his handkerchief. "They should be a case study in every business school in this country.

"It's remarkable," Moe continued, "year after year, with a very occasional exception, the Cubs organization puts a lousy product on the market. Then they sell that product as rich in tradition, as loveable, and all that other happy horseshit, and year after year they pack this joint. They've raised ineptitude to a commercial art form.

"Oh, once in a blue moon they'll win their division. But never the pennant. And they haven't won the World Series in ninety-five years. Think of that, Jack," Moe said, poking Doyle's arm with an index finger for emphasis, "ninety-five years! And yet they raise their prices almost every year, and people line up to pay them! Futility. Failure. But bale up the money and send it to the bank!"

Moe turned away from Doyle to exchange greetings with a portly, red-faced man in a light blue seersucker suit who had come down the steps from behind them. The man's face was shiny with sweat. After a few moments of soft conversation, during which the man knelt on one knee like a supplicant while whispering into Kellman's ear, Moe waved him away. "Take care of yourself, Judge," he said, as the man retreated back up the aisle.

Moe turned back to Doyle. "My grandfather on my mother's side, Morrie Greenburg may he rest in peace, although he's a longshot for that, Morrie would have bowed low in admiration to these guys that run the Cubs. Bowed low, I'm saying.

"For over fifty years, Morrie sold cheap jewelry at inflated prices to the schvartzes over on Maxwell Street. But even Morrie gave more value than these guys," Moe said, as the Cubs short-stop sailed his throw to first base into the third row behind the visitors' dugout. Two runs scored, putting the home team down 5-0 to the St. Louis Cardinals in the top half of the first inning. When the ninth Cardinal batter of the inning finally flied out against the ivy in dead center, the crowd cheered and clapped enthusiastically.

Doyle ordered beers from a vendor who was several exits past seventy on his roadway of life. As he handed one of the cups to Kellman, Doyle said, "Look, I know we're not here to discuss contemporary corporate economics. What's our business today?"

"Jack…Jack," Moe said, a pained expression on his face, "it's not business here today. I just wanted to make sure that you know my people had nothing to do with that ripoff of your twenty-five grand.

"According to the story I get—no, no, don't ask me how I know this, just believe me that I do—there was a white woman and a colored guy seen running out of your garage that night, probably right about the time you hit the deck.

"We've made inquiries, you might say, but we don't have a clue as to who these two were. Maybe they were looking to mug somebody and just stumbled on you. Who knows?

"What I do know is that when you do business for us, and do it right, you've got nothing to worry about," Moe emphasized.

Nothing to show for it either, Doyle thought as he sat there, feeling like an idiot. Somehow Maureen and E. D. had smelled out the plot involving City Sarah and had combined forces to take dead aim at one of the plotters—him. Doyle couldn't escape feeling another silent wave of deep embarrassment.

Moe said, "The point, Jack, is that we don't *owe* you a goddam thing. But we owe you. You know what I mean?"

He shook his head as he saw Doyle's puzzled expression. "It doesn't make any difference if you understand or not. The thing is, here's five grand—it's to tide you over till you find something else." Moe slipped an envelope into the side pocket of Doyle's sport coat. "No, it's not a loan," Moe said before

Doyle could speak, "don't worry about that. Let's just say it's a belated bonus."

Moe looked thoughtfully toward the Cubs bullpen, a beehive of activity all afternoon. "Another thing, Jack. I heard you had some visitors early the other morning. Representatives of one of the nation's law enforcement agencies." He smiled slightly, noting the look of astonishment on Doyle's face.

"That's okay, Jack," Kellman continued. "Everybody gets unwanted visitors every once in a while. But you don't want to get too cozy with people like that."

"Moe, I have to—or I might have to," Doyle hurriedly amended. Looking at his little companion, Doyle suspected that here, too, Kellman was probably running head to head with him in the knowledge department.

"We understand that, Jack. You're in kind of a bind here, or"—Kellman smiled—"what at the racetrack they call a blind switch. Great old term. A blind switch is when a jockey gets himself caught in a pocket during a race, trapped maybe down on the inside, looking for a way out. Jocks just have to keep looking to work their way out when they're in those spots. Otherwise they lose for sure. Looks like the feds have you boxed in."

Kellman took off his sunglasses and turned in his seat to face Doyle. "Let me get back to 'too cozy' with the feds, as I just mentioned. Too cozy as it might pertain to me and my people. Sometimes you tend toward the blunt side. That wouldn't be good in your dealings with those people you're being forced to deal with now. There's a lot to be said for the vague approach, if you know what I mean."

After putting his sunglasses back on and draining his beer cup, Moe again patted dry his mustache. "Don't thank me, Jack," he said as he stood to leave. Then he leaned down and added: "But don't look for anything more either.

"One of Grandpa Morrie's favorite quotes—I can almost hear him saying it—was from Benjamin Franklin. Franklin said 'There are three faithful friends—an old wife, an old dog, and ready money.'

"All you've got is one out of three, Jack, so try to hang on to it, okay?" Moe turned away.

"See you at the gym."

◇◇◇

After Moe had gone, Doyle sat half-watching the game. He bought a cold hot dog and a warm beer, but didn't finish either. He thought of the money in his pocket, then of E. D. and Maureen. He had really liked both of them, and had believed the feeling was at least close to mutual. How had he so badly misread that situation?

As the Cardinal batters continued to feast on a procession of Cubs pitchers, Doyle concentrated on the game only occasionally. He had a final beer, this one cold, and, still thinking of his assailants, realized that he was quite capable of forgiving them if their actions were ever explained to him. Doyle shook his head. "I must be going soft," he said to himself. "Anybody else robbed me like that, I'd be looking forward to flaying them."

Doyle left Wrigley Field just prior to the start of the bottom of the seventh inning. The home team trailed 11-1. Yet the crowd was on its feet, waving at the panning WGN-TV cameras, singing along with an apparently half-demented one-time rock star as he led them, clueless as to the lyrics, in a genuinely horrendous rendition of "Take Me Out to the Ball Game." Their team trailing by ten, Cubs fans were still having a grand old time.

Moe's Grandpa Morrie would have envied this scene.

Chapter 8

Doyle waved at a nearby polar bear as he walked the concrete path, deftly dodging a couple of baby strollers, then a child waving a cotton candy stick. The bear, splayed out on a rock in white-furred splendor, moved his head as if to respond. Doyle knew that was not the case, but smiled to himself at the thought.

He was, that sunny afternoon, making his way through Chicago's Lincoln Park Zoo because of a phone call he'd retrieved on his answering machine the previous evening.

The voice on the phone had been quick, the message abrupt, delivered in an accent that Doyle realized was that of New Zealand. The voice belonged to Aldous Bolger, and informed Doyle, "We'll meet Tuesday afternoon, half-past two, Lincoln Park Zoo, in the part they call the Farm. I'll spot you, not to worry. If this doesn't suit you, leave a message at 708-864-0854."

The FBI agents had told Doyle to expect this call from Bolger. It was necessary, they said, for Doyle and Bolger to meet before Doyle applied for work at Willowdale Farm.

"You two need to talk, to go over the details of the job in advance, in case Rexroth has any questions for you," Karen Engel had said. "Rexroth will definitely interview you. He talks to everybody but the landscape helpers before he hires them. It's a peculiarity of his. By no means his only one, by the way.

"The fact that you know racehorses, from being around them at the track, will of course come in handy. But farm work, the procedures there, are something you're not familiar with. That's what Bolger can brief you on. He seems to be a pleasant enough fellow. I think you'll get along with him. He can also go over the details of the Willowdale horses."

Doyle stopped at one of the zoo's concession stands. He bought a bag of popcorn that he nibbled at as he continued to stroll the tree-lined walkways. It was a little after two o'clock, so he had plenty of time to reach the meeting spot. Doyle's apartment was located a couple of miles to the north. He'd always liked this place, and in fact often visited it after he'd jogged along a path in the adjacent park. In contrast to the Chicago area's other zoo, a comparative megalopolis located in a western suburb, the Lincoln Park Zoo was accessible and compact enough to easily be traversed, and most of its inhabitants viewed, in the course of a leisurely afternoon.

Twice, Doyle remembered, he had met women here whom he'd subsequently dated: a wealthy divorcee with an obnoxious young son, and an unmarried veterinarian who worked in the zoo's small animal house. He'd had a fairly lengthy relationship with the veterinarian until she took a job at the San Diego Zoo.

A breeze ruffled the baggy T-shirts of a group of black children in front of Doyle as he walked alongside the little zoo lake, over which a colorful flotilla of paddle boats moved in erratic fashion, guided by pilots with various degrees of proficiency. The kids, all between the ages of eight and ten, looked wide-eyed at the paddle boats, then at the sheep and cows that grazed behind fences near the red, wooden farm building.

A couple of the kids excitedly asked questions of one of the counselors who moved calmly among them. The kids' shirts said *Better Boys Foundation*, a local organization Doyle knew was headquartered on Chicago's poverty-ridden west side. "Must be an interesting field trip for them," Doyle thought. He remembered reading a magazine article about gang members from that area of Chicago, only a few miles west of the Loop; several of the gang-bangers had admitted they'd never once in their lives seen Lake Michigan.

Doyle sat down on a bench near a water fountain. The bench was just to the side of the farm building, so he figured he should be visible to Bolger. Doyle remained there nearly fifteen minutes and was beginning to wonder if he'd been stood up. Suddenly, he felt a large hand grip his shoulder from behind him.

"No, no, mister, don't get up. Sit right there," Doyle heard the man say.

A man with hair so blond it was almost white moved around the bench to face him, large hand outstretched, broad smile spread across his tanned, pleasant face. He was wearing a short-sleeved blue shirt, blue jeans, and western boots. The man was a couple of inches taller than Doyle, about six feet two inches, but he looked to weigh at least forty pounds more than Doyle's one-sixty. He looked extremely fit, Doyle thought, not from gym efforts but from years of hard, outdoor work.

Beside him stood a slim, very attractive woman in her early thirties, probably four or five years younger than the man, her hair almost exactly the same color as his. She, too, wore a blue denim shirt, opened slightly to reveal a slender neck, but instead of jeans had on a cream-colored skirt. She smiled at Doyle in friendly fashion, a smile that he found himself warmly returning. Standing between the man and woman were a young girl and boy; like the adults, they had white-blond hair, even features, and deeply tanned skin.

The man said, "Mr. Doyle, I'm Aldous Bolger. Pleasure to meet you."

Doyle said, "My pleasure. And call me Jack, will you…er, Aldous?"

Bolger looked at Doyle with an expression of resigned amusement. "Let me explain the name," he said. "Our old man thought *Brave New World* was the most important bloody book since the Bible, and Mr. Huxley was one of his all-time heroes. My father read Huxley's novel to our family at least once a year. I know long passages of the bloody thing by heart." He gave a short laugh.

Doyle said, "Do I call you Al?"

Bolger turned very serious. "Not even once," replied the New Zealander. "Out of respect to my father, and Mr. Huxley, it will be Aldous, if you don't mind."

Doyle nodded in assent. He recognized Bolger as being one of those lifelong horsemen whose years of hard physical work made them gristle-tough and fiercely independent. *I doubt I could dent this son of a bitch with a hand ax,* Doyle thought. "Aldous it is," he said aloud.

Bolger turned to the woman. "Caroline," he said, "meet Jack Doyle. Jack, my sister, Caroline Cummings. And these are her children, Helen and Ian."

"'Ello," the children said, almost as one.

"Are you visiting, or do you live in the States, too?" Doyle asked their mother.

Caroline shook her head, her blond bangs moving across her forehead. "No, we don't live here. This is actually our first time in your country. No, we're on what you might call an extended visit to my brother down in Kentucky. Longer than he may have anticipated." Her smile was somewhat apologetic. Doyle noticed that Caroline's strikingly large, widely set eyes were brown-gold, while the children's eyes were a very light shade of blue.

"Nonsense," Aldous said. "Caroline," he added, "as you know, Jack and I have some talking to do. Why don't you take the kids in to those farm buildings. We'll come back for you in a bit."

"Right you are." As the three of them moved off, one of the zoo workers announced over a portable microphone, "Our goat-milking begins in three minutes. Watch the milking and try some," she invited. Helen and Ian dashed on ahead of their mother.

As Doyle and Bolger began walking in the opposite direction, Bolger said, "The 'long visit' my sister mentioned has only been about three weeks. She's more than welcome to double that or more, if she wants. I'm not married. I've got plenty of space for

her and the kids. They seem to like it at Willowdale. And they
need the time away from home."

Doyle looked at Bolger inquiringly. Bolger said, "Caroline's
husband, Grant Cummings, was a jockey, and one of my oldest
friends. He carked it in a bloody awful spill back home at
Ellerslie, that's the track in Auckland, a little over a year ago.

"A terrible, shocking tragedy, it was. Grant was only just
turned thirty. He was coming into his own as a rider, just starting to get the best mounts from the top stables. Grant was a
great bloke, and a great husband and father as well. It's been
very tough on Caroline and her kids.

"I invited them over here after Grant's funeral, trying to give
them a change of scenery, something to help them along. It took
them a long time before they finally decided to come. But I'm
glad they did. They seem to be brightening up a bit every day
they're here. Thank God for that," he said.

Seeing the earnest expression on Bolger's face, Doyle felt
himself warming to the man and his obvious sincerity.

"Caroline's no bludge," her brother continued. Seeing the
look of incomprehension on Doyle's face, he quickly amended,
"I mean she's not here to spend time with me because she's in
any financial straits. Her husband left her a goodly packet, and
he was well insured. No, Caroline and the kids have got big
bickies—what I mean is, more than enough money. They've no
worries on that score, believe me.

"And for the kids, it's not all holiday they're on. It's winter
back home, and she made them bring a term's worth of lessons with them. She spends hours with them on their school
work near every day. Caroline's a remarkable woman," he said.
"She's got her own real estate business in a suburb of Auckland.
Started it herself and built it up, dealing mostly with the high
end properties."

Bolger shook his head admiringly. "Sometimes I can hardly
believe she's what my little sis grew up to be."

Strangely, Doyle found this glowing description to be somehow depressing. He realized he'd been immediately attracted to

Caroline, but learning that she was a wealthy widow served to dampen his interest. *A bit too high up the financial ladder for me,* he thought regretfully, and abruptly changed the subject.

"What about you, Aldous?" he asked. "What's your story?" It sounded ruder than Doyle had intended.

Bolger gave him a startled look at the sudden shift in tone. His ordinarily open and good-natured expression fled his face, replaced with a frown. Doyle realized he'd succeeded, however unwittingly, in hurting Bolger's feelings.

"Well, then," Bolger said gruffly to Doyle, "let's try this path up to the right and I'll try to sum things up as quick as you'd like. We'll try to have you home and hosed in an hour."

Doyle thought, not for the first time lately, that there was a thin line between being a self-protective cool operator and being just a wise-cracking asshole. There were so many "thin lines" in his life—another of the major ones lying, as his old buddy Olegaard back at Bass, Sexton used to say—between "bull-dozing and charisma." Doyle forced himself to concentrate on what Bolger was telling him.

"I came to the States six years ago," Bolger said. "I'd gotten started in the horse business back home when I was a lad, mucking out stalls when I hardly came up to the horse's belly. I worked for an uncle of mine, Duane Hatch, for years. He eventually lined me up with a job in England, and I learned a lot working there on some of the major breeding farms.

"But I was always aware that the best horses, and the best farms, were in the States, especially Kentucky. So, when I heard about an opening at Willowdale, well, cor blimey, I fired off a resume. I figured I had enough experience by then to take on a manager's position at a major farm. All I knew about Willowdale was that it was owned by a very wealthy man, that he was interested in breeding top horses, and the pay packet was quite nice, indeed. It's what I'd hoped of doing all my life, man.

"Maybe I should have caught on to the fact that something was wonky when…." Bolger was interrupted by Doyle. "Something was *what?*"

Bolger said, "Wonky. I mean, you know, *crooked*. Wonky's something we say at home."

"Like cor blimey?"

Bolger grinned at Doyle, his innate good nature back in evidence. "You'll have to forgive me, friend. Like they say, you can take the lad out of the country, but you can't take the country's talk out of the lad. If I confuse you too much, just stop and ask me what I mean. No offense will be taken. This happens to me a lot."

Doyle nodded. He felt himself starting to like this big, good-natured man. Then Bolger's normally amiable face creased with concern as he resumed talking.

"Once I got to Willowdale," he said, "I was damned surprised to learn that I was the third farm manager hired in eighteen months. I'd had no idea. Maybe I was too eager to grab at this opportunity. Maybe I should've done some research of my own. But from where I was, in England, this looked like a dream job.

"Anyway, when I later asked Rexroth about the two managers who'd been there before me, he just shrugged it off. 'Personality clashes,' is how he'd put it, 'very common here in America.' Then he'd say, 'Let's not let that happen to us, eh, Aldous,' and give me a thundering clap on the back. And I'd go back to my air-conditioned cottage and riffle through my check stubs, and kind of park under the rug any concerns I had about Willowdale's job turnover.

"I just said to myself, it's the same thing here as anywhere else I'd been. You work for a man with big bickies and you take your chances. Some of them will like you, some won't, and with the money they've got they can afford to change employees like they change their woolies. That's the risk of being in the employ of the rich, if you follow me here, Jack.

"And," Bolger added, "Rexroth can be a very charming fella, when he wants to be. Just one of the 'common old workin' men'—he's got an act like that he trots out every now and then. But down deep I think he's got the inborn contempt for others that's bred into so many of these privileged bastards. Don't get me started on that subject."

They had walked to the middle of one of the bridges that spanned the park's meandering lake. Doyle paused and leaned his arms on the railing. "So where did your problems start with Rexroth?"

"Not right away. The first year was grand," Bolger replied. "We foaled some nicely made young horses. We went to the Keeneland breeding stock sale and bought some very fine mares. Rexroth told me, 'If you see a mare you think is worth the money, *pay* the money.'

"I'll admit it, I was pretty impressed by this—not only that Rexroth had the money, but that he'd trust me with spending it the right way. I'll admit, too, that I got kind of caught up in the grand spirit of things. I mean, we were riding around in a limousine, eating at the best restaurants. It was quite a leap for a Kiwi lad like myself.

"The trouble started the next year. And it had nothing to do with me. What was happening was that some earlier horse purchases, made by my farm manager predecessors, turned out very badly. Well, you know, this happens in the business. Bound to. As my uncle Duane always used to tell me when I worked for him back home, 'Aldous, this is not an exact science—neither the breeding nor the betting.' He had another saying, too: 'The dumbest horse can make the biggest fool out of the smartest man.'"

Bolger paused to light a cigarette, casting a sideways glance at Doyle that combined both embarrassment and defiance. "God help me, man, I know how dumb this is. But I'm not ready to quit the smokes just yet."

Doyle made a deprecating gesture. "I don't know why you don't quit," he joked. "Quitting's easy. I must have done it twenty times before I got it right. Anyway, don't worry about it. I know how it is. I finally kicked it about ten years ago, but you're not talking to a member of the international tobacco police."

"Well," said Bolger, "there's an officer of that department right over there on the park bench—Caroline. And I can see she's waiting for us."

Bolger turned to face the other way from his sister, inhaled hugely with his back bent like a jazz saxophone player bending deep into the melody, then surreptitiously dropped the cigarette under his boot. As he crushed the butt, he said, "That girl's got the eyes of a hawk. Let's start heading back over there. I'll finish telling you about the Rexroth situation as we go along."

It was after he'd been at Willowdale about a year, Aldous said, that the first suspicious horse death occurred.

"I don't mean the first horse to die," he emphasized. "We had a couple of mares die while foaling, we had a yearling killed when he was hit by lighting out in the field one night. Those sort of things are not unnatural on a breeding farm where you've got two hundred or more horses. These animals are given to all sorts of mischief and misadventures, even when they're not on the racetrack and competing.

"But," Bolger went on, "there then came this one incident—a horse named Uncle Francis. We found him one night down in his stall with as bad a shattered rear leg as I'd ever seen. All we could figure was that he had been frightened somehow and lashed out with it, kicking terrifically hard against the stall wall. But, still, even though that's what the vets said…well, it was goddam unnatural. I hated to see that horse put down. But that's all we could do. He was ruined."

Doyle said, "As I understand it, the insurance company paid up. Right?"

"Yeah, they did," Bolger replied, "but not without nosing around for weeks and, I might add, giving me and my staff a pretty good questioning.

"Anyway, about two months later we lost another stud horse, Prince Fennimore. He was found in his stall one morning, stone cold dead. There wasn't a mark on him. The vets and the insurance people concluded he'd died of a heart attack, which is not unheard of, but I knew this horse. Hell, he was only nine years old. He hadn't done much as a stallion, but he was a big, strong, healthy specimen, at least to the naked eye. They performed a necropsy—that's an autopsy for horses. It didn't show any heart disease, but they just figured his heart quit on him.

"Finally, a few weeks back, we find a mare named Signorina Goldini dead in her paddock. It was located right behind a barn. Not a mark on her, either. Again, it looked like a heart attack, and that's what they decided it was, even though she'd appeared to be in a glowing grand health. Her only problem had been that, despite being bred to the farm's best studs each year, she never got in foal. She'd been a real commercial flop.

"At about this point, the old light bulb goes off over my thick noggin. I'd been thinking about these deaths, off and on, for weeks. Finally, it comes to me. These are heavily insured animals, ones that had been thought to have great promise as breeding prospects when they retired. But not one of the three came close to living up to that promise. Believe me, every one of them was expendable from a financial standpoint."

Bolger paused, then looked away, his jaw tightening. Turning back to face Doyle, he said bitterly, "Rexroth came down to wring his hands over every one of these cases. And he'd look appalled, and concerned, but his act just didn't play with me. There was something phony about it and about him.

"After I'd tussled with this and chewed on it, I finally called the FBI. I didn't want to go to the state police, or the local authorities, because I was afraid Rexroth would get word of it. Through his media business, he's got connections everywhere.

"If I was wrong, I didn't want to lose my job over it. If I was right, I didn't want to expose myself to risk, if you know what I mean. A person who will murder horses will murder men as well.

"But I'm pretty damn sure I wasn't wrong," Bolger said with emphasis. He smiled at his sister and her children as he and Doyle approached them. "Just a minute or two more, then I'll buy you lunch," he called to them.

Doyle, arms folded across his chest, cast an appraising glance at Bolger. "What about a pattern—is there any kind of pattern involved here, other than the fact these horses had dropped off sharply in value?"

"The only so-called pattern I could come up with was that I was not at Willowdale when the last two horses, Prince Fennimore and Signorina Goldini, died. When Prince Fennimore died I was at a horse sale Rexroth insisted I attend down in Florida. When the mare died, I'd gone with one of our crews to bring a shipment of two-year-olds up to the racing stable at Heartland Downs."

Doyle digested this for a minute. Then he said, "Okay, this could be looked at in a couple of ways. One, Rexroth thinks you're on to him and wanted to keep you out of the way so there was no chance that you'd discover the horse killers in action.

"Of course, there's also possibility number two. That you're involved in masterminding these killings and conveniently scheduled absences for yourself when they were to take place."

Bolger stopped walking. Gripping Doyle's arm, and powerfully squeezing it, he exclaimed, "If that's a joke, my friend, it's sure not funny. And if it's not…well, what the *hell*, man. You think that if I was involved in this terrible business I'd be the one calling your FBI and asking for help?" he said angrily.

Doyle shook off Bolger's hand. "Only kidding, buddy," he said. "I get your point. And, yeah, I believe you."

As much as I believe anybody these days, Doyle added to himself.

Chapter 9

After picking up their rented Taurus at the New Orleans Airport, Karen Engel and Damon Tirabassi began the nearly four-hour drive north and then west on Hwy. 10 to the heart of Louisiana's Cajun country. This area was home to the quarter-million descendants of French-speaking, Roman Catholic settlers who fled there after having been thrown out of Nova Scotia in the mid-eighteenth century for refusing to pledge their allegiance to Britain's Protestant king. They were an independent lot then, and not much had changed about that strain of their character since.

Acadiana, as this area is known, stretches from Lafayette on the east to Lake Charles on the west and is home to some of the most fun-loving, colorful citizens and memorable food that the United States has to offer.

Damon drove as Karen worked to adjust the air-conditioning. Outside the car, the morning air was thick with humidity. Oak trees seemed to shimmer and sag in the bright sunlight, and moss-covered cypresses looked similarly lethargic. The terrain varied between prairie and swamp, its common bond an enveloping layer of heat.

The two FBI agents had flown south from their Chicago base after a long phone conversation with Clayton Fugette, an agent in the Bureau's New Orleans office. Fugette said he had received a tip from what he termed a "normally reliable informant—or as reliable as the damned snitches ever get to be"—that the horse killer, or killers, sought by Engel and Tirabassi was "from down around here, over by Lafayette. That's in Cajun country. My man said the horse killer is supposedly an ex-jockey who went bad. Said the guy was now making a real good living killing horses for rich people for the insurance money.

"I think you should take a trip over there," Fugette advised. "I don't have anybody to spare right now myself. You've never been there, right? Well, it's a whole different world. *Bonne chance, mes amis,*" he added with a chuckle before hanging up.

As Damon drove rapidly up the interstate, Karen reached into her briefcase and took out a file. "According to the postal records, there must be nearly as many Mortvedts around Lafayette as there are catfish in the bayou."

Damon nodded. "Yeah, it might take some time. But we'll find the right family, or somebody who can tell us about this guy," he said, his mouth tightening. Karen had little doubt that this would be true, for Damon was widely known in the Bureau as being one of its most tenacious agents. Before Karen was assigned to the Chicago office and teamed with him, she had heard numerous admiring references to the man they called Tirabassi the Terrier because suspects were unable to shake him off.

Damon was a native of Chicago's Little Italy, a tightly knit neighborhood on the near west side of the Loop. He had developed an anti-crime attitude as a young boy, its source the fact that his father's tiny sandwich shop was forced to pay "tribute" to the arrogant, "made" guys who strutted around Taylor Street like, as Damon used to sneer, "little Mussolinis." He developed a powerful contempt for these small-time hoods who preyed on their fellow Italian-Americans, secure in the knowledge that they would not be "ratted out" to the law.

That contempt never left him through the years when Damon earned a business degree at the nearby University of Chicago-Illinois, then a law degree on scholarship at Northwestern University. At age forty, Damon had now been an FBI agent for twelve years. He was happily married, with three sons, all of whose youth soccer teams he helped to coach.

Two years earlier, after they had progressed through the early months of their partnership, Damon had finally felt at ease enough with Karen to begin kidding her that the reason they would work well together was that she had "been brought up with enough Dagos to know what to expect."

It was true that Karen had had several good friends among the sizable Italian-American community in her home town of Kenosha, Wisconsin. She had certainly stood out from most of them physically, with her Swedish-American complexion and her size: at five feet ten inches and one hundred forty-five pounds, she had the athletic build and the ability to earn a volleyball scholarship at the University of Wisconsin, from which she'd graduated with a degree in criminal justice. She'd also taken her law degree there, and it was at the UW law school that she'd met and married Dan Litzow.

That ranked as her only real mistake made in Madison, she once told Damon; she and Litzow had divorced after three years. At thirty-three, Karen entertained few thoughts of marrying again. She dated occasionally, but for the most part found herself satisfied with making her work the overwhelming priority of her life.

Karen smiled to herself as she glanced sideways at her super-serious partner. Damon's only real flaw, as far as she was concerned, was his major lack of a sense of humor. He wasn't dour, but rarely did Damon permit himself even a chuckle, even when smack dab in the middle of situations that cried out for laughter. Karen remembered Damon's all-business attitude when the two of them had apprehended a missing Chicago grain exchange dealer hiding in the canvas-covered jacuzzi of his hunting lodge in the northern Wisconsin woods. Once they'd pulled the cover back off the steaming jacuzzi, the finance felon had leaped to his feet from the roiling water, hands in the air, wearing only a Green Bay Packers ball cap. "Don't shoot, I'll pay it all back," he had said loudly. Karen could hardly retain her grip on her revolver as she took in this ludicrous scene.

Damon had responded by looking impassively at their dripping-wet quarry. "You're damn right you will, Cheesehead," was all he had said.

A few days later, back in Chicago and describing this arrest scene to their supervisor, Karen had commented, "And Damon, well, he was the epitome of cool." She had meant it as a compliment. Hearing her say that, Damon shook his head and sighed. "I'm not cool," he insisted quietly. "I'm like most people. I spend my life bouncing back and forth between boredom and hysteria. I just cover it up pretty well," he had added with a small smile.

Damon, driving with his usual calm precision, was not devoting any thought to his partner's psyche. He had immediately accepted Karen as a required presence in his career, one whose ability to perform her job was, to his mind, never jeopardized by the fact that she was tall, intelligent, and right on the border of beautiful, despite her practical hairstyles and understated makeup.

Nor, in spite of the kidding remarks of envious male colleagues, had Damon ever thought of Karen in any way other than as that of trusted partner. Damon had grown up in a household with four very bright older sisters, a circumstance that had early on given him an abiding liking of and respect for women. And once he had, ten years before, married Marie Romano, Damon Tirabassi had never evidenced any hint of a roving eye. In his marriage, as in his professional life, Tirabassi was steadfast.

Damon shifted slightly in his seat. "You've read what there is on this Mortvedt," he said to Karen. "Sum it up for me, will you?"

Karen said, "It's not much. Just a summary of reports and rulings from the Thoroughbred Racing Protective Bureau, the horse racing industry's security arm."

Mortvedt, she said, early on was the subject of the normal number of suspensions for occupational infractions—rough riding, careless riding, failure to exercise proper judgment. But as his career settled into the trough of mediocrity, his temper often took hold of him in public, and the young Cajun was fined for "striking his horse on the head" after three different losing races. On two other occasions he was suspended for viciously kicking his mount in the belly after dismounting. In his third year as a jockey, Mortvedt drew a six-month suspension for blatantly attempting to put a rival rider over the rail during a race at New Orleans' Fair Grounds.

Alphonse LeBeau, a trainer who for some time employed Mortvedt as his regular rider, later told the track stewards that he had "never known a rider to hate horses like this little bastard."

When Mortvedt was twenty-four, he was discovered to have ridden a series of favorites in such a way as to prevent them from finishing in the money in trifecta and exacta races. He was working at the time in conjunction with a small ring of New Orleans-based professional gamblers who used to their benefit the knowledge that certain horses would finish "nowhere" in specified races when Mortvedt was riding them.

Trainer LeBeau, who had parted company with Mortvedt three years earlier, was one of several honest horsemen who reported their suspicions to investigators. Eventually Mortvedt was arrested, tried, and convicted of race-fixing and sent to Oakdale Prison. He served seven years of a fifteen-year sentence before being paroled. Because of his conviction, Mortvedt was banned for life from ever again working as a professional jockey.

"Mortvedt appealed that ban twice to the state racing commission," Karen said, "but was turned down. His last unsuccessful appeal was three years ago."

"Not long before the horse killings began in Kentucky," Damon said.

"That's right," Karen said.

What was not a part of the Ronald Mortvedt file was anything explaining how he, a convicted felon from deep in America's south, had ever gone into business with Harvey Rexroth, press lord and prominent Kentucky horse owner and breeder. Their unlikely alliance arose from two shared traits: both men understood the value of horses, while not respecting them any more than they would any other commodity; and through each of these otherwise disparate individuals ran a broad streak of larceny parallel to a sizable streak of cruelty.

Mortvedt, like dozens of jockeys before him, hailed from the rural area near Lafayette, where young boys begin to ride horses in match races when they are so small they have to be tied on to their mounts.

But unlike the vast majority of his Cajun colleagues, Ronald Mortvedt harbored no love of horses: he saw them only as a way out of a life he despised. He had enough physical talent to have realistic hopes for escape, too.

Besides his ability as a hustling, hard-hitting little rider, Ronald Mortvedt brought with him into the world outside his native Acadiana a truly venomous attitude toward his fellow human beings in general. This undoubtedly had its source in the years of physical and mental abuse Ronald had suffered at the hands of his alcoholic father, Maurice. Or perhaps he had, in the words of his beleaguered mother, Audrey, just been "born mean, like his daddy." Ronald had coal black hair, the same color as his father's, and the same icy black eyes that seemed to state to the world, "I don't trust you. And if you're any way smart at all, you'd better not trust me."

Ronald was an only child. One was more than enough for Audrey, who fled the company of her sociopath husband and son when Ronald was fourteen, running off with an East Texas truck driver she had met at the Abbeville match races one Sunday.

Young Ronald himself moved away barely a year later, some two months before Maurice Mortvedt killed himself by driving into a concrete abutment while en route home from Guidry's Tavern early one Tuesday morning. At that time, Ronald was working at Evangeline Downs Racetrack for trainer LeBeau. Informed by phone of his father's death, Ronald accepted the news without comment, hung up the receiver in LeBeau's office and went back to work, a wicked little smile on his narrow face. "He's a cold-hearted little coon ass, ain't he?" LeBeau said to his assistant trainer when the screen door of the office had slammed behind Mortvedt.

Nineteen months later, Ronald Mortvedt rode for the first time in a race at a recognized racetrack. LeBeau had put him up on an old, sore-legged gelding named Friar Tuck, who went off at nearly fifty to one in a cheap claiming race at Evangeline Downs. Under Mortvedt's furious whipping, the old horse got up to be second. LeBeau was livid. "Goddam you, boy, I told you not to abuse that old horse. He always tries his best. Don't have to whip that horse." Mortvedt barely acknowledged his boss' words before swaggering back to the jockeys' room, eminently pleased with himself.

Thus began a riding career that could best be described as checkered. It produced a decent number of victories, for Ronald Mortvedt had "some talent," as Alphonse LeBeau had noticed early on. Mortvedt was also fearless, ruthless, and ambitious. And, like most professional jockeys, he was blessed with amazingly quick reflexes and a level of strength inordinate for his size—five feet four inches, one hundred ten pounds.

But Ronald Mortvedt's level of riding skill proved to be far below that of such famous fellow Cajuns as Eddie Delahoussaye, or Kent Desormeaux, who went on to fabulously successful careers at the major California tracks. Young Mortvedt realized that much early on. He adapted by looking to find ways to make money illegally. It was not just an attempt to enhance a modest income, but a form of revenge against the sport that he had hoped to use as his meal ticket.

◇◇◇

Ronald's conviction was welcomed by his co-workers. "I'm glad they nailed that bastard," said Evangeline Downs' leading rider, Ray Moreau. Privately, Moreau admitted to friends his amazement at Mortvedt's skill in "stiffing" horses. "You gotta watch him close," Moreau said. "I tell you, he's awful good at it.

"If he worked at hard as trying to win as he does trying to lose, he'd make a decent living for himself. That boy's so strong he could hold an elephant away from a barrel of peanuts."

Chapter 10

As the Taurus neared the outskirts of Lafayette that afternoon, Karen said, "It's after two o'clock. I'd like something to eat."

"Sure," Damon said. A few blocks later, he pulled into the small, dusty parking lot of Guerin's Café. Seated at one of the six tables inside, they discussed strategy over bowls of gumbo and a shared platter of fried catfish—barbue frittes, as the worn menu described it. As usual, Karen ate with rapid relish, while Damon worked his way methodically through his meal.

Besides the friendly, heavy-set waitress, the only other people in the place were two elderly men in work clothes. They were sitting at the small counter, talking quietly and drinking bottles of Dixie beer. An ancient black radio, positioned on the shelf dividing the kitchen from the counter, played Cajun music from station 1050-AM. "The races?" replied the waitress to Karen's question. "Sure, they goin' on now."

Following the waitress' directions, the agents drove a couple of miles to LaCombe Downs, one of Louisiana's last remaining bush tracks, meaning horse racing at its most rudimentary: amateur jockeys wear T-shirts, jeans, and gym shoes; a handwritten, mimeographed track program lists the day's races and entries; and the horses have been trained on their owners' farms, then trailered over to the track for the day. No pari-mutuel betting adds to the excitement, as at the larger, recognized tracks; instead, all the wagering done here is up front and personal between interested patrons.

As they slowly walked on a sand path that led from the little paddock to the railing that rimmed the racetrack, Engel and Tirabassi observed racing fans of all ages, from very small children to extremely senior citizens, all rooting on their favorites, then talking about the next race to come. Women sat in lawn chairs, fanning themselves against the heat as they watched lively, laughing children. Groups of men wearing straw cowboy hats talked softly, so softly that Karen could barely discern that the language they were employing was French. As Clayton Fugette had said, Karen thought, this *is* a different world.

Damon made inquiries as they advanced through the crowd; the third one produced directions to the tented area in which food and drink were served. "You can't miss her," Damon was told by a helpful young girl. "Old Alice Cormier's big enough to take up two chairs. She's that Mortvedt boy's aunt."

The agents approached a corner table at which sat a middle-aged white woman who appeared to weigh at least two hundred fifty pounds. She was wearing a flower-patterned yellow dress. Her bright, brown eyes were almost lost in the folds of fat that served as her cheeks. A small, red mouth above a triple layer of chins widened into a guarded smile when Tirabassi introduced himself and Karen, being careful to display his badge discreetly so that onlookers could not see it.

"Don't have to show me no badge," Alice Cormier said. "If you weren't FBI or some such, don't think you'd be out here in your business clothes on a afternoon hot as this."

She motioned for them to sit down across from her, then pushed forward a plate of meat. "That's barbequed raccoon," Alice said. "Help yourself. If you don't like that," she added, "the red beans and rice are awful good here." Alice briskly transferred three forkfuls of food into her mouth, her eyes never leaving their faces as she did.

Karen learned forward. "We just had our lunch, Ms. Cormier," she said, "but thank you anyway.

"The reason we're here," Karen continued, "is to try to get an idea of how to locate a man you're related to. His name is Ronald Mortvedt. We understand he's your nephew."

Alice Cormier slowly lowered her fork onto her plate. She looked pained under the weight of unbidden memory. "Oh Lord," she sighed, "what's that boy gone and done now?"

◇◇◇

In the sweltering south Louisiana afternoon, as a portable fan swept back and forth nearby, making ripples in the fetid air but cooling nothing, Karen and Damon listened patiently as Alice Cormier recounted her recollections of "my sister Audrey's only child."

"Ronnie," she said, "was an unhappy baby, crying all the time, poor little fella, and as he got older he was just a real mean-tempered little boy. And he got to be meaner every year, it seemed.

"Ronnie's daddy, Maurice, would come home drunk and beat on the both of them, Audrey and Ronnie. It was terrible, what went on there for years. Audrey went to the sheriff a lot of times but never got no help that I remember. I don't know why. Finally, Audrey just up and run out on them, and later on Ronnie left here, too. I ain't seen him since. I read about him the papers, though. Last I heard he was over in that prison west of here. I wrote him some letters up there, but I never heard back from him."

Alice paused to run a kerchief across her forehead. She took a long drink of iced tea before continuing. "Ronnie's a boy that probably was no good just from his father's blood—them Mortvedts are nothing but trouble. Never been nothing else. But I always felt sorry for Ronnie. There's many a time, Audrey told me, that Maurice would whup him for no reason at all. So he was never surprised when he got whupped for something he did do.

"By the time he was nine or ten and starting to ride in the match races around here, he was as hard as oak. There didn't seem to be anything he was scared of or could bother him—even the beatings from his daddy. Boys four or five years older than him was afraid of Ronnie."

Over the course of the next hour, Alice took considerable pains to emphasize that Ronnie Mortvedt's character was in no way representative of his mother's side of the family. "I'll tell you all day long that them Mortvedts was the matter here," Alice said forcefully. "Our people hardly never got into no trouble with the law. And we sure didn't enjoy it when we did.

"We had people in racing, too," Alice emphasized. "My daddy, Mervin Cormier, was a very, very well respected horseman. He was known over in New Orleans. He raced his horses there for many years and made a lot of friends doing it.

"I'll never forget when daddy died. Before they brung him back here to be buried, they had a service for him right there at the Fair Grounds racetrack in the morning. We all drove over there for it.

"It was kind of a memorial service. They held it right after the workouts was over. All daddy's friends from the racetrack turned out, even though it was a rainy morning, and kind of cool, too. The racetrack chaplain gave a little talk, and then the hearse with daddy in it drove all the way around the track. That's a mile around there, I believe.

"When that hearse turned into the homestretch one of daddy's old friends, a horse owner named Jack Muniz, he hollered out, "'Yeah! *Here* he comes, *here* comes the winner!'

"And everybody else started joining in, saying the same thing: "'Here comes the winner!' I remember standing right by the winner's circle when that hearse moved by real slow. I was crying, and so was most of the rest of them."

Alice Cormier sat back in her chair. "When you think of what kind of people Ronnie came from—at least on *one* side," she said with a snort—"it is hard to believe he turned out so bad, it truly is."

"So he left to work at the racetrack about"—Karen paused to consult her notes—"eleven or twelve years ago?"

"That's about right."

"Has he ever come back here for a visit?" Karen continued.

"Not that I know of," Alice answered. "From the time he snuck out of here as a boy, I don't believe Ronnie's ever been back. One of the Romero boys told me a year or so back that he heard Ronnie was working on some farm up in Arkansas, or Kentucky. Ronnie can't never be a jockey again, and he can't get a license even to exercise horses at the racetrack. But he can work on farms, I guess.

"But," Alice said, "I'm not even sure that's true. Rumors 'round here are thicker than skeeters in the swamp. All I could say is that, if he ain't in jail again, he's probably doing something with horses. That's all Ronnie knows. He's smart enough to stick with what he understands.

"Thing is, Ronnie was a pretty bright boy. Could have stayed in school and done well. They was always testing him over to the grade school after he'd get in trouble. They found out that his brain was okay, but his mentality tests, well, they used to get them counselors all worked up."

Alice Cormier shook her head sadly. "Swear to you," she said earnestly, "it all goes back to that damned Mortvedt blood. Why my sister ever married into that bunch is something I won't understand if I live till Huey Long comes back."

◇◇◇

Driving back to New Orleans, Karen said, "This Mortvedt must be a real sicko."

"I won't argue with that," Damon replied as he pulled out to pass one of the horse trailers that had also recently departed LaCombe Downs.

Damon drove in silence for several miles before Karen said, "There's one thing that really bothers me about this whole case."

"What's that?"

Karen said, "It's that, from the start, the whole emphasis seems to be on apprehending Rexroth. I mean, I know he deserves it if he's been defrauding insurance companies by having his poor horses killed. But everything seems to be aimed at him, from the time this investigation was launched. He's the primary target.

Looking for Mortvedt, well, it seems like that is seen as just an avenue to get to Rexroth. My question is, what about Mortvedt himself? As the creep doing the dirty work, why doesn't he have the bull's eye on *his* chest?"

Damon gunned the Taurus into the passing lane and sped past a pair of semis before responding.

"I know where you're coming from," he said. "The emphasis from the top has been on Rexroth from the very beginning. I can't tell you why. And it's not 'ours to wonder why,' either.

"All I know is that Rexroth is the big enchilada on this plate, Karen. Mortvedt's on the menu, but Rexroth is the main course as far as the Bureau is concerned."

Chapter 11

After angling across the frenzied Dan Ryan Expressway traffic and exiting onto the Calumet Expressway, heading for Indiana, Doyle glanced out of his car window to the left, seeing the remnants of Gary's industrial age, the empty foundries and factories. The Skyway was dotted with signs for the area's current boom industry: casinos. Doyle thought he'd rather be fishing for the industrial-strength carp that inhabited the waters of Wolf Lake to the right of the Skyway than shooting craps on a summer afternoon.

He figured about six and a half hours to Lexington and Willowdale Farm following the tollway to Indianapolis, a quick stop there to pick up a couple of pastrami sandwiches from Shapiro's Delicatessen, then I-65 through the Hoosier State to New Albany, other side of the Ohio River from Louisville. Then it was an easy seventy-five miles or so from Derby Town to the heart of the Blue Grass.

Doyle moved the radio dial off an all-news station after hearing the announcer begin to describe "an Oak Park woman who was the victim of a *home invasion gone terribly wrong.*" Doyle tried to imagine a home invasion going smoothly to the satisfaction of all concerned.

As Doyle tuned in Gary's good jazz station, in the middle of an Oscar Peterson tour de force titled "Nigerian Marketplace," he began to review his assignment. He went over what Engel and Tirabassi had told him about the horse killings, went over his meeting with Aldous Bolger. Then his thought-train quickly went onto a siding marked by Doyle's pleasant memory of meeting Bolger's sister.

"Caroline," he said to himself, "nice name…nice girl… Wonder how many other New Zealand women are as great-looking as she is?"

Doyle's car, at the suggestion of Maggie Howard, was unwashed and unkempt, the interior packed haphazardly with his possessions, backseat strewn with horse industry magazines and old copies of the *Racing Journal*.

"You got to make it *look* like a horseman's car," Maggie had said.

This advice Doyle had received the previous morning after he'd driven out to Heartland Downs. He had wanted to say goodbye to City Sarah and Maggie, not necessarily in that order, and also ask that if any word was received in the Zocchi barn of former employee E. D. Morley, it be forwarded to Doyle in Kentucky.

Doyle had caught up with Maggie right after training hours. "I got on ten this morning," meaning she'd exercised ten horses, she said happily, "and I'm starving. I'll even let a suspicious character like you buy me breakfast." Her black eyes crinkled with good humor.

Once they were seated in the track kitchen, where the morning orders were just about evenly divided between fried eggs and huevos rancheros, with bottles of beer being sold to many members of each faction, Doyle said, "What do you mean, suspicious?"

Maggie smiled at him from over her platter of ham and eggs. "Jack, you know what I'm talking about," she said. "Ever since you came to work for Angelo, everybody around here figured you were up to something. Like I told you from the get-go, you weren't any kind of horse person then.

"Sure, you picked up the routine pretty fast. And you showed up and worked hard, I'll give you that. But that didn't change the fact you weren't really one of us."

Doyle stepped away from the table for a coffee refill at the cafeteria counter. When he'd returned to his seat, he said, "Maggie, what you say may be true. But I'll tell you this, my dear, I better look the part where I'm going next." Without coming close to getting into the subject of his involvement with the FBI, Doyle recounted how he had found a position on a farm in Kentucky.

"Doing what?" said the incredulous Maggie Howard.

"Working for a friend of mine. Name is Bolger."

"What farm you going on?" Maggie asked.

"It's called Willowdale."

Maggie looked even more amazed at this statement. "Jack, that's one of the major farms down there." Taking off her black exercise rider's helmet, Maggie shook her black curls in another sign of disbelief. Then, her eyes narrowed as she regarded Doyle across the scarred plastic table.

"Jack Doyle, you're up to *another* something, aren't you?" she said accusingly.

"I'm just going about making a living, Maggie," Doyle replied. "I don't know how this is going to work out for me. But I haven't got anything else going. I refuse to go back to the kind of bullshit jobs I used to do. And Angelo hasn't exactly offered me any bonus money to return to work for him. So, I figured I'd give it a try down in the old Blue Grass." He reached for his coffee cup, avoiding her gaze.

Maggie went back to the counter, evidently convinced she wasn't going to elicit any more useful information regarding Doyle's upcoming employment. She returned with two bran muffins nearly the size of croquet balls, then quickly polished them off. Doyle shook his head admiringly; the girl had about a twenty-inch waist. "Don't tell me," she said, laughing at the look on Doyle's face. "I know, I know, it's what everybody says—I've got the metabolism of a hummingbird. Well, enjoy it is my theory."

"So," Doyle said, trying to be as nonchalant as possible, "anybody ever hear from E. D. Morley?"

Chapter 12

Once he'd identified himself over the intercom at the huge stone gates, Doyle pointed his car up a long, winding driveway that led through Harvey Rexroth's Willowdale Farm.

Doyle had driven the eleven miles out from Lexington on a blacktop county road that was flanked on each side by miles of rolling green pasture divided by expensive white fencing. Many of those miles had nineteenth-century stone walls still in place nearer the road.

In contrast to the boom times of the nineteen-eighties, not all of the pastures were replete with thoroughbred horses; many of the fields were empty, others contained grazing beef cattle. While the city of Lexington had experienced a tremendous growth of business in recent years, Fayette County's most visible and famous industry, horse production, had tailed off sharply.

Still, the scenery was striking. Spring sunlight glistened on dew-laden grass, on which lay, lazed, or romped a variety of thoroughbred horses—from mares in foal, to those with foals at their sides, to the stallions isolated in the imperious splendor of their own paddocks. The white fences bordering the lush acreage of the Willowdale property extended for miles.

When Doyle's car had curved around the white-gravel driveway and up to the columned portico of the farm's red-brick mansion, the front door of the enormous structure opened and a small, dark-haired, dark-suited man wearing gold-rimmed glasses

Maggie shook her head. "Not a word," she said. "That was real strange. E. D. worked for Angelo for four, maybe five years. That's a long time these days on a racetrack backstretch to work for the same man. Everybody figured they got along real good.

"But then E. D. just never showed up one day. Never even picked up his last check, Angelo said. And that was *real* strange, because E. D. was as tight as they come. Not cheap, mind you; he'd always chip in for guys down on their luck, or something like that. But tight, is what I'm saying. I guarantee you, E. D. knew where his every dollar was, and why it was there.

"Say," Maggie said, frowning at Doyle. "Wasn't it just about the same time you left the stable that E. D. did?"

"Right about the same time, I guess. I'm not positive," Doyle shrugged.

Maggie's big black eyes burrowed into Doyle. "Jack, there's something here you're not telling me about, something funny. Am I right?"

Doyle stood up, smiling. "You'd know a lot more about me if you would have accepted my kind—no, make that *heartfelt*—invitation to dinner back when I first met you. But now," he said, hands raised apologetically, "I've got to leave the state and head to my new job. I just don't have the time to exchange any confidences with you now. Come on, I'll walk you back to the barn."

As they headed toward the track kitchen door, Maggie said, "Somehow, Jack, I get the feeling I did the right thing. Don't get me wrong," she added, "it's not that I don't like you. But you remind me of a story an old boyfriend of mine told me."

Maggie waved hello at a trainer coming their way, then resumed talking as they walked.

"This fella, this one-time boyfriend, grew up in Detroit and went to school with the son of one of those Mafia dons, or whatever they call them. Anyway, Jimmy, my friend, stayed in touch with this guy, his name was Mario, over the years. Jimmy wound up as a horse trainer, Mario went into the family business.

And about five years ago, Mario got nabbed in a big crackdown in Detroit, and he got sent to prison.

"My friend Jimmy kept in touch with Mario. And Mario wrote him back these long letters. He was a real good letter writer. Jimmy said Mario had been the editor of their high school newspaper.

"Anyway, Mario is in prison for about three years, and near the end of his sentence, he gets to know a new arrival—a congressman from near his home back in the Detroit area. They get to be good buddies.

"The congressman reads one of Mario's letters one day, and he tells Mario, 'You're a terrific writer. I'd like to write a book—about my experiences in politics, and my bad luck that brought me here, and so forth.' And then he says to Mario, 'Would you help me write this?'

"According to Jimmy, Mario tells the congressman, 'No, I can't do that, as much as I'd like to. The reason is, there's not enough time. I'd like to help you, Congressman, but I'm getting paroled out of here in two weeks.'

"I guess the congressman was pretty disappointed at this. He says to Mario, 'Well, that's too bad. I wish I would have gotten to know you sooner.'

"And Mario takes a long look at this guy, this congressman, and he says to him: 'Believe me, if you would have known me longer, you would have *been* here sooner.'"

Maggie stopped walking. They had nearly reached the south end of Angelo Zocchi's barn by now, where her car was parked. She looked up at Doyle.

"Jack, I can't hardly help but think that there's something about that story that brings you to mind. I don't know what you were up to when you were here before. And I don't know what you're up to taking this farm job in Kentucky. Tell you the truth, I'd rather not know.

"You're a cool guy, Jack. But I do believe that getting into your life could be a risky thing."

Maggie Howard extended her strong, brown, ri
and Doyle gripped it briefly. He couldn't argue with he
seemed like a very nice, straight-ahead young woman, c
with one of those built-in bullshit detectors like the k
Jack Doyle carried through life.

motioned Doyle to park in a spot beside the steps. "Good morning," the man said after Doyle had stepped out of the car.

"I am Byron Stoner, Mr. Rexroth's executive assistant. If you will please follow me, Mr. Rexroth is almost ready to see you."

Doyle removed his sunglasses, placing them in a pocket of his tan sport coat. He wore a white short-sleeved shirt, khaki trousers, and Western boots. The complete assistant farm manager's look, he hoped. He followed Stoner down a long hallway where walls of dark wood were covered with paintings of horses. The hall led to the rear of the mansion.

Glass doors, like those in airports and hotels, slid open as Doyle and Stoner approached. Then they were at the entrance to an enormous tinted-glass structure covered by a retractable dome. The building housed a huge swimming pool, its border dotted with some comfortable-looking beach furniture.

Circling the area that bordered the pool was a beige-colored, slightly banked track around which sped a gorgeous, long-legged, young redhead on inline skates. Doyle did a double take. All she was wearing was blue knee pads, blue elbow pads, and a red headband.

"Well, good morning America, how are ya?" Doyle muttered to himself as the nearly nude figure flashed past him.

He said to Stoner, "Isn't that kind of dangerous? Without a helmet?"

"She's a real daredevil, that one," Stoner said. "She's one of Mr. Rexroth's secretaries and companions. As you may have read in the popular press, Mr. Rexroth is a bachelor who loves women."

"Likes them active, eh?" Doyle said as the redhead zipped through the far turn of the track and headed toward them up the left straightaway. As she swung her arms from side to side, her breasts shifted sideways like cantaloupes in motion.

"Active they must be," responded Stoner without a trace of irony on his serious face. "Their assignments are considerably more physical than clerical, but Mr. Rexroth demands devotion to duty in all his employees, no matter what those duties may be. Mr. Rexroth is over there," Stoner said, gesturing toward the far end of the pool.

Doyle saw a thick-bodied man, five feet nine or ten and over 200 pounds, somewhere in his late thirties. He looked to Doyle to have been one of those naturally pudgy children who grew up packing on firm layers of blubber each year into adulthood, where they topped out in the portly section of their tailor's files. Rexroth was talking on a cellular phone. His resonant baritone voice was angry and loud. The sun, shining through the open dome, bounced off Rexroth's large, hairless head. Daddy Warbucks in the Blue Grass, Doyle thought.

Rexroth wore a dark-green velour robe. On his feet were gray Nike cross trainers. In his left hand was a baton-sized cigar that he gestured with as he talked into the phone. Asleep next to Rexroth's right Nike lay a brown and white bulldog. Like Rexroth, the dog had a broad head, big shoulders, and a large, fleshy jaw. Doyle found himself momentarily gawking at the similarity of appearance between man and beast.

About fifteen feet to Rexroth's left, leaning forward on a white wicker couch and apparently impervious to the phone tirade taking place nearby, was a very large young man who Doyle, from the description supplied by the FBI agents, recognized as Rexroth's bodyguard, Randy Kauffman. He looked as ominously stupid and strong as they had said. Kauffman was intently watching, on a small color television, the *Jerry Springer Show.*

Doyle recalled Damon Tirabassi's description of Kauffman as being "wider than a warehouse door, and just as dumb. He pumps more iron than the Packers, and he eats steroids like popcorn."

Damon had gone on to say that a Willowdale worker, later fired, reported Kauffman to the Society for the Prevention of Cruelty to Animals. "This woman," Damon said, "called in that she had seen Kauffman knock down a horse with one punch. Evidently Rexroth had ordered him to do it, so Kauffman cracks this old mare right between the eyes with a right hand, and down she goes. The ex-worker said Rexroth just was hopping around, laughing at this, calling Kauffman 'Mongo.' The point," Damon said, "is don't ever let him get his hands on you."

Doyle returned his attention to Rexroth. The media mogul sat behind a large, marble-topped desk, an impressive piece of furniture completely at odds with the rest of the mini-pavilion's casual decor. The top of the desk was piled with computer printouts, notepads, newspapers, and a computer that Rexroth impatiently pecked at as he continued to shout into the phone.

"Phillips," he said, "the reason I made you editor of *Horse Racing Journal,* the reason you have a huge salary plus an expense count that you've padded so much it could win the Pulitzer Prize for fiction—was to boost, that's BOOST, circulation. Goddamit, my papers don't LOSE readers, they GAIN them—all except the one you're editing.

"What? What was that. Bullshit! I don't want to hear about the *Racing Daily* having a built-in advantage because it's been around for five fucking centuries or whatever. It's ready to be driven out of business, goddamnit. Are you hearing me?

"I want you and that bloated staff of yours to come up with new, different, sensational stories from the racing industry...the Dark Side of the Sport of Kings...jockeys with batteries, crooked trainers, drugged horses...I want those stories and plenty of them.

"I don't give a shit if they don't exist. Find them! Fake them! Then put them on page one in headlines you can read from across the street. I want people fighting with each other to buy the *Horse Racing Journal* every goddam morning, Phillips.

"'Man Fucks Mare!' 'Horse Rapes Jockette!' Ninety-six point type. That's what I'm looking for—the racy stuff behind the races, the dirt, the filth, THE STUFF PEOPLE LOVE TO READ!" Rexroth roared.

Finally lowering his voice and allowing the veins in his neck to recede, Rexroth said, "Find those stories, Phillips, or find another job." He then threw the phone into the swimming pool. Without hesitation, Kauffman got up, grabbed a long-handled fishing net, and adeptly retrieved it. Doyle recognized this as a practiced motion.

Rexroth rose to his feet, briefly shook Doyle's hand, then motioned him to a chair in front of the desk. The nearly -nude redhead whizzed by on the track behind Rexroth's chair, her wheels whirring. She peered straight ahead. She was working up a pretty good sweat, Doyle noted, asking himself, I wonder what the other FBI moles are looking at this morning?

Rexroth interrupted this brief reverie with a question, spoken in a voice turned somewhat raspy from the strain of his recent phone call.

"I've read your resume, Mr. Doyle," he said. "Now, I want you to tell me why you want to go to work at Willowdale."

Spotting the redhead on another revolution of the track, Doyle couldn't help but respond, "Well, the scenery certainly is attractive."

"Yes, she's a winner," Rexroth agreed. Then he called out, "Darlene, you can take a break now."

"It's Darla," the redhead shouted over her shoulder, irritation obvious in her voice. "Do you need me anymore today?"

"No," Rexroth said. "I'll see you tonight. Please send out Deirdre."

Darla did as she was told and, within seconds, much to Doyle's amazement, another neo-naked blader appeared on the track, this one a diminutive brunette with legs muscled like those of an Olympic sprinter. How many has he got lined up back there, Doyle wondered, as Deirdre began zipping around the track with quick little strides.

"If you don't mind me asking," Doyle said, "how often do the shifts change?"

"As often as I want them to," Rexroth growled. Then his expression cleared.

"I find the presence of such active beauty to be a remarkable tonic—both physical and mental. Variety...variety kick-starts creativity.

"VARIETY KICK-STARTS CREATIVITY," he suddenly shouted, startling Doyle, the dozing bulldog, and even the television-watching behemoth.

Rexroth jumped to his feet. "Stoner," he said to his assistant, "write that down and have bumper stickers made of it for every RexCom employee. Display will be mandatory on each employee's vehicle. Have the bumper stickers distributed along with pay-checks. They'll be taken more seriously that way."

Rexroth shook his head, recalling past promotional and motivational schemes that had fallen short of his expectations. "It's a shame, I sometimes think, that you have to have people working for you in order to run a business."

Doyle remembered reading, in the background informa-tion on Rexroth that the FBI had given him, how the RexCom chairman made it a practice of once each year arriving at each of his major corporate offices to harangue the employees—his "troops." as he referred to them—while dressed like his hero, General George S. Patton. Rexroth would strut up and down the auditorium stage in front of a huge American flag, snapping a riding crop against his polished boots, bald dome covered by a gleaming silver helmet.

Attendance was mandatory at these performances, so much so that one worried RexCom office manager, hospitalized for hemorrhoid surgery, had himself delivered by ambulance to the auditorium one year in an attempt to demonstrate his fealty. Rexroth fired him anyway once the man had returned to his job. "The troops were paying more attention to that suckass Schullman that day than they were to me," Rexroth said, in explaining this dismissal.

After Rexroth had riffled through papers that Doyle recog-nized as his phonied-up resume created by the FBI agents with the cooperation of some prominent West Coast breeders who were eager to be of aid to the agency, the publisher again turned his attention to Doyle.

"I see that Aldous Bolger knows you," Rexroth said. "He's quite complimentary about your abilities."

"Aldous and I go back a long way," said Doyle, lying resolutely. He then went on to mention other aspects of his fictional career on some of California's leading horse farms.

"Have you ever trained horses?" Rexroth asked.

"I've had some experience on the racetrack," Doyle replied truthfully, "but I got tired of the traveling around. I'm engaged to be married," he lied again, "and I thought it was time I tried to find a job with more permanence to it." He gave Rexroth his most sincere, polished at Serafin Ltd., look. Rexroth didn't seem either impressed or unimpressed. He looked more uninterested than anything else.

"You know the salary," he said. "I'll review your performance with Bolger after your first month, and we'll see where we stand. Welcome to Willowdale," Rexroth added, dismissing Doyle as he turned to pick up the slightly damp cellular phone.

Stoner accompanied Doyle out of the pool area and toward the front door. He must have read his boss' body language, for he said, "Congratulations on your new job, Mr. Doyle."

Doyle nodded. Then he said to Stoner, "Is that some sort of whirling harem Rexroth has going back there?"

"No, not necessarily. I wouldn't describe the situation quite in those terms," the secretary replied. "It's true that one of the girls occasionally falls into what might be termed Rexrothian favor, and as a result takes up residence in the house. But, by and large, these women are hired for exactly what you see them doing.

"In addition to the rollerblading," he continued, "Mr. Rexroth's favorite of their public exercises, they also perform aerobic routines during the course of the day. He insists that the sight of them, the aesthetically pleasing counterpoint they provide to the labors required of him in operating a giant business enterprise, serve to sharpen his acumen."

"That redhead would have my acumen standing at attention," Doyle remarked. Stoner ignored it. He said, "Mr. Rexroth does, however, as is quite widely known, have a mistress at his New York City residence, another one on the old family homestead in Montana." Stoner supplied this information with a touch of pride, perhaps even the hint of a vicarious thrill of possession, Doyle thought.

"Has Rexroth ever been married?"

"No, he has not." He paused.

"As Mr. Rexroth has commented on more than one occasion, a man of his financial stature has to be extremely cautious. At the same time, as he puts it, the thought of a prenuptial agreement, something de riguer in his level of society these days, causes his 'cock to shrivel up like a retractable telescope.'

"Not a condition a man with Mr. Rexroth's appetites would relish," he added.

As Doyle took one more glance back toward the girl circling the track, he saw a portly black woman, dressed as a hospital attendant, wheeling a food cart toward Rexroth's desk. Once she'd reached it, the woman lifted a tray off the cart and placed it before Rexroth, who was rubbing his hands in anticipation. He looked up at the black woman, said something to her that Doyle could not hear, gave her a broad smile, then dismissed her with a wave of his hand. Rexroth then began to eat, with obvious relish.

Doyle looked inquiringly at Stoner. The secretary was silent, but Doyle saw that Stoner was watching him out of the corner of his eye. Stoner was waiting for Doyle to bite on this, Doyle just knew it.

"Dare I ask?…" Doyle began, but Stoner interrupted him, perhaps eager to get this explanation over with.

"Since a childhood skiing accident that put him in the hospital for an extended period," Stoner said, "Mr. Rexroth's favorite food has been…hospital food. He likes the servers to be as authentic as possible as well."

Doyle said, "You're jerking my chain here, aren't you, Stoner?"

"I am *not* making this up," the secretary hissed, shaking his head from side to side.

Doyle said, "Hospital food? In the tradition of, well, hospital food? We're talking mystery meat, vegetable remnants, jello parts? That's what you're telling me?"

Stoner nodded, shrugging his narrow shoulders. In defense of his employer, he said, "It's obviously one of those acquired tastes that few people ever acquire."

Stoner smiled thinly as he waited on the front door threshold for Doyle to descend the broad steps of the mansion to his car. The smile left his face as Doyle's car disappeared down the long drive, and Stoner frowned as he re-entered the mansion and walked to his office. There was something about Jack Doyle—he couldn't put his finger on it, but it was there—that Stoner found troubling. This, despite the fact that Doyle's impressive resume and list of references checked out perfectly.

Byron Stoner came from a business background in Toronto where he had worked in RexCom's Canadian division, specializing in labor relations. Later, this field changed into "human relations," but the work remained the same: finding the most effective ways to beat down the unions and slash personnel costs.

Stoner's successes in Toronto brought him to the attention of Harvey Rexroth, and Stoner accepted the offer to become the publisher's executive assistant, i.e. number one trouble shooter. A lifelong bachelor, with no close family remaining, Stoner had no compunction about crossing the border and eventually becoming engaged in far more serious acts than framing union officials or bribing shop stewards.

Rexroth realized early on that Stoner could be entrusted to do anything, thus leaving his employer at a presumably safe legal remove from possible recriminations. Rexroth once remarked to the little Canadian, "I'm not sure I understand how you know the kind of people we occasionally need to hire for special jobs."

"Oh, I don't, Mr. Rexroth," Stoner had replied. "But I know how to *find* people who do know what we're looking for. For the money you're willing to pay, we can find people willing to do just about anything."

Rexroth took great pride in having secured the services of Byron Stoner. "Look at him," Rexroth once commented, "with his thinning hair and those glasses, that expressionless face, he looks like the chief accountant in some backwater button factory. But he's got no more morals than a musk melon."

When Stoner entered his office, his phone message light beaconed. It was time for the various RexCom managers to deliver their midday business reports. Stoner was soon immersed in his work, thoughts of Jack Doyle dismissed.

Chapter 13

Among the numerous targets of RexCom's recent cost-cutting program was Thaddeus "Red" Marchik, a thirty-year veteran of racing journalism who had been in RexCom's employ for nearly five years, and fully expected to remain therein until the arrival of what he deemed to be his well-earned retirement.

The "well-earned," however, was not an assessment shared by Marchik's immediate supervisor, managing editor Paul Lipscomb. When Lipscomb had received the most recent staff reduction order from RexCom corporate headquarters, he began to compile a list of potential firees. Marchik's name led off.

As Lipscomb told one of his assistants, "I don't know why in hell we've kept him as long as we have. Marchik has been dogging it since Lassie was a pup. No matter where we assign him, he finds a way to slow down the pace, all the while complaining about how he's overworked and underpaid. We used to have a summer intern take care of all the racing commission rulings that we publish in two hours a day. Marchik has somehow managed to turn this function—an almost mindless function, I might add—into a full-time operation requiring overtime, for Chrissakes! "

He drew breath. "Marchik has got to go."

Co-workers who heard the howl that erupted from Marchik upon being informed of his firing cowered in their cubicles. "You can't treat a Navy veteran like this," Marchik shouted, pounding a large fist on Lipscomb's desk. A broad-shouldered six-footer, Marchik, even at age fifty-nine, made for a formidable sight with his sweaty face as bright as his full head of red hair.

"Red, face the facts here," Lipscomb advised. "You just haven't worked out for us. I couldn't do anything to save you if I wanted to," Lipscomb lied. "These are orders from the top."

Marchik looked at him incredulously. "You mean Mr. Rexroth himself?"

In an attempt to mollify Marchik by making him feel important enough to be a personal concern of the media kingpin, and also anxious to get Marchik out of his office, Lipscomb nodded his head affirmatively. "He just felt it would be best for all concerned if you took your talents elsewhere." Lipscomb struggled to keep a straight face.

Red Marchik rose to his full height. "That tub of guts will regret the day he decided that. He'll learn you can't fuck over a Navy veteran." He then stormed out of Lipscomb's office.

"Send in the next sheep for slaughter," Lipscomb said into the intercom on his desk.

◇◇◇

Red Marchik came from an extended family of occupational malingerers, one dotted by union officials with phony jobs, ghost payrollers on the municipal side, and a couple of cousins whose careers had been devoted to winning phony accident lawsuits against insurance companies.

Those members of the Marchik family who, like Red, actually held real jobs, usually considered these positions to be either "beneath them," or "too much for them," or flagrantly ill-paying. Their working lives were replete with indignation at what they considered to be slights or insults suffered at the hands of supervisors who had no business giving orders.

Someone once said of the late television announcer Howard Cosell that, if he were a sport, "he'd be roller derby." Similarly, if the Marchiks were considered as an historical entity, they'd be seen as a continually pissed-off but immobilized peasantry.

Later on the day he'd been dismissed by Lipscomb, while sitting at the poker table in the basement recreation room of his modest ranch home on Louisville's west side, Red Marchik pondered his fate as he tossed down a succession of shots of Jim Beam followed by gulps of Pabst Blue Ribbon. His berating of his former employer become increasingly embittered as the afternoon, and the alcohol, wore on. But no matter how loudly he decried his fate, Red's wife, Wanda, maintained her composure. She sat across from Red at the felt-covered table, rolling and smoking one marijuana joint after another and nodding her head in agreement at her irate husband.

The recreation room, refinished by Wanda years ago, was the Marchiks' pride and joy. On shelves dotting the fake knotty-pine paneled walls sat an amazing array of stuffed carcasses—raccoons, coyotes, various other mammals—along with the head of a small deer.

The prized trophy, an albino squirrel with a strikingly malicious look in its eyes, held center stage between a huge National Rifle Association poster and a blown-up photo of one-time Nixon henchman Charles Colson, whom the Marchiks were convinced had been railroaded to prison where he became a born-again Christian.

Red peered blearily at Wanda. "They're not gonna get away with doing this to me, Wanda. They're going to pay for this." He again recounted to her his meeting earlier that day with a member of RexCom's Human Resources Department. "They ripped me off on severance pay, insurance, pension—the whole eleven yards, the bastards.

"Human Resources, hah! What a fuckin' name for what they do! Their motto should be Bend Over and Spread Those Cheeks."

Wanda Marchik was used to hearing such tirades from her husband of twenty-three years, and paid them no heed. She looked upon Red as a delightfully harmless, terribly attractive man, one she had been crazy about since literally bumping into him one night between beer frames at JJ's Bowling Lanes many years earlier. Wanda didn't spend time analyzing why she adored her lazy, perpetually put-upon husband. "There's no explaining it," she often told her girl friends. "He's just a beautiful hunk of man, isn't he?"

Wanda, a diminutive brunette, had wide-ranging interests that Red would have been hard put to explain, had he been asked. He just accepted them. In addition to owning and operating a thriving carpet-cleaning business, one that employed a battalion of industrious Polish immigrants, Wanda was an active member of the NRA, the Sierra Club, the Coalition for the Retention of the Death Penalty, Planned Parenthood—the Marchiks themselves were childless, the result of what Red openly admitted was his "shooting blanks in the sperm division"—and the National Association to Legalize Marijuana.

Such a diverse dossier of memberships never struck either of the Marchiks as unusual; this undoubtedly explained the theme of mutual content that permeated their marriage. Some people are indeed "just made for each other," and the Marchiks—Red, a lifelong malingerer and discontent, and the ambitious Wanda—qualified on these counts.

Wanda rolled up the sleeves of her Chicago Bears sweatshirt. She then started rolling another joint. "Honey, you really don't have to work anymore. My business is going great. You're getting close to retirement anyway. Why not just sit back and enjoy this? Why are you making this so, you know, personal with Mr. Rexroth?

"Those big companies dump people all the time. Good people like you," Wanda quickly added.

"That tubby turd is going to pay for this," Red vowed. "Stay out of my way on this one, Wanda." Red lurched to his feet and stumbled toward the plastic-covered white couch that faced the forty-two-inch color television set. After flopping down, he quickly went to sleep, still muttering.

Wanda smiled fondly at the love of her life. She had heard Red promise punishment to a variety of employers, or foremen, or co-workers, over the course of his career spent performing the simplest tasks in a variety of small-time journalistic jobs. Frankly, she had been surprised when Red had landed—through the help of a friend of his, Chester Langenbach—a position on the *Horse Racing Journal*, part of the Rexroth empire. Wanda was further surprised that Red had lasted in the job so long, considering what she tolerantly accepted to be his combination of semi-ineptitude and bilious attitude toward work.

"Oh, you'll get over this, too, honey," Wanda whispered to her hubby as he rested peacefully beneath a haze of marijuana smoke and a small cloud of beer and bourbon fumes.

Ordinarily an accurate assessor of her mate's moods and intentions, Wanda Marchik proved to be way off the mark this time.

◇◇◇

As the weeks following his firing by RexCom went by, and his severance pay dwindled, Red Marchik's fury lingered. Predictably, his half-hearted attempts to find another job produced nothing, and Red appeared to be home free with his twenty-six weeks of unemployment checks. Wanda's business continued to thrive, so the Marchiks were not confronted by financial worries. It was the bitterness billowing from what he considered to be the huge personal insult that was his firing that stoked Red's anger. Try as he might, he could discern no reason why he should have been found wanting at this stage of his working life. "I wasn't doing any better—or any worse—than I ever did," he repeatedly complained to Wanda.

In the second month of his forced retirement, Red began to soothe his ego with the theory that his firing had been "a goddam hate crime by that fucking Rexroth." The more he thought about it, the more sense it made to him. Over the course of several days one week, Red struggled to compose a letter to his former employer.

"You will soon hear from my attorney regarding charges of age discrimination and ethnic prejudice that I intend to bring against you," the letter began. It continued:

If you think that you can operate your evil conglomerate without fear of reprisal, think again. Understand that fighting evil is nothing new to me. I am a U.S. Navy veteran.

After my years of dedicated service to RexCom, I was abruptly terminated. The only reason I can think of for my firing is that you have carried too far your hatred of Lithuanian Americans. I proudly happen to be one. It was not lost on me that another employee fired, Mr. Harry Lopke, has a widowed mother he supports, she, too, being of Lithuanian-American heritage.

If you think you can get away with your cancerous practices, think again. Your prejudicial perpertrations are comparable to those fostered in years past in Nazi Germany and Communist Russia, and today in sinkholes like Chile and China. I will show that your vicious actions have caused me to suffer a near heart attack, tremendous emotional and mental stress, and a condition of semi-impotency. I shall prove that my wife and I were almost hospitalized as a result.

I shall have my counsel subpoena you and your clique which have employed Nazified tactics for years, and which vicious activities you vermin have approved of and encouraged. I will produce documental evidence.

A copy of this letter has been sent to every member of Congress, and the Secretary of Labor, and the President of the U.S. himself, for bigotry and hate such as you spew embroils all races and all religions and all must be warned. A copy of this letter has been sent to newspaper editors, to columnists, to television and radio talk show hosts throughout this country and parts of Canada.

If you think you can smirk behind the walls of your house of hate, think again. There are some people who are dedicated to wipe out evil wherever it exists.

       Best Regards,
       Thaddeus "Red" Marchik

Three days later a messenger service delivered an envelope to the Marchik house. It contained Red's letter to Rexroth, across the top of which in large writing scrawled the following reply: "I will be happy to pay for the psychiatric help you so sorely need, you raving asshole." It was signed with the initials HR.

With his vicious hiring and firing practices, Rexroth was used to being occasionally harassed. Among the most irritating of his ex-employees had been a business department clerk named Matthew Dow. For weeks after he was let go Dow would telephone the publisher in the middle of the night and drunkenly sing *A Letter Edged in Black*. This ceased only after Randy Kauffman had been dispatched to talk things over during some of Dow's rare sober moments. Dow had gotten the point, as all of them did. Rexroth didn't give another thought to Marchik or his letter.

◇◇◇

Soon after his letter to Rexroth was so rudely returned, Red began to lay plans for a different kind of revenge. He knew he stood little chance with the courts, and financing a lawsuit claiming age and ethnic discrimination would be expensive. Furthermore, bloodless justice was really not what he sought. Red's plans came to fruition on a summer night, at Willowdale Farm, not long after the death of the horse Uncle Francis.

The previous month, Wanda Marchik had spotted an item in the Louisville paper about an upcoming charity fund raiser to be hosted by Rexroth at Willowdale. She had innocently mentioned this to her husband, almost immediately wishing that she hadn't—because Red seized upon this event as an ideal opportunity for his promised act of fatal revenge.

The fund raiser didn't promise to be as exciting as memorable Kentucky Derby week debauches thrown by one of the Blue Grass area's most flamboyant hostesses, events featuring semi-nude dancers, high octane cocaine, and blow jobs in the bushes. But it nevertheless seemed certain to draw a large crowd and guarantee its host's appearance—in public, on a designated date. The fact that Rexroth was obviously spending a huge chunk of money to sponsor this event served to further infuriate Red. "Some of that money came out of my hide, Wanda," Red said. "He's going to pay for that."

In preparation for the charity dinner-dance, Red retrieved his old Ruger deer-hunting rifle from the Tuck-Away Storage bin west of town. The weapon had been willed to him by his father. Red and his dad, Walter, had spent many autumns in fruitless quest of deer. Walter Marchik was a terrible marksman. Red was worse.

Fortunately for him, the only shots he had been required to produce in the U. S. Navy were as a medical assistant.

With the old rifle, now cleaned and oiled, in hand, Red spent several mornings on a public shooting range near Nicholasville, blazing away at a relatively nearby stationary target. For the most part the targets, like the deer of his past, remained unscathed. Gus Potros, proprietor of the shooting range, warned his assistant to keep an eye on "that red-headed fella out there. He's liable to drop his rifle and then hit something for the first time," Potros said, adding, "If there's a worse marksman in Kentucky than that man, he's walking the streets behind a seeing-eye dog."

One evening Red brought home a rental from the video store that he insisted Wanda watch with him. It was the movie *The Day of the Jackal*.

"The real one," Red emphasized, "not the puny remake with the *Die Hard* guy."

The next weekend, he and Wanda signed up for an open-to-the-public tour of Willowdale Farm. Red described this as an opportunity to "examine the layout." He took "mental notes about the terrain," he whispered to his wife, who had twice been asked by the tour leader not to deposit her cigarette butts in the water trough near the broodmare barn.

On the eve of the Rexroth charity gala, Red declared himself completely satisfied with their preparations. "The Tubby Tycoon is a dead man walking," he announced as he and Wanda shared a homemade burgoo pizza in their recreation room. Wanda just nodded. Long, long ago she had concluded that Red didn't need a whole lot of encouragement in order to carry out his various loony schemes. The natural buoyancy of the classically bile-ridden malcontent was enough to carry him along. And the best part, as far as Wanda was concerned, was that she could usually count on Red to somehow screw up and emerge, if unfulfilled, at least unscathed.

◇◇◇

Red parked their car well clear of the wide circle of light that marked the Willowdale entrance to the charity bash. Red had borrowed camouflage uniforms for both of them from his neighbor and fellow NRA member Oscar Belliard, now in his twenty-seventh year of unsuccessful attempts to recruit a powerful local militia aimed at the overthrow of the Kentucky Senate, which he considered a "cancer on the liver of the Commonwealth." Belliard had managed to round up far more uniforms than bodies to fill them.

"These are brand-new uniforms," Red proudly told Wanda as he tenderly applied face-black to her broad forehead.

With Red in the lead, deer rifle in hand, they skulked through the first field of the farm, then a second, and reached a knoll overlooking the Willowdale swimming pool, which tonight was flanked by two large tents, one with a band and dance floor, one with a lengthy buffet line.

"Hand me the binoculars, honey." After Wanda had done so, Red—prostrate on the ground, peering intently just as the Jackal would have—suddenly yelped with excitement. "There's Rexroth," he whispered. Red took the safety off the rifle.

As he did so, Wanda began to hear noises in the night, noises that grew increasingly louder somewhere behind them. It was a rumbling, muffled sound, at the same time both new to her and somehow strangely familiar. Suddenly, Wanda thought of movie Westerns she had seen, where the scout holds an ear to the ground before announcing, "I hear horses."

"I hear horses, Red," Wanda said. They both turned. Approaching was a large group of Willowdale broodmares, a collection of convivial equines spurred on by curiosity to inspect these intruders in their pasture.

The Marchiks did not know, of course, that they had nothing to fear from these mares. The Marchiks' joint knowledge of horse behavior was extremely minimal. But their unease was at the maximum, for in the dark of the night the approaching horses looked as big as boxcars, especially to Red. He leapt to his feet and frantically led their retreat, beating Wanda over the fence and to the car by thirty widening feet. Red threw the rifle into the backseat, the car into gear, and away they sped, Wanda fumbling to pull her door shut.

As he drove home Red fulminated about the "goddam bad luck" that had served to bring "those goddam beasts right up on us." Wanda noticed how her husband's hands trembled on the steering wheel. Rexroth, she realized, to both her relief and satisfaction, was safe from any Red Marchik rifle shot, tonight or any other night.

Then Wanda heard heard her husband announce, "But there's more than one way to skin a cat as fat as that. Rexroth'll pay, oh yes, he'll pay. Shooting may not be the answer."

Red took a sharp exit off the Circle Beltway. He continued talking, but Wanda wasn't really listening. She was concentrating on two questions: which frozen casserole she would take from the freezer once they reached home, and whether the comforting toast they would share would be libations of Pabst Blue Ribbon or of the pear brandy she kept under the kitchen sink for special occasions.

She had another question, too, one that made her smile as she rode: how long would it take her designated driver and fledgling assassin to cool off from this night's intense excitement and fall asleep in her loving arms.

Chapter 14

It had been nearly two months since the death of the Willowdale stallion Wilton Lad when Jud Repke picked up his phone one afternoon and heard the cold, calm voice of Ronald Mortvedt.

"Got us another job. I'll pick you up Friday morning," Mortvedt said curtly.

"You in Louisville?"

"Never mind where I am," Mortvedt answered. "Just be ready Friday morning. You'll be back home in a couple of days."

Home for Jud Repke was an aging apartment complex on the north side of Louisville, Kentucky. Repke had lived there for seven years, rent free, serving as the building's superintendent. He'd gotten the job through his brother, a friend of the building's owner. Jud set his own hours, working as few of them as he could get away with, so he had no trouble fitting a Mortvedt-procured job into his schedule.

Like Mortvedt, Jud Repke was an ex-convict who had never been married, having settled instead for a succession of live-in women friends over the years. Jud had met Mortvedt in the federal correctional center at Oakdale, in the southwestern portion of Louisiana. Repke was serving a three-to-five year term for transporting stolen goods, luxury automobiles, across state lines, a trade he had successfully practiced for much of his adult life before slipping up when a deal went bad with a New Orleans Mafia bigshot named Joe Angelici. The Mafia guy walked, but

Repke was convicted and sentenced. Mortvedt was already in Oakdale doing his race-fixing time when Repke arrived.

At a well-worn thirty-eight, Jud Repke was a year younger than the ex-jockey who, he realized after they had known each other for less than a week, was both much smarter and tougher than he was. A natural follower, Repke gratefully buddied with Mortvedt for eighteen months in Oakdale before the ex-jockey was released. Repke was granted parole a year later.

When, two years ago, Mortvedt had tracked Repke down at a grandstand bar at Churchill Downs late one blustery fall afternoon, Repke was not only delighted to see his old jailmate but to hear his plans for work. It didn't take Repke long to agree to go into business with Mortvedt. As Jud later would gratefully say during some of their late-night bar visits, "Ronnie, you been a regular money machine for me, and I thank you for it."

Repke was also unaware of what had gone on in Mortvedt's life after the two of them left prison, unaware that Mortvedt had joined a burglary ring that operated in the New Orleans area. Repke was unaware that, one winter night, Mortvedt had killed a home owner who discovered him, beating him to death with the crowbar he had used to gain entrance to the house.

It was at that point in his life that Mortvedt confirmed for himself, once and for all, that killing didn't bother him in the least. Had Repke known that, he would still have been eager to go into business with the little man.

◇◇◇

Harvey Rexroth had also been eager to go into business with Ronald Mortvedt—or at least someone like him. Their unlikely alliance dated from a horse sale four years earlier, one of the major Kentucky auctions. It was a hot, humid July night, and bidding for the best stock was equally torrid throughout the premier portion of the sale. That session concluded with the offering of a mare named Donna Diane.

A champion runner, Donna Diane was now retired from racing, had been bred, and was carrying a foal sired by a famed male champion. This mix of blue chip past performances and golden-hued promise combined to make for an extremely attractive prospect. Donna Diane was valuable in her own right, and the anticipated foal could correctly be expected to have tremendous value as a runner, then a breeding prospect, no matter what its sex. "By a champion, out of a champion" began the auctioneer's sales spiel. All these factors added up the expectation that Donna Diane would attract the highest price at the sale. She did not disappoint.

In the weeks leading up to the auction, Harvey Rexroth had boasted to several industry people that he was determined to buy Donna Diane. He saw her as the potential leading light of his growing broodmare band, a name acquisition that would further underline his stated desire to become a major player in horse racing.

As Donna Diane was led into the crescent-shaped sales ring that night, Rexroth mopped his face. Despite the air-conditioning inside the pavilion, he was sweating heavily. Seated next to him, Byron Stoner had never before observed his boss at anything approaching this level of anxiety.

When the bidding began on Donna Diane, the first shouted offer was a whopping one million—unheard of for an opening bid. The crowd buzzed. The price rose rapidly after that, shedding bidders along the way. Finally, it became clear that there were really only two serious factions remaining: Rexroth and a partnership made up of wealthy Irish breeders and English bookmakers. This partnership had dominated the sale in recent years, spending millions on horses that it shipped back for eventual racing in Europe.

The bidding on Donna Diane climbed to four million, then five million. When the man representing what Rexroth resentfully termed the "foreign conglomerate" coolly indicated that six million dollars was fine with him, Rexroth realized he was not going to outbid these rivals.

Without even a glance at the expectant auctioneer, Rexroth suddenly rose from his seat and stormed out of the pavilion into the steamy night, Stoner and Kauffman struggling to keep up with him. Approached by reporters as he awaited the arrival of his limousine, Rexroth rebuffed them all, including Ira Meyer, who worked for Rexroth's own *Horse Racing Journal.*

For days after the sale, Rexroth fumed over his failure to purchase Donna Diane. Stoner had never seen him so bitterly distraught. Stoner attempted to counsel Rexroth to look beyond it, but his advice earned him only a tirade of curses. Finally, one night, Rexroth summoned Stoner to join him poolside. His massive jaws grinding with intensity, Rexroth said, "I am going to have Donna Diane. That mare should belong to me, and she will."

"That partnership will never sell you the horse," Stoner cautioned. Rexroth just looked at him. "I'm well aware of that," he replied. Then he described what he wanted done, emphasizing to Stoner that "they're due to ship her abroad at the end of the month. That's how much time we have."

The next morning, Byron Stoner flew to New Orleans. There, through the expensive offices of Daniel Delacroix, a powerfully connected attorney employed by RexCom to represent its interests in that section of the South, Stoner was introduced to Lou Tenuta, a high-ranking member of the Tornabene crime family. Over dinner that night in a private room of one of the city's legendary restaurants, Stoner explained the purpose of his visit.

Lou Tenuta listened impassively for several minutes, his thick hands folded before him on the linen tablecloth. He wore an expensive light blue suit, a dark blue custom-made shirt, and a white tie. With his black pompadour and narrow black mustache, he looked to Stoner like a prototypical French Quarter pimp.

Tenuta beckoned to the waiter watching from across the room. The waiter snapped his fingers to a busboy. The ripple of command reached the kitchen, from which plates of food quickly emerged, drawing Tenuta's rapt attention. Stoner, always a light eater, paid as little attention to this food as he did to most.

Several minutes elapsed before Tenuta momentarily halted his attack on a platter of barbequed shrimp and said, "I got the guy for you. But it'll cost you—not just for him, for us. A finder's fee."

"We have no problem with that," replied Stoner, feeling relieved. This had not been as difficult as he'd feared. He was anxious to phone Rexroth and report mission accomplished.

Stoner slid an envelope across the white linen surface of the table. "That's a down payment, plus expense money for this man to come to Kentucky and meet my employer. The man is to call me first, at the number on that piece of paper. His meeting with my employer will have to be carefully arranged and completely secret from all but a few of our people. We'll wire your people the remainder of their fee tomorrow, to the usual account."

Tenuta nodded as he reached for the just-delivered plate of steaming crawdads.

"What is the name of your man?"

Between bites, Tenuta said, "His name is Mortvedt. They call him the Sandman."

"Why?" Stoner asked.

Tenuta methodically worked his way through the mound of crawdads, keeping Stoner waiting for an answer. Stoner knew this game. Tenuta, after all, was playing on his home court. Like most of the lowlifes Stoner had had to deal with over the years, Tenuta was intent on displaying his power in his town. Finally, Tenuta mopped the last of the sauce remaining on the platter with a slice of French bread, which he chewed and swallowed before speaking. Then he said, "Because he puts horses to sleep. Maybe people, too. The Sandman. That's what they call him.

"They tell me he'll do the kind of work you've got in mind," Tenuta continued. "Here's how you get to him." He flipped a small piece of paper onto the tablecloth between them, making Stoner reach to retrieve it. "You call him, tell him what you want. We don't have no contact with him on this, *capice*? And I got no interest in whatever you want him for either.

"Don't have time for coffee," Tenuta said as he rose from his chair. He nodded in the direction of the wait staff. "You want some, or some dessert, go ahead." He left without saying another word.

◇◇◇

As always, Mortvedt arrived in Louisville right when he said he would. He and Repke walked down the street from the apartment complex to a nearby chain restaurant advertising Breakfast All Day, Every Day, $1.99. They made an odd-looking pair, Repke towering over the ex-jockey, yet bending deferentially to listen to him. It was funny, Repke sometimes thought to himself, that he was always talking down to this man that he looked up to like no one else he'd ever known.

Seated in the restaurant, Mortvedt described the upcoming job as they ate.

"How much is this job worth?" Jud asked.

"Your cut is three grand," Mortvedt answered, looking hard at Repke, his eyes cold. Mortvedt's longish black hair was combed straight back, without a part. There was a bluish cast to his white cheeks even this early in the day, evidence of the heavy beard he shaved off each morning. This was a face that would never play host to any laugh lines near eyes or mouth. Not for the first time, Repke found Mortvedt's look to be unsettling.

Jud let his glance shift to the clock above the deserted salad bar, then rubbed a large hand through his lank, brown hair. No question about it, the little man could make him nervous in a way that those dago gangsters in New Orleans never had during his car-stealing years with them.

Mortvedt had never revealed to Repke what the total take was from any of their jobs. And Repke never could quite get up the courage to press him about it. He didn't want to anger Mortvedt—not since the day he'd seen the smaller man pull a concealed shiv and open a series of slices in a big black iron-pumper called Gator Man one afternoon at Oakdale. The dispute was over the delegation of duties in the prison laundry. It was over so quick hardly anyone had to lie to the guards when they said they hadn't seen anything. Gator Man healed up and kept quiet, too, swearing he never got a good look at his attacker.

Jud had concealed Mortvedt's weapon after this flash fight. "Be first. You *always* got to jump the bastards first," was the little man's practiced theory.

Despite the fear that he often felt in Mortvedt's presence, Jud counted himself fortunate to be involved in these remunerative and relatively risk-free jobs. He wasn't making as much money as when he drove the stolen Mercedes and Jaguars from Cincinnati and Chicago to points south and west, but he was getting by nicely, and sleeping better, too. Unlike Mortvedt, who in Oakdale had seemed to regard his surroundings stoically, just another place to be as his life played itself out, Jud had hated prison from the bottom of his Kentucky hillbilly heart.

Mortvedt stirred his coffee. Then he said, "We'll do it Sunday night. I got to talk to a man later today, see about some details."

He got to his feet and laid a ten on the place mat in front of Repke. "Breakfast's on me. You don't have to leave no tip in a dump like this. I'll meet you after nine tonight over to that titty joint you like."

◇◇◇

Mortvedt arrived on time at the Red Velvet Swing, a gentleman's club that Repke patronized whenever he had enough money to pay $7 per beer. Its marquee advertised body painting, a deep soak room, stripper slaves and "much more."

Jud had already "established a beachhead," as he drunkenly put it to Mortvedt, with a couple of the establishment's lap dancers who had worked the noon to eight shift and were eager for some off-the-premises action.

The women regarded Mortvedt somewhat warily as he jerked a chair over from a nearby table and sat down, appraising them silently.

"This here is LeeAnne," Repke said, one arm around a tired-looking woman in her late twenties with long, straight black hair and a pouty mouth, lavishly over-lipsticked. Mortvedt looked at LeeAnne and said, "I guess you're not the one that's the life of the party." She glared back at him as Jud continued to massage the back of her neck.

Jud said, "Betty Lou's her name," nodding at a small woman with tight-curled, dark blond hair that glistened beneath the revolving strobe light over their table. She looked to be about the same age and just as battle-fatigued as LeeAnne, but she mustered a welcoming look, and Mortvedt nodded in approval. He was partial to the ones with big breasts and big, sloppy smiles.

"You like being a dancer here?" Mortvedt asked.

"Oh, yessir," Betty Lou said, brightening at the question. "My body interprets rhythm in a personal way," she added softly, as if she were repeating something she'd first thought of long, long ago.

There were a pair of empty margarita pitchers on the table, and a third one about a quarter full. Mortvedt said, "Let's get out of here and get us a real drink." He got to his feet, placed a $50 bill beneath one of the coasters.

When LeeAnne made a quick and clever move toward the $50 as she scooped up her purse and started to leave, Mortvedt suddenly turned back and looked at her. She quickly withdrew her hand. *Bastard must have eyes in the back of his head,* LeeAnne thought. She put her arm around Jud Repke's waist as the four of them exited the Red Velvet Swing. Mortvedt opened the door for Betty Lou.

◇◇◇

They rode in Repke's red Chevrolet across town to the interstate and checked into the first cheap motel Mortvedt spotted. He paid for two adjacent rooms and tossed the key to one of them to Jud. "Later, man," he said. "I'll come get you when the fun's done."

As soon as he and Betty Lou had entered their room, Mortvedt crossed the worn blue carpet to the battered television set. He flicked it on, then turned up the volume. A famous big-jawed comedian was just starting his ego-stroking stroll down the front-row line of studio fans who reached eagerly to shake his hand, like supplicants trying to touch the hem of a holy man's robe.

Taking a bottle of Wild Turkey out of the paper bag he'd brought in, Mortvedt ripped the cellophane off two of the plastic motel-issue "glasses," then filled both of them with the amber whiskey. After handing one glass across the bed to Betty Lou, Mortvedt drank his straight down, his throat contracting effortlessly. Betty Lou said, "Can I have some sweet soda to go with this?" He ignored her request and moved around the double bed, with its faded, flower pattern spread and cigarette burn dots, to face her.

"Get your clothes off," Mortvedt commanded. He had already shed his shirt and shoes and was working on his slacks before she finished slowly pulling off her T-shirt with its drawing of a near-naked woman poised in mid-air in a red velvet swing. Betty Lou was proud of her large breasts. She took her time, giving Mortvedt a good long look at them.

When she'd stripped off her panties, Betty Lou smiled coyly at Mortvedt, her eyes roaming his muscled body until they fell on his emerging erection. She smiled admiringly, her plucked eyebrows raised. "Well now, honey, I guess you ain't such a little man after all. Whoeee! Look at that big thing standing up to look at me."

Mortvedt said nothing. He motioned for Betty Lou to lie down atop the worn coverlet. She extended her arms behind her and arched her back slightly as Mortvedt roughly fondled her breasts. He increased the pressure, then began squeezing her nipples. "Hey, baby," Betty Lou said, "not that hard, okay?"

Mortvedt ignored her pleading. When Betty Lou sharply complained again, he suddenly slapped her across the face with his right hand. "God*dam* you," she cried, face flushed with anger, the imprint of his hand visible on her left cheek. "What'd you think your doin'?"

Mortvedt dismounted momentarily. With a quick move, he flipped Betty Lou over on her stomach, then thrust his knees up between her legs. "I don't like it there, not back there," Betty Lou screeched. As she continued to protest, Mortvedt took her

T-shirt and wound it roughly around her face so that it covered her mouth, muffling her cries.

Betty Lou tossed her head from side to side, her body squirming, but she could not get out from underneath Mortvedt, who was far too strong for her. As she tried to pull her knees up under her, he hit her a cracking punch on her right cheek. Betty Lou fell forward onto a pillow, tears of pain and anger beginning to pour down her rapidly swelling face. The laughter from the audience on the television drowned out the rest of the noises she made.

"Little man, eh?" said Mortvedt, thrusting his penis into Betty Lou's anus. He pistoned into her, grinning at her whimpered sounds of pain that stretched over the minutes.

Mortvedt watched his face in the pock-marked mirror that stretched the length of the bed's headboard. The louder Betty Lou wailed, the wider his smile became.

Chapter 15

In March of the year after Ronald Mortvedt, on Harvey Rexroth's instructions, had pulled off the widely publicized and never solved theft of the in-foal mare Donna Diane—and three years before Jack Doyle went to work at Willowdale—the mare produced a sprightly brown foal without a mark of white anywhere on him. The birth of this very plain-colored youngster took place on a section of Willowdale Farm known as the Annex, a piece of property that at the time housed only Donna Diane and an old gelding that had been placed there to keep her company.

As the birth of the bay foal represented, to Rexroth, a furtherance of his revenge, it also signaled the imminent demise of Donna Diane. The mare was simply too valuable, her unsolved theft still too fresh in the minds of Kentucky horse people, for her to remain alive and possibly be discovered. So Ronald Mortvedt was summoned from Louisiana. He found Donna Diane in her dark field one night and silently dispatched her with a fatal dose of pentobarbital supplied to him by a ruled-off New Orleans veterinarian named Karl Classen.

Unlike the insurance claim-driven horse deaths that were to come at Willowdale, Donna Diane's demise was of course not reported. Instead, Mortvedt and Jud Repke winched Donna Diane's carcass onto the back of a flatbed truck, covered it with a tarpaulin, and drove to the farthest reaches of the Willowdale property, an area once used as a dump before environmentalists hounded Rexroth into abandoning it. There, they buried the champion mare Donna Diane. Mortvedt drove back south that night, $10,000 richer even after he had paid Repke his share.

The orphaned brown foal, an avid eater, was placed with a nurse mare. The Willowdale groom Pedro Ramos was given as his assignment the full-time monitoring of and caring for this pair. One night that fall, the brown colt was ushered unobtrusively by Pedro into a field of other weanlings. Only Rexroth's farm manager at the time, Bob Brokopp, was made aware of the fact that the weanling band at Willowdale had been enlarged by one. Other observant workers noted the presence of the newcomer, but were told by Brokopp that Rexroth had bought the youngster privately from a small breeder up in Maryland. Such purchases were not uncommon.

When Brokopp was given his walking papers, as well as a large cash settlement to his contract, direct knowledge of the brown colt's background remained with Pedro Ramos. At Rexroth's instructions, Pedros' wage package had also undergone considerable enhancement, so much so that he was the proud owner of a new Jeep Cherokee, which made him the envy of his fellow grooms. "I won a big trifecta over at Keeneland," Pedro said, explaining his newfound riches.

◇◇◇

In the months immediately following the theft of Donna Diane, Rexroth had relished the situation purely from the revenge angle. The outrage and anguish evidenced by the Irish-English combine when Donna Diane was discovered missing from her paddock one morning gave Rexroth tremendous satisfaction. "Hear the howls from across the ocean?" he happily asked. When the mare remained undiscovered, at first her angry owners charged carelessness, if not malfeasance, on the part of the well-known Kentucky farm which had boarded her after her sale. Later, they accused area law enforcement officials, who had unearthed no hint of Donna Diane's whereabouts, of gross inefficiency.

Rexroth chortled mightily at these developments, although only privately, or occasionally in the presence of Stoner and

Kauffman. The dense bodyguard had no interest in the matter, other than the fact that it put the boss in good humor, but Stoner asked Rexroth, "What do you plan to eventually do with this colt?"

Leaning back in his chair at poolside, Rexroth paused to light one of his hefty cigars before replying.

"Keep him out of the hands of those goddam foreign raiders," Rexroth said. "That's satisfaction enough for me.

"If they'd just had the class, or courtesy—I'm talking amongst gentlemen, now—to offer to go partners with me on Donna Diane, they'd still have their six million dollar mare.

"But I've got her colt now, and I don't care if he's not worth a dime on anybody's market. I've got him and those sons a bitches don't." Rexroth pounded his big fist on the desk for emphasis, his broad face aglow with the sheen of triumph.

This situation, one that involved Rexroth playing dog in the manger with a stolen horse, remained unchanged until one day early in June, two years later, when the publishing tycoon received a phone call from Douglas Phillips, beleaguered editor of the *Horse Racing Journal.* Phillips, as had been the case ever since he had held his post, remained under intense pressure from Rexroth to produce sensational stories involving the "dark side" of racing.

"Mr. Rexroth," Phillips said nervously, "I know you want to be kept informed of any major series that we might run in the paper. That's why I'm calling. I think we've got a good one," Phillips said nervously.

"I'll be the judge of that," Rexroth growled.

After a brief period of silence, during which he took a hearty swig from the flask of Cutty Sark combined with Maalox that he kept in his desk, Phillips continued: "We're thinking along the lines of a three-part series, based on a file of old clippings one of our librarians came across when she was doing research at the public library. She kind of stumbled on this packet of stories from 1909, all from Midwest newspapers and all having to do with a huge scandal involving racetrack fraud."

"Nineteen hundred and nine?" Rexroth thundered. "The *Horse Racing Journal* isn't an historical magazine, Phillips, it's a racing daily. Have you forgotten that?"

Aided by another larrup of the Maalox-Cutty fortifier, Phillips stubbornly persisted. He said he thought the more than eighty-year-old case could be vividly recalled in a series to be authored by Clyde Senzell, one of *Horse Racing Journal's* feature writers.

"Mr. Rexroth," Phillips pleaded, "it's a sensational story. Nobody on our staff had ever heard of this case. What these guys tried to get away with, well, we think it has real appeal. Racing's Past Thieves, we could title it. And remember, Mr. Rexroth, the *Racing Daily* won't have this."

"All right," Rexroth barked, "send Senzell out here with the clippings. I'll go over the material with him before I decide if we'll run this." He hung up on the hapless Phillips without a goodbye.

Senzell arrived at Willowdale from his New York City base the next morning, having flown coach class, as he hastened to assure Rexroth. After Senzell, a very thin, tightly wound man of forty-five, had opened his briefcase and extracted a folder of fragile, faded clippings, Rexroth waved him away and began to read. Almost immediately, Rexroth found himself fascinated, intrigued, even somewhat jealous of the larceny and imagination that had been displayed decades previous by one John B. Cabray.

The first story in the file was dated Sept. 24, 1909. Like all the others, it bore a Council Bluffs, Iowa, dateline and the byline of Richard Lloyd-Brown, who was identified as staff reporter. Lloyd-Brown wrote:

```
DES MOINES, Iowa—John B. Cabray and eighty-
four alleged associates were indicted by a
federal grand jury here today in a case
that is believed to involve one of the most
gigantic swindles in the police annals of
the country.
    The indictments were for conspiring to
defraud by illegal use of the mails, to wit,
```

persuading people to send money through the postal system, money that was supposed to be bet on what Cabray and his far-flung ring of accomplices promised would be a "fixed" horse race, one with an outcome Cabray claimed had been determined in advance.

Unfortunately for the naïve investors, Cabray arranged so that the actual outcome of the fix would be for all of them to lose their money because of an unexpected development leading to an "upset."

When those duped began to communicate with each other in the days and weeks after the race, and after Cabray and his ring had gone to ground, the fraud victims went to law enforcement officials with their complaints. None of the money sent to Cabray to be "bet" has been recovered.

Enticed into this scheme by Cabray and his slick-talking confidence men were prominent businessmen and civic leaders all over the country. Victims in eighteen states, the territory of Alaska, and the Dominion of Canada are named, indicating the wide range of territories over which Cabray and his associates are alleged to have plied their vocation.

Although specific amounts are not mentioned in the indictment, the amounts lost by the alleged victims reportedly exceed one million dollars. The sums lost by individuals range from $1,500 to $30,000, the latter amount having been placed on the race by a Missouri bank owner named C. D. Arnett.

Harvey Rexroth placed the file of clippings down on his desk for a moment, shifted his glasses to his forehead, and began pondering these facts from eight decades ago. After a minute or two, he said aloud, "My God! A million dollars in 1909…what would that be worth today?"

Senzell, who had been goggle-eyed for the past few minutes as Deirdre skated through her paces wearing nothing but a serious expression, came to attention at the question. He'd done his homework. "In the neighborhood of thiry million, Mr. Rexroth."

Rexroth shook his head admiringly as he considered the scope of Cabray's larceny. "What a nice neighborhood!" he said. He then resumed reading from the file.

```
    Cabray is in custody here, along with three
of his associates: Harlan Kornkven, James
Draeger, and Stafford Appleby. The names of
the other eighty-one people indicted were
not made public. It was stated, however, that
the list includes many persons known in the
criminal annals in all parts of the country,
and that nearly every such name is followed
by from one to four aliases.
    Each of these alleged confederates appar-
ently had a coded number by which they were
referred to in Cabray's complicated file of
records, recovered by U.S. Marshall Marcus
Gordon from Cabray's temporary headquarters
in Altoona, Iowa.
    It is expected that the trials will begin
in Des Moines during the November term of
court. Patrick Rafferty, special assistant to
the Attorney General of the United States, at
the insistence of the Department of Justice,
is taking part in the prosecution and will
doubtless have entire charge of the case when
it comes to trial.
```

That concluded Richard Lloyd-Brown's first report. Examining it more closely, Rexroth said, "Senzell, where's the rest of this? Part of this last page has been torn off. Goddamit, man, I want to know what *kind* of fix went on? How did Cabray pull this off?"

Senzell ventured a small, nervous smile. He was beginning to sense that he had the boss hooked on doing this series.

"The bottom part of Brown's first story is missing, Mr. Rexroth," Senzell said, "but keep on reading. Not all of Brown's coverage was retained for the file. Or else parts of it were lost, or stolen, over the years. But the sequence is solid enough to paint the picture. It all becomes clear—how Cabray did it."

Senzell sat back in his chair, keeping one eye on the circling Deirdre, the other on his engrossed employer.

DES MOINES, Iowa—As the date draws near for trial of people accused in one of the most gigantic and sensational frauds in the nation's recent history, more details have emerged regarding the case.

The million-dollar swindle of numerous prominent citizens, allegedly masterminded by John B. Cabray, was spread over at least eighteen states.

Cabray and his associates are alleged to have used as bases of operation such towns as Council Bluffs, Burlington and Davenport, Iowa; St. Louis, Little Rock, Seattle, Denver and New Orleans, to which sites many victims were either taken by Cabray's numerous "steerers" to deliver their betting money, or to which places they were instructed to mail their funds.

All were assured that their promised "profits" could either be picked up in those towns, or would be mailed to them if they so chose. No profits, of course, were ever delivered to the duped investors in this so-called "fixed" race that took place at a track in the eastern part of the country.

Included in the court documents are copies of many sensational letters alleged to have been exchanged between Cabray and his associates, missives that refer to alleged "deals" and specify various sums of money as having changed hands as the result of the operations of those mentioned in the indictment.

One of these letters is dated from a New York City hotel and invites "Friend John," who, it is alleged, is Cabray himself, to go to New York, declaring "I have a town right across the river in New Jersey, a swell

track, and absolute protection. The sheriff
and prosecutor and police will be absolutely
right on the job for us during our working
hours."

In a letter written four days later, the
same man informs "Friend John" that the race
"fixing" can be done "for $750, which will
cover everything—that is, the sheriff, his
brother-in-law the police chief, and the
prosecuting attorney."

Rexroth leapt from his chair. "Seven hundred and fifty dollars!" Rexroth shouted. "This man Cabray was a genius!" With a thump of his fist on the desk, Rexroth said, "Senzell, now *here* was a man who understood how to KEEP DOWN OVERHEAD—something I've been trying to get across to you *Horse Racing Journal* buffoons for years!"

As the dog Winston began to snore, Rexroth plunked himself back down in his chair and resumed reading.

DES MOINES, Iowa—The eagerness of criminal
mastermind John C. Cabray's victims became
evident in federal court here Monday when some
of their letters were read into the record.
This was over the objections of Cabray's
attorney, Charles McStone of Chicago, objections denied by presiding Judge George H.
Stevens.

A letter from Moline, Ill., signed by Oscar
Farley, said "am inclosing $3,000 to apply to
our deal, pending. I am looking forward to a
fine, and prompt, result and return."

Another letter, this one from Eugene S.
Hunter of Antigo, Wisc., said: "I have made
my check on the bank here for $7,500. My
father-in-law is the president of the bank,
to which proceeds may be forwarded. We are
looking forward to their arrival."

Rexroth flipped through a few more reports from Richard Lloyd-Brown before he found the one he was seeking. Brow furrowed, jaw clenched, he read it through twice. Then he threw his head back and erupted in laughter, a cascade of sound that startled Deirdre, Senzell and the dozing Winston.

Reaching for the intercom on his desk, Rexroth ordered champagne. Next, he buzzed for his executive secretary. When Stoner had emerged from his office, nodded at Senzell, and taken a chair, Rexroth slid most of the clippings across the desk to him. Stoner began reading. Rexroth poured champagne for himself as Stoner perused the material. After several minutes, Stoner looked up, a puzzled look on his face.

"I grasp the situation," Stoner said, "but only up to a point. A sharp con man puts together a dishonest scheme to clip some of the nation's greediest burghers. You could call it the Rape of the Rotarians, except I'm not sure the Rotary Club existed back then."

"Or, Clipping the Kiwanians," Rexroth said with another booming laugh. "Mauling the Masons in their pocketbooks. Eviscerating the Elks. Oh, yes, W. C. Fields had it right, you can't cheat an honest man. But as Cabray knew, that left plenty of material to work with. He knew there were suckers mooning in pools all over the country, primed and ready to make what they thought was a dishonest fortune.

"Here, let me read to you about one of these pillars of the community," Rexroth said. He searched the folder of clippings until he found the one he wanted. "I'm quoting from Lloyd-Brown's story," he said.

> Millionaire banker W. T. Baillew, of Jefferson City, Mo., the star witness in the case against John C. Cabray, was on the stand all day Thursday detailing the manner in which he lost the money.
>
> Baillew acknowledged that, although he believed the race had been "fixed" and that he and his friends thought they were sure to

```
win their bets, he considered it "legitimate"
that he had bet on the outcome of the race.
     Baillew said he had been approached by a man
named Martin, who brought a letter of intro-
duction from Cabray. After much discussion,
it was agreed that Baillew should travel to
St. Louis and make a bet for Martin on the
supposedly fixed race. Baillew was to bring
$30,000 of his own money to show that he was
a "man of affairs."
     After Baillew had bet many thousands of
dollars of Martin's money, he grew excited,
he said, and put up his own cash as well.
```

After he'd finished reading from the clipping, Rexroth took another gulp of champagne. As was his custom, he was drinking out of a beer stein in order to save time on replenishing. Stoner had seen the man quaff quarts of the stuff in an afternoon before beginning his cocktail hour. He must have a liver the size of a bowling ball, Stoner thought. Rexroth interrupted this reverie when he said, "But Stoner, that's not the point of interest here. It's not so much *who* Cabray conned, as it is *how* he conned them. Therein lies the beauty of this."

Rexroth reached across the desk and took the file of clippings from Stoner. "You don't have to read the rest of them," he said, "I'll sum this up for you. Listen, and marvel at Cabray's chicanery.

"After getting all those boobs to send him their money," Rexroth began, "money he and his people have convinced them will be at least tripled as the result of the race, Cabray goes to New Jersey and sets things up.

"Now, with all these prominent people on the hook, he's got to put on some kind of race or they'll be pursuing him all over the country. He can't just disappear with the loot without going through his illegal motions. That would be too crude for this artiste.

"So, Cabray arranges for this match race to be held on a July afternoon at the track in New Jersey. He tells the investors that all their money is going on a horse named Bradford Baron, a horse that Cabray has shipped east from Chicago in order to take advantage of the arrogant, provincial Easterners who traditionally look down their noses at Midwest talent. This long-prevalent attitude, he tells his backers, will boost the price they get on Bradford Baron.

"Cabray tells them that he owns Bradford Baron, which is true, and assures them that the Baron will beat his rival, a horse named Rex of Racine, which could never happen.

"Rex is actually a pretty decent little stakes horse, and he figures to leave Bradford Baron in his dust. Cabray knows that, all right, but his investors don't.

"Cabray has also gone so far as to assure all the suckers that the race is fixed. He tells them Bradford Baron is a cinch, because the connections of Rex of Racine are in on the deal. This is not true, either. Actually, Rex of Racine's owner was an honest gent named Garson Carleton, who thought they'd been invited into an easy spot to pick up a little purse between stakes engagements. According to his later deposition, Carleton privately told friends he thought Cabray was crazy to challenge Rex of Racine. He considered Cabray to be a pigeon!"

Throwing back his head, Rexroth let loose another barrage of laughter. He drained his stein of champagne. After refilling it—still failing to offer any to Stoner or Senzell—he resumed his description of the coup.

"The day of the match race arrives. Cabray's got everybody in that town paid off, from the DA on down. Riding Bradford Baron is an old drunken jock on his last legs named Bobby Mitchell that Cabray has resurrected for this race.

"They lift the barrier—there was no starting gate in those days—and Rex of Racine scoots into a big lead. This should be no surprise, since he's a stakes-class horse facing a little old allowance runner.

"When Rex of Racine starts pulling farther away, Bobby Mitchell takes a nice little gymnast's tumble off Bradford Baron near the far turn and lies on the track, still as a silver dollar. The screaming crowd suddenly goes silent. Rex of Racine zips down the stretch and crosses the finish line as the easy winner.

"Now, there are other bettors on hand besides Cabray and his boys, bettors who out of honest stupidity have wagered on Bradford Baron. They begin to voice their suspicions regarding the gentle tumble taken by Bobby Mitchell. Their voices grew louder, and according to one of the stories in the file it was 'feared that unruly elements might burn down the grandstand in their furor over the outcome.'

"But Cabray—oh, what a blue ribbon rascal—is ahead of them here. All of a sudden a so-called doctor, medicine satchel in hand, rushes from out of the crowd onto the track. The doctor pushes aside the attendants that are peering at Bobby Mitchell, who is face down in the loam and hasn't moved a muscle.

"The doctor, of course, is another guy Cabray has hired, a down and out New York actor named Ned Robinson. Robinson does a terrific job. He examines the still prostrate Bobby Mitchell, shakes his head sadly, gets to his feet, and loudly proclaims, 'This man is dead. A heart attack apparently caused him to fall from his horse. Please, gentlemen, step away from the body.'

"At this point the crowd, even the clucks who have lost money on Bradford Baron, fall silent. They leave the track talking about the terrible tragedy they have witnessed. Cabray's suckers, some of whom have traveled to Jersey all the way from Cow Flop, Iowa, or whatever, were the most dumbfounded by this turn of events. They trooped out of the track in various stages of dejection.

"Bobby Mitchell's 'body' is transported to the county morgue by the paid-off sheriff. When the wagon nears the steps of the building, Bobby Mitchell suddenly springs to life and enters a waiting coach. Cabray is in that one, holding Mitchell's payoff, and they drive away, never again to be seen in that part of Jersey.

"The next day—and you can imagine what kind of night Cabray's losers must have gone through—a couple of the brighter lights inquired as to the funeral plans for the dead jockey. 'No dead jockey ever was brought in here,' says the coroner, and shoos them away.

"'What about the doctor who pronounced him dead on the racetrack?'

"'Nobody around here like that,' said the district attorney.

"Finally, a couple of days later, after the sheriff and police chief have told them to haul their asses out of town, these fellows returned to the Midwest and West. Some of them then found a sympathetic prosecutor in Des Moines. Later, the Attorney General's office gets interested. And, two years after the race, the indictments are handed down for Cabray and his pals.

"Cabray was arrested in Hot Springs, Arkansas. The only reason the authorities ever located him was that he had gotten in touch with one of the original pigeons, an Oklahoma oil tycoon named Prentice O'Bannon. Cabray wrote O'Bannon a long letter, apologizing for what he described as the 'mix-up' in New Jersey, but promising that he would make up for it with a better, tremendously more profitable fixed race at the track in Hot Springs that fall. Cabray had either blown his ill-gotten gains, or lost his marbles, or had the biggest set of balls in the U. S. Whatever, he tried to go back to this well once too often, and the oil tycoon went to the cops. That's how they came to nab Cabray."

Stoner sat forward in his chair. "All right. They had the trial. Cabray and three of his cohorts were present. That's what one of the first stories in the file said. What happened?"

Rexroth reached into the glistening ice bucket for the second bottle of champagne. He smiled broadly as he carefully filled his stein to the brim.

"What happened was that John B. Cabray and his three associates on hand were found guilty. By a jury of what obviously could not have been their peers, I might add, since I don't think they produce world-class con men by the dozen in the Hawkeye State. Anyway, they were sentenced to fifteen years in prison and ordered to make restitution.

"Found guilty in absentia were the eighty Cabray accomplices not in custody but named in the indictments. The shitkicker judge there in Des Moines permitted Mr. Cabray and his buddies to post bond. Can you imagine? Bond was set at $5,000 per man. Out there in the corn belt, the judge must have thought that was major money.

"But it wasn't for these lads, of course. Naturally, Cabray and his boys soon departed Des Moines, Iowa, never to be seen again. For them, $5,000 in bond money was an incidental expense. None of the money bet by the greedy Babbits of the Midwest and other regions was ever recovered."

Rexroth swirled the champagne in his stein, looking pensive. "John B. Cabray," he said softly. "Oh, how I would have liked to have known that man."

After a few minutes of silence, Rexroth put his stein down on the desk. Senzell looked expectantly at his employer.

Rexroth gazed benignly back at Clyde Senzell. He said, "This is excellent stuff. Should make a terrific series. Go to it, Senzell, give it your best. We'll publish this over the weekend of July Fourth. Tell Phillips to promo it heavily in advance.

"And," Rexroth added, "tell Phillips to give that librarian a good pinch on the ass for finding this material."

After Senzell had gone, Rexroth sat without speaking for several minutes. Stoner busied himself reading that day's RexCom financial summaries which he'd retrieved from the nearby fax machine. As usual, the figures looked good.

Rexroth leaned back in his chair, his right hand, with its Ivy League Squash Champion ring gleaming in the light, resting lightly on Winston's cranium. As Rexroth ruminated, the slumbering bulldog silently passed some powerful gas, something that only Stoner seemed to notice.

Finally, Rexroth looked at Stoner and said, "I can't get over this Cabray story. What an achievement it was to pull off a caper like that! He was brazen, and bold, and thoroughly dishonest and, best of all, he got away with it! He took their money and got away with it!"

Rexroth realized that nothing in his already privileged life would please him more, bring him more satisfaction, than to somehow emulate Cabray in some strikingly larcenous way. He poured the last of the second bottle of what he called "Donny P" into his stein.

It was then that Rexroth's thoughts turned to the royally bred son of Donna Diane, grazing these days in total obscurity in one of the far Willowdale pastures.

Rexroth had originally orchestrated the theft of Donna Diane only to exact revenge on his hated foreign rivals. It had been, up to then, simply a matter having the mare's offspring for himself, and fuck those Micks and Brits. Now, with Cabray's caper fresh in his consciousness, Rexroth's mind fastened upon the plain bay yearling.

And then the Grand Plan suddenly arrived full-blown in the devious mind of Harvey Rexroth, a criminal epiphany that caused him suddenly to leap to his feet and thrust his thick arms into the air.

"Ah…fucking…hah!" Rexroth shouted, loud enough to cause the surprised Stoner to drop the sheaf of financial reports, to startle the bulldog Winston, who awakened with another vicious fart, and to cause Randy Kauffman to turn away from the television screen whereon a group of dwarf transvestites of different races were embroiled in a scuffle that had carried them, along with the talk show host, into the front rows of the studio audience.

Chapter 16

"It's going okay," Doyle said. He was at an outdoor wall phone of the Wildcat-Jiffy-Shopper gas station and convenience store located at an intersection of country roads three and a half miles from Willowdale. It was early dusk of a warm summer evening, and Doyle was talking to Karen Engel in Chicago. He thought the FBI agent sounded a little anxious. This prompted Doyle to play it as cool as he possibly could manage. "Nada to worry about so far," he said.

"Nothing I want to talk about," Doyle might have added, but did not. Embarrassed as he was at what had happened, Doyle had decided to refrain from mentioning the major *faux pas* he had committed the day before.

He had been standing outside the Willowdale stallion barn, leaning on a paddock fence and rubbing the nose of a friendly black horse named Chisox. It was nearly lunch time. Doyle, having completed his morning duties under Aldous' supervision, was passing the time talking with the stable assistant named Pedro. He asked the young Mexican-American about Chisox' stud record.

There wasn't any such record, Pedro said, shaking his head. Chisox, he said, was a teaser.

"Huh?" Doyle responded. After a few moments during which Pedro looked quizzically at Doyle, he proceeded to briefly describe the teaser's role, to which the amazed Doyle said, "A teaser does fucking *what?*"

Pedro gave him another puzzled look. "No, no, he does *no* fuckeen," Pedro emphasized. He informed that it was the role on every stud farm of at least one male horse to be used to excite the mares sexually, then be removed from their presence prior to ejaculation so that a valuable stallion could be slotted in to polish off the breeding job.

Doyle cringed as he recalled how he'd become indignant on behalf of the teaser—much to Pedro's astonishment, Pedro having been long aware of such a traditional breeding practice. When Doyle realized he had revealed a huge gap in his knowledge of animal husbandry, he'd attempted to pass it off as a joke, slapping Pedro on the back and laughing. "Pulled your leg pretty good there didn't I, amigo?" Doyle said. Pedro had responded by looking at Doyle with the impassive expression many Latino busboys reserve for the gringo customers in upscale American restaurants.

Engel and Tirabassi had asked Doyle to report to them at least twice a week. "And if anything looks like it's going to break, call us right away, any time," Damon had emphasized. "This number is good twenty-four hours a day. And always use a public phone."

As he cupped the receiver in his hand, Doyle looked across the store's crowded parking lot. It was filled primarily with pickup trucks, some owned by workers Doyle recognized from Willowdale. They emerged from the store carrying packages of groceries, or six-packs of beer, or both. They then drove off in the direction of the farm, where they lived either in the two-story dormitory on the north side of the property or, if they had families, in one of the small wooden cottages near the east border.

This was Doyle's fourth telephoned report to the agents in Chicago, and it was as uninspiring as those preceding it.

The calls had begun at the end of Doyle's second full day at Willowdale, a day he had spent in the good-natured and informative company of Aldous Bolger. Putting his best efforts into first creating, then teaching, a crash course in farm management,

Bolger had given Doyle a tour of nearly every yard of Willowdale's six hundred acres and most of the structures thereon.

There had been capsulized descriptions of the roles of the employees, from top to bottom. Bolger showed him grooms at work, described the various aspects of breeding season "in case anybody brings it up," Bolger had emphasized. "We're past the real breeding season now. Otherwise, I wouldn't have the time to trot you around the place like I'm doing."

Other topics touched were the horse sales held at various times each year, and the preparation of horses to be sold; the function of the on-site laboratory and its adjacent X-ray facility. Doyle was shown the feed barns, stallion barns, broodmare barns; the tool and machinery sheds; even the lake stocked with fish and home to a pair of swans. Doyle shook hands with dozens of people whose names he attempted to memorize.

Toward the end of the tour, Bolger led Doyle over to the railing of Willowdale's one-mile training track, a meticulously manicured strip of loam that lay just outside an equally neat turf course.

"Not many places in the country have training tracks the quality of these on their property," Bolger said.

Doyle watched as a lone horse headed into the homestretch of the dirt course. He was going very fast, very smoothly. The rider was hunched down on the bay horse's withers, hands still. When horse and rider sped past the spot where he and Bolger stood, Doyle was very surprised to see that the rider of the brown colt was Willie Arroyo—City Sarah's jockey. Doyle ducked behind Bolger. "Let's get out of here," he said urgently. "I don't want that jock to see me here. He could recognize me." Bolger and Doyle then walked rapidly back toward Bolger's office.

"You know Willie Arroyo?" Bolger asked as they hurried up the road.

"Kind of," Doyle said. "I won't bore you with the details. But it wouldn't be a good idea for him to see me here. He might think something was going on, and he might talk about it. I don't want to take the chance."

"I'll tell you one thing," Bolger replied as they entered the air-conditioned haven of his office, "there's something 'off' about that colt we just saw. Rexroth is very interested in that colt's workouts. Everybody around here calls the horse Boomer. I know that can't be his real name, but I've not been able to find any record of him in the farm's files.

"He's a big, strong youngster, and from what I've seen of him, he can run like hell. But I don't see that much of him, and that's another strange thing."

Doyle said, "What do you mean, you don't see much of him?"

"You know that piece of the property I told you about called the Annex?" Bolger said. "It's a couple of hundred acres about five miles west of here. That's where Rexroth keeps his oldest mares and, for some reason, this horse you just saw working out. He's got him hidden out there back of beyond.

"I don't know bugger all about this Boomer—why he isn't up with the racing stable, why he's being kept here," Bolger said. "I asked Rexroth about this. Twice, I did. Both times, he said that it was a matter of no concern to me. The second time he made it quite clear that he didn't want to be asked again.

"So," Bolger said, "I don't know what the hell's going on with him. The jock flies all the way down here from Chicago to work him at least once a week. But Arroyo won't talk about Boomer, either. One day I tacked up the horse myself and had him ready for Arroyo when he drove in. Willie just nodded pleasant like at me and, when I asked something about how the horse felt to him, he motioned for me to give him a leg up to the saddle and trotted off, as if he hadn't heard my question. S'truth, Jack, there's something wonky going on with this horse."

Doyle sat back in the leather chair, holding a half-finished can of beer. He let thoughts of the brown colt drift away as he attempted to review everything he'd seen that busy day. Then he said to Bolger, "If I remember a tenth of what I've heard and seen today, we'll both be lucky."

Bolger smiled at Doyle. "I know, it's far too much to take in completely. And that's for anybody, not just a city creature like yourself.

"The major piece of advice I can offer you, Jack," Bolger continued, "is keep your mouth shut as much as possible. That will both enhance your learning and conceal your ignorance. No offense meant, by the way."

"I know what you're talking about," Doyle responded glumly. "If I can pull off this caper, masquerade successfully as a knowledgeable horseman, well, I'll deserve an Academy Award."

"You deserve another cold lager just for listening to me all day," said Bolger. "C'mon, lad, let's go up to my place and put our feet up on the porch railing."

Now, standing in the convenience store parking lot, Doyle wondered if the exasperation he felt was evident in his voice as he said, "There's been no sign of anything out of the ordinary."

He heard the click of another extension, then Damon's voice. "Jack, you can't rush this sort of thing. Just take it easy. Do the work that Bolger gives you to do. As I understand it, a lot of it will be clerical work and phone calls, done in his office—stuff you can easily handle. I know Bolger's told his workers that you've been brought in to ease his burden of paperwork.

"Just go about your business quietly, with a strong hold on that Irish temper of yours," Damon advised.

Doyle held the phone receiver away from his face. He looked at the setting sun, which had ribboned the invading dark with bold streaks of deep gold. He took a deep breath.

"If I need a lecture on rage-control, and I don't think so, I wouldn't ask for one from a representative of one of God's most hotheaded tribes. Talkin' to you, Tirabasssi," Doyle said.

Karen said, "Jack, take it easy, we're just...."

"I'm doing the talking right now, lady," Doyle said, still seething. "You're up there in civilization, hundreds of miles from the inaction. Don't lay this 'take it easy' crap on me." He paused to exhale, then took another deep breath. There was silence on the other end.

"All right. Okay," Doyle said. "Maybe that was a little harsh. But what you've got to keep in mind is, this is getting real old in a big hurry. Remember, I'm a city boy. Down here, the only bright lights are over the barn entrances. You hear what I'm saying, Damon?

"I've been out to eat five times, man, and let me tell you, there's only so much chicken-fried steak, or steak-fried chicken, or mush puppies or whatever, that I can handle.

"You ever hear of something called a 'Kentucky hot brown'?" he asked. "I didn't think so. I'll spare you the description."

More silence on the other end. Doyle exhaled, feeling his blood pressure and anger levels descending steadily. He scuffed one of his western boots in the gravel of the parking lot. "Okay, folks," he said in a normal voice, "I'm done. Rant's over. Lost my cool, there, but it's come back. Go ahead, either one of you."

Karen said, "How about Bolger? How's he doing with this? And with you?"

"Fine," Doyle replied. "Actually, he's a real good guy—and plenty sharp. He's got it set up so that I never do any work that would reveal my astounding ignorance of the breeding farm business.

"To tell you the truth, though, I think he's getting a little tired of babysitting me. And we don't ever go out at nights, get off the farm, except Fridays. The rest of the time he pretty much stays home in his house there, with his sister and her kids.

"I've had dinner over there several times. Must say that I've enjoyed those family evenings, as alien to me as they might seem, if you know what I mean," Doyle said. Damon coughed on the other end of the line, but said nothing.

Doyle paused as a red pickup, its truck bed replete with teenage boys, came to a sliding halt near where he was standing. He tried to wave away the cloud of dust thrown up by the truck's wheels. The driver hit the horn twice to emphasize his arrival.

"What's that?" Damon said sharply.

"Nothing. It's nothing. Just some of your local youths, stopping to pick up some suds." What the hell else do they have to do out here in the country, Doyle thought to himself, ride around and count hay bales? He fleetingly recalled stories he'd read about a popular rural pastime involving tipping over cows as they stood, sleeping on their feet, in their pastures.

Damon said, "Jack, any sign of the ex-jockey we told you to keep an eye out for? Ronald Mortvedt?"

"Nothing," Doyle said. "There's plenty of those little guys around here, but they're involved in breaking and training the horses. Aldous knows them all. I told him what you told me about Mortvedt, so he's got an idea of what to look for."

It was after Karen and Damon had returned from Louisiana and their trip to Cajun country, and prior to Doyle's departure for Kentucky, that they had met with Doyle and briefed him on the background, habits, and criminal dossier of Ronald Mortvedt. The agents had not had any luck in locating Mortvedt, but everything they heard about Mortvedt had served to make him a possible suspect. He "profiled out big time" was how Damon phrased it.

"One of the New Orleans racetrack snitches told our man down there he heard Mortvedt was doing business with some rich Yankee horse owner. From what we've learned, Mortvedt could very well be the guy doing the horse killing for Rexroth," Damon had said, adding: "And be careful if you ever spot this guy. He may be about half the size of Randy Kauffman, but from what we've heard of him, this little sucker may be twice as bad as that oaf."

Over the Wildcat-Jiffy-Shopper phone, Doyle heard Karen ask, "How often do you see Rexroth?"

"Every two, three days."

"Does he ever say anything to you? Pay any attention to you?"

Doyle said, "Not really. I'm not saying he's not polite. He knows who I am. He always says hello. But he's usually in and out of the barn area in a few minutes. Sometimes he'll grab a cup of coffee in Bolger's office, or have that Neanderthal, Kauffman, get it for him, but he never stays around to drink it."

"It's almost as if Rexroth needs to take a quick inventory every day or so—you know, to make sure all his toys are in place."

Karen said something, but Doyle couldn't hear her over the noise made by the departing red pickup truck. It looked to Doyle as if the truck-bed attendance count had almost doubled. Maybe they're on a recruiting drive, he thought, need some extra hands to help topple a big Black Angus.

Doyle said, "I've got one piece of intelligence for you regarding Rexroth." Doyle was grinning now. He could almost feel the high level of expectation emanating from the two FBI agents.

He waited until Damon said, impatiently, "Well, what *is* it, Jack?"

"You know the poolside rollerblading setup I told you about before? With the naked girls? Rexroth's secretary, Stoner, told me something interesting the other day concerning that.

"Aldous had asked me to go up to the big house to deliver some notes he'd made about broodmares, mares of Rexroth's that Aldous thought should be sold at the fall sales.

"The butler lets me in. He directs me to the indoor pool, and that's where Stoner meets me. He says Rexroth is too busy to see me, that I should just give him Aldous' report on the mares. Fine, I say.

"While we're talking, I can't hardly help but notice some kind of ruckus on the other side of the glass doors involving a couple of members of the Rexroth Roller Derby. I can hear Rexroth bellowing at one of them, Darla, the redhead. And I can hear her giving it back to him pretty good before she clomps off the track and out the door. Meanwhile, I can see little Deirdre, the one built like a sprinter, kind of simpering and smiling on the sidelines until Rexroth gives her a signal and she starts zooming around the track without a stitch on. So I say to Stoner, 'What was all that about?'"

Doyle stopped talking as another pickup pulled up near the phone, its front bumper halting about a yard away from him. "Nice driving, Ace," he said to the driver, who ambled into the store without taking any notice of Doyle.

"Anyway," Doyle said back into the phone, "Stoner fills me in on this situation. He says, 'Mr. Rexroth is an extremely superstitious man. Each week that the financial report for RexCom is up over the corresponding week of the preceding year, Mr. Rexroth keeps the same skater working for that full day and rewards her with a handsome bonus.'

"'But if a week comes that profits are down, Mr. Rexroth immediately changes bladers. If the news is not good and Darla, let's say, is the designated skater that day, well, whoosh, she's dismissed and replaced and put on the sidelines for at least two days without pay.'

"'Most of the girls have come to recognize this as equitable and just part of their job assignments. Some, of course, occasionally react rather bitterly,' Stoner says.

"Is this the damndest thing you've ever heard?" Doyle said. "I wonder if Rexroth learned this at Harvard Business. It could be the basis of a real popular course, providing visuals are included."

There was a momentary silence on the line after Doyle finished. Doyle then heard Damon say, as if to himself, "This Rexroth truly is nuttier than I'd thought."

Doyle looked out at the store's parking lot. Much of it was now completely in shadow, and most of the vehicles were gone. He was about to begin another quiet night alone at Willowdale. Then, motivated as much by the desire to keep talking to the agents as to inform them, Doyle said, "You know that Chicago jockey, Willie Arroyo? Well, he's been making these kind of quick visits here once a week to work some mystery horse for Rexroth. Aldous doesn't know what the story is on this horse, can't even find out its real name. And Rexroth won't tell him anything about it, either. Kind of interesting.

"Arroyo knows me from when I groomed City Sarah," Doyle added. "I've made sure he hasn't spotted me, because he sure as hell would think something was up if he saw me working here. But as to this mystery horse, I don't know what the deal is with him."

Karen said, "If you learn anything else you can tell us when you call Friday. Unless something comes up. If it does, call right away. And be careful, Jack."

"Will do," Doyle said, regretting that this communication with what he had come to regard as the real world—even if it was populated by FBI agents dedicated to manipulating his life—was about to end.

Chapter 17

Following his *faux pas* with Pedro regarding Chisox the teaser, Doyle took to heart Bolger's advice about doing more listening, less talking. Rather quickly he picked up the daily routine of life on Willowdale Farm, although he never found himself adjusting completely to the fact that his shift, along with those of the vast majority of the farm's employees, began before six each morning. As he pointed out to Bolger, "My life used to find me coming home at the time you've forced me to get up." Bolger would smile good-naturedly, commenting, "The horseman's life is not for the lazy man."

"I was never lazy regarding my nightlife," responded Doyle.

After the first few weeks, life at Willowdale proved to be a pleasant surprise to Doyle. The steady rhythms of outdoor work, plus the warmth of the Bolger family, were starting to smooth out some of his hard edges. This change did not go unnoticed.

Aldous said to Jack one morning when the last horse had been fed and watered, "After observing you these weeks, laddie, I've decided something."

"What's that?" Jack said. He bent down to retrieve a rubrag one of the grooms had dropped.

"You remind me of an orphaned colt I was given when I was a boy. I was young, and so was he, and he'd been mistreated in some way or other at the farm my father bought him from.

"When I got him he was the meanest little critter you'd ever see. He didn't trust anybody and he lashed out at everybody every chance he had. It took me months to convince him the world wasn't the hell hole he thought it was. Once I got through to him, he'd still pretend to keep his mean ways, but he really didn't have his heart in it anymore. He'd changed, and we both knew it."

Jack turned away to hide his grin. "You're a cheeky lot, you Kiwis," he said over his shoulder as he walked away.

◇◇◇

The more Doyle got to know Bolger, the more he appreciated the man—for his work ethic, his fair treatment of his work force, for the joy he took in spending time with his sister and her children. Bolger's energy supply was apparently inexhaustible. Not only would he work twelve hours most days, he would reserve the time to spend with Helen and Ian almost every evening, usually taking them to fish in the Willowdale Farm lake, or else monitor their riding of the Shetland pony he had acquired just for their use during their stay.

Doyle sometimes accompanied Bolger and the kids to the fishing hole, but he rarely remained for long. He could appreciate the calm and peaceful setting, and the feel of the lush green grass that draped the sides of the blue lake, and, no question, the obvious joy evidenced by Caroline's children as they competed with each other to catch the most, or biggest, fish. But as Doyle put it one evening to Bolger as they observed Ian and Helen in their dead-serious competition, "Fishing just doesn't do it for me. You know what I mean?

"There was a guy I used to work out with, he loaned me a book about some New York newspaper editor who 'found himself' fly-fishing? I went fly-fishing once with this guy, spent a whole morning and most of the afternoon up to my balls in icewater, we didn't catch enough to feed a small cat breakfast.

"Fishing, for me, is about in a dead heat with watching yacht racing, cooking shows, or the first three quarters of NBA basketball games."

"Keep those opinions near your vest, man," Bolger said seriously. "A lot of horsemen are serious fishermen, both here and back home. To say otherwise makes you sound even more suspect than you usually do."

Doyle looked at Aldous. "Really?" Concern showed on his face, until he realized that Bolger was exaggerating nearly as much as he. "Naw, you've been cracker," Bolger reassured him. "I've heard some muttering from a couple of the lads, them wondering how I'd picked you for my assistant over them. But that's been about it—more jealousy than doubt. You're not a bad actor, Jack Doyle. I'd say it's good on ya so far."

On a few of those evenings when Doyle didn't accompany Uncle Aldous and niece and nephew to the lake, he walked back up the little hill and headed toward his apartment, which was located on the top floor of the Willowdale dormitory. Most times, he walked past Bolger's two-story brick house. Sometimes, he was happy to discover, Caroline Cummings would put down the book she was reading, wave to him from her chair on the front porch, and invite him to "stop for a drink, if you'd like?" He had yet to refuse her.

Caroline would usually make easy conversation, asking him about his day, about how Doyle liked working with Aldous.

"Suppose I said I hated working for him?" Doyle said to her once. "Suppose I said I can't stand how overbearing he is, and rude, and bullying to his help? Suppose I said that? Then what would *you* say?"

Caroline cocked her eye at him—she was looking toward the lake, and he had been admiring her profile as he kidded her, the soft-looking white-blond hair pulled back from her tanned forehead, her long eyelashes—and replied, "What would I say? I'd say you aren't talking about Aldous Bolger." She added, "His boss, maybe, yes."

As the weeks unfolded with Doyle held hostage, as he thought of it, in the heart of Kentucky's Blue Grass country, he began more and more to look forward to two things: finding the incriminating material needed to hang Rexroth out to dry and thereby get the FBI off his case, and, two, his twilight conversations with Caroline.

In addition to admiring her beauty, and easy and good-humored way of conversing with him, Doyle was impressed with her strength. When the subject of her late husband came up, usually in the context of something to do with the children, Caroline calmly addressed it, never attempting to shield the pain she felt over his loss, but never dramatizing it, either. Grant Cummings must have been a hell of a man as well as a hell of jockey to win this woman for his wife, Doyle thought.

As Doyle sat chatting with Caroline one evening, the telephone rang in Bolger's house. Caroline went inside to answer it. When she returned to the front porch, she said, "That was the man at the front gate. He said there is a Federal Express package there for you, Jack. He can't leave his post there. He wants to know if you will go down there and pick it up. What shall I tell him?"

Minutes later, Doyle made his way down the long driveway to the front gate of Willowdale. As he moved past the grazing horses in the broad fields on either side of him, he wondered who might be sending him something via Federal Express. Had Karen or Damon planned to mail him something, he was sure they would have informed him in advance. "This could be Publisher's Clearing House, or a letter bomb," he said to himself.

After Doyle had retrieved the package, he opened it as he began his return walk. When he saw what was inside, he abruptly stopped. There were six cashier's checks, each worth $5,000. Doyle riffled through them twice, his initial disbelief giving way to a growing tide of exultation. "Damn, these things are for real," he said to himself. "I can't believe it!" He checked the address label on the front of the package. The addressee was definitely Jack Doyle. The return address was in Hallandale, Fla.

Doyle looked inside the package again. He then extracted a folded-over piece of white paper. The writing on it was from a typewriter. It said: "Dear Jack. Sorry we did what we did to you, but we had a very, very good reason. Look up a three-year-old named Bunny's Al. If you wish, call this number."

He read this note two or three more times as he stood in descending dusk. Then Doyle hotfooted it to Bolger's office. The door was unlocked. Doyle entered and headed for the stack of *Blood-Horse* magazines Bolger kept on a shelf behind his desk chair. He began to leaf through recent stakes results in the back of the publication. Three issues back, he found the name of Bunny's Al.

Underneath the name, which was in white type on a black background, was the following: "Whirlaway Stakes, Florida Park, June 22, $75,000 added, value of race $83,200, three-year-olds, seven furlongs, 1:23 4-5, track fast."

Doyle read further. The next entry repeated Bunny's Al name, then gave his color (chestnut), age (three), and weight carried in the race (118), plus his winner's share ($49,920).

The names of his sire and dam were next, but they meant nothing to Doyle, nor did the name of the horse's breeder.

He continued to examine the *Blood-Horse* entry. On the next line, after the letter "O" for the horse's owner, Doyle read "M. Hoban." No clue there, he thought at first, although something was niggling at his memory. But the next piece of information jumped out at him. After "T" for trainer, was this: "E. D. Morley."

Stunned, Doyle looked around the area in which he stood, as if he were going to suddenly find someone there to consult with concerning this astonishing revelation. "Didn't Maureen tell me her last name was Hoban?" He ransacked his memory. Doyle was pretty sure he was right about that.

"I'll be a triple-decker son of a bitch," he said aloud. Then he began jogging up the drive to his Accord. Doyle couldn't wait to get this pair on the phone, although he knew he'd much rather have his hands around their necks.

Chapter 18

The parking lot where Doyle stood, outside the Wildcat Jiffy-Shop station and store, was relatively quiet. Not so the background noise on the other end of the receiver when, after several rings, it was finally picked up and a woman's voice said hurriedly, "Fado. How can I help you?"

Doyle said, "Fey-dough? What the hell does that mean?" He hadn't intended to be impolite to this stranger, but the thought of the thieving twosome bit at him. The woman replied, in a chilly voice, "Fado, that is spelled F-a-d-o, means 'long ago' in Gaelic."

Long ago and far away, with my money, Doyle thought. "What *is* the Fado you're talking from?" Doyle asked. "I mean, what sort of business is it?"

There was a pause on the other end of the line. Somewhat impatiently, the woman said, "Fado is an Irish bar and restaurant. And a very popular one."

Doyle said, "Isn't that Bob Marley and the Wailers I hear on your sound system?"

"Yes, it is."

"And this is an Irish bar and grill?"

For a moment it seemed she was going to take the time to explain Fado's choice of music. Instead, though, she said, "It is indeed an Irish bar. Now, again, how may I help you?"

"Let me talk to your lady bartender from Cork by way of Chicago," Doyle said. "Tell her it's Mr. Doyle. From Immigration."

There was another lengthy pause, then Doyle heard the phone being set down. He waited, tapping his foot to the reggae beat and looking up at the star-packed Kentucky sky. Finally, he heard a familiar voice say, "Jack Doyle, you lovely man. Isn't it a great thing now that you're calling?"

"Hello, Maureen," said Doyle.

After adding a few more sentences on to her warm greeting, Maureen said, "Jack, I can't talk to you from this phone. Give us your number up there, please, and I'll call you back in five minutes. I'll be paying for the call that way."

"You should be," Doyle growled. He waited eagerly for the phone to ring. When a pickup truck pulled into the parking lot, he snatched up the receiver, making it look like the phone was in use, then replaced it. Seconds later, the phone rang.

"Jack, we're both on here now," Maureen said. Then Doyle heard E. D. Morley's deep voice, on another extension, say, "Hey, mon, what you op to?"

"Don't start that Jamaican jive with me," Doyle snapped. "E. D., I want to know what the hell you were doing when you robbed me of my money. And hit me with that dose of knockout juice." Doyle could feel the heat rush to his face as he relived the ambush in his parking garage.

"Aw, sheet, Jack," E. D. said in his rumbling bass while reverting to his natural Chicago West Side accent, "it's a long story." There was a pause, then Morley said, "But you got a right to hear it."

"True that tis," chipped in Maureen. Doyle was about to lash out at his one-time counselor from Cork when he decided it was best for him to just shut up and listen.

What Doyle heard over the course of the next half-hour or so was a combination of explanation and justification, interspersed with elements of sincere apology. All this was jointly offered by Maureen and E. D., who vowed repeatedly that they had never intended to keep the money they stole from Doyle, only use it as the basis for an investment that "couldn't go wrong—and didn't."

Maureen said she had first met E. D. the previous year at a St. Patrick's Day party hosted by one of Angelo Zocchi's clients, Jim Dunleavy, for all the stable help. It was held at O'Keefe's Ale House. Maureen, of course, had been working on this busiest night of O'Keefe's year, and she helped serve the Dunleavy party.

"It was brilliant, Jack," Maureen gushed. "We hit it off right away. E. D. came around the next night, and then we started going out, and now—well, we've been together since right before we left Chicago."

Interjected Morley earnestly, "My mama's grandma really was from Jamaica, a white woman name of Cullerton."

"Look," Doyle said, "don't take this as being anti-romantic, or anything, but I'm not real interested in this reggae version of Abie's Irish Rose, if you know what I mean. Why'd you take my money?"

Morley and Maureen had seen their chance, they explained, when Jack had confided in her about his deal with Moe Kellman. "What ever made me trust you?" Doyle said, groaning into the phone.

Spurring them on, they said, were Maureen's desire to get out of the barmaid's life and E. D. Morley's long-harbored hope of obtaining his own trainer's license and horses to train. "I groomed and did the scut work for years," Morley said. "I worked as Angelo's assistant. I wanted to go out on my own. Only two things standing in my way: my color, and my bank account."

"Your color," Doyle said, "what're you talking about? There are black trainers, I've seen them at Heartland Downs."

"How many you seen?" Morley shot back. Doyle realized that the number was, indeed, very small. "I guess, well, two," Doyle said, thinking of Clifford Spraggins and Scotty Hunter.

"I'm telling you, it's almost impossible for a black man to get a good stable to train," Morley emphasized. "So, I was looking to get started with horses of my own. All I needed was the capital."

E. D. had gotten a call from a friend of his in Florida, telling him that there was a promising, obscurely bred but well put together three-year-old gelding for sale.

"Horse had never started, the owner had died, the widow was anxious to sell off this gelding and a couple of other horses her husband had owned. My buddy told me this gelding, Bunny's Al, could be a steal at the price. The widow lady would let him go for $20,000 and throw in one of the old claiming mares to boot."

E. D. said he'd taken a week off of work and driven to Ocala, Fla., to examine Bunny's Al. "I liked this horse from the get-go," Morley said. "I told the widow lady, 'give me a week to get you the money.' She promised she would. Then I drove back up north fast as I could and talked this all over with Maureen."

"So this is where I came into it," said Doyle.

Once Maureen and Morley agreed that they knew what Doyle was up to, they simply sat back and watched the plot unfold. When City Sarah won her "target" race after the maneuverings of Zocchi and Doyle, they had indeed bet on her.

"But we made our big bet on you, Jack," Maureen said. She then went on to vow that "we had always, always intended to pay you back. The proof is in those checks we sent in the Federal Express. Jack, it was just kind of a loan we had of your money. That's all it was." She sounded sincere.

"That's the stone truth, man," added Morley. "We didn't like to do you that way, but we were careful not to hurt you when we took the twenty-five off you. And we've put that money to good use, Jack, you got to admit that."

Bunny's Al had turned out to be "all racehorse," his proud owner-trainer said. "Maybe he's no classic horse, but he's been good enough to win us more than $125,000 so far. Fact that he's done so good for me has gotten me some other owners. I'm training ten head down here at Florida Park."

Maureen could hardly wait to announce her plans. "If E. D.'s stable keeps going along well, we may buy into Fado. I've already been given an option on twenty-five percent of it. How's that for a fookin' brilliant prospect?"

Doyle pondered all that he had heard. His silence brought a rebuke from Maureen.

"Jack, don't be that way," Maureen said. "It's all water over the stones, now. You got a bump on the head is the worst thing, really. Now, you've got all your money back."

"Plus interest," E. D. rumbled, "let's not forget the extra five grand we sent you."

A question occurred to Doyle. "How'd you find me?"

"We talked to Maggie Howard. Called her at Angelo's barn," E. D. replied. "She told us you were working for that guy Rexroth, on his farm. At first I thought she was jivin' me. Maggie said she could hardly believe it either."

"You know," said Doyle, "I could just keep that anonymous money and still go back to Chicago and file a complaint against you two."

The words were hardly out of his mouth before he recognized the fallacy of that strategy. And Maureen and E. D. were not far behind him. "Now, Jack, would your Mr. Rexroth like to know he's got a boyo working for him that's thought to have fiddled with a horse race up in Chicago?" Maureen mused. "One that had a lot of the lads in Vegas chewin' on their cufflinks?"

Doyle knew she was right. But he couldn't resist a parting shot. "When you take over that bar down there, be sure and change its name from Playdough or Fado or whatever. Maybe make it Ebony and Ivory. Or, better yet, Assault and Robbery."

Maureen's hearty laugh resounded over the phone. "Oh, Jack, you sound just like yourself."

Driving back to Willowdale, he couldn't help but smile at the conversation he'd had, with all its various elements of desire and deceit. Maureen and E. D., he thought, who'd of believed that? He'd pulled something off, but they had trumped him easily.

With so much that had been unexplained now clear, Doyle felt a lightened mood as he sped down the dark country road. He liked both E. D. and Maureen too much, and admired their gutsiness, to hold a grudge.

Once he'd turned into the Willowdale property, Doyle slowed his car. He waved his hand out the window at a row of broodmares peering out at him from one of the pastures, lined up along the white fence like chorus girls at ease.

The thirty grand now in hand, he admitted to himself, also served to influence his newly benign view of Maureen and E. D.

Chapter 19

"BUT JEEZUS HAD A JUMP SHOT!!!…"

Hearing this, Red Marchik awakened with a start. He sat straight up in bed, heart pounding. For a moment he looked about him wildy, the words ringing in his ears. Jesus had a *what?*

Then he listened again to the booming voice, saying "AND JEEEEEZUS ROSE UP AT THE TOP OF THE KEY, AND SHOT OVER OLD SATAN'S OUTSTRETCHED HANDS…AND JEEEEEZUS SCORED!!!…"

Fully awake now and aware of where he was and what he was listening to, Red Marchik reached across the still form of his peacefully sleeping wife and turned off the radio.

The clock read 7:01. Wanda always set their alarm on the station that featured Reverend Roland Ruland, the famed Sports Preacher. Reverend Ruland was a widely popular radio and television minister in the South, tying together as he did two of the great passions of the region: religion and sports. All of Reverend Ruland's sermons—"available only on videotape or cassette, no printed versions"—involved scripture combined with athletics. The more far-fetched these connections, the more tenuous his analogies, the more popular Reverend Roland Ruland became.

As Red Marchik sank back against his pillow, he smiled to himself at Wanda's devotion to the Sports Preacher. She'd never been particularly interested in religion during the early years of their marriage, but once she'd heard Reverend Ruland roaring through "Old Testament game summaries" and various biblical "box scores," she had insisted that Red travel with her to hear the Sports Preacher in person.

Red vividly remembered pulling up next to an auditorium in Clarksville, Tenn., and seeing Reverend Ruland's semi-trailer with its huge mural depicting Christ and the Apostles. The thirteen towering figures were in an oversized, fluorescent red, white, and blue painted bass boat on a body of water identified, in bold writing, as the Sea of Galilee. Christ, as the Fisherman for Souls, was shown reeling in a human figure from the roiling blue waters. The Apostle Peter stood next to Christ, net in hand and gaff at the ready.

And the Reverend's service that night, complete with laser light effects and some Las Vegas magic show touches, had impressed them both. Reverend Ruland was not a handsome man, with his florid, flat-featured face and a tall, black pompadour big enough to hide a partridge in, but Lord, that man could flat out preach.

As Red reminisced in silence, Wanda suddenly woke up. Rubbing her eyes, she said, "We've overslept, Red." She looked at the clock, then turned on its radio. The Sports Preacher's choral group, a barbershop quartet known as Jocks for Jesus, was just beginning the reverend's theme song. The Marchiks smiled at each other and relaxed again, listening to what had become a great favorite of theirs:

> *There's a football game in heaven,*
> *where they fight for every yard,*
> *with Jesus playing fullback*
> *and Moses playing guard...*
> *Oh, rock 'em...sock 'em...*
> *Jeeeeezus knock 'em...*
> *Stick with God.*

When the last note had faded away, Wanda poked Red in the ribs. "Heaven sakes, honey, get up," she urged. "We've got to get out there and talk to your cousin about killing Mr. Rexroth."

◇◇◇

In the weeks following the Marchiks' Night of the Jackal fiasco in the Willowdale broodmare pasture, the experience continued to rankle the redhead. "Who thought horses could be that big?" Red said to Wanda. She clucked and cooed sympathetic replies, assuring her husband that there are many different brands of bravery. Just because horses scared him did not mean he was a coward, or in any way lacking as a man. Red gratefully agreed with her assessment.

But the desire for revenge continued to burn. One cool Wednesday morning, Red and Wanda drove over to Versailles to visit Red's cousin Junior Kozol, a gas station attendant who served as a colonel in General Oscar Belliard's Underground Militia. Red explained he was looking for guidance in how to eliminate "a true threat to this nation and," he added, "a man who has done personal harm to yours truly."

"Stealth and guile, guile and stealth," Junior told Wanda and Red as the three of them sat at the fold-down kitchen table of Junior's small house trailer on the outskirts of town, a trailer whose jumbled interior reeked of gun oil and dirty socks. "That's the way to do these things.

"Now," Junior continued, "I don't want to know who your target is, Cousin Red. In fact, I don't need to know. Security reasons," Junior whispered. "Just let me ask you this, is he or she the kind of individual that goes out in crowds a lot?"

"Sure is," Red said. "Very prominent man, one of the leaders of business and society in this area." He spoke almost proudly of his hated former boss.

"Well, that's real good," Junior said. He looked thoughtful as he began to energetically itch inside the left armpit of his gas station coverall, meanwhile using the other hand to plow a Q-tip deep into his right ear. Wanda looked at him wide-eyed. "Let me do some research on this, Red," Junior said. He gestured to a shelf that took up most of one of the side walls of the trailer. It was packed with products from the burgeoning How to Kill/Maim/Dismember Your Fellow Citizens branch of American publishing.

"I'll report back to you next week, if that's all right with you," Junior said, now starting to scratch his way downward from his armpit. Red said, "That's fine, Junior. You know how to contact me." Then he and Wanda exited as quickly as politeness permitted.

Said Wanda as she shut her car door, "I'll bet that boy scratches his balls more than a major league first baseman."

Red shook his head. "He's not the brightest youngster," he said of his thirty-two-year-old relative, "but he's right on the cutting edge of this professional killer stuff. Oscar Belliard speaks very highly of him, very highly. And Junior's daddy, you know, was a Navy vet—just like me."

Wanda turned her head and looked out the car window as she rolled her eyes.

◇◇◇

Junior called the next Tuesday. He told Red, "I've got your answer, Cuz. I've nailed it down. It's called cue-rah-ray."

Red responded angrily. "Goddamit, Junior, I'm too old to learn one of those sneaky slant-eye marital arts things. How am I going to jump up in the air and kick anybody backwards? I got bad knees from my days in the United States Navy.

"And," Red added, "I just can't take on the Target in hand-to-hand combat. He's got people around him all the time."

"Well that, Cousin Red," Junior chortled, "is exactly my point. C'mon down to the station later, I've got the four-to-twelve shift. I'll fill you in, and you can fill up your tank on the house." Junior laughed again, obviously in a fine mood.

◇◇◇

The Marchiks made their way slowly and carefully toward the clubhouse entrance of Heartland Downs racetrack. It was a beautiful July Fourth afternoon, and a large holiday crowd was on hand in eighty-degree weather beneath a cloudless blue sky. A slight breeze ruffled the flags in the racetrack infield. As the throngs moved through the turnstiles, they were serenaded by a six-piece Dixieland band, its members sporting straw hats. Strolling jugglers and balloon artists labored to entertain the horse players' children who were along for the afternoon of races that was to be followed by an elaborate, and free, fireworks show come nightfall.

Red Marchik, wearing a red sport coat, white slacks, and blue American Legion cap, was aware of the comfortable temperature. But he was not enjoying the sight of the cloudless sky, nor the looks of pre-race anticipation on the faces of his fellow Heartland patrons, for he couldn't see them. With Wanda guiding him by the right elbow, Red was cautiously advancing, a blind person's long red and white cane poking the path in front of him, his eyes hidden behind a coal-black sunglasses.

"How'm I doing, Wanda?" Red asked. Wanda, looking more wary than festive in her pink polyester pants suit, kept her gaze straight ahead. Without looking at her husband, she whispered, "You're doing just fine, Red. Just give us a coupla more taps with the cane every few yards, will you? You know, make it look as realistic as you can."

Red inadvertently complied when he tripped on the first step of the clubhouse stairs. Desperately seeking to regain his balance, Red swung his free arm widely, nailing the man beside him directly on the nose. As the man's nose spurted blood, he began to curse Red. But then, noticing the glasses and cane, he stopped, and said, "Sorry, pal, I guess I got in your way. Have a good one," he added lamely.

The man's white shirt was spattered with crimson as, handkerchief held to his nose, he turned to a cigar-smoking man next to him. "Lou, how much time we got to bet the double?" he asked. "They're almost at the gate," came Lou's answer. Hurriedly, the man with the bleeding nose reached into his pocket. He handed a bill to the cigar smoker, a look of desperation on his face. "I ain't had time to handicap. I just got here, and then this blind guy pops me in the nose. Run in there and get me a $20 daily double, willya?"

The man with the cigar said, "Whadda you want in the double?"

"Get me…well, you know…hell, get me *anything!* I gotta go to the john and stop this bleeding, Lou."

Red and Wanda, meanwhile, had quietly removed themselves from this scene and passed through the clubhouse doors into the air-conditioned interior. They then took the elevator to the third floor of the clubhouse. Everyone in the elevator gave Red plenty of space. A woman in a broad black hat smiled sympathetically at him and said, "Mister, you can probably pick them as good as me even if you *can't* see them." Her male companion groaned and nudged her in the ribs as the elevator door opened. The other passengers pretended they hadn't heard her.

Once the Marchiks had been ushered to their reserved seats near the stairway leading to the paddock, Red sat down with a groan and mopped his brow. "I'm sweating bullets, Wanda," he said. "This isn't easy, walking around like a blind man when you're not blind. The ones that really are blind got a cakewalk compared." His lifelong reservoir of resentment, with its base of imagined imposition, had begun to froth in the Fourth of July sun. "I need a beer," Red added piteously. He groped for Wanda's hand.

She removed her hand from Red's reach. "You're just sweating out all that beer you guzzled last night," Wanda said. "No beer for you right now. Remember what Junior said: we've got to be at our 'lethal best to meet the test.'"

The previous night, sitting around the poker table in their basement, the Marchiks had watched as Junior Kozol put the finishing touches on the weapon he'd obtained for use in the intended murder of Harvey Rexroth. This item, which Junior had discovered in one of his assassination textbooks, was a cane for the visually impaired, modified to contain at its end a retractable needle. Junior had mail-ordered it from a dealer in Alabama. The needle, as Junior had promised, contained curare.

"This is full proof, Red," Junior had insisted. "The KGB used this, the CIA, everbody. Remember when that Adelaide Stevenson was killed under mysterious circumstances, you know, when he was our ambassador to somewhere?"

"You mean Adlai Stevenson? The guy Ike kicked the shit out of twice for president?"

"That's who I said. Anyway, he got bumped off, maybe by the Russians, or the Kennedys, maybe it was the Rockefellers, whatever. He was walking down the street and keeled over. They all said it was a heart attack. But the word was he was nailed by a secret needle gun. The needle had poison in it that killed him on the spot. I don't know if it was cue-rah-ray, probably not, or it might have showed up in the autopsy. But that don't matter. What we're using is the method. You don't give a shit what it is puts the Target down, do you?" Junior asked.

Red reached for his ninth beer of this planning session. The Pabsts, coupled with a smattering of Jim Beam shots, were not having a calming effect on him. Wanda, observing her husband closely, realized he was just working himself up into the mood of fury that he believed would propel him through the next day's planned act of revenge.

"This here thing is full proof," Junior repeated, proudly displaying his handiwork. "All you do to release the needle is lift the end of the cane off the ground and press this here little button right near the handle. Then, it's two-shay and sigh-a-nara. Soon as you poke the Target with this, turn away and head out for the exit. You can drop the cane and the glasses in a trash can on your way. They might remember a blind man at the scene and start looking for him," Junior cautioned.

Red put on, then took off the dark sunglasses Junior had also supplied. "I can't see a goddam thing out of these," he complained.

"Cuz, you ain't supposed to," Junior said. "Remember— you're blind. The glasses, being so dark, give you something they call very-simmily-tude. I read about it in one of the books.

With these glasses you can't hardly see through, you'll feel and act more like the blind man you're supposed to be. Get it?"

As he sat in the sun-drenched box seat, Red said to Wanda, "You'll have to keep an eye out for Rexroth."

"I can see him from here," Wanda said. "He's about twenty yards away, over in one of those terrace areas. I guess that's where the horse owners sit. When he heads down to that paddock, we'll just follow along and get close to him on the pathway." Rexroth, wearing a tan suit, about the color of his bulldog Winston, who sat at his feet, was engaged in animated conversation with a group of boxholders to his right. He waved a giant black cigar as he talked, his big bald head glistening in the afternoon sunlight.

Rexroth's three-year-old colt Old Flossmoor was to run in that afternoon's seventh race, the sub-feature on the card headed by the Stars and Stripes Stakes. Rexroth, the Marchiks had learned, never missed an opportunity to visit the paddock on the days his horses competed.

Rexroth enjoyed preening among the other owners, usually with one of his attractive young bladers at his side. He frequently gave detailed instructions to the jockey who was to ride his horse. One time, Rexroth had gone so far as to hand a jockey named Frankie Sheehan a map of where he wanted him to be at every point during the course of a mile and one-quarter race. Sheehan, deeply insulted, and notorious for his fiery temper, had ripped the piece of paper to shreds and flung them down at Rexroth's feet. That was the last horse Sheehan ever rode for Rexroth.

The Marchiks sat tensely for most of the next three hours. Wanda made some $2 show bets on horses whose looks she liked, cashing two of them. She permitted Red to have a beer prior to the fifth race, but that was all. When the sixth race was over, she saw Rexroth rise from his seat and descend the steps leading to where the horses would be saddled for the seventh.

"This is it, Red," she said. Wanda took a longer look at their quarry. "Rexroth has got a redhead with him, and he's got a dog with him too, on a leash. Bulldog, I guess. Jeez, what an ugly puss on that one. The dog I mean. C'mon, baby."

Red growled, "Just point me at that sack of shit." With his cane tapping and his free hand on Wanda's shoulder, he followed her in Rexroth's wake.

When the procession of paddock-goers reached a roped entrance, their credentials had to be checked before they could be admitted to the area by track security. Rexroth and his companion were fourth in line to be given the go-ahead. As they waited while those in front of them showed their passes to the security men, Wanda had Red edge ahead, Red clutching her arm tightly. The more polite people, noticing the blind man, stepped aside to allow Red and Wanda to advance. "We're right behind him now, honey," Wanda whispered. Red hastily lifted his glasses for a quick peek. Rexroth was about three feet from the point of the lethal cane.

Junior, relying on his manual, had instructed Red to aim at the Target's lower leg; that way, Red wouldn't have to raise his cane more than a foot or so off the ground in what should be a relatively indiscernible motion to any bystander.

Red quickly glanced at the target area. Then he dropped the sunglasses back down on his forehead into their original position. When he did so, there was a movement in front of him that Red, of course, did not spot.

Red heard Wanda hiss in his ear, "Do it, Red." He responded instantly. Red thrust forward with the lethal cane, and the needle hit dead center in the leg muscle. Red smiled as he felt the contact being made by his weapon.

Unfortunately, Red, aiming blindly and from memory, had hit a leg muscle belonging to Winston the bulldog. The dog, feeling a tug on its leash, had moved closer to his master's side just as Red struck. Winston dropped like a sack of cement, killed instantly.

Rexroth, meanwhile, having impatiently displayed his paddock pass to a security guard and wanting to move forward, gave a yank on Winston's leash. He was startled by the leaden lack of response. Then Rexroth looked down and let out a yelp.

"What in the living hell," Wanda heard Rexroth say as she guided Red away from the commotion that immediately erupted: Rexroth examining Winston in disbelief, his redheaded companion breaking into tears, the security men making a circle so as to shield the view of this scene from other paddock spectators.

"We got us a dead dog here at the paddock gate," one of the security guards barked into his portable phone. There was a crackle of incredulous reply from the main security office. "Yeah, you heard me right," the guard said angrily into the phone.

Wanda gripped Red's right elbow hard as she continued to steer him across the walkway and toward the nearest exit. Her face was bright red.

"Dammit, Red," said Wanda as she elbowed their way through the crowd, "we gotta get out of here! Take off those damn glasses and follow me quick!"

Chapter 20

Friday night of that week, Doyle was desultorily watching a heavyweight boxing match on cable television, the audio off, and scanning the thoroughbred industry trade publications in an attempt to keep as current as possible in his new occupation.

As the two over-muscled and under-skilled behemoths flailed occasionally, and for the most part unsuccessfully, at each other between their lengthy exchanges of glowering looks, Doyle sat, trying to recall if he'd made any major slip-ups in the course of his work day. None, he concluded, to match his *faux pas* regarding Pedro and the teaser. He took this as a sign of at least some progress.

Doyle was relieved to hear a light tapping at his door—anything to break the monotony of another tediously uneventful night. On the other side of the screen door he saw the shyly smiling face of Caroline Cummings. A breeze was blowing lightly, carrying with it traces of soft summer rain, and her face was moist. Before he could open the door, Caroline had pulled it open and was over the threshold and into his living room.

"Come right in." But as she turned to face him, Doyle bit back further irony. He knew Caroline was here on some kind of mission that he would be wise to meet with other than his standard cavalier approach.

"Have a seat," he said, motioning toward the couch. "Can I get you anything to drink?"

She shook her head, so Doyle closed the screen door behind her, then the oak door. He'd waved Caroline to the old leather couch, his apartment's major piece of furniture. Doyle turned off the television and clicked on the CD player. The dark satin baritone of Johnny Hartman, John Coltrane's tenor sax floating beneath it, started "They Say It's Wonderful."

Caroline nestled into the other end of the couch, sandals discarded, tanned legs folded up beneath her. Caroline was wearing white shorts which contrasted nicely with the beige, scoop-necked T-shirt she had on. He thought, not for the first time, that this was a beautiful, intelligent, and very appealing woman. Unfortunately, Doyle thought, she appeared to have something serious in mind.

Years before, Doyle had read with interest some rules for living laid down by the Chicago novelist Nelson Algren, who advised that a man should never play poker with a man called Doc, eat in a restaurant called Mom's, or get involved with a woman with more troubles than his own. Doyle had adhered to the first two, but had never been much good about following the third, as his marital record attested. Attracted as he was to Caroline, he briefly considered reining in his interest. Then the thought came to him that while the woman was widowed and a single mother, she at least was not under the thumb of the FBI as race-fixer. Maybe they were at least equal in the troubles department. He felt better immediately and turned his full attention to her.

Caroline brushed a hand through her hair. She looked first across the room, then back to Doyle. She started to say something, paused, then began again.

"Jack, I came here tonight because I'm concerned about, well, the situation here involving you and Aldous. It's taken me days to come on to it—I should have been more alert or aware when we met in that grand zoo in Chicago—but my mind was on other things."

Caroline paused and shifted slightly on the couch, her eyes never leaving Doyle's face.

"I've had a lot to be thinking of here on this visit, especially my children and how they're faring. It never occurred to me that Aldous might be involved in something dangerous, something he could hardly bring himself to tell me about. After all, I came here at Aldous' invitation to get away from a place that was wearing me down…the memories…the problems of a mother raising children without their father…."

Doyle said, "What has Aldous told you—about this dangerous situation?"

"He's told me that you're working with him on trying to establish whether or not horse killings are taking place here. And I know that he thinks you are up to the job, even though you two met such a short while ago."

She sat back on the couch and laughed softly, shaking her head. "Aldous is such a trusting soul, you'd not believe it. He's always been that way. He's just a great person—as a brother, as an uncle to my children. They think he's a bloody god," she said.

"What I've come to ask, Jack, is that you be very, very sure the two of you know what you're doing here. I don't know what brought you into this, or what your motivation is. Aldous has told me nothing about that. If he even knows.

"I know why *he's* involved. Because he's as honest a fellow as you'd ever meet. If he thinks bad things are happening to horses under his care, on this farm, well, he'd do anything to prevent it. And not quit, mind you. No, never that. He's never walked away from a problem in his life."

Caroline got up and walked over to the window. With her back turned to him, she lowered her face into her hands. Doyle admired the sleek, tanned length of Caroline Cummings' legs.

Doyle said, "Whatever Aldous has told you about me and the situation here, well, that's as much as it's probably wise for you to know."

He was slightly shaken by the sight of his beautiful, concerned visitor. He was also, he realized, despite every warning bell ringing out the angelus in his psyche, about to make a move on her. He got up from his couch and walked over to where she stood near the window. As Caroline turned to him, Doyle realized that he was not going to be an unwelcome aggressor.

"I want to know that I trust you to watch out for my brother." Caroline's eyes searched Jack's face.

"He'll be foremost among my thoughts," Doyle assured her.

"No, I'm *serious*," Caroline protested, her lovely face now within inches of his own.

"I know you are. So am I."

Doyle put his hands on her shoulders. Before he could gently pull her forward, Caroline gave him a look both questioning and resolute. "Is this going to be all right?" He held her close for a few moments as she rested her head on his chest. Her hair smelled like lilacs in May, Doyle thought. He felt a slight trembling at the back of his knees. She moved willingly against him.

"You can trust me. I've got his best interests at heart," Doyle murmured to Caroline, his mouth pressed to her ear.

"What about mine?" she said, smiling up at him. Caroline looked searchingly at Doyle, shaking her head slightly. "I've not been with anyone since my husband…since then…."

"Yes," said Doyle.

"So," she continued, her lips on his neck, "no offense, but this isn't exactly a matter of love that I'm feeling. At this point."

"At this point," Jack said, his hand now up inside the T-shirt, fingers brushing her left nipple.

"You might…You might," Caroline murmured, beginning to unbutton Doyle's shirt, "describe mine as a case of unrequited lust."

Doyle said, "I have a suggestion. Let's requite it."

Later, as she was dressing and preparing to leave his bedroom, Caroline said with a smile, "Jack, you're not the awful hard case you make yourself out to be." Then, realizing the multiple meanings her remark, she let out a whoop of laughter.

"That wasn't too ladylike, now was it?" Caroline said. "You were hard enough for me tonight, laddy." She reached down and brushed her lips against his. She was still giggling as she exited the front door.

Doyle remained in the rumpled bed. He lay still, hands behind his head, relishing the lingering scent of lilac and woman.

With a grin, he began humming to himself the first bars of the jazz standard "Out of Nowhere."

Chapter 21

"The air-conditioner in this tin can ain't hardly breathing. Motherfucker's on life support, and it's fadin'. Gotta be a hunnert degrees in here," Jud Repke said.

Ronald Mortvedt, at the wheel of the white pickup truck he'd bought off a Louisville used car lot, glanced over at his complaining companion.

"You turnin' into some kind of pussy? Little heat ain't gonna kill you."

Repke's light blue denim shirt had sweat crescents spreading under each arm. Repke's forehead glistened with heat-produced moisture. Mortvedt sat chilly behind the wheel, his black T-shirt dry against his muscular torso. Mortvedt never sweated.

"Open the damn window if you have to," Mortvedt added.

"We got a layer of dust in here already sifted through the cracks of this piece of shit," Repke grumbled. "I ain't opening no damn window."

They drove on in silence through the late afternoon, the only sound for miles that of the pickup's engine straining up the highway that rose toward Colorado Springs. Interstate 25 would take them south into New Mexico, their next stop on what Mortvedt called their "horse hunt."

Repke shifted restlessly in his seat. He rubbed out another Marlboro butt in the rapidly filling ashtray, which wobbled as he did so. "Look at this plastic crap. Don't know why you bought something made by them hillbillies down in Tennessee."

"That's no way for you to talk about your people," Mortvedt said. "Your folks, they were from up in them Kentucky hills, where the mines were. That's what you told me, right?"

"*They* did their living up there. I don't. I'm a former hillbilly," Repke said, settling back in his seat, his right shoulder against the door, red NASCAR cap brim down over his eyes.

Mortvedt shook his head. "There ain't no such thing," he said.

Repke reached behind him to the ice chest on the floor behind his seat and took out a can of Coors. He said, "Why didn't we rent one of those new Chevy pickups, the ones with all the doodads on 'em? Bet the air-conditioning works in those suckers."

Mortvedt's eyes remained on the road as he answered. "Don't make no sense to spend that kind of money until we find our horse. Why put all those miles on a rental? Clunky as this thing is," he said, tapping the dashboard, "we can sell it when we're done. Stoner gave us a nice chunk of 'spense money. What we don't spend, we'll split.

"Once we've found our horse, we'll buy a used one-horse trailer, probably get one off somebody at the racetrack. We'll haul the horse back to Chicago in that."

"If we find the right horse," Repke reminded.

Mortvedt said, "We'll find the son of a bitch, don't you worry about that."

The sound of Repke fumbling in the cooler caused Mortvedt to turn to him for a moment. "The beer just pops out on you in this here heat. You drink too much beer."

"There ain't no such thing."

◇◇◇

Their mission had begun with a summons from Harvey Rexroth. Mortvedt flew into Louisville, then had been picked up by Randy Kauffman and taken to Willowdale Farm.

Without going into detail, Rexroth told Mortvedt, "I want you to buy a horse for me."

Mortvedt's stoic face did not reveal the surprise he felt. The functions he'd performed thus far involved killing horses, not purchasing them. "What kind of horse?"

"Let's take a little drive," Rexroth said.

The two men entered the waiting car and Kauffman drove to the part of Willowdale Farm known as the Annex. Kauffman pulled the car up to the fence of a paddock that contained one horse, a dark bay colt that was grazing in the middle of the damp field.

"Take a very, very good look at him," Rexroth instructed Mortvedt as they walked through the lush grass toward the grazing horse. "I want you to buy a horse," Rexroth repeated, "that looks as much like this colt as possible. He's got to be a racehorse, a three-year-old, one that can compete at least at the allowance level at a major track like Kentuckiana or Heartland Downs.

"This one," Rexroth said, gesturing toward the field, "is three years old. As you can see, he hasn't got a distinguishing mark on him—no blaze, no white feet, nothing that stands out from the standpoint of color or markings. He's not real big, not small either. Being a bay, he's in the majority of the horse population as far as color."

Mortvedt's eyes narrowed as he looked at the horse. "He's plain, all right. But he's put together right," he said appraisingly. The little man walked around to the other side of the horse, which was casually grazing while keeping one eye cocked on him. "Damn good balance, good hindquarters. He's got a helluva shoulder on him. Nice clean legs, too. Bet he can run a little. Am I right, boss?"

Disregarding the question, Rexroth resumed issuing his instructions.

"I don't care where you look for this horse's double—in fact I don't want to know—but you can pay whatever it takes. Stoner will give you ample expense money when we return to the house. When you've found our horse, contact Stoner and he will wire the purchase price. Naturally, the sale would have to be private, and there must be absolutely no hint of any connection to me.

"When you've got the horse, call me here. If I'm not at Willowdale, they'll reach me. I'll want you to deliver the new horse to my racing stable at Heartland Downs. Leave him there with my trainer, Kenny Gutfreund. I'll have made the arrangements so that he'll know you're coming. As far as he's concerned, you're just bringing in a new horse that I heard about and decided to buy."

That night, Mortvedt drove to Louisville. After buying the white pickup truck the next morning, he met Repke, described the job, and within an hour the two men left for Des Moines, Iowa. Two days at nearby Prairie Park, a combination racetrack-casino facility featuring 1,001 slot machines, served only to diminish Repke's bankroll as he gambled while Mortvedt checked out the horse population. He found nothing they could use. From Prairie Meadows they drove to Oklahoma City, whose Sooner Park racetrack proved similarly barren of eligible equine prospects.

Repke was relieved to get out of Iowa. "I lost a bundle back there," he said. "I never seen so many quiet white women in one place in my life. Just stare at those slots, stare at those slots, that's all they did. Threw me way off my game."

"How do you know they was women?" Mortvedt said.

Repke said, "You got a point there, partner. They get to a certain age out here in this farm country, they sure start to look alike. From the back, there was a lot of them I couldn't tell if it was a pointer or a setter, swear to God. Sometimes from the front, either."

Two more tries were similarly unproductive, one in Wyoming at a little track named Evanston Downs, the other at Pioneer Park outside Denver.

Mortvedt had explained to Repke, "I can't be looking to buy this horse in Louisiana or Texas, where too many racetrackers know me. And I want to be as far away from Kentucky or Chicago as I can when I go after this horse. But I never been to California or New York, don't know shit about the tracks or the people there. So we'll try somewhere else, where a couple of country boys like us won't stick out like tits on a bull."

They'd watched a Sunday program at Evanston Downs, then two days of racing at Pioneer Park, plus attending the workouts at both places. A horse named Joyce's World that won the feature the day they were at Evanston Downs, the $15,000 Werblin Memorial, looked "a helluva lot like what we're after," Mortvedt said, "but he's five years old. Can't use him." Now, they were headed to New Mexico.

"Don't know how they can call Wyoming the Big Sky country, like they got a fuckin' patent on it," Repke said as he looked out his window. "How could a sky be any bigger or higher than this one?"

They were still heading south on Interstate 25. They would pass Raton, New Mexico, just over the Colorado border, without stopping, since the racetrack there had long ago closed. This long, smooth highway would carry them to their next destination, the little track located a few miles south of Santa Fe.

On Sunday afternoon, their second day at Santa Fe, Mortvedt sat forward in his grandstand seat and said to Repke, "I must have missed this s.o.b. if they galloped him this morning. Check out the number seven horse here."

As the field for the eighth race walked past the stands, Repke looked at horse number seven, then at his program. "Name's Lancaster Lad. Bay three-year-old colt. Owned and trained by W. L. Connaughton. Bred here in New Mexico."

Mortvedt said, "What's his record look like?"

"Only started three times. Won two of them, all this year." Repke looked up at the tote board. "He's the favorite here, two to one."

"Let's hope these cowboys know what they're doing with the betting," Mortvedt said, now scrutinizing Lancaster Lad through binoculars as the field assembled behind the starting gate on the other side of the track. "Because this one looks like what we're looking for."

Two hours later, the deal was done. Lancaster Lad had won his race by four lengths. As he posed for the traditional winner's circle photo, Mortvedt leaned across the chain-link fence and called to Lancaster Lad's owner-trainer, "Mr. Connaughton, could I speak to you when you have time? I'm interested in making an offer for your horse there."

Connaughton tilted his Western hat back on his head as he moved over to the fence. He was a lean, middle-aged man with a long, deeply sun-tanned face. He wore a white, long-sleeved shirt, a bolo tie under a turquoise clasp, dusty jeans and boots, and an expression of slight shock that was quickly being over-taken by major avarice. "Mister, you just come back over to Barn Fourteen in about a half hour and we'll talk some business."

◇◇◇

Negotiations lasted until dusk started to obscure the mountain range to the north of the pretty little track. They started in the track kitchen, continued in Connaughton's tack room office, then concluded back in the track kitchen over a round of beers.

Connaughton had begun by inviting Mortvedt to "make me an offer." Mortvedt responded by requesting that the angular horseman "set a price." The figure initially announced of $40,000 was for what Connaughton described as "the fastest three-year-old in New Mexico. Lancaster Lad's just coming into his own, fellas. Took my time with him, but it was worth it. He'll blow the doors off anything around here."

Mortvedt didn't even respond, merely looking disdainfully at the ceiling. He left it up to Repke, who said: "Maybe you didn't get our drift, mister. We don't want to buy your whole *stable*—just this one horse. Forty thousand would be about the total worth of all the damn horses you got here, and I'm probably going a little high at that.

"We're interested in just this one. And we're not going to be keepin' him around here so he can dust these hammer heads."

Back and forth they went, in the protracted tradition of horse dealing, before finally agreeing that Mortvedt would deliver to

Connaughton the next afternoon $28,000 in cash for Lancaster Lad and another $2,000 for a beat-up, but usable, one-horse trailer to be used for hauling their acquisition to Chicago.

"This horse is tattooed, right? And you got papers on him?" Mortvedt said as their meeting neared its end.

"Son, you ain't out in the Territories," Connaughton said. "Course I got those things. I'm giving you a helluva deal here. If my grandson wasn't suffering under leukemia and I didn't need the money for the hospital bills, you'd never be able to buy this horse off of me. He's the fastest horse I've *ever* raised.

"See you fellas tomorrow," he said as he got up to leave. As they watched the screen door of the track kitchen bang shut behind Connaughton, Repke said, "What is this Lancaster Lad going to do up in the big time?"

"Probably not much," Mortvedt replied. "The fastest horse in New Mexico these days is probably no better than a lower-level allowance horse up north. They ain't got the talent down here."

"So why would a guy like Rexroth have us go to all the time and trouble to find this sucker?"

Mortvedt gave Repke an icy stare. "None of our fuckin' business," he said. "Remember that."

On their way toward the door, Mortvedt stopped at the lunch counter and addressed a stocky Navajo man, a backstretch worker who had been quietly monitoring their negotiations with Connaughton.

"Chief, let me ask you something," Mortvedt said. "How bad off is Mr. Connaughton's sick grandchild?"

The man snorted, then turned back to his beer. "That old tight pockets never been married in his long and sorry life."

When they pulled away from Santa Fe the following morning, Repke looked back. He could see through the window into Lancaster Lad's trailer stall. "Horse's doing fine back there," he said.

Mortvedt drove slowly away from Barn 14. Repke watched as Connaughton's barn receded in the right-side mirror of the pickup.

Repke said, "Twenty-eight grand for this little horse? Man oh man…."

"Didn't want to bargain with the bastard any longer than we did," Mortvedt said, turning the wheel of the truck out of the stable area and onto the service roadway. "What do I give a shit whether we paid too much? What we paid wasn't our money."

"Shake hands with that man, better ask for a receipt for your fingers," Repke said, as W. R. Connaughton continued to enthusiastically wave goodbye. "He thinks he's pulled off the biggest score in these parts since the Spaniards rode in.

"That old son of a bitch," Repke concluded admiringly, "would sell the grazing rights on his grandmother's grave."

Chapter 22

When Ronald Mortvedt had begun killing horses for a living, back in Louisiana a few years earlier—piece work that he picked up from an old friend of his who was training on the show horse circuit—his methods were crude.

Early results were mixed and rough, involving horses driven into fences, others inoculated with toxins that would develop into fatal diseases, some urged onto well-traveled highways through holes created in farm fences.

Some of these results passed the post-mortem scrutiny of the insurance companies. Others did not. After collecting his up-front money, Mortvedt would only receive the remainder of the agreed-upon payment if the policy was paid off in full. It bothered Mortvedt, and his friend and business scout, Chuckie Lanier, to be what they considered short-changed if the insurer did not come through.

So, Mortvedt worked to improve his murderous technique. A dead horse wasn't worth much to him or its owner if it appeared to have been clumsily slaughtered. These horse deaths, Mortvedt realized, had to be as natural or accidental appearing as he could make them. Calculating and thorough, Mortvedt spent months devising ways to meet the standard of efficiency required.

Not long after he first came to Kentucky to do his killing work for Harvey Rexroth, Mortvedt fastened upon a neater, cleaner method than before. He began suffocating his equine victims.

At first, Mortvedt used a practice he'd heard about from Chuckie Lanier, his Louisiana cohort. This involved stuffing ping-pong balls up the nostrils of the horse so that air-flow was halted and suffocation followed. The problem here was the time involved: too many minutes—between ten and fifteen minutes, usually, during which discovery was always a possibility—spent with the terrified, struggling horse, trying to hold its head in place and keep it from crashing around the stall in its frantic attempt to breathe. The horses made too much noise as they thrashed about, terror-driven, their hooves resounding off the flooring. There was no way to keep that from happening. Mortvedt came to believe the risk of this technique, no matter how effective it was as a means of so-called natural death, was too great.

Mortvedt switched to plastic garbage bags. This was another tremendously effective method, leading to suffocation and the resultant "death from natural causes" perceived by those who did not have a clue as to what was going on, but it, too, had its drawbacks. It was difficult and dangerous work to keep the garbage bag tight enough over the head of the panic-stricken horse who would fight so desperately for life.

Both of these methods required the enlisting of a muscular assistant, for as strong as he was for his size, Mortvedt could not manage this alone. Thus it was that Jud Repke had been sought out and signed up. "You got the strength, Jud," Mortvedt rather grudgingly admitted.

After their joint venture had been in full swing for many months, Jud Repke found himself becoming increasingly reluctant to go on these jobs, despite what he regarded as the amazing amount of money he made working with Mortvedt. Jud would get a summoning call from Mortvedt, agree to a meeting, then try to figure out a way to get out of it.

Jud was never much good at that kind of figuring. But Ronald Mortvedt was awfully good at reading the thoughts and intentions of Jud Repke.

One night, as they sat drinking beer in the parking lot of Repke's apartment building, Mortvedt said, "Goddam it, Jud, what's wrong with you? Every time I tell we got us another one to do, you give me that hangdog, hound dog look of yours. I don't fucking get it. Your daddy had to work half a year up in those coal mines where you're from to make what I get you in a couple of hours. Hours!

"Now, you never did come straight with me about how much money you made stealing those fancy cars. But I sure as hell doubt it was any more than I'm putting into your pocket. And the risk factor…shit! You see any risk factor in this?

"That's why I don't get what your problem is," Mortvedt said, angrily crumpling his empty beer can.

Repke realized, somewhat uneasily, that this was probably the longest statement he had ever heard from the close-mouthed Cajun. He was further unnerved when he heard Mortvedt say next, "And I don't like it a goddam bit, man," giving Jud that slit-eyed sideways look that never signaled anything good as far as Repke had observed.

Jud looked out the window of the car. He said, "It's not that I mind *what* we're doing. It ain't that. And the money is goddam golden, man, I know that. I appreciate that." He turned to face Mortvedt and said, "I just don't like the *way* we're doing it. I hate to see those horses suffering like that, it just bothers the shit out of me. I see their eyes rolling around in their heads, their chests bulging out.…I don't like it. It stays with me."

The memory of Mortvedt patting, and chirping to, and otherwise distracting the horse named Wilton Lad so Jud could suddenly slip the deadly garbage bag over its head came back to Repke with a horrifying flash. He couldn't help but shudder. He hoped Mortvedt hadn't noticed.

Jud nervously took a short pull on his quart of beer. He didn't like to complain to his benefactoring buddy, that was for sure, but he didn't like the dreams he was having, either. However, weighing Mortvedt's menacing expression against his need to express himself, Jud figured he'd gone far enough on this subject.

And he sure as hell didn't want to admit to Mortvedt that he was dreaming about dying horses.

That was why he was relieved to hear from Mortvedt, who had stopped silently gazing at him, "Shit, man. You ain't got to worry no more about *that* stuff. I got a new way of doin' them, won't bother you at all."

"What is it? How does it work?" Repke asked.

"You'll see," replied Mortvedt. "It's fuckin' foolproof, man. Don't leave a mark on 'em, and it makes it look like they colicked."

"Colicked? What's that mean?"

"Horses die of it all time. They get sick and their intestines get twisted up, it's called getting the colic," Mortvedt said. "But the way I kill 'em now, they don't hardly feel nothin' and, bang, it's over."

Repke nodded his head slowly, looking at Mortvedt with renewed respect. He thought to himself again how lucky he was to have met old Ronnie down there in Oakdale.

◇◇◇

Aldous Bolger, never a heavy sleeper, was awakened by the sound of a rain-bearing wind coming in from the west. The wind ebbed and flowed, then was followed by the sound of the raindrops arriving in a steady tip-tap against his bedroom window. When Bolger cocked an eye at the electric clock, it read 1:47 a.m.

Bolger lay there for some three minutes, unsuccessfully trying to burrow his way back into sleep. Then he got up, dressed quietly so as not to awaken Caroline and the children where they slept in the two other bedrooms, and sat briefly on the screened porch of the house, enjoying the sweet smell and discreet sound of the soft night rain. Finally, growing restless, he donned his green windbreaker with the Willowdale logo above the left breast pocket. After he'd put on a cap and stepped off the porch, he decided to inspect the barn area. There was nothing to arouse his suspicions, nothing he was consciously aware of; rather, his decision to patrol the grounds and visit the stud barn was prompted purely by restlessness.

At first Bolger lowered his head as he walked down the gravel drive toward the stallion barn. But the smell and feel of the warm rain on his face was pleasant, spurring memory. For a few moments, he raised his face to the night sky, eyes closed, relishing the sensation of the drops falling, remembering how he'd done this so many times as a boy back in the hills of New Zealand.

The first thing Bolger noticed as he neared the stallion barn was a briefly flashed beam of light that raked across the window near the broad doorway. He wiped the rain off his forehead. He wondered if he might have imagined seeing the light.

Then he heard one of the horses whinny loudly, and the sound of a human voice responding in a harsh, low tone, saying something he could not discern.

Bolger felt his heart rate accelerate. There was a surge of adrenaline, a welcome feeling that coursed its way through his body and into his big hands. He wondered briefly where Alan Henry, the night watchman, was; probably on patrol near the broodmare paddocks. That must be it, because the Ford pickup normally parked near the stallion barn entrance was absent.

Bolger ran silently forward. After flattening himself against the wall of the barn, he moved carefully toward the open doorway.

There was another small sound, followed by other movements by several of the obviously disturbed horses. An odor of fear emanated from them. They were shuffling their feet, their big bodies banging against the sides of their stalls.

Bolger felt a surge of anger: that these harmless creatures should be frightened and trembling at the obviously unwanted presence of strangers infuriated him. Before slipping through the doorway, he took off his boots. Although the floor of the barn was covered with expensive rubber bricks, he didn't want to risk making any sound. He crouched down and moved inside, knowing someone was in there with his horses.

The bastards are here and I've found them, finally, Aldous thought. *Don't go wobbly now, man*, he said to himself, *stay cool, stay cool.* He slipped into an empty stall across the broad aisle from where he'd heard the noises, then dropped to his knees and peered out carefully past the wooden partition. What he saw then both astonished and enraged him further.

Unaware of Bolger's hidden presence only yards away, Ronald Mortvedt was preparing to employ his new, improved method of horse murder: death by electrocution. He had run an extension cord from the outlet near the far doorway to the stall in which lived an aged, no longer very productive stallion named Burlington Boy. With his back to Bolger, Mortvedt was whispering to the horse as he approached him, electrical cord in hand.

From where he crouched across the way, all Bolger could see was a small man, dressed all in black and wearing a black mask. He couldn't see that the extension cord Mortvedt carried had been sliced down the middle, or that Mortvedt had fastened alligator clips to the ends of the exposed wire strands that were now ready to deliver a jolt of electricity, one that would surge from the horse's nose to tail. All Aldous could discern was that the little man was talking softly to Burlington Boy, who was shifting restlessly about even though Mortvedt had a good grip on his halter. Mortvedt then reached up and clamped one of the alligator clips to the horse's left ear. He then began to move to the rear of the stall. There, he placed the other clip in the horse's rectum.

Horrified, Bolger realized what he was witnessing; realized that, once the two clips were in place, what was coming next was for the extension cord to be plugged into the wall socket. Burlington Boy would be instantly electrocuted.

Bolger had but an instant to regret that there was no weapon at hand for him to use, that he had left his house without picking up his otherwise ever-present cell phone that Rexroth demanded that he carry during work hours.

Briefly Bolger debated whether to slip back out of the barn and get help. He could summon the absent Alan Henry by phone. He could even call the big house, ask for the bodyguard, Kauffman, to come down.

But if he did that, Bolger knew, the gallant old horse Burlington Bob would surely be dead before he could return. Aldous Bolger, horseman through and through from the days of his New Zealand youth, made his decision. He moved quickly from his hiding place and across the barn's broad aisle.

As Bolger hollered toward the little man, "You bastard, drop that cord," he thought he heard a sound behind him. He couldn't be sure, for his concentration was on Burlington Boy and the little man dressed in black. The little man dropped the cord. Bending down, he yanked a knife from inside his right boot. He turned quickly, glaring at Bolger from behind his mask.

Bolger saw the knife but moved forward anyway. There was another sound behind him. He had just begun to turn to look over his shoulder when Jud Repke struck. The last thing Bolger heard was the whistling sound of a heavy pitchfork handle cutting through the air, its handle leveled at him in a high, flat swing.

That thwacking blow rendered Bolger instantly unconscious. Blood began trickling from his right ear, which was now flattened against his skull.

"Bastard's breathing," Repke said. He looked wildly around the barn. His chest was heaving and his hands were awash with sweat. It was easy for Mortvedt to take the pitchfork from him.

"Can't do this horse *now*," Mortvedt said, his mouth twisted with anger. "Who the fuck is this motherfucker coming in here on us? Goddam, the old man won't pay us for this fuck-up.

"We got to get out of here," he added.

"What about this fella?" Repke asked. He didn't want to look down at the man he'd just attacked so violently. He wanted to get away from this place as quickly as he could. But Jud found he couldn't move his feet; it was as if they were locked in quicksand. Part of it was Mortvedt, standing there coiled up with fury at what had developed, this blown job, the first they'd ever had.

Mortvedt's grip tightened on the handle of the pitchfork. He looked across Bolger's prostrate form at the shaken Repke. "Don't turn pussy on me now, Jud. Not now. I'll teach this old boy not to mess us up," Mortvedt said, his chest heaving.

Repke paled as he saw Mortvedt raise the pitchfork. "Ronnie, wait, *don't* kill him," Repke pleaded. "I'm not in this with you for no murder charge."

Mortvedt paused, the fork at shoulder level. "All's I said was teach him a lesson. And I will." He looked across Bolger into Repke's face, grinning that terrible little icy grin of his, the meanness of him thick and tangible in the darkened barn.

He brought the pitchfork handle down with a sickening thud on Bolger's left knee. The sound was like a muffled gunshot. Mortvedt raised the fork again, this time slamming it down on Bolger's right knee. Bolger cried out from the depths of his unconsciousness. Mortvedt hooted with satisfaction. Repke, stunned by the terrible damage he'd just seen done, was barely aware of Mortvedt shoving him toward the barn entrance.

"Let's get the fuck out of here," Mortvedt said. He motioned to Repke to pick up the electrical cord and clips. He handled the pitchfork himself. The only sound as the two men exited the barn was that of the unsettled horses, moving about in their stalls.

Chapter 23

Just after 2:30 that rainy morning, Doyle was awakened from one of his rare dreamless sleeps by the sound of the phone near his bed. As he reached for the receiver in the dark, the thought flashed to mind that never in his life had he ever answered a phone call in this section of the night that signaled good news.

"Jack," he heard Caroline's voice saying, speaking low so as not to awaken her children, "Jack, I'm terribly sorry to call you at his hour. But," Doyle heard her whisper urgently, "Aldous has gone out, and not come back, Jack. I think he went on one of his late-night inspection tours. I was reading in bed, and I barely heard the front door open and close. He said nothing before he left."

"How long ago?"

"More than a half-hour. He never takes that long usually. And I just rang his cell phone but there's no answer. Jack, could I ask you to go and take a look for him?"

"No problem," said Doyle. "I'm sure nothing's wrong," he added, wishing that he felt a bit more confident of what he'd told her, "but I'll go right out. We'll be back soon," he assured Caroline before hanging up. He slipped on his jeans and boots, reached for yesterday's T-shirt, and was out the door in his poncho a minute later. Before he started down the cottage steps, however, he turned back, went inside and grabbed the heavy flashlight he kept in a pantry cupboard. It was the only weapon-like object he owned. He hoped he'd need it only for its illuminating powers.

Doyle trotted through the rain to the stallion barn and entered through its open door. The horses stirred and shifted noisily in the darkness. Doyle felt for a light switch to the right of the door. Unable to locate it, he switched on the flashlight, then the lights. Moving forward slowly he approached the body centered on the barn floor with horrified disbelief.

The right side of Bolger's head was so swollen and disfigured Jack briefly thought it was another man, one he did not know. But then he recognized the New Zealander's blood-spattered windbreaker, the one with the Willowdale Farm logo, and his eyes fastened on the distinctive white-blond hair turned dark by the pool of cranial blood in which it lay.

But he could see Bolger's chest heaving. He was alive. Then Doyle's gaze fell on Bolger's legs. Both knee caps were grotesquely inverted. A shard of bone projected through the torn khaki pants over the left knee. Doyle involuntarily retched.

The physical violence Doyle had known in his life was confined to the boxing ring, both during his fighting days and in the time since, when he still followed the only sport that had ever really appealed to him. He had seen men drubbed, noses smashed, eyes swollen shut. Doyle was familiar with such evidence of pain inflicted and suffered. But he'd never witnessed the results of such explosive brutality as he was looking at here, in the Willowdale stallion barn, as he looked down at Aldous Bolger.

After flashing the light through the barn, Doyle sensed no danger. He knew he was alone with the horses, that whoever had done this was gone.

Doyle shook his head as if to clear it. He rubbed a hand over his eyes that were now filled with tears of rage and sorrow at the horrible sight in front of him. He heard the shuffling feet of the nearby horses, huge, confined beasts terrified by what had unfolded before them.

Then he turned and ran to summon help, dreading the impending moment when he would have to knock on Caroline's door.

Chapter 24

The hours immediately following the attack on Aldous Bolger were a blur to Doyle as he gave his account of discovering his battered friend to the sheriff's deputies, then repeated it to Karen Engel and Damon Tirabassi, first over the phone, then face-to-face following their arrival in Lexington from Chicago. There was also the tortuous time spent attempting to deal with the shattering effects of this crime on Caroline Cummings and her children. Doyle knew he would never be able to forget the look of shock and then soul-tearing sorrow on Catherine's lovely face when he told her what he'd found in the Willowdale stallion barn.

It was his "hard Kiwi head" that saved him, Aldous whispered to Jack in Lexington's Central Baptist Hospital a few hours after regaining consciousness. Bolger's speech was painfully slow, his eyes reflecting his desire to communicate faster and better than his concussed brain made possible.

All he remembered, he said, was the small man dressed in black "about to do something to one of our horses." The physicians said Bolger's head injury was "miraculously" less severe than the blow he'd received could normally be expected to cause. "A powerful blow that caused the equivalent of a temporary, minor stroke," was how Dr. Howard Sill had described it to Caroline and Jack. "There's trauma, but his speech patterns can be expected to return to normal in time," Dr. Sill had assured them.

The doctor's prognosis concerning Aldous' other injuries was far less sanguine. Dr. Sill had called in a team of orthopedic specialists to examine Aldous' shattered knees. The tissue trauma was so severe that CT scans were needed to disclose the extent of the damage.

Their opinion was that Aldous would require knee replacements if he were to walk again. "They are very effective procedures," Dr. Sill told them. But the operations could not be done for several months, during which Aldous would need to recuperate from the damage he'd suffered.

Doyle was amazed at how stoically Aldous had accepted this news. When Jack was first allowed into the critical care unit, he was both appalled at the paper-white hue of his friend's face and amazed at the look of defiant cheerfulness in his eyes. "Down, but not out, laddie," were the first words Aldous had whispered to Jack. Couldn't kill him with a hand axe, Jack thought again.

Rexroth had dispatched Byron Stoner to express his concern to Caroline and Jack. "Mr. Rexroth was, of course, appalled and saddened by what happened," Stoner said in his prim way. "He would have told you that himself, but he was called away on urgent business early this morning." Rexroth insisted that Willowdale pay all expenses involved in Bolger's treatment.

"Mr. Rexroth wished me to also tell you," Stoner said to Jack, "that he would appreciate it if you would remain on here at Willowdale temporarily, serving as acting farm manager until a successor to Mr. Bolger can be hired. You are, naturally, invited to apply for the position yourself," Stoner added, "although I must tell you that it calls for a person with more extensive experience than your own."

The brutal beating of Aldous Bolger caused a sensation. The story was extensively covered by the local and state newspapers, which had a major interest in anything that occurred in Kentucky horse country, especially an event of this nature.

Naturally, the crime was given continued attention by the national racing press, Rexroth's *Horse Racing Journal* leading the way. The fact that it had been committed on Willowdale property resulted in Rexroth expressing his outrage in a number of media settings. Rexroth himself authored a ringing front-page editorial for *Horse Racing Journal,* decrying this "despicable act against this outstanding horseman of international reputation," and offering a reward of $100,000 for information leading to the arrest and conviction of "the criminal or criminals involved, whose motives remain as mysterious as their methods were heinous."

Doyle was infuriated by what he considered to be Rexroth's sanctimonious posturings. While he didn't suspect Rexroth of attacking Bolger, or ordering the attack, Doyle felt in his gut that Rexroth was tied to it somehow, probably through his employee, Mortvedt.

Doyle said nothing about his theories to Caroline, for early on in Doyle's working relationship with Aldous Bolger the two men had agreed to keep from Caroline any knowledge of Jack's connection to the FBI, and the FBI's interest in an ex-jockey ex-convict named Mortvedt.

"If she knows that," Aldous had said, "she's going to worry about me. I know that. This girl has had to go through more than enough already. I don't want to add to her burden. And," Aldous had noted, "there's no real reason for her to know anyway. Let Caroline enjoy herself as best she can while she's here."

Bolger had also cautioned Doyle against "trying to pass your-self off as a lifetime horseman" to Caroline. "She'd sniff that out as a lie in a minute. You can tell her, and truthfully, that you've had some experience working on the racetrack. But don't go past that, it'll never fly.

"Caroline's taken a bit of a fancy to you, Jack," Bolger added, grinning at Doyle. "That's good on ya, mate, as far as I'm concerned. But I'll give you this piece of advice if the feeling is at all mutual. Don't try to bullshit this girl. She'd suss that in a second."

"My story is supposed to be that I decided on a midlife career change," Doyle said. Thanks to the FBI, he added to himself.

"Jack," Aldous had said, "I don't give a boiled banger why you're doing this. Those agents just told me I was going to be given some help. You don't have to tell me any more than that, man."

Approximately thirty-six hours after Doyle found the New Zealander, Karen, Damon, and Doyle were seated at a table in a conference room in the Dalton House Hotel on the outskirts of Lexington.

"Never," Doyle said slowly, "never would I have gone ahead with your plan if I thought Aldous Bolger would be at risk. What was done to him...I can't believe it." Doyle rose so abruptly from his chair that it fell over behind him. He walked over to the curtained window and stared out, palms on the sill.

After a glance at Damon, Karen said, "Jack, ease up a little bit, won't you? I know you're furious. I know your Irish is up. But we have to get past those emotions and approach this situation in a professional manner. We had no idea Aldous would wind up like this. How could we have envisioned that? But there's nothing to be gained from looking back on that now. What we've got to do is concentrate on finding who did this."

Earlier, Karen and Damon had spent considerable time commiserating with Doyle. Embittered as he was, Doyle's skeptical streak made it hard for him to accept the truth—which was that their sorrow was sincere. Both Karen and Damon had admired the New Zealand horseman for his courage in calling them into the case of the horses being killed, for his bravery in agreeing to work with Doyle in a combined effort aimed at nailing the culprits.

Damon had said, "Jack, these are not courtesy condolences we're feeding you here. Bolger was a stand-up guy. What happened to him was terrible. But we've got to move on here together, and that includes you."

Doyle finally turned away from the window and faced the agents. "All right," he said. "I'm sorry I lost it there. Sorry I blew up at you. Deep down, I know damn well this wasn't in your plans.

"But I'm having a hard time with this. I can't get over what was done to that good man. I can't get out of my head the look on Caroline's face when I told her about her brother."

Doyle began pacing back and forth on the brown carpet of the conference room. He said, "Aldous must have discovered the horse killers at work there in the stallion barn. Or preparing to work, anyway. There's no other way to explain what happened to him.

"The man didn't have an enemy on either side of the world. You know that from all you've learned about him. No, those bastards must have jumped him after he stumbled on them. Why in hell Aldous didn't come and get me before he went down to that barn...we were working on this together...that was the whole idea. He should never have gone there himself.

"And why they had to batter him like that...." Doyle shook his head. "I just don't understand something like that. What kind of animals would beat a man that way?"

No one spoke for several moments. Doyle, tired as he was from nearly two days without sleep, was energized by his agitation. He continued pacing. Finally, Karen said, "Jack, I'm sure that Aldous acted on the spur of the moment. Maybe he couldn't sleep and decided to patrol the grounds. He was known to do that.

"Then, he must have spotted something out of the ordinary. Aldous was a big, strong man, and a pretty independent fellow. You know that about him, certainly. I'm sure he was confident that he was capable of handling anything that he ran into on that farm.

"As to the beating he took...well," Karen said with a grimace, "if you saw some of the things we've seen...." She looked over at Damon, who said, "Jack, my friend, you've got no idea what's out there. I could give you war stories from here to Christmas morning."

Tirabassi shifted in his chair. After sipping from his coffee cup, he turned to look out the window at the motel courtyard, a pensive look on his long face. He said, "It's absolutely no comfort to anybody involved but, believe me, what happened to Aldous Bolger is not some unique phenomenon. Not in this world."

Doyle recognized the validity of Damon's statement. He also realized that the two FBI agents did not deserve the anger he had leveled at them. In addition to Bolger's murderer, there were other elements feeding his fury.

Immediately after news of the attack spread, the Kentucky horse industry rumor mill, a machine rarely dormant, had cranked up big time. Bolger, it was said, had been beaten for not paying gambling debts....He'd been assaulted by thugs hired by the irate husband of a local woman he'd secretly been seeing....The attack was an attempt to silence him before he began cooperating with officials who were attempting to crack a horse country cocaine ring.

Doyle had heard various versions of these and other rumors. He knew there wasn't a scrap of truth attached to any of them, and they bothered the hell out of him.

Suddenly, Doyle banged his fist down on the table with a force that startled both agents. "Where in the hell is Mortvedt?" he said loudly. He looked first at Karen, then at Damon. "I can't believe that the vast resources of the FBI can't locate this little crook. *You* know in your heart Mortvedt killed those horses, and probably attacked Aldous, and *I* know it. Why can't you track him down?"

Karen's face reddened. She said, "Contrary to what you think, we don't *know* anything for sure about what Mortvedt's done. It's all speculation, speculation based on pretty solid background, yes. Certainly we suspect Mortvedt of killing those horses. And he may well have done Bolger, too. But we don't have a speck of proof regarding either matter. We can't put Mortvedt on a most-wanted list if we've got nothing to back up our suspicions. That's not the way it works, Jack."

"If we had anything solid to go on," Damon said emphatically, "we'd have issued a bulletin on Mortvedt from minute one. I guarantee you that."

Doyle took a deep breath. He felt as tired and frustrated as he'd ever had in his life. "How do you see all this?" he asked. "You've got to believe—I mean, it has to be obvious—that Aldous nearly paid with his life for finding somebody in that barn that shouldn't have been there. Who do you think it was, if it wasn't Mortvedt?"

Karen glanced at Damon before replying. "It could well have been Mortvedt. It probably was. And *if* it was, he might have had a motive for attacking Aldous besides just the fact that Aldous accidentally discovered him in the Willowdale barn.

"Mortvedt may well have suspected Aldous of knowing something he wasn't supposed to know. Something having to do with another horse there, not one of the devalued stallions."

Doyle said sharply, "What the hell are you talking about?"

"Let me tell you about a man named Lucas Collier," Karen said.

Chapter 25

Lucas Collier was a fifty-seven-year-old white male native of nearby Woodford County who had bounced around the Blue Grass horse industry scene for most of his working life.

"High school dropout…married and divorced twice, total of four children…series of menial jobs on Kentucky horse farms, including cutting grass, repairing sheds, painting fences, et cetera," Karen said. "No hands-on experience with horses—evidently nobody trusted Lucas' brain power to do that kind of work. I doubt Lucas has got many more IQ points than he has teeth. And he's in short supply in the tooth department," she said.

Collier's previous record was a series of small-time crimes, Karen continued, "mainly bar fights, one breaking and entering that was dismissed, a couple of DUIs, one that stuck." He most recently had come to the attention of local law enforcement when a field behind the falling-down farmhouse he'd inherited from his father proved to be the site of a thriving marijuana crop.

Collier was "very, very anxious to avoid a prison sentence," Karen said, "so he tried to deal. He volunteered information regarding a theft he'd engaged in four years ago. It involved a horse, and what he believes was a valuable one. According to records, the theft Collier described coincides time-wise with the theft of a famous mare named Donna Diane. Collier played a minor role in this, but he was there when the horse was taken and he described the other men involved."

Doyle said, "I don't get what you're getting at here. What's the connection?"

Damon reached over to a stack of papers on the table and extracted a folder that he handed to Doyle. "This is Lucas Collier's confession. It's long and rambling, so you can skip over a lot of it. I've tagged with a blue marker the parts that are of interest to us."

According to Collier, he'd been approached one night in a rural beer bar by a man who identified himself only as Jud. Collier had been asked if he was familiar with the physical layout at Sheridan Brothers' Farm. "Hell yes," Lucas had answered, "I worked there about three years. What do you need to know?"

What the man named Jud wanted to know was the location of the broodmare fields, the rotation schedule for the horses that was used by the Sheridan Brothers' farm manager, and the location of the roads that ran through the property. Jud spent several hours over the next two nights interviewing Collier and making notes. After giving him some instructions, Jud said he would contact Collier in a week or so. He paid Collier $1,000 "in cash money" for the information and said that a similar payment was possible for future services.

As Doyle read further, he learned how the men—there were three of them—had stolen this horse. First they ascertained which field held the valuable mare Donna Diane. For three straight nights, the smallest of the three spent an hour or so at the pasture fence, feeding Donna Diane and her companion gelding sweet alfalfa from a plastic bag. Sheridan Brothers' Farm, like most breeding farms, employed only a few night watchmen who made occasional rounds of the property. The watchmen were easy to spot as they checked on the sixteen- to twenty-member groups of mares in each pasture.

Collier told the interrogators he had parked his pickup at the intersection of two farm roads about a half-mile from where Jud and the little man had left their car. Collier was instructed to flash his lights and drive off immediately if he spotted any vehicle or anyone approaching, but he never was required to do that.

Doyle looked up from his reading. He shook his head. "Can you imagine having millions of dollars' worth of horses being guarded by five-dollar-an-hour night shift guys? Man, these farm owners down here are a trusting lot. Or stupid. Or cheap."

"Not anymore," Damon replied. "After the Donna Diane disappearance all the farms beefed up their security systems."

"Was there a reward for her?"

"Only a million dollars," Karen said. "But they never found out what happened to her."

On the third night, Lucas Collier's confession continued, when Donna Diane had again enthusiastically come to the fence, eager for company and food, Jud quickly and quietly sawed off three boards where they joined the fence post. He swung them outward, creating a gap. The little man, who had slipped a lead rope on Donna Diane, silently led her through the opening.

"I was too far away to see exactly how they done it," Collier said, "but that was what Jud told me they was going to do. Jud, he took those board ends and tied them back onto the fence post with rope. They wouldn't hold against any pressure, but there wasn't any of that. And from where I stood, the fence looked okay, like there was nothing wrong with it."

The mare nickered anxiously as the little man led Donna Diane carefully down the embankment to the one-horse trailer attached to Collier's pickup truck. Since he was known in the area, the idea was, Lucas said, that "anybody seeing me hauling a trailer wouldn't be much suspicious. I guess that was why they needed me. Course, I was a pretty good lookout, too," he added.

As soon as the mare was in the trailer, Collier said, the little man "stuck her with a needle," which he assumed contained a tranquilizer.

Then, Collier said, the men drove cautiously down the dark country backroads in their two-vehicle procession. They went just a few miles, he estimated, before they pulled off the asphalt and up a narrow dirt road leading onto a property Collier had never seen.

Jud motioned for Collier to get out of his truck. Jud and the little man then unhooked the trailer from Collier's pickup and sent him on his way, another $1,000 in his jacket pocket.

"I don't know what they done with the trailer," Collier said. "I asked the little fella where we were when Jud gave me my money. But he never said. He just give me this real hard look, so I didn't ask him nothing else. I just took my money and got out of there."

But, Collier said, about a year and a half later he was hired on a short-time basis to work cutting back undergrowth on an off-the-road piece of property. The road leading to the work site looked "mighty familiar," Collier said, and he eventually became convinced that this was where he and Jud and the little man had parted company.

"I found out it was land owned by that Mr. Rexroth, the Willowdale fella," Lucas Collier said.

Doyle closed the folder and looked at the two agents across from him at the table.

"We had Lucas Collier going over mug shots last night," Karen said. "He didn't come across the man called Jud. But he absolutely, positively ID'd the 'little man' as Ronald Mortvedt. He said that was a face he could never forget."

Damon leaned forward, arms on the table. "Do you see it now, Jack? We've got Mortvedt, the horse killer, tied to Rexroth, the collector of insurance premiums on murdered horses.

"We're in business here, Jack."

It was the first time Doyle had ever seen Damon Tirabassi grin.

Chapter 26

It was a few minutes before eleven o'clock on a cloudless Thursday night. The nearly full moon gleamed a Velveeta yellow in the high summer sky. The retractable skin of Willowdale's pool/pavilion complex was pulled back to reveal the relatively bright night, which in turn made visible the female form that circled Rexroth's blading track. As bright as the moonlight was, her face was still not discernible in the darkened pavilion. All that was visible were the iridescent elbow and knee pads, glowing a light green, as she skated in leisurely fashion, throwing in a pirouette or two in every other loop.

Rexroth, who sat behind his vast desk reading computer printouts, occasionally raised his head to glance at the circling figure, but did not speak. The only sounds in the building were of the whirling of her wheels and of the woman's breathing as she made her rounds over the track.

At five seconds before eleven, Rexroth heard movement behind one of the ceiling-to-floor curtains that hung from the expanse of windows back of his desk. He knew who it was, but couldn't help turning to look.

Ronald Mortvedt slipped into the pavilion. His entrance, as always, served to send a shudder through Rexroth. No matter how many times he met with the ex-jockey ex-con, Rexroth could never come close to feeling comfortable with him—this, despite the fact that in almost every moral and ethical sense they were blood brothers. Maybe that was why Mortvedt made the publishing magnate so uncomfortable.

Also disturbing, Rexroth had found, was the little man's great gift of stealth. He always arrived right at the appointed time, easily eluding the Willowdale security setup. *That's what makes him so good at the jobs he does for me*, Rexroth thought, with a mixture of admiration and unease. Rexroth well understood that Mortvedt was, to the unsuspecting—as his victims almost always were—as deadly as cobra venom.

Rexroth realized from the start of their relationship that the only way to meet with Mortvedt was like this, at night, at Willowdale, where secrecy was best maintained.

Mortvedt, as always, remained out of sight behind one of the pavilion's drawn curtains until Rexroth dismissed the blader.

"Darlene," Rexroth announced, "that's enough for tonight, sweetheart. You're excused. And thank you."

After Rexroth heard the far door close, he signaled Mortvedt to come forward.

As was his custom for these night meetings, Mortvedt was dressed all in black: long-sleeved jersey, jeans, cowboy boots, all the color of his slicked-back hair. His eyes were impassive and he sat perfectly still, strong hands on the arms of the chair. He was not there to apologize for the Bolger disaster, that was clear to Rexroth.

Rexroth said, "What went wrong?"

Mortvedt shrugged. "Motherfucker picked the wrong night for a walk in the rain," he said nonchalantly. "Bad luck for us—I couldn't do the horse—but worse luck for him."

"Yes, I'd say worse luck for him," Rexroth replied. "And damned bad luck for me, too, and Willowdale. The Bolger incident has been all over the media. The fact that you apparently covered your tracks, that they have no leads or suspects—well, that's fine, but…."

"But fuckin' *what?*" Mortvedt said quietly. "Ain't no way to pin that thing on me, and you should know it. You should *know* it," he repeated. Mortvedt shot a steady, black-ice look at Rexroth, who not for the first time felt a powerful feeling of regret that he'd ever decided to welcome Mr. Ronald Mortvedt into his employ.

Mortvedt said, "Boss, where you hidin' your nearest john in this here mansion?"

"Oh," Rexroth said, standing to point. "Take that door at the far end of the pool. There's a sauna room, then a washroom."

Sometimes Rexroth, when making his motivational speeches dressed in his General George Patton regalia, advised his employees that "there are different ways of looking at looking back.

"A philosopher named Santayana used to say that if you didn't know history, you were doomed to repeat it. A baseball pitcher named Satchell Paige, on the other hand, advised never to look back because something might be gaining on you.

"Both men were right, in their own way," Rexroth-as-Patton would shout, "both men were wise. It's up to RexCom employees to distinguish between the validity of these views when applied to the situation at hand. Deciding which wisdom fits at the proper time is what makes for a leader in the mighty media army of RexCom troops. It is all about *choice*, people!" Like all of Rexroth's utterances, this one was always greeted with a wave of orchestrated applause from the carefully prepped employees.

In Mortvedt's brief absence, Rexroth wondered to himself exactly what kind of a choice he had made when he launched his alliance with the little Cajun killer. Even now he had to fight off the memory of Aldous Bolger's horribly battered features that he'd been forced to view when visiting the crime scene in the Willowdale stallion barn.

◇◇◇

Mortvedt slipped back into his chair across from Rexroth's desk. Eyebrows raised, he asked, "You been sick, boss?" He nodded at the hospital cart and tray of food nearby.

"No, I haven't," replied the suddenly irritated Rexroth. Ordinarily, he limited the knowledge of his hospital-like cuisine preferences to members of the immediate staff. Rexroth could not imagine how he might explain this idiosyncrasy of his to Mortvedt, and he did not attempt to do so.

As he looked at Mortvedt's lean, sharp-featured face where the little man sat at the edge of the lamplight, Rexroth thought, *I've known him four years now, and in every one of those years his sociopathy has become more obvious.* Rexroth realized just how fearful he was of the ex-convict.

Rexroth noticed that his desk clock read 11:23. The end of their association was very near.

He said, "Ronald, I've got one more job for you. Then, I think it will be in the best interests of us both if we stop doing business together."

Mortvedt's always morose face darkened even further upon receipt of this news. The little man leaned toward the light. His hands tightened on the arms of the chair.

"What's the problem?" Mortvedt said. "Yeah, I laid the wood to that clumsy farm manager of yours. That was his fault for being in the wrong place at the wrong time. And I didn't leave a goddam trace of anything in that barn. These hayseed cops ain't got a clue," he said dismissively. His eyes locked onto Rexroth's, challenging him. "So, what's the fuckin' problem?"

Rexroth attempted to summon all his powers of amelioration and persuasion. He didn't want Mortvedt to become an enemy. Rexroth needed to usher him out of his life as smoothly as possible.

"The problem is this: we've stretched the envelope, you and I. Oh, certainly," Rexroth continued expansively, waving his huge cigar, "our work together has been ultra-efficient and effective. You've done a marvelous job, accomplishing everything assigned you. But," Rexroth said with a shake of his head, "I'm convinced that we're at that point where we are uncomfortably close to pushing our luck past where it will go.

"What you did to Bolger, no matter how much it needed to be done considering the circumstances you were in, raises the stakes for us considerably. Insurance fraud that involves dead horses is one thing. Action bordering on the murder of a human being is quite another.

"Nothing lasts forever, Ronald. I've decided that we are just about at the end of our line together. I want you to kill one more of my equine liabilities. His name is Uncle Francis. He's in stall five in the stallion barn. You can do it any night you choose within the next two weeks. And that will be the last one you do for me. That's why," Rexroth said, reaching into a desk drawer for an unmarked envelope. "I've readied this for you." Mortvedt took the envelope, noting, without expression, the thick packet of bills it contained. He looked at Rexroth expectantly.

"There is seventy-five thousand dollars there, all fifties and hundreds. You may count them if you wish. This represents your final fee, plus a bonus for excellent work done in the past. Consider the latter a farewell gift."

Mortvedt saw that Rexroth was determined to end their relationship in this abrupt way. He felt a wave of resentment. *All the dirty work I've done for rich boy here, and he calls the final shot without asking me?* he thought. His expression darkened, but he said nothing.

Mortvedt tucked the cash-filled envelope into his boot. When Mortvedt did so, Rexroth noticed the ankle holster on Mortvedt's right leg. Then he realized it wasn't a holster for a gun, but a knife scabbard. Light briefly reflected off part of the knife blade before Mortvedt pulled his jeans leg back down over his boot. Rexroth felt himself hosting another involuntary shudder.

But knowing now that Mortvedt was, indeed, going to go along with this parting of the ways, Rexroth began to relax. This was going to work. Mortvedt was not going to present a daunting obstacle to his plans, or any kind of obstacle at all.

Mortvedt stared at Rexroth for a moment. Then he quickly rose from his chair and left without a backward glance. Rexroth stared at the curtained doorway through which the little man had slipped. The curtains continued to shift for several seconds after Mortvedt had disappeared, though Rexroth was unable to discern the presence of any summer breeze. The night, Rexroth knew, was dark, deep, and as silent as the black-clad figure that must be now moving to his car, hidden as always on one of Willowdale's farthest borders.

Chapter 27

Jack drove Caroline and her children to Lexington's Blue Grass Airport, following as closely as he could the ambulance transporting Aldous from the hospital. A midday summer rainstorm had just subsided, but no rainbow followed. As Helen and Ian talked quietly in the backseat, Caroline looked straight ahead from her passenger seat, eyes shielded behind dark glasses. The weight of depressed reaction to what had happened to Aldous bore down on all of them.

Turning onto New Circle Road, Jack said, "Well, at least Aldous seems happy to be going home."

Caroline thought for a moment before replying. "Relieved, disheartened, terribly disappointed—all those things more likely," she said. "That big dream he had of making a mark on American racing as a brilliant farm manager, to have that torn away from him, it's almost as bad as the crippling. He wanted it so badly."

"Don't say crippling," Jack responded. "You can't say that yet. You don't know that to be true."

Caroline reached over and patted Jack's knee. "You're right, we don't," she said. "I hope I'm wrong and the doctors are right, that he'll get his speech fully back, that the knee replacements will work out over time. But what was done to him will be with him all the rest of his life. And all our lives as well. There's a crippling involved in all that, I can tell you."

She turned to look out her window, attempting to muffle an involuntary sob.

Traffic entering the airport was light. Jack pulled up to the curb behind the ambulance, whose attendants were carefully lowering Aldous' wheelchair to ground level. He sat in it with his legs in their casts straight in front of him, his big hands gripping the chair handles. Discomfort was evident on his broad face, but he attempted to reassure the watchers by smiling.

The Bolgers were to take a series of flights from Lexington to Auckland, arranged to accommodate Aldous and his wheelchair. Aldous had insisted on this plan. "If I'm to be chopped and chiseled, I want it done on home ground," he'd told Dr. Sill at Central Baptist. Dr. Sill had okayed Aldous to travel three days earlier. He told Jack admiringly, "This man's got the pain tolerance of a Thai kick boxer. He'll be able to make that journey all right."

Jack waited as the Bolger party checked in at the Delta counter. It was a slow Tuesday morning and the process was quick. Caroline politely waved off an airport attendant who volunteered to wheel Aldous to the gate. "Thanks, we'll handle it ourselves," she said politely. "Jack, are you coming?" she asked.

"I'll say goodbye here," Doyle replied. He moved forward to kneel and embrace the children. "Be good, you Kiwi rascals," he grinned. "I'll be checking up on you." Standing, he turned to Aldous, who began to speak. Aldous' voice was soft and halting as he struggled to convert ideas into sound. Jack winced at the painfulness of this slow process, then tried to hide his reaction.

"Keep your eyes open wide," Aldous finally managed to get out. "Guard those horses—and yourself, Jack." He fell silent after this taxing effort, then turned his head to look down the corridor to the Delta gate. It was their signal to leave.

Caroline smiled at Jack, who took her in his arms, face pressed into the fragrance of her hair. He felt her tremble as he held her tightly. "We hardly got out of the starting gate," he whispered to her.

Caroline laughed quietly. She kissed him briefly on the lips, then put her head on his chest for a moment. "Maybe there'll be another start another time, Jack," she said. "Thanks again for all you've done for us." Then she turned away and began to wheel her brother down the corridor, her kids on either side of Aldous' wheelchair. None of them looked back.

Doyle exited the terminal and walked to his car in the airport parking lot. He sat for nearly an hour, restlessly drumming his fingers on the Accord's steering wheel, turning the radio on and then, quickly, off. Blue Grass Field was so compact he had no trouble spotting the Delta aircraft when it finally taxied away down the runway, then lifted off.

As the plane faded out of view, Doyle turned on the ignition and started the car. He felt as if something had again been lost to him. He realized he hadn't experienced such a feeling since his brother Owen died. But the spreading emptiness in his chest, the tightening of his mouth, even the reflexive narrowing of the eyes to thwart tears—"tough guys don't cry," his father had insisted in his drunken rages—were terribly familiar to him.

He put the car in gear and sped out of the airport.

Chapter 28

The phone call from Byron Stoner's impeccable office at Willowdale to the thoroughly messy kitchen of Earlene Klinder's weather-beaten one-story home on the outskirts of Louisville went through at nearly ten o'clock at night.

Stoner sat at his orderly desk, having completed his review of that day's RexCom business results. All had gone well, he was glad to find, so there was no need for him to go through the process of ordering a change in the blader line-up.

This was the end of a typical working day for Stoner, one that extended from seven in the morning until well after the dinner hour, and he was tired. He just had one more thing to arrange, then he could repair to his second-floor suite of rooms in the Willowdale mansion. Stoner was re-reading Robertson Davies' *Deptford Trilogy*, thoroughly enjoying again the depiction of life in his native Canada. But, first, a phone call.

When, two days earlier, Rexroth had told Stoner what he needed done, he did so with "complete confidence that you can find a way. You are truly a marvel at this sort of thing, Byron," Rexroth had said, and Stoner couldn't help but feel the flush of elation that always accompanied one of his employer's infrequent compliments.

Earlene Klinder was tired, too. Resting her forearms on the dish-laden kitchen table, she was tempted to put her head down between them and go to sleep. Her teenage twins, Earl and

Earlette, were in the living room squabbling over which television show to watch. The twins had fought once they'd learn to talk, and hadn't stopped in the dozen years since. Earlene tuned them out as best she could.

Reaching for the radio dial, she flicked on the Reverend Roland Ruland's program. The Sports Preacher was segueing from a dissertation on Samson and Delilah—"Samson, the premier power lifter of his time, until he was brought down by the ayerobic dancing wiles of old Delilah"—into what he termed his "feature presentation lesson of the night.

"Picture the Orange Bowl on a New Year's night," Reverend Ruland boomed, "Florida 'gainst Nebraska, and a huge and hungry crowd on hand. But all the concession stands are locked up tighter than a miser's safe! There's no food or beverage to be had!"

"Then imagine your lord and savior, the one and only JEEEEEZUS Christ, appears at mid-field, the fifty-yard line. Brothers and sisters, do you remember the wedding at Cana? Well, that's what I'm talking about here….I'm talking about the Greatest Concessionaire of All Times, feeding and slackening the thirsts of the parched and hungry multitudes. But it is their *souls* that cry out for sustenance from the Great Concessionaire, JEEEEEZUS Christ…."

This was the windup of another twelve-hour work day for thirty-eight-year-old Earlene Klinder, the kind she'd been forced to endure since the death of her husband, Leroy, in a motorcycle accident eight years earlier.

Stoked on methamphetamine and rye whiskey, Leroy had pulled out of a roadhouse parking lot early one Sunday morning directly into the middle of a fast-moving National Guard truck convoy on the way home from once-a-month nighttime maneuvers.

"Maybe Leroy had a flashback and thought he was entering the service of his country again," the minister had said at the funeral, putting as good a spin as he could on the situation.

Leroy had been in the U.S. Army during the Gulf War. He attributed his subsequent passion for pharmaceuticals to post-traumatic stress disorder, although in his role as an Army mechanic he'd never gotten farther from Kentucky than the motor pool at Fort Benjamin Harrison in Indiana. Earlene had made no attempt to play the role of grieving widow. "He'd turned into such an asshole," she volunteered to everyone who offered condolences.

Leroy's contributions to the Klinder standard of living had been spotty at best. Even so, their disappearance forced Earlene to find a second job. At the suggestion of a childhood friend, Mary Hendrickson, who worked as a horse identifier at Kentucky racetracks, Earlene went through training and then became a licensed horse tattooer, one of the few women in the country doing that work. Earlene and Mary had been friends since the time when, ages twelve and thirteen respectively, they'd worked around a third-rate riding academy named Upson Downs in exchange for free riding lessons.

Mary Hendrickson had explained to Earlene that every thoroughbred, in order to be allowed to compete in races, must carry identification: five numbers and a letter applied to its upper lip by dye-filled needles. Most horses undergo this procedure when they are two years old.

Each horse's lip tattoo is unique, matching the identification number that appears on it's official registration papers. Each time a horse enters the paddock to race, Hendrickson said, the "lip tattoo is checked by the official identifier—that's me." If these inscriptions do not match up, Mary added, "that horse don't run."

Earlene visited the Kentuckiana track for three and a half hours each morning to tattoo horses. Sometimes, she drove to area farms to keep appointments. Mornings at ten she was at her post in the K-Mart checkout line, where she remained until six. Her combined income from these two jobs was just enough to keep her family afloat.

"Mrs. Klinder," said the smooth voice over the phone, "my name is Byron Stoner. I'm calling from Willowdale Farm over near Lexington. I'm interested in making an appointment for your services as a horse tattooer."

"Kind of late at night, isn't it?" Earlene replied, her fatigue manifesting itself in irritability. "Hold on a second; I'll get my appointments book." She thumped the receiver of the phone down on the kitchen counter.

A minute later, Earlene said, "Mr. Stoner? I'm scheduled to be down your way next Tuesday. I can put Willowdale on my list of stops."

Stoner said, "No, that won't do. We need you to make a special trip here, this week." There was a pause. Then Stoner said, "You see, we need you to tattoo only one horse."

Earlene, disbelief in her voice, said, "A special trip? At night? Mr. Stoner, I only get paid $12 a horse. Look, why don't we wait until I've got some other appointments lined up? Croft Lane Farm has got a bunch of two-year-olds they want done. That's near you. I just haven't figured out a time yet. But I could hook you in with them.

"Otherwise, it's just not worth my while to drive all the way down there to tattoo just your one horse."

There was another pause. Stoner then told her what the job would be worth. "I've got a messenger on his way to your home right now with a down payment of $1,000—in cash—just to get you to come down here and discuss this, shall we say, unique situation," he said. "No strings attached. The $1,000 is yours regardless of what you decide."

"Is tomorrow night soon enough for you?" Earlene asked.

◇◇◇

Randy Kauffman met Earlene Klinder's car at the front gate of Willowdale. He introduced himself and, without asking, opened the passenger door of her seven-year-old Yugo and sat on the front seat, his bulky body bringing a squishing sound out of the worn cushion as he squeezed in. Kauffman directed her through the dusk over a road well removed from Willowdale's main barn complex. Minutes later, Earlene pulled up in back of the large equipment shed on the portion of Willowdale known as the Annex. Waiting for her were Byron Stoner, the groom Pedro, and a bay horse who moved his feet restlessly as he watched her approach with her tattoo kit containing its needles and dyes.

Kauffman held the horse's shank as Earlene showed Pedro how to position the clamp that kept open the horse's mouth.

Stoner said, "This is the tattoo you are to apply," showing her a plain piece of paper with the letter B and five numerals on it.

"This is no two-year-old," Earlene muttered as she readied her equipment. She could tell that by the horse's teeth as well as its size and musculature. None of the men responded.

Two-year-olds, Earlene knew from experience, were the easiest ones to deal with. The older the horse, the more time they'd had to learn tricks, as she called them. Still, this horse stood calmly for the most part, and Earlene went about her work with cool efficiency. She finished the job in less than fifteen minutes.

Stoner walked with Earlene back to her car. As she opened the driver's side door, he handed her an envelope. "This the remainder of your payment," Stoner said. "May we never meet again." He turned away without another word.

Earlene rapidly counted the $4,000 in cash in the envelope. She had just committed a criminal act, one that could lead to her being in prison and Earl and Earlene in foster homes if it were ever discovered, but she couldn't help but feel excited, triumphant even! This was like winning the lottery, something she knew in her heart she'd never do.

Earlene was confident Byron Stoner would never reveal any details of her illegal doings here at Willowdale tonight, and she was damn sure she wouldn't. Several times during the drive home, she riffled the bills between her fingers as they lay in the envelope on her lap. She couldn't help but wonder to herself about who the bay horse really was.

Chapter 29

With his host busy talking on the telephone, Jack Doyle sat back in one of the comfortable chairs that flanked a long glass table positioned near the large window of Moe Kellman's north Michigan Avenue business office. Directly in front of the table, also facing north toward a spectacular, eighteenth-floor view of the Chicago skyline, was an expansive, comfortable, dark leather couch.

Kellman had waved a greeting as Doyle was ushered in, but continued his phone conversation. He was elegantly dressed as usual, white linen shirt agleam under a gray silk suit, two huge diamond cufflinks sparkling as he shifted the phone from one hand to another.

Kellman perched on a chair behind his desk. But there were no chairs in front of it. Kellman preferred to do business from the couch, located several deep-carpeted yards from his desk, where he could easily reach over and give an encouraging pat to a customer's knee or hand.

Still talking on the phone, Kellman motioned across the room to Jack. The late afternoon sun behind Kellman's back served to back-light and further emphasize his startling head of frizzed white hair. He was urging Doyle to help himself to the lavish platter of fresh fruit that just been delivered. Responding in pantomime, Doyle waved off Kellman's offer of something to drink.

This was Doyle's first visit to Kellman's place of business, and he was impressed by the prestigious Michigan Avenue address, the two glossy receptionists in the outer office, the extensive collection of modern art that graced the walls of the spacious, tastefully furnished room.

Doyle walked over to the north-facing window, admiring the view. When his gaze fell upon a church steeple in the distance, Doyle remembered the shock he'd felt early that morning. After informing Byron Stoner that he had personal business in Chicago and would be away for the day, Doyle had gotten into his car at Willowdale and turned on the radio as he pulled out of the driveway.

"And JEEZUS, driving old CAR NUMBER ONE, he leads the JERUSALEM 500, you better believe it, brothers and sisters.…"

The voice had jumped out of the speakers, startling Doyle. *How'd I get this station on my dial?* Doyle thought, quickly reaching for the knob. He found hard to believe the popularity of the man he thought of as "Elmer Gantry in a jockstrap." Doyle silenced the radio and inserted a Gene Harris tape. Doyle smiled as the gospel-influenced jazz pianist's music replaced the preacher's bombast.

"That's right, sweetheart," Kellman cooed into the phone, eyes alight as he winked at Doyle. "That's the price. Rosemary is going love that coat. You'll have to take her out every night next winter, show her off." Kellman laughed loudly at the short response to that suggestion.

"Okay, that's how we'll do it. Tomorrow afternoon, I'll messenger it over to you. Same to you, Feef."

Placing the phone down, Kellman said, "Fifi Bonadio." He shook his head. "Cheapest son of a bitch in the Outfit. Every time he buys a coat as a present for one of his punches, it's like you're negotiating the fuckin' Louisiana Purchase. And with all the money he's stolen and hidden.…"

Moe crossed the room. First he shook Doyle's hand, then reached up to pinch his cheek fondly. "This is our City Boy?" he said, glancing at Doyle's farm manager outfit, short-sleeved white shirt with no tie, tan khakis, western boots. "You're dressed like Ronald Reagan on vacation," Kellman said. "All you need is a red neckerchief." He took a seat on the couch, plucked a pear from the tray on the table, and sat back.

"So what is it, Jack?" Kellman smiled. "You miss me? That why you drove all the way up here from Kentucky to talk?"

"Not quite," Doyle replied.

The reason for Doyle's visit, as he had explained to agents Engel and Tirabassi prior to departing Kentucky, was to pick Kellman's brain regarding what he thought Rexroth might be up to with Willowdale's mystery horse—the fast, bay colt of unknown origin that Willie Arroyo was still flying in to work out. "If anybody would know, it would be Moe Kellman." The agents did not disagree.

Doyle spent the next quarter hour recounting to Kellman the details of Aldous Bolger's beating, an event Kellman was very curious about, having seen the various media accounts, and the confession of Lucas Collier. "We're looking to tie together Mortvedt and Rexroth," Doyle said.

"You mean you and your FBI buddies."

"Yeah, me and my FBI buddies," Doyle answered glumly. "You probably know all about that, how they've got me by the balls because of the City Sarah thing."

Kellman held up his hands defensively. "I know about how they reeled you in. That's all I know, and all I want to know. All I'm assuming, Jack," Moe added with great seriousness, "is that you've been very, very discreet regarding our dealings."

Doyle said, "They know more about you than I do, I guarantee you that. No, they haven't laid all over me regarding our...what could you call it, association? More important to me right now is Rexroth, what he might be doing."

"That's great, Jack," said Kellman. He settled back on the couch and began to talk. He said that of course he had no way of knowing "exactly what Rexroth was planning," but one possibility came to mind.

"Are you familiar with ringers in horse racing?" Kellman asked.

"No," Doyle said. "Thanks to you, my knowledge of racetrack crime is confined to stiffing horses."

Kellman let that pass. "Well," he said, "it's hard to do, but it's not impossible. Simply put, it involves the substitution of a fast horse, the ringer, for a slow horse. And it involves two horses that look very much alike.

"The last case like this that I remember involved some guys out west. Two guys. They got their hands on a set of the equipment that's used to tattoo horses—you know, identify them. You saw City Sarah's lip tattoo, right?"

"Right."

"So," Kellman continued, "these guys went to Mexico, either Juarez or the track in Mexico City, I don't remember, and paid cash for a pretty good runner, plenty fast enough for what they needed. They brought him back to northern California. This Mexican horse had no tattoo. So they tattoo him with the registration number of this bum they'd been racing up there. The horses looked almost exactly alike, and I think they were the same age. The slow horse hadn't finished in the money in six months.

"They enter the slow horse under his name, but they lose him someplace and run the fast one, and he wins big. Twice. The horse checker at the track sees that the tattoo matches up with the one on the slow horse's papers, so he doesn't suspect anything's out of line. He thinks the horse is legit. Believe me, this is the kind of caper that is very rarely attempted these days. It was more common seventy, eighty years ago. Hell, they had a guy years ago that *painted* horses so they could be used as ringers. Paddy Barry, I think his name was.

"Anyway, these guys cash two huge bets before the authorities get wise to them and determine that no registered tattooer had ever worked on the Mexican horse, that his tattoo was really the tattoo of the slow horse. Both of the guys were kicked out of racing and convicted. One of them did time. Before the other one had a chance to serve, he turned up as a floater in San Francisco Bay."

Kellman paused to deftly tong an ice cube from the silver bucket to his tall glass of Perrier. "The floater was related to a friend of mine, a third cousin of this guy I know. But that's another story.

"Now, besides the tattoo as identification," Kellman continued, "horses registered in the United States can be traced by blood types. Their parents' blood sample records are on record—both the sire's and the mother's, or the dam's, as they call them.

"As I understand it, that system was put in mainly to protect against mix-ups with young horses. If a guy bought a horse that was supposed to be sired by, say, Uncle Sam, who'd knocked up Miss Liberty or whatever, and for some reason the guy has doubts that this is true, he can check it out. The foal's blood sample has got to be consistent with the blood types of its parents. If not, then something isn't kosher and the alarms go off."

Doyle shifted in his chair. "This is all very interesting, Moe. But what could this have to do with Rexroth?"

Kellman said, "I'm coming to that.

"Suppose—just suppose—that Rexroth has got a horse that nobody knows about."

"What do you mean?" asked Doyle.

Kellman said, "I'm talking about a horse that nobody, or hardly anybody, knows about. A horse that has not been registered, or officially named. A horse that for racing purposes *does not exist*. And suppose this horse is owned by Rexroth, and Rexroth is giving this horse secret workouts, flying in a professional jockey to work him, staging simulated races.

"And suppose this unknown horse is supposed to be the fastest item to come along since Cigar?" Kellman sat back again on the couch, looking self-satisfied bordering on smug.

Doyle said, "I'll be damned. You've heard something, haven't you?"

Kellman didn't answer that. He just smiled at Doyle, his eyes twinkling. "Try a pear?" he asked.

Getting up from his chair, Doyle walked slowly over to the north window of Kellman's office suite, deep in thought. He was not even slightly aware of the impressive flotilla of pleasure boats maneuvering in the green-blue waters off Oak Street beach, or the giant white clouds, looking like deformed dumplings, that moved before the steady northwest wind, being pushed across the lake toward Michigan.

All of Doyle's thoughts were concentrated on the bay horse housed back at Willowdale, the horse that jockey Willie Arroyo flew in to exercise each week, the horse that Aldous Bolger had been instructed by Rexroth to ignore.

He turned back toward Kellman. "Okay, let's say Rexroth has got this unofficial horse, or mystery horse, or whatever you want to call him. What could he do with him?"

Moe reached to the silver platter and began expertly to quarter a red apple as big as a bocci ball, using a long, thin knife sharp enough to skim fuzz off the nearby peaches. He said, "If this animal has talent, there could be a special use for him. It would be tricky, but it could be done."

"You're talking about as a ringer."

"I'm talking about as a ringer, yes."

Doyle paused to think this over. "What about the horse's registration papers? The lip tattoo? How could Rexroth work around those things?"

"The registration papers? Simple. You just use the slow horse's papers. They're on file at the track. All they have to show is the description of the horse in question. And if I'm right, Rexroth would have a horse in his racing stable that looks a helluva lot like the unknown horse—as close to identical as he could find.

"So the official papers aren't a question, not considering the advances in technology along those lines."

"Say what?" said Doyle.

"I'm saying that forged documents are all over the place. You don't need printing presses any more. All you need is some larcenous computer genius with an inkjet printer and a scanner. Jack, from what I've been told, nearly half of the counterfeit money passed in this country is made that way. Papers for a horse would be no problem for the right guy to produce."

"The tattoo. What about that?"

"No problem. Not for a guy with Rexroth's money. That guy Stoner he's got working for him could find an abortionist in the Vatican. They've got resources, my friend.

"What they could do is buy, on the sly, the services of one of the official horse tattooers. Maybe they use muscle, or blackmail. Maybe just money. But they get the guy to put the correct tattoo of the slow horse on the unknown horse, who has never been tattooed because he's never been near a racetrack. Yet. Then they switch the horses, and they run the fast one under the slow one's name. Get it?"

Doyle slumped back in his chair. All that Kellman had theorized, Doyle realized, could very well become reality under Rexroth's guidance. The bay horse from the Annex...that must the betting tool that had been polished up and honed over the past few years.

"But what I still don't get," Doyle said, "is why a guy like Rexroth would go to all this trouble. Get involved in something like this? The bastard's got all the money he'd ever need."

Kellman said, "Jack, why does Rexroth kill horses for the insurance like you think he does? You tell me what this guy's all about. I've got no answers for that. He is what he is."

"I don't know where to go with this stuff," Doyle said. He felt overwhelmed. He went over to the window again, gazing out as unseeingly as before.

Doyle's formerly ultra-high self-confidence level, for years near the top of the charts, was in free fall, a descent that was picking up enough momentum to qualify as a plummet. Aldous' beating, the FBI tie-in, the hovering factor of Mortvedt—all this had invaded his life in just a few months, changing everything for him. Mentally, he tried to gather himself, as in his boxing days, when after being caught with a good wallop he'd always say to his opponent, "Is *that* all you've got?"

Doyle took a deep breath. Before turning away from the window he found himself wondering again why Moe Kellman was being so helpful. Kellman wasn't the sort who would feel any great guilt over Doyle's being robbed of his City Sarah payoff. He was too practical for that, though he had been generous enough with the added five grand. He'd also suggested that Jack not get too cozy with the FBI agents who had visited him. A bribe in a velvet glove, Doyle considered it.

No, Kellman's willingness to help must have its source elsewhere. Perhaps it was traceable to something else that he'd once said to Doyle: "I like to know things. A lot of what I learn winds up making money for me."

Doyle sat down again. "What could we do to stop Rexroth and his ringer caper?"

"Not *we*," Kellman replied, the twinkle in his eyes obvious once more. "*You.*"

He offered another neatly quartered piece of apple to Doyle.

"Can I suggest something to you, Jack?"

Chapter 30

It was late on a Saturday afternoon, the end of a perfect early autumn day on the west side of Louisville.

Had he still been employed by Harvey Rexroth's *Horse Racing Journal*, Red Marchik would have been complaining bitterly about being required to work so late on such a beautiful afternoon, especially with the Kentucky Wildcats football team playing at home. "Love them 'Cats," was a Marchik family mantra, mostly during basketball seasons when the teams were usually excellent, but in football season, too. Red was a fan who "bled Kentucky blue."

But now, still out of work and with more time on his hands than he'd ever had to deal with before in his life, Red gave no thought to the state university's football fortunes as he emerged, blinking, from his basement bunker and started slowly raking the leaves that carpeted his backyard.

The ESZT-3 sports network had just finished its fourth consecutive hour of auto racing, all of which Red had tuned to; the channel was now offering a fifteen minute infomercial on oil-changing. Red was confident he knew all there was to know about oil-changing, so he had turned off the TV.

He then switched on the radio. It was Reverend Roland Ruland's re-run of his early morning show. "Raisin' the bar… Raisin' the bar…" Red heard the Sports Preacher thunder. "We hear that so off-ten these days. Comes from your track and field, the high jump or maybe the pole vault…whatever….We know they're talkin' about a higher level.

"You want to talk about really raisin' the bar? Then, brothers and sisters, let's talk about RAISIN'—when JEEEEEZUS high-jumped over the top of death, when he pole vaulted way, way, way, way over the top of death, and raised old LAZARUS from the dead. JEEEEEZUS CHRIST ALMIGHTY DID THAT, PRAISE GOD."

Red knew Wanda would have listened to more, but she was out shopping. So Red had turned off the Sports Preacher and headed for his backyard, where he continued to wrestle with the problem of how to deal with his yet unsatisfied lust for revenge against Harvey Rexroth.

Wanda kept urging Red to "let it go, honey," but Red just couldn't bring himself to do so. The Marchiks never took insults lying down, he told Wanda, "never have, never will." Hearing this for the umpteenth time, Wanda usually interrupted the cleaning of her handgun arsenal to light a joint. Eyes slitted against the smoke, she would regard her husband and try to figure how long it would take him to get to the point in his life where he could turn to other concerns.

In the years Wanda had known and loved him, Red had entertained a number of obsessions—video poker, the self-improvement guru Diplok Shewphat, bait worm farming on a share-cropping basis by mail—but they eventually evaporated. She was sure this one, too, would pass. The question was when.

Red, with two failed revenge attempts against Rexroth behind him, felt stymied, and he didn't like it. So far, he had succeeded only in killing his former employer's bulldog Winston. The mystery surrounding that incident ("What Had This Dog Done to Deserve to Die?" was a question posed by Rexroth in an uncommonly personal Letter From the Publisher) had caused a furor, the publicity serving to make Red lie low for weeks, considering options. Now, Rexroth had trumpeted his plan to win the upcoming Heartland Derby with "my rejuvenated horse Lancaster Lad."

"You're right about me being out of the assassination business," Red said one night to Wanda. "That man is not worth a murder charge in case something went wrong."

His options now, Red thought, pushing the leaves into a pile at the back corner of the yard, were either to somehow put this whole matter behind him, and lose face with Wanda, or come up with a new idea. It was at that moment, just as Wanda pulled up to the carport and began unloading groceries, that the lead squadron of the South Louisville Hot Air Balloon Club hove into view in the sky over the Marchiks' yard, brilliant in its monthly flight on this clear day. Soon, the first four balloons were joined by several dozen others.

As the richly colored balloons sailed south over the gawking Red, he put down his rake and began waving at the figures gliding past, some of whom waved back. Red thought he'd never seen a more beautiful sight than these vehicles of the air smoothly traveling across the vivid, blue sky.

"Damn, that looks like fun," Red said to himself. He waved some more, and more pilots and passengers waved back, much to his further delight.

Then a thought came to Red. He bounced it around for a few more minutes as he watched the tail-end of the airborne procession. Why not? he concluded. Then he yelled, "Wanda, come on out here. And bring a bunch of Pabsts along with you."

What had just occurred to Red was that his friend Oscar Belliard, commandant of the Underground Militia, was an avid balloonist. Often at Militia meetings General Belliard had invited Red and Wanda to "come on out some day and we'll give you all a ride. You haven't seen anything till you've been up there in the azure blue."

As the empty Pabst Blue Ribbon cans piled up in the nearby garbage can, the possibilities multiplied in the mind of Red Marchik.

Chapter 31

The Heartland Derby plan had first come to Harvey Rexroth a week earlier. On a bright October morning, as Darla whirled around the indoor track enthusiastically, Rexroth summoned Byron Stoner to poolside at Willowdale.

Rexroth, wearing a lavender velvet jumpsuit and brandishing a huge Cuban cigar, proceeded to unveil his Grand Plan. His little pig eyes danced with excitement. He rose to his feet and began pacing vigorously up and down alongside the track that bordered the massive swimming pool, talking loudly all the while.

Stoner never took notes, never needed to, for his memory was first-rate. And caution, to which the Canadian was devoted, also suggested that there never be anything in writing that might come back to plague him.

Over the years, Stoner had been privy to a number of amazing Rexrothian schemes, many of which he'd helped bring to fruition. But this one boggled the mind of even the cautious, ultra-pragmatic Stoner. *I've never him seen as full of himself as this*, Stoner thought with a shudder.

"This will be the single greatest, most audacious stroke of brilliant planning and execution in horse race cheating since John Cabray's remarkable coup of 1909," Rexroth boomed. "It will make me famous—strike that, *more* famous—and it won't be a matter of me taking advantage of a bunch of ravenously greedy small town businessmen, like Cabray did.

"Instead, Stoner, I'm going to provide a sure-thing winner for readers of the *Horse Racing Journal*, whose numbers I predict will swell dramatically after this is over. I'm going to invite the great unwashed and everybody else to share in a *winning bet*—that Lancaster Lad will win the Heartland Derby! A publisher predicting—no, *guaranteeing*—a win by his own horse! Who's ever done anything like *that*, I ask you?

"Or at least," he said in an aside to the attentive Stoner as Darla rounded the near turn and headed for them, "the horse purporting to be Lancaster Lad."

Stoner said, "I don't know that much about the racing part. I trust your judgment, Mr. Rexroth. But, isn't this kind of a, well, a *stretch*, to think that Donna Diane's colt could win a Derby in the first start he'd ever made at a racetrack? Could he actually be that good?"

Rexroth's expression hardened. He hated being questioned. Angrily, he threw his cigar into the center of the pool. Randy Kauffman immediately reached for his retrieving net.

Stoner was steadfast. "Mr. Rexroth," he intoned, looking straight ahead and not at his boss, who hovered over him, "that is what you pay me for—to ask questions of this sort."

Moments passed before Rexroth said, "You're right, Stoner, to raise that point. Of course you are." Rexroth sat down in the chair behind his desk, and his expression softened. "Of course you are," he repeated. "That is, as you say, your job.

"But worry not, Stoner, worry not, my friend. I know exactly what I'm doing here."

Rexroth, relaxed again, resumed describing his plans. He said to Stoner, "I want Douglas Phillips down here tomorrow morning so I can personally give him my instructions. Phillips is so dim sometimes that I want to be looking into his eyes so that I can tell for myself *exactly* what isn't registering. Can't do that over the phone, right? Har har har!"

Stoner chuckled in agreement. He was positive that Phillips was much smarter than Rexroth gave him credit for, but that the *Horse Racing Journal* editor was for the most part nearly stultified by terror when dealing with his boss. Stoner couldn't help but ask, "Why don't you just replace this Phillips?"

Rexroth gave Stoner an incredulous look. "*Replace* him? As cheap as Phillips works?"

◇◇◇

When *Horse Racing Journal*'s executive editor Douglas Phillips heard the red phone ring on his desk, he reflexively reached for his flask. The red phone was for one thing only: direct calls from Phillips' employer. The sound of this instrument, which might ring twenty times in one day and then not at all for a week, invariably made Phillips feel as if he were undergoing a colonoscopy without benefit of anesthetic. To combat this feeling, he administered his own. Phillips took a lengthy swig before saying, "Yes, Mr. Rexroth."

When Phillips reached Willowdale the next morning, he was astounded at the orders he was given. "I want you to turn your best writers loose on this story," Rexroth sternly instructed. "This is to be played at the top of page one of the *Journal* every day from tomorrow to race day.

"I will personally author a front-page piece in which I promise that Lancaster Lad, up to this point a pretty ordinary performer, will come to life and carry off the Heartlands Derby a week from next Saturday. His remarkable improvement will be the result of a startling new training regimen that will be revealed later. Or maybe not. We'll iron out those details down the line," the publisher said, puffing expansively on his cigar.

"Each day's edition of the *Journal*," he continued, "will carry several photos of Lancaster Lad, his jockey Willie Arroyo, trainer Kenny Gutfreund, and, of course, me.

"Other angles will be daily interviews with horse racing people, most of whom if I know them at all—except for the reliable cadre of suck-ups we can always count on—will be pooh-poohing Lancaster Lad's chances. That's fine. That's great. Give their opinions plenty of play, so that they'll look like the fools they really are once this horse wins the Derby.

"Also...." Rexroth interrupted himself to look at Phillips, who was frantically scrambling to record every word of his boss' orders on a yellow legal pad that was becoming blotched by drops of sweat falling from his brow. *"Are you getting all of this, Phillips?"* Rexroth suddenly shouted. The editor jumped in his chair, dropping his ballpoint and barely managing to hold on to his notepad. "Yes, sir, I am," he responded. Rexroth grinned maliciously.

"Summing up, Phillips," he said, "the repeated emphasis—the guts of this story—is that I will make history by guaranteeing a victory by my thus far ordinary horse. That is my vow, that is my promise. And this amazing triumph," he added grandly, "will be my racing legacy."

Douglas Phillips' reaction to Rexroth's Grand Plan was to think, "He's *really* gone over the edge now. He can't do this." Of course, Phillips kept his thoughts to himself.

Rexroth, some years earlier, in overruling an objection Phillips had meekly lodged, quoted the late press critic A. J. Liebling, a man Rexroth despised for his liberal politics. "That leftist looney made just one accurate statement in his life," Rexroth had shouted at Phillips. "I'm going to quote it to you now, and I want you to remember it: 'Freedom of the press is guaranteed only to those who own one.'

"Well, goddamit, I own a bunch of them. And I'll use them the way I want to. Get it, Phillips?"

The massive publicity campaign got into high gear two weeks prior to the Heartlands Derby. Phillips dutifully saturated the *Horse Racing Journal* with the story, and all the rest of racing's trade publications reported it to a lesser extent. So did other media outlets: *People Magazine* and the *Wall Street Journal* both carried items describing Rexroth's "unique promise to the public."

Chapter 32

Doyle had been back at Willowdale not five minutes that Thursday night after having had dinner in Lexington when the phone rang in his apartment. The caller's voice was faint against a din of thumping background music.

"Don't you even have an answering machine?" said the woman resentfully. "I've been calling for almost two hours."

"Who's this?" Doyle said.

No words came back, just some hushed breathing. Then she said, "I'm calling you to tell you that you all better keep on the sharp lookout out there. There's a man going to do some damage out there, kill some kind of horse, I believe....He is a small man, and terrible mean. You'd best keep on your best watch."

Before Doyle could again ask "Who is this?" the connection concluded abruptly from the woman's end. "What in the hell is going on now?" he said to the silent receiver.

Fourteen miles away, Betty Lou Blackmon put down the pay phone in the lobby of the Red Velvet Swing. Quickly, she slipped back to her dressing room to prepare for her upcoming shift. Tired as she was physically, Betty Lou felt a surge of emotional energy. She wriggled as she checked herself out in the mirror, then grinned at her reflection. "Hope to *God* they catch that little fucker," she whispered to herself.

The night before, Betty Lou and her best friend LeeAnne had some drinks, then dinner with Jud Repke. Jud and LeeAnne had been spending time together in recent weeks. Betty Lou liked Jud, because he didn't mind including her for the occasional late night, after-work meals before he and LeeAnne headed back to his apartment. She liked Jud, too, because he continued to invite her even after she had made clear to LeeAnne that she never, ever again wanted to be within ten country miles of Ronald Mortvedt. The memory of what Mortvedt had done to her in the hotel was enough to make her weep with anger and mortification.

LeeAnne had passed this information on to Jud, and Jud didn't say anything to Betty Lou about it, never chided her for not liking his buddy. Betty Lou took Jud's silence on this matter as an indication of understanding. "He's got so much more class than that Mortvedt," Betty Lou remarked to LeeAnne.

But the fact that she liked Jud did not deter Betty Lou from placing him in what she hoped was trouble with his partner. That opportunity had presented itself the previous night, when Betty Lou, LeeAnne, and Jud were having "just one more nightcap," as Jud put it, in the Stoned Pony Lounge of the Walnut Suites Motel.

A boisterous bunch of young Rotarians had just paid their bill and exited the ringside table midway of the female piano player's medley of *Elvis in Vegas* songs. They'd held their monthly meeting in the hotel dining room earlier in the evening.

Jud looked resentfully at the men, all well-dressed, with recent haircuts and pressed suits, as they headed for the door. "Bastards're just full of themselves, ain't they?" he said. "World by the balls."

He drained the rest of his Bacardi and Coke. "Well, they ain't the *only* ones." Jud's rum-glazed eyes brightened. "We got us a pretty goddam good little money maker going down next week out there at Willowdale." He elbowed LeeAnne in the side, just beneath one of her silicone-enhanced breasts, winking broadly. She winced. Jud waved forward the cocktail waitress.

Betty Lou leaned toward Jud. If LeeAnne wasn't interested in this drunken disclosure, as least she could pretend to be. After all, Jud was paying for her drinks again tonight.

"You and Ronnie got something going?"

"Bet on it," replied Jud. "We got a *gooood* thing going. You know what those horses are worth out there at Willowdale? Well, most people don't know it, but some of them are worth a hell of a lot more dead than alive," he snickered.

Jud picked up his new drink, raising it in a toast. "Here's to good things," he smiled drunkenly. "And I'm lookin' at a couple of 'em right now," he added with a giggle as he buried his face in LeeAnne's bosom.

LeeAnne shrugged at Betty Lou, as if to say "Well, I have to let the boy play when he pays," but Betty Lou wasn't paying her any mind. Betty Lou's mind was clicking out ideas the way it always had, in the fashion of an overworked copying machine that had lost smoothness but retained the ability to keep slowly churning.

Twenty hours later, Betty Lou made her call to Willowdale. She asked for the "manager in charge." The gate house guard transferred her to Doyle, whose car he had waved through only minutes earlier.

"That's what the woman said," Doyle repeated. He was seated in Damon Tirabassi's room at the Dalton House Hotel, having called the agent from Willowdale before rapidly driving the fifteen miles to town. Doyle had just finished describing in as much detail as he could the phone call of warning he'd received from the mystery woman.

Karen Engel, in jeans and a UW-Madison sweatshirt, perched on the sofa in the mini-suite. It was the first time Doyle had seen her not wearing her FBI business suit, and she looked about ten years younger. Tirabassi on the other hand, although casually dressed for him—slacks, shirt, tie but no jacket—appeared as official as ever.

Karen said, "Let's talk about this new information. Damon, what do you make of it?"

Tirabassi said, "I'm not surprised. This is why we put these people in prison; they're stupid, and they make mistakes. If this woman is talking about Mortvedt, we've finally got a shot at him. Even if she isn't, we've got to set up surveillance out at Willowdale for whoever might show up. But I'll bet it's going to be Mortvedt."

Doyle had emphasized to the agents, "We can't have some SWAT team crashing around out there at Willowdale. If Rexroth gets wind of any FBI presence, he'll call off Mortvedt for sure. You better figure out a way to do this real quietly."

What finally unfolded was a schedule that saw either Karen or Damon be picked up by Doyle at the hotel each evening, then transported to his apartment on the Willowdale property while crouched down on the backseat of Doyle's car. Whichever one it was that accompanied him stayed the night in his place, where Doyle tried to sleep so that he would be ready for his regular duties in the morning. The agent not with Doyle communicated by radio with the other team leader, who was positioned in a car located a mile down the road from Willowdale.

Meanwhile, two other FBI agents slipped onto the property each night and made their way to the stallion barn without being observed. Doyle had sent the barn's security guard on a surprise one-week vacation with pay, telling him he would "check on these horses every night, don't you worry." The guard, Alan Henry, gratefully agreed to this plan. Doyle felt better once Henry had been removed from any potentially dangerous situation.

Ralph Ebner and Ed Kamin were the FBI agents stationed in the stallion barn. One was positioned in an empty stall midway of the north wall, the other in the hayloft that ran the length of the building.

On the fourth night of this surveillance schedule, Doyle had again finished hammering Damon Tirabassi at gin rummy. As much as he liked winning, their card games were beginning to bore him. Shaking his head in mock sympathy, Doyle said, "I'm beating you like a drum, man, like a drum. I'm going to have mercy on you and call it a night."

Although he would again have to rise at five the next day to fulfill his acting farm manager duties, Doyle did not feel like going to bed. At the beginning of this week, Doyle had felt energized, full of that good impatient feeling he used to get before his fights. He'd loved those adrenalin-packed minutes as he entered the ring and warmed up, casting sidelong glances at his opponent, every cell in his body seeming to cry *let's get it on!* It was one of the best feelings in the world as far as Doyle was concerned.

Now, four days into the vigil, he was growing increasingly impatient and losing faith in the plan as well. He'd slept fitfully the past two nights and was more restless than ever this night. Putting down the deck of cards, Doyle announced, "I'm taking a walk."

"Stay away from that barn," Tirabassi warned. "I don't want Kamin or Ebner coming down on you."

"Remember, Damon, this is Willowdale. There are five hundred ninety-nine other acres here I can use," Doyle said as he went out the cottage door.

It was twenty-one minutes after midnight when Doyle began strolling under the starless autumn sky. He stopped in front of the silent house that had been shared by Aldous and Caroline and her children. For a moment or so, he visualized them all on the front porch, at their ease of a summer evening, so innocent in their ignorance of what was to come. Doyle shuddered at the memory. Then he moved away on the gravel path, intending to circle the pond. He wished he had brought a flashlight.

Suddenly, Doyle heard movement in the darkness off to his right. There was an empty paddock there, so he knew it was not a horse he was hearing. Quickly he crouched down at the edge of the viburnum bushes that lined the path. There was another rustling sound, closer now. As Doyle knelt on the damp grass, he could feel drops of sweat beginning to trickle from his armpits, just as during the nights when he'd stood in the ring corner, looking across at his opponent, both of them riding adrenaline highs as they waited for the opening bell.

Doyle took off his boots and crawled closer to the bushes. He heard a harsh whisper, "Jud, creep up into that barn and make sure our horse is where he's supposed to be at. Fifth stall on the right was what the man told me. If he's there, flick on that flashlight for a second to let me know. I'm not gonna move our stuff up there till I know we can use it."

Doyle strained to hear more. He thought he heard a muttered "You got it," then departing footfalls. Doyle crawled closer to the break in the hedge. The damp grass felt cold on his hands and feet; his socks were becoming soaked with the dew.

Doyle rose silently to his feet when he'd advanced to the point where a path split the hedge. At precisely that moment, Ronald Mortvedt arrived at the hedge opening from the other side. For a split second, they looked at each other, equally startled. Doyle let out a grunt. Mortvedt was silent. He was dressed completely in black, from ski mask to gloves, and Doyle didn't see the beginning of his movement. Mortvedt dropped the canvas bag he carried in his left hand. As he did so, he dipped his right shoulder and reached down toward the knife in his boot.

Doyle slipped slightly as he tried to set his feet on the wet grass. The left uppercut he unleashed missed its target, Mortvedt's jaw, landing on Mortvedt's right temple.

But it served to raise Mortvedt's head. Right behind that punch Doyle delivered an overhand right that arrived with a satisfying *thwack*. The little man dropped face-forward to the ground and lay still.

"Damn," Doyle said, "what a living I could have made fighting bantamweights!" He was so pumped it was several moments before he realized he'd probably broken a knuckle on his left hand. He flexed the hand, winced, then bent to examine the man in black, who remained still.

There was no wallet in the man's pockets. But when Doyle unzipped the canvas bag, he knew the figure at his feet was the one they were after. Amid the extra pair of gloves and the bags of peppermint candy used to entice the horses was an electrical extension cord and a pair of alligator clips.

Doyle remembered the veterinarian, Dr. James O'Dea, who had speculated to agents Engel and Tirabassi that the killer was "electrocuting horses, making it appear as if they've died of heart attacks. I'm sure that's what he's doing. It's a method that leaves no marks."

He heard Mortvedt stir as he continued to rummage through the black canvas bag. Quickly, Doyle took out a section of rope and tied the little man's hands behind him, then lashed together his ankles. He twisted the rope as deep into Mortvedt's skin as he could, relishing the groan it elicited. Then he tore up the little man's ski mask.

From somewhere in the distance—it must have been at the stallion barn—Doyle heard shouts, the sounds of feet scrambling through gravel, and somebody hitting the ground hard.

"*On* the ground! *On* the ground! Hands behind your head," Doyle heard one of the agents shout. They must have done their job, Doyle thought.

Doyle hooked his left arm around Mortvedt's feet and began dragging the little man, face down, through the wet grass. As they proceeded toward the patio behind his building, Mortvedt began to mumble. What Doyle heard as he stopped and let Mortvedt's feet thump to the concrete floor of the patio was "You *cock*suckah." Mortvedt shifted his body, straining against the rope. His eyes were wild, darting about, then concentrating on Doyle like malevolent lasers as he regained full consciousness.

Doyle went to one knee, his left, and jackhammered two punches with his right hand into Mortvedt's left kidney. Mortvedt screamed after the first punch landed, a quick gulping sound that he tried to call back, but couldn't. He only gasped when Doyle's second blow struck him.

"If you were going to live any longer you'd be pissing blood, you piece of shit," Doyle said, getting to his feet. Then he pivoted and dropped down and again buried his fist into Mortvedt's side, same place as before.

"I don't know which way to do you," Doyle said. He was breathing hard now, not so much from the exertion as from the hate-fueled energy that raced through him.

Looking down at Mortvedt, he said, "Should I fry you? Fry you like you fried those poor horses you killed for the money?

"Should I do that?...I could do that."

Doyle was breathing like he'd just spent ten minutes pum-meling the heavy bag in the gym.

Mortvedt had recovered his breath. Trussed up tightly, on his back, he looked up defiantly. "Don't know what horses you talkin' about, Cuz," he sneered.

Doyle began to unbolt an arm of one of the redwood chairs that bordered the metal patio table. He had trouble at first, but then the club-like apparatus came off in his hands. It was damp with the night dew. Doyle's hands were dry. He took a good, strong grip on the piece of wood.

"Or," Doyle said to Mortvedt, his voice hurried, "I could just beat your fucking face in. Beat you like you beat Bolger." Doyle was on his feet now, chest heaving as he stood over Mortvedt.

Doyle raised the piece of wood to his shoulder. It weighed at least as much as a baseball bat, or a rake handle, he knew that. It would do.

Mortvedt's mask of hate briefly disappeared as he looked up at Doyle. For an instant all of Mortvedt's defiance was wiped away, replaced by a surprised expression of acknowledgment that he knew exactly what Doyle was talking about.

Mortvedt recovered quickly. But both men realized what had just been confirmed in that moment.

"His name was Aldous Bolger," Doyle said slowly. "He was a friend of mine. If Bolger were here, he'd never do to you what you did to him. He wasn't that kind." The words were coming out more rapidly now. "But I am. Oh yeah, I am."

Doyle bent down, leaning closer to Mortvedt. "Bolger was one of those men that guys like you laugh at. He was this straight shooter, he'd go to the wall for his friends. You know what I'm saying?

"No, you don't know, you miserable little shit."

Doyle turned away from Mortvedt. Quickly, still breathing rapidly, he started to uncoil the electrical extension cord.

"Aldous Bolger respected horses," Doyle said. "It cut him to the heart, the way you killed those animals. Way you made them *suffer!*"

Doyle pivoted, then hurled the piece of armchair redwood into the darkness.

He reached into the canvas bag and took out the extension cord. Moving more slowly, so Mortvedt could see what he was doing, Doyle placed the extension cord's plug on the floor right below the electrical outlet near the patio grill. Then Doyle picked up one of the sets of alligator clips. He attached it to the cord. In the light from the patio fixture Doyle could see Mortvedt watching him, silent again, his face contorted by hate.

With a quick movement Doyle clamped the alligator clip onto Mortvedt's scrotum. The little man twisted frantically on the patio concrete, trying to free himself.

Doyle brought the prongs of the plug up to the electrical outlet.

Chapter 33

Doyle grimaced as he looked at his face in the bathroom mirror of his Willowdale apartment. Under the streak of dirt that charred his forehead, part of his nose glistened where the skin had scraped off when he had hit the patio concrete face first. He was busy attending to the latter matter, dousing the raw surface with Bactine.

Damon Tirabassi, along with fellow agent Ed Kamin, sat in the living room. Mortvedt, still trussed up, was laid out on the floor between them. The other agent, Ralph Ebner, who'd been stationed in the stallion barn with Kamin and had joined in the capture of the fleeing Repke, had handcuffed Jud to the refrigerator door in the kitchen. Ebner sat on a kitchen chair near Repke, arms crossed, face expressionless as he regarded his silent and docile captive.

"Thanks a lot, Damon," Doyle said from the bathroom doorway as he pasted a Band-Aid over the bridge of his nose. "This thing has only been broken about five times before you took your crack at it."

Twenty minutes earlier Tirabassi had come hurtling out of the darkness, throwing himself forward as Doyle held the extension cord whose clips were attached to Ronald Mortvedt's balls. Tirabassi's charge hit Doyle in the back, driving him face forward to the floor. Tirabassi had then pinned down the stunned Doyle.

Right behind Tirabassi onto the patio had come Kamin, who landed directly on the prostrate Mortvedt.

Tirabassi was breathing heavily as he heard Doyle say from beneath him, "Damon, get the hell off me. I already nailed the little bastard. It's Mortvedt. That's him lying there under your man. Why in the hell are you kneeling on my shoulder blades?"

When he'd arrived at the patio edge and seen Doyle moving the extension cord outlet toward the socket, Tirabassi explained, he'd accelerated his advance.

"I thought you were about to kill the little bastard, Jack. I didn't want to lose our star witness."

As Doyle walked out of the bathroom, one hand still applying pressure to the Band-Aid, Tirabassi gave him an appraising look. He said, "Jack, would you have"—he nodded toward Mortvedt—"if I hadn't jumped you?"

"Would I have what?"

"Hit him with the juice."

Doyle shifted his gaze from the waiting Tirabassi to Mortvedt, who also seemed interested in his answer.

"I was tempted, I'll tell you that. But with the FBI right on top of me? Are you kidding? Fry Mortvedt, and risk spending time for it? Not a chance, Damon. There'll be somebody dumber than me will come along and rid the world of this little bottom feeder, then wind up paying for it instead of getting the medal they deserve."

Doyle feinted as if he were going to plant a kick on Mortvedt's side. Damon jumped to his feet, but Mortvedt didn't flinch. Doyle smiled at the two of them as he sat down on the couch.

◇◇◇

Damon took a call on his portable phone. When he snapped the phone shut, he said, "That was Karen. She's informed the sheriff of the capture of these two, but told them to stay away from Willowdale, that we'll bring Mortvedt and Repke in to them."

Earlier Tirabassi had walked up to the mansion himself to inform Harvey Rexroth of the capture of the two horse killers, eager to observe the reaction on the publisher's face. But, Tirabassi had been informed by Byron Stoner, "Mr. Rexroth is out of the state on business. I'll certainly let him know as soon as possible. He'll be immensely relieved these criminals have finally been apprehended."

"I'd hate to play liar's poker with Byron Stoner," Tirabassi said after returning to Doyle's apartment.

◇◇◇

Jud Repke saw the light early the next afternoon. Facing charges of horse theft, thanks to the confession of Lucas Collier, and insurance fraud for killing Rexroth's horses, he heeded the advice of his attorney and agreed to testify against Mortvedt. Repke was promised, in the most general and potentially deniable terms, a fine, a suspended sentence, and lengthy probation in case he didn't come through.

"I always hated killing those horses," Jud said. He added, "Afraid as I am of Ronnie, there ain't no way I'm going back inside if I can help it."

Mortvedt was another story. He refused to answer any questions and, as a result, was bound over for trial in federal court. He was represented by a Louisville lawyer named Ed Boniface. At the urging of the government attorneys, Mortvedt—considered not only a threat to society, but a prime prospect for fleeing the country—was denied bail, despite Boniface's stentorian objections.

Doyle was far from heartened by these developments. As he complained to Damon and Karen over lunch one afternoon, "Repke did plenty of this dirty work, and he gets away with a slap on the wrist. What if his testimony doesn't convict Mortvedt? Then what have we got?

"I'll tell you what we've got—nothing. They both could walk, even though they probably attacked Aldous. And without Mortvedt linked to him, how are we going to nail Rexroth for having his horses killed?"

Damon said, "Jack, be realistic. We've got no way of tying Mortvedt and Repke to Bolger's beating, no matter how much we suspect them. Repke denies being there that night, Mortvedt won't even answer questions about it. We've got no physical evidence whatsoever.

"But with Repke going against him on the other matters, we've got a good case against Mortvedt. They were both apprehended at Willowdale, with their horse killing tools. And Repke admits to why they were there, and what they had done there on previous visits. I think a jury will believe him and put Mortvedt away."

"Yeah," said Doyle, "but not for what he *should* be put away for. There's no doubt in my mind Mortvedt beat Bolger to a pulp. That's what he should be going up for."

Karen shifted her glass of iced tea on the place mat, then began drumming her fingers on the table. They were in the only deli Doyle had located in Lexington, a place called Mama Goldberg's, and it was a far cry from Shapiro's in Indianapolis, or any of several Chicago delis he frequented. "The pastrami here tastes like it was made from a recipe left by Daniel Boone's mother. Stay off it," Doyle had warned the agents, adding: "The turkey sandwich won't kill you. The chicken soup might."

Karen said, "Let's not give up on Mortvedt yet."

Damon gave her a puzzled look. "What do you see that I don't?"

"I've got a feeling he'll deal," Karen answered. "He's been inside seven years of his life already. He's a very independent individual, a guy who has always gone his own way. And I know how ruthless he is. But I think, just like with his buddy Repke, a long stretch inside is something he desperately wants to avoid. I've seen hard cases like him cave in before.

"And there's something else," Karen said. "Mortvedt's got a real hatred of rich people. And Rexroth certainly qualifies on that point. I'm telling you, Jack, Mortvedt'll turn. When we get across to him that he's going down, that Repke's testimony will put him away for twenty years, he's going to change his mind. You watch. You'll see."

"In our dreams," said Doyle, sliding the luncheon check toward Damon.

But Doyle, as he happily admitted a week later, was "dead wrong on this one." Karen's prediction proved to be on the money. Following Karen's third interview session with him, and under continued pressure from prosecutors, Ronald Mortvedt joined the succession of toppling tenpins just as Karen predicted he would. Faced with a long string of successive sentences for insurance fraud, Mortvedt finally agreed to testify against Rexroth. His confession was detailed and decisive, citing dates he'd met with the publisher, and how his payoffs had been wired to his account in a New Orleans bank.

Mortvedt signed his confession on Saturday, October third, or two weeks prior to the running of the Heartland Derby. Under the terms of his agreement with government prosecutors, Mortvedt was to be given a five-year sentence in return for his testimony against Rexroth. While the prosecutors were eager to file charges against Rexroth as soon as possible, Karen and Damon prevailed upon them to hold off until after the upcoming race.

"Rexroth has begun this huge publicity campaign about how he's going to win that Derby," Damon told the Justice Department lawyers. "Jack Doyle insists Rexroth's got something kinky going with this, too. I think Doyle is right when he says we should wait and see how this plays out. We may be able to nail Rexroth even a little higher up on the wall."

"Rexroth isn't going anywhere, anyway," Karen added. "We've still got Mortvedt in custody. There's no reason we can't delay bringing in Rexroth for a few days."

◇◇◇

The following evening Doyle got a phone call from Damon, who had returned to Chicago with Karen. "We need you up here early tomorrow morning," Damon said. "There's someone I want you to meet, someone who wants to meet you. Someone who can answer some of your questions about Rexroth's importance.

"Don't drive," Damon instructed. "Take the first flight out. Come to our office on the tenth floor of the Dirksen Building."

Jack grimaced. "What am I going to tell Rexroth?"

"Think of something, Jack," Damon said. The line went dead.

A few minutes later, Doyle called Stoner. "Byron, I have to go up to Chicago first thing in the morning," he said. "Personal business. I'll be back late tomorrow afternoon."

Stoner said, "What kind of personal business?"

"There's a reason it's called personal," Jack replied, slamming down the receiver.

◇◇◇

It was an extraordinarily warm Indian summer morning in Chicago's Loop, the street musicians already sweating, pretzel sellers looking as limp as their product. Inside the Dirksen Federal Building, Jack stood gratefully in the slow-moving metal detector line, enjoying the air-conditioning.

When he was ushered into a tenth-floor office, Karen and Damon were already there. So was a stocky, middle-aged woman wearing a dark blue pants suit over a glistening white blouse, who was talking on the phone in a decisive tone. She had close-cropped white hair, a ruddy complexion, and a look of intense concentration as she conversed.

Jack sat down between the agents in one of the three chairs lined up before the woman's desk. The nameplate on her desk read *Florence Farley*. Leaning over to Karen, Jack whispered, "She looks like a cross between Willa Cather and Gertrude Stein. Who the hell is she?" Karen pretended not to hear him.

Then the woman put the phone down. "Good morning, Mr. Doyle," she said. Under her unflinching gaze, Jack felt as if he'd been Twilight Zoned into another appearance before his grade school principal back at St. Mary's Parochial. "Good morning," he replied.

"I am an assistant United States Attorney, criminal division, based here in Chicago," Farley said. "I've been monitoring the

progress of this case from the start. I will be the attorney seeking federal grand jury indictments. You have provided valuable
service to your government, Mr. Doyle. Voluntarily or not,"
she added. Farley stood and reached across the desk with her
right hand extended. Doyle got to his feet. She had a grip like
a steelworker.

"I understand you have some misgiving about the case,"
Farley said when they were both seated again.

Jack shifted in his chair. "Not the nature of the case," he said.
"But the way it's being handled now that we're close to closing
the cage on these vermin.

"Look," he continued, "I'm not complaining about the work
I've been asked—make that forced—to do for you people. I
committed a crime in stiffing that horse, though you couldn't
prove it, and you all know that. But in helping you nail Rexroth
and Mortvedt, well, I feel like I'm making up for what I did with
City Sarah. Maybe even doing some good for a change.

"But let me be clear about this, Ms. Farley. As I've told my
Feeb pals here, it makes my blood boil that Mortvedt is getting
to plead down. How does this guy deserve a break? Why are you
letting him do it? He's a horse killer, and he would have been a
murderer if Aldous Bolger had died. And you people have made
a deal with this piece of crap? I don't get it."

Farley leaned back in her chair, fingers steepled under her
square chin, eyes measuring Doyle.

"Harvey Rexroth," she said, "is a dangerous and evil man. He
has committed crimes you have no knowledge of, but because
of his cleverness and the acuity of his expensive attorneys, he's
gone unscathed for years.

"The crimes he's committed with these horses is a form of
fraud that is very, very difficult to prove. There are some people
out there, wealthy but nevertheless greedy, in both the thoroughbred and show horse fields, who are pulling the same horrible
stuff as Rexroth. We need to make an example of Mr. Rexroth.
Make clear to these people that we *will* pursue them."

Florence Farley leaned forward, arms on her desk, head lowered, eyes boring into Doyle's. She said, "And now, at last, in the case of Harvey Rexroth we have proof. It comes from a despicable source, Mortvedt, and his dim-witted accomplice Repke. That is true. But we'll take it, and use it. We have taped and signed confessions from both of them implicating Rexroth. And he's worth cutting a deal to get," she emphasized, slapping her hand on the desk for emphasis.

When Farley had finished, Doyle silently looked out the window behind her. Then he said, "A man I know, Moe Kellman, tells me that years ago Rexroth made serious enemies of a couple of men who are high up in the government today." The implication hung in the air.

Farley smiled but said nothing. "Could it be possible," Jack pressed on, "that politics has reared its ugly head here?"

Florence Farley rose to her feet. She shook Doyle's hand again. With a little smile cold enough to freeze a chunk of warmed brie, she said, "Thank you for coming, Mr. Doyle."

Chapter 34

Exiting the Dirksen Building, Doyle hit a wall of Chicago heat. It was nearly noon, the thermometer on a nearby bank building read a near-autumn record ninety-three degrees, and he had three hours to kill before his flight back to Lexington. His frustrating session with Florence Farley had ratcheted up his blood pressure so much that he stopped in the plaza and took a few deep breaths of the pollution-laden downtown air. That didn't seem to help. He loosened his tie and took off his sport coat as he walked to the line of cabs on Dearborn Street. Still seething at the government's rationalization for going easy on Mortvedt, Doyle decided to vent in the company of the only man in town who knew what had been going on with him. He gave the cabbie the address of Moe Kellman's office.

Hillary, another one of Kellman Furriers' standard-issue beauties working the front desk, smiled when Doyle walked in, then shook her head. "You just missed him, maybe five minutes," she said. "Shall I call Mr. Kellman on his cell phone?"

"That'd be great," Doyle said. "Thanks."

When the connection had been made, Hillary handed the phone to Doyle. He heard Kellman say, "Jack, welcome back again. How was your command appearance at the Dirksen?" Doyle could picture Kellman's sly grin at this statement.

I'm not going to give him the satisfaction of asking how he knew about that, Doyle thought.

After a pause, Moe said, "Friend of mine spotted you going in there this morning. I'm glad you got in touch. Here's where you can meet me. I'll send my driver for you." Kellman gave him an address on Sheffield Avenue.

"Wrigleyville, right?"

"You'll see," Kellman said, cutting the connection.

Fifteen minutes later Kellman's driver, a retired Chicago police sergeant named Pete Dunleavy, pulled Kellman's white Lincoln town car over to the curb in front of a brownstone on Sheffield on Chicago's north side. It was one the properties directly across the street from Wrigley Field. "You'll find Mr. Kellman on the top floor," Dunleavy said.

The front door of the old but recently refurbished structure was open. So was a gate in front of the stairwell. There were apparently two apartments on each of the first three floors of the structure. Doyle read the names on the mailboxes. Scarlatti, Greenberg, Angelici, Grossman, DiCastri, Kellman…. Maybe this is a chapter of the Jewish-Italian Mutual Aid Society, Doyle thought as he began walking up the carpeted stairs.

The top floor proved to be a large loft space with two washrooms, a long bar, and several couches and chairs, the west doorway leading to the spacious front porch. Moe was standing outside, leaning against one of the sturdy wooden railings that bordered the large space.

Doyle had previously viewed these special Cubs-watching venues only on television. Seeing one of them up close, he was impressed. The porch area contained rows of stadium chairs as well as more tables, all overlooking the nearby ballpark. There were two large Weber gas grills adjacent to wash tubs meant to hold kegs of beer. This site was high enough so that most of the interior of Wrigley Field could be seen. Now, of course, with the Cubs season recently concluded in an all-too-familiar deluge of heartbreak and despair, the park was empty.

Moe waved a greeting, then punched some more figures into a handheld calculator. Finished, he smiled and walked forward, extending his hand. "Great to see you, Jack. You look tip-top."

"Don't be deceived," Doyle said.

Kellman said, "Let's get into the air-conditioning." They walked into the loft and sat at a table, Doyle reaching for his handkerchief to wipe the sweat from his forehead. Kellman's face was dry beneath his bushy head of white hair.

"You got a relative living here, Moe? I saw 'Kellman' on one of the mailboxes downstairs."

Kellman nodded. "That's one of my nephews. Goes to law school at Loyola. He kind of keeps an eye on things for us here. Supervises crowd control on game days."

Doyle grinned. "I suppose 'us' stands for your 'people.'"

A look of irritation flitted across Kellman's face before he said, "Yes, Jack, 'my people.' We bought this property a couple of years ago. The old owner had been selling a few lawn chair seats on the porch for some Cubs games. We spent some money and moved the place up several notches."

"How much business do you do up here?"

Moe pointed at the calculator that lay on the table. "I just did some numbers," he said. "If we add six more seats, we'll bump the per-game gross to over thirteen grand."

Doyle was stunned. He knew Kellman wasn't given to exaggerating. The little man said, "The clientele is mainly young, professional people—traders, brokers, lawyers, they get together and form partnerships that rent the space for games. We've got room for ninety people up here for a game, on the roof and inside watching on those big TVs. We charge a hundred and fifty bucks a head. For that they get free drinks from thirty minutes before the game to thirty minutes after, free barbecue all during the game served by a good-looking wait staff. And they get the chance to look at the game from up here on high—when they're not schmoozing, or hustling, or working their cell phones, or trying to pick each other up."

"Jesus," Jack said, as he began calculating. "The Cubs have eighty-one home games a year. But you don't have a full house up here for every game, right?"

"Wrong. There's so much young money floating around this town you wouldn't believe it. And don't forget the power of the attraction. A year ago the Cubs only won sixty-five games and *raised* their ticket prices. This year they got into the playoffs, so I *guarantee* you they'll raise their prices again. And the joint will still be packed for most of the season. It's incredible."

Doyle reflected on the recent spate of Cubs mania. Only days before, the team had been within five outs of winning its first pennant since 1945. Then Lady Luck stepped in, wearing a malicious grin. A fan sitting in the front row of the grandstand deflected an apparently catchable foul ball away from the Cubs left fielder. Given new life, the opposing hitter reached base, and the Cubs collapsed, losing that game, then the next one, thus being eliminated. The hapless fan who had touched the foul ball was vilified throughout Cubdom, his suburban residence even being picketed after it was shown on a local television station. The notorious ball, recovered by an opportunistic spectator, was auctioned off for more than one hundred thousand dollars, its new owner vowing to destroy it in a public ceremony. Reading of all this while in Kentucky, Doyle had said to himself, "What a rube town I come from."

Moe broke the silence. "You remember Mike Royko?"

"Naturally," Doyle responded to this mention of the late, famed Chicago newspaper columnist.

"Royko was a huge Cubs fan," Moe continued, "and he wrote about them a lot. One time he said, and I quote, 'I always believed that being a Cubs fan built strong character. It taught a person that if you try hard enough and long enough, you'll still lose. And that's the story of life.' Unquote.

"But that depressing thought," Moe said, "is completely lost on this generation of Cubs fans. It makes no difference to them what the Cubs do next year, or whenever. They will pack the

park—and this place," he said, gesturing to the porch. "They come like lemmings to the sea, all bringing money."

"'Wait until next year,'" Moe said, "the Cubs fan's mantra. What a beautiful thought."

Doyle walked over to the refrigerator behind the bar and took out a Heineken. "Bring me a bottled water, will you, Jack?" Moe said. Doyle returned with the drinks and sat down at the table. He was still running the building's financial figures through his head. He said, "So, if I fixed another horse race for you—at my old rate—I could rent this joint for maybe a two-game series, right?"

Moe looked hurt. "Jack...Jack," he said, "I'm surprised at your bitterness. I thought we'd gotten past all that."

Doyle didn't respond. He clutched the beer can, eyes aimed down at the table. Finally, he said, "I've got a right to be bitter. Especially after my meeting this morning with that gorgon from the U. S. Attorney's office.

"The government," he told Moe, "has struck a deal with that little bastard Mortvedt. They're letting him plead down in order to get his testimony against Rexroth for insurance fraud."

Doyle slammed the beer can down on the table. "Damn it, Moe, this is hard to swallow, after what Mortvedt did to Aldous, what he did to all those horses. It's just grinding on me. The idea of Mortvedt getting any kind of break at all—I can't come to grips with it."

Moe said softly, "But there's nothing you can do about it. Rexroth is the government's target, the big catch for them. Media bigshot takes precedence over a crooked jockey, any day of the week. That's the way it is, Jack."

"So it seems," Doyle said. He drained the Heineken and crushed the can in his hand. "So it seems."

They sat silently for a minute or so. Moe poured the last of the Evian water into his glass. "You're how old now, Jack?"

Doyle frowned. "I'll be playing the 4-1 daily double for my age next year," he replied. "What the hell does that have to do with anything?"

Moe said, "Maybe it's time you learned how to accept the fact that some things just have to be accepted. Period. Because otherwise they turn into little worms in your psyche, burrowing into you, paralyzing you mentally. I've seen it happen. Not a pretty sight."

"Psyche!" Doyle snorted. "Don't be worrying about my goddam psyche. This issue is burning in my goddam gut."

Moe looked pityingly across the table at Doyle. He said, "When I was younger I was a lot like you, getting myself fucked up concentrating on things I had no chance of ever controlling. Chewing on questions I could never answer. Big ones, small ones. How did human life begin? Who taught Oswald how to shoot like that—if he did that shooting? Why is the underside of the pillow always cool?"

He paused, then added in a low voice, "Why did I survive the retreat from Chosen Reservoir and three-quarters of my Marines platoon didn't?…Why did my mother die of breast cancer when she was forty-one years old?"

Moe got to his feet and buttoned his black silk sport coat, then put on his sunglasses. "It was making me nuts, so many questions. Once you start asking them, they multiply. They start to take over. So I finally wised up. I stood back. I decided to concentrate on controlling only things I had at least a chance to control. It probably saved my life, that decision. Do yourself a favor and think about that, Jack."

Doyle followed as Kellman walked to the doorway leading to the porch. The two men silently looked down and across Sheffield Avenue at Wrigley Field, its green seats, green grass, and ivy-covered brick walls gleaming in the afternoon sun.

"To you, it looks like an old ballpark," Moe said fondly. "I see a genuine, certified, bona fide gold mine.

"C'mon, Jack," Moe added. "I'll have Pete drive you to the airport."

Chapter 35

The morning after he returned from Chicago, Doyle walked into his office at Willowdale and activated his answering machine. First thing he heard was a message from Rexroth.

"They'll be bringing our horse Lancaster Lad down from Heartland Downs late today," Rexroth said. "He's not been running well. Probably needs a change of scenery. When he arrives, put him over on the Annex with Boomer until further notice. Good place for him to relax. The van from Heartland should arrive about four."

"Relax, my ass," Doyle said to himself. "Change of scenery! Change of identity is more like it."

After he'd cleared the remaining messages, he sat down in his desk chair. He decided to slip away for a nap that afternoon, for he knew he was going to be on the alert each night and morning at least the rest of that week, his last at Willowdale.

◇◇◇

Arriving two days later from Chicago via Rexroth's private jet was jockey Willie Arroyo, who climbed aboard Boomer at 6:15 a.m. and worked him over the training track together with Lancaster Lad, who was ridden by exercise rider Gwen Goran. At least the two started out in company. However, not a quarter-mile of the six-furlong trial had elapsed before Boomer began to pull rapidly away from Lancaster Lad. Arroyo sat still as a statue on Boomer, never urging him, but the margin increased anyway.

Goran frantically hustled Lancaster Lad in an attempt to keep up, to no avail. Boomer crossed the finish line more than sixteen lengths in front, going easily.

Only two grooms and Pedro Ramos, recently promoted by Rexroth to assistant foreman, watched this from the viewing stand next to the training track rail. Jack Doyle took in the action from a stand of trees located on a slight incline across from the eighth pole of the track. The emerging sun was behind him, so he didn't worry about his binoculars glinting and giving away his presence. When he checked his stopwatch after Boomer passed the wire, he whistled softly. Then he sneaked away through the trees, smiling to himself.

As he made his way back to his office, Doyle thought hard about the principals involved in this caper. He doubted that Kenny Gutfreund, trainer of the Willowdale horses at Heartland Downs, knew what was transpiring here on the farm; Gutfreund had a strong reputation as a straight shooter.

On the other hand, Doyle had every reason to believe that jockey Willie Arroyo knew quite well what was going on, for he'd ridden both horses, Lancaster Lad in his mediocre races at Heartland, Boomer in his sensational early morning trials at Willowdale. Still, if things played out the way Doyle thought they would, it would be hard to pin anything on the jockey, who was known to feign ignorance with the best of them.

But that realization didn't bother Doyle for long. As he circled the base of the berm that obscured the training track from the nearby road, Doyle recalled the words of his Uncle Pete O'Connor, his mother's older brother. An avid fisherman, Pete loved to intone, "One big fish is worth a whole bunch of little ones."

Doyle had always considered Uncle Pete one of the most boring humans he'd ever known. But today, particularly, he saw the value of this little piece of philosophy.

◇◇◇

Rexroth phoned Doyle in his office that afternoon, some nine hours after the so-called secret workout on the Willowdale training track.

"Change in plans, Doyle," Rexroth said curtly. "Lancaster Lad has definitely come to life after his R&R here at Willowdale. Good thing, too," Rexroth added with a phony chuckle, "or I'd have a lot of egg on my face come next Saturday night after the predictions I've made about him winning the Derby.

"But now," Rexroth continued, "it's all systems go for Saturday. The horse is doing fantastically well. They can't run the Heartland Derby any too soon, far as I'm concerned."

Rexroth then instructed Doyle to have Lancaster Lad ready for loading on the van by five Wednesday morning.

"I'll have him ready," Doyle promised. "I'll take care of it myself."

Rexroth responded, "That's what I like in people working for me, Doyle—the hands-on, personal responsibility approach." As he listened, Doyle looked out the office window. In the parking lot, he saw Pedro's Jeep Cherokee with its bumper sticker proclaiming *Variety Kick-Starts Creativity*.

"Variety," Doyle began to quote. But he realized he was about to go too far. He thought of Moe Kellman counseling him not to be such a wiseass. Doyle stopped the sentence with a cough. He heard Rexroth say, "If you'd like to fly up to Chicago with Stoner and me in the Willowdale plane Saturday morning, you're welcome to do so."

"Thanks for the offer," Doyle replied, "but I'll be driving up. I've got some personal business to take care of on Sunday. But I'll sure see you at the races."

Chapter 36

After a final look at the odds-board, which showed that Lancaster Lad was holding steady at three to one, a lukewarm favorite in the betting, Harvey Rexroth turned his binoculars to the head of the stretch where the gate was positioned for the start of the $500,000 Heartland Derby. Never removing his gaze from the track, Rexroth nudged Byron Stoner with his right elbow.

"Are we set?"

"Just as you directed," Stoner answered. "We've got one hundred thousand to win on Lancaster Lad and fifty thousand in exacta keys with him on top. Randy is holding the tickets." Kauffman, standing to Rexroth's left, nodded importantly as he patted his sport coat's inside breast pocket, which was bulging.

"Three to one," Rexroth said, cigar in his teeth, "and the so-called experts had him pegged at fifty to one. Talk about the power of the press—especially mine! Is this one for the books, Stoner?"

Byron Stoner said, "You couldn't be more right. It's one for the books."

It was one of those gorgeous autumn afternoons, temperature seventy-six, the maple trees in the track infield ablaze with color, that the Chicago weather gods annually provide as precedent to another long, brutal winter. But Rexroth was oblivious to anything but the impending race.

"Good work, men," Rexroth said. He placed the binoculars before him on the shelf of the private box in which they sat, then snapped his fingers. Kauffman produced another one of Rexroth's mondo cigars and carefully lit it.

"It's all over but the counting," said the publisher, smiling broadly between puffs on his cigar.

◇◇◇

As Rexroth exulted in anticipation in Box Three of the Heartland Downs stands, seeds of chaos began to be sown in sky to the south of the track.

The flight of *Right to Bear Arms*, General Oscar Belliard's balloon, had started in fine fashion. The general had charted a course featuring a beautifully predictable wind flow that promised to carry the balloon from its launching point five miles southwest of Heartland Downs, over the track and its crowded stands, to the spot another three and one-half miles northeast, the Ross County Fairgrounds, where it would be met by the retrieval team, comprised of two other members of the Underground Militia with their four-wheel utility drive vehicle and trailer.

A slight distraction the previous day had been quickly overcome. General Belliard's regular assistant pilot and longtime ballooning companion, Marcia Raybelle Pratt, had called in sick on Friday afternoon.

This development forced General Belliard to hurriedly recruit Junior Kozol as a substitute flight assistant. Junior had flown with the general before, but always as an open-mouthed passenger, not one assigned aeronautical tasks. Nevertheless, in these comfortable weather conditions, all had gone smoothly, starting with the pre-dawn departure from Louisville and the five-hour drive that brought them to the launch site.

With General Belliard expertly manning the controls, Junior Kozol standing anxiously by, and Wanda and Red clinging uneasily to the sides of the swaying wicker gondola, the early part of the flight had proceeded without incident. Junior was responding to the general's instructions very nicely, and the Marchiks, after their first gulps when the basket rose heavenward, were smiling, however uneasily. Red was emboldened enough to comment, "This is a lot easier than we thought it would be." The general gave Red a stern look. "Balloons are not toys," General Belliard intoned, adding, "They are deceptively powerful, make no mistake about *that*."

◇◇◇

As requested, Heartland Downs general manager Niles Milbare had reserved a box for the FBI team, one located seven rows below Rexroth's. By the time Karen, Damon, and two agents they'd summoned for assistance, Tom Sheehan and Ray Rosengren, had found their way to their seats, Damon was looking decidedly uncool in his dark suit and tie. Karen, as usual, appeared as calm and confident as if she were again about to ace her opening serve in a UW volleyball match. "Save one of the front-row seats for Doyle," Karen instructed Sheehan.

The attraction of a $500,000 race had helped lure the largest Heartland Downs crowd of the season—more than thirty-five thousand. Contributing greatly to the presence of this throng had been the publicity generated by Harvey Rexroth's headlined promise that Lancaster Lad would "reverse his fortunes in amazing fashion" and score a "resounding victory" in this important event. Some sports media, not just in Chicago and Kentucky, had echoed his claims straight-faced, while others had poked fun at what they termed his braggadocio. Whatever the interpretation, the result was a flood tide of publicity that had helped produce the large crowd this afternoon.

◇◇◇

Fifteen minutes earlier, Doyle had been waved past the paddock checkpoint by an old security guard, Art Schwartz, who remembered him from his days as City Sarah's groom. Actually, Doyle had to tap the guard on his shoulder to get him to lift the chain across the entrance. As usual, Art was half asleep in his chair.

"How you doin', son?" Art had finally asked once he'd looked up. "You been in a scrap?" he asked, pointing at Doyle's nose, with its Band-Aid covering the bridge.

"Just a little one," Doyle grinned. "I'm fine." He moved to extract himself from the grip of the garrulous old-timer and walked over to the No. 1 stall, which housed Bunny's Al.

Had Doyle not known who he was looking for, he might never have recognized the pair that confronted him. Under a broad white hat was the broadly smiling face of Maureen Hoban. The former O'Keefe's Ale House waitress/counselor was fashionably gotten up in a bright flowered dress, white stockings, shoes, and gloves. Just a touch of makeup, this in sharp contrast to the days she used to show up at O'Keefe's looking like she'd applied her cosmetics with a trowel.

Linda Tripp could have used Maureen's makeover maven, Doyle thought. He grinned as Maureen leaned forward to kiss him on the cheek.

Over her shoulder, Doyle looked at the imposing figure cut by E. D. Morley. Gone were the Rastafarian dreadlocks, the wispy goatee, the eye-concealing sunglasses. When Morley doffed his Panama hat in an exaggerated motion of greeting to Doyle, his shaved head shone like an ebony bowling ball. Morley was wearing a glistening white linen suit over a black silk shirt and white silk tie.

"You look like the overseer the old Colonel up and left the plantation to," Doyle said. E. D. reached for his hand, saying softly, "No soul shakes here, my man, just a straightforward handclasp among upstanding citizens." Doyle's hand disappeared inside E. D.'s big mitt.

Doyle couldn't help but laugh softly as he looked at his two assailants. "The last time you approached me was to steal twenty-five grand and put me to sleep in a damned garage," Doyle said. "Now look at the two of you! Talk about re-inventing yourselves—at my expense."

"Now, now, Jack," said Maureen, "sure and it's bygones be bygones by now, 'tisn't it, seeing how we sent you that tidy packet? No real harm done in the long run, am I right?" She looked quizzically up at Doyle's damaged nose, but said nothing about it.

Maureen took Jack's elbow and began to walk with him over the grass closer to stall No. 1. "I hope you'll not be like what some of them are at home," she said. "You know the saying over there? 'What's Irish Alzheimer's disease?' The answer is, 'They forget everyt'ing but the grudge.'" Maureen laughed merrily, peering up at Doyle.

Morley caught up to them, walking on Jack's other side.

"We're both damned glad to see you, Jack," E. D. said. "Now come take a look at what you helped us to get our hands on."

Bunny's Al, a medium-sized chestnut, was pawing the ground and tossing his head about restlessly as he was held by a groom. A well-muscled horse, his gleaming coat evidenced his terrific condition. He was jumping out of his skin, as the racetrack expression has it.

But Bunny's Al settled down as soon as Morley approached him. The big man handed his Panama hat and white suit coat to the groom, then expertly put the saddle on the now calm horse and cinched it securely. They had brought their own jockey with them from Florida, a youngster named Jesse Black, who had ridden Bunny's Al ever since E. D. and Maureen bought him.

"Do it again, Jesse," E. D. told him as he boosted him aboard Bunny's Al. Those were Morley's only instructions to the jockey.

The crowd of owners, trainers, hangers-on, and racing officials began to leave the paddock in the wake of the horses who headed through the tunnel toward the track. "Will you watch the race with us, Jack?" Maureen asked.

"Can't," Doyle said. "I've got another little matter to settle." He glanced at the paddock odds board. Bunny's Al was four to one. Doyle looked at the horse's beaming co-owners. "In spite of everything," Doyle said, "good luck to you."

"I think he means it," E. D. said to Maureen.

"Acourse he does," Maureen said. "That's a heart a gold beatin' away in there behind that cobbly front the man puts on."

"Watch where you're stepping, Maureen," Jack said as he left them. "The horseshit can get high around here, especially with you contributing to it."

◇◇◇

As the *Right to Bear Arms* smoothly advanced, Wanda shifted her gaze from the ground far below to the man at the controls. General Oscar Belliard was a short, squat, gray-haired and gray-bearded man of fifty-five. Tufts of gray hair protruded from his large nostrils, his large ears, and the backs of his little hands. Looking at him as they soared over Chicago's western suburbs, Wanda thought the general reminded her of some character, she couldn't quite pin down which one, in a book she used to read to her nieces, *The Wind in the Willows*.

General Belliard made his living managing one of Louisville's discount club grocery stores. His only direct exposure to things officially military had been as an ROTC cadet during his brief stint in college. A congenital heart murmur, he said, had prevented him from enlisting in any branch of the service. But his interest in everything military—including his vast collection of war textbooks, games, weapons, and films—along with his ballooning hobby, consumed most of his non-working hours. His role as founder and leader of the Underground Militia was the most important thing in the life of this lifelong bachelor.

Confidently, General Belliard gave Red and Junior the go-ahead to attach their banner to the stainless steel cables at the rear of the gondola. The banner contained the messages their flight was designed to deliver. "Target in sight," cried the general as he looked through his binoculars toward Heartland Downs. "Prepare to unfurl!"

Having issued that order, General Belliard relaxed and reached into his knapsack for his lunch. He removed a ziplock baggy from the supply he issued to Underground Militia members when they went on backcountry maneuvers. It contained a handful of gherkins and a bulging sandwich of fried squirrel in white bread.

"Love eating these little critters—and hunting them, too," the general said as he munched enthusiastically. Between bites he asked, "You folks hear about the scare those pointy heads over at the university are talking about? Some nonsense about a virus connected with eating squirrel brains? Can you believe that? What a load of manure, pardon the expression, Wanda.

"My Uncle Merle," continued General Belliard, "probably ate a thousand or twelve hundred squirrels in his life, brains and all. No exaggeration. I can't begin to estimate how many pounds of squirrel that'd come to.

"Late in his life, when he found his gums could not tolerate dentures, Uncle Merle used to skin his squirrels after he'd shot or trapped them, take the bones out, cut the meat up in little pieces, and put it all in this big blender he had. Said it made for the most refreshing drink in the world.

"And Uncle Merle lived in just darned good health to ninety-seven and three-quarters. Hunted right up to the end, too," the general said proudly, before he suddenly clutched his chest and keeled over sideways onto the floor of the gondola.

◇◇◇

Jockey Willie Arroyo, who normally chattered away to Beth Anderson, the pony girl accompanying the Willowdale horses in every post parade, was silent this afternoon. Beth usually just nodded without really listening to Willie's rapid talk, but she found its absence now to be somewhat unsettling.

"What's wrong, Willie?" she grinned, her blond ponytail swishing as she turned to face him from her big white pony as they proceeded toward the starting gate. "It's only another half-million-dollar race. Those little nuts of yours aren't shriveling up even smaller, are they?"

Arroyo barely heard her. His usually laughing and expressive countenance was grim, marked only by a frown. He patted Lancaster Lad on the right side of his neck, then stood in the stirrups to begin jogging the horse slowly forward. When the brown colt responded, Arroyo looked even more worried than he had moments earlier.

Seeing Arroyo's concern, Beth Anderson turned serious. "Hey, babe, I was only kidding with you," she said. There was no reply, so Beth asked: "Willie, what's wrong here? Do you feel something? Is this horse sore, or what?"

They were almost at the gate, now, where the eight other Heartland Derby starters already waited to be loaded, some patiently, some having to be rotated in circles by members of the gate crew before their turns came. A dark bay filly named Nurse on Call balked and had to be hustled forward by assistant starters who locked arms behind her and pushed her into her slot. The others began to enter willingly, Bunny's Al whinnying eagerly as he moved forward.

Beth reached over and unhooked the shank from Lancaster Lad. Willie Arroyo finally turned to face her. "Theez horse don't," he said, "theez horse don't seem…."

Then Arroyo stopped talking. As the assistant starter took hold of Lancaster Lad's bridle and pulled him forward, Arroyo took one last look back at Beth Anderson. He lifted his shoulders in a mighty shrug, flipped his goggles down and turned to face the racetrack that stretched before him beneath the bright October sun.

◇◇◇

As the first of the Heartland Derby horses was being loaded into the starting gate, track announcer Calvin Gemmer momentarily interrupted his memorizing of the jockeys' colors and lifted his binoculars skyward. He spotted a red, white, and blue hot-air balloon that was heading toward the track property in distressed fashion: zigging, zagging, yo-yoing up and down.

Gemmer switched on his in-house intercom and reached track publicity director Dan Zenner. "Have we got some kind of balloon promotion I should be mentioning?" the announcer asked. "Not that I know of," came the reply. "Okay, just checking," Gemmer answered.

Gemmer took one more quick, concerned glance at the balloon, which continued to weave and lose altitude as it approached. It was now about three-quarters of a mile south of the track's main parking lot. With his high-powered glasses, Gemmer could discern uneven writing on the long, broad banner that trailed behind the balloon. What he saw was *ROOt AGAINST LaN. LAD—THE TYRANTS HoRSE.*

A sudden wind shift revealed the message on the other side of the same banner: *LITHUANIA.... 4eVER.*

"What the *hell* is that all about?" the announcer said, startling his audience, for he had uncharacteristically forgotten that his microphone was turned on. But, old pro that he was, Gemmer quickly got back in his normal groove. "They're all in the gate....*Aaand they're off!*" began his description of the Heartlands Derby.

"It's a good thing geldings can't understand that term," Doyle grinned, speaking to the grim-faced Karen who was concentrating on the horses passing before her, "otherwise they might be too embarrassed to run.

"Oh, come on, Engel, ease up," he added, "it's only a horse race. In about thirty seconds or so, take a look back up there at Rexroth—I guarantee you'll start enjoying this."

"*That's Agile Andy going right for the early lead,*" Gemmer announced, "*Jean's Tom lapped on him to the outside. Next comes Bunny's Al, who is down on the rail and saving ground. He's followed by Nurse on Call, Jimminy Quicket, Kaplan's Dream, Pennoyer Park, Friar of Foxdale and Capper Rick. As they curve into the backstretch favored Lancaster Lad is the trailer, ten lengths behind the leader.*"

Karen now had turned from watching the race to watching Rexroth. Above his binoculars, trained on the field as it approached the far turn, she could see the look of concern on his face. He momentarily dropped the glasses and, looking perplexed, said something to Stoner, who shrugged without answering. Rexroth's jaw tightened as he put the binoculars back up to his eyes.

"*Midway of the far turn, Agile Andy is drifting out and beginning to tire. Moving through the hole on the inside is Jean's Tom, who takes command by a length. Bunny's Al is also on the move along the rail. The rest of the field remains strung out and Lancaster Lad continues to trail, although Willie Arroyo is already asking him for his best...."*

"Check him out," Karen said excitedly to Doyle. Jack stood up and turned around to look at the Rexroth box. As he did, he saw the red-faced publisher throw his binoculars to the floor of the box, then begin pounding his big fists on the railing in front of him. A man in the adjacent box said something to him, and Rexroth snarled a reply that caused the man to hurriedly turn away.

"Bunny's Al and Jean's Tom are head and head for the lead as they reach the eighth-pole. Friar of Foxdale has found his best stride and is putting in a big run and Pennoyer Park is also gaining ground.

"With a sixteenth to go, Bunny's Al begins to edge clear as Jean's Tom gives way. But here comes Friar of Foxdale with a tremendous late charge! He's eating up ground with every stride. Jesse Black is asking Bunny's Al for everything he has. They're neck and neck approaching the finish line.

"Here's the wire. Bunny's Al hangs on by a head over Friar of Foxdale in a tremendous running of the Heartland Derby. Capper Rick closes well to take third money, another three lengths back, with Pennoyer Park in fourth....Bringing up the rear of the field is favored Lancaster Lad, who just didn't have it today."

Ignoring the exciting race that had gone on behind them, Doyle and Karen kept their eyes on Rexroth. Before Bunny's Al was called the winner and Lancaster Lad the trailer, Rexroth had already begun to leave his box and head for the racetrack apron.

"Let's go," Karen said. "We'll follow him down there."

She and Jack began to move. But Damon Tirabassi still stood, transfixed, watching the video replay of the Heartlands Derby finish on the jumbotron television in the track's infield. He was completely caught up in it.

Doyle said, "Maybe Agent Straight Arrow bet this winner. Look at him!"

Karen grabbed Damon's arm and yanked. "For God's sakes, Damon," she said, "let's go!"

"That was something!" Tirabassi said, excited by the thrilling contest he'd just witnessed. Then Damon resumed what Karen termed his Hoover mask and they all moved swiftly down the aisle to the winner's circle.

◇◇◇

Frantic now as the balloon continued its zig-zagging course, Red Marchik looked down at General Belliard. Then he knelt awkwardly in the cramped gondola and put an ear to the stricken man's chest. The general's face was fish belly white, his eyes rolled up in his head. Red said excitedly, "He is still alive. He is still alive!"

Red struggled to his feet, his big red face now the color of a hydroponic tomato. "We're going to…We're going to…Junior, goddammit, do you know to drive this thing? Of course you don't. What the *hell* kind of a deal *is* this?" Red shouted.

He again looked down at their motionless leader. "You suppose he got hit by that squirrel virus?" Red asked.

Junior, ashen, remained silent. Wanda said, "Looks more like a heart attack to me."

The balloon basket lurched sideways, then downward. Junior fumbled with the fuel controls, looking wildly about him. The general's head lolled on the floor of the gondola.

"Jesus, Wanda," cried her panicked husband, "give him some of that CRP."

"That course I took was CPR, Red," Wanda said as she gazed warily down at General Belliard. "Cardio-Pulmonary Resurrection. But I don't know that I'm about to CPR a man with part of a squirrel hanging out of his mouth."

Suddenly the gondola dropped several more feet. Red's face lost its deep crimson shade, converting rapidly to a hue reminiscent of lime Gatorade. Seeing this, Wanda reluctantly bent to her task. She felt the general's heart leap back into proper gear, but he remained unconscious.

Red and Junior, meanwhile, began battling for control of the blast valve, Junior attempting to open it up, Red struggling to close it. In the midst of this standoff, as the combatants almost trampled Wanda and the general, the balloon began descending rapidly in the direction of the Heartland Downs racing strip.

◇◇◇

Harvey Rexroth rolled down the aisle steps toward the racetrack like a boulder down a mountain. The people who didn't see him coming he bumped out of his way. Stoner and Kauffman struggled to keep up.

Rexroth was recognized as he descended the stairs. "Guaranteed winner? Guaranteed my ass, you big phony," one man shouted. Others began to boo and curse. Suddenly, in the midst of this beautiful afternoon, it began to sound like a drunk and disappointed football crowd at Soldier Field in the late minutes of another Chicago Bears drubbing.

When Rexroth and his men arrived at trackside, Bunny's Al was being led into the winner's circle. Rexroth brushed past the winning owners, Maureen Hoban and E. D. Morley, and rumbled through the opening leading to the racing strip. He waved vigorously at jockey Willie Arroyo. "You, rider, bring that horse over here," he ordered.

One of trainer Kenny Gutfreund's grooms put a shank on Lancaster Lad's halter and held the horse as Arroyo dismounted. There was no jubilant, high-flying leap this time; the jockey slithered off the sweaty, tired horse. He started to say something to Rexroth, but when he spotted Doyle and the agents approaching, Arroyo neatly stepped around them toward the scales and weighed in. He then scurried up the tunnel and out of sight.

The flustered Rexroth, turning and seeing Doyle, did a double take. "What's going on here, Doyle? Who are these people with you?"

Without waiting for answers, Rexroth turned on trainer Gutfreund. "What have *you* got to say about what happened here?" he shouted. Gesturing toward Lancaster Lad, he said, "That can't be my horse. Not the way he ran. There's been some kind of foul-up here, Gutfreund. I'm holding you responsible."

Damon Tirabassi said, "No, it's you, Rexroth, who is going to be held responsible."

"For what? Held responsible for what? And who the hell are you?"

As Karen stepped forward to join Damon in showing their FBI badges, Doyle said to Rexroth, "You're going to be held responsible for a list of things as long as your upcoming prison serial number. Including running the *right* horse this afternoon—not the *wrong* one that you planned to run."

Rexroth's jaw dropped. He watched as Damon Tirabassi waved down the track at a groom who was waiting with a bay horse. Tirabassi motioned the young woman forward. Rexroth took a step backward as they approached.

The bay horse pranced and danced as he moved toward them, his coat glistening in the late afternoon sunlight. Muscles rippled as he stepped lightly along. Playfully, he threw his head from side to side, eyes alight. Bred for the racetrack, the son of Donna Diane was finally on one for the very first time.

Karen Engel called out, "Will the horse identifier help us here now?"

Chuck Tilton stepped forward. The longtime identifier for the state of Illinois looked almost as puzzled now as when, a half-hour earlier, Karen had phoned him in his track office and requested that he come to the winner's circle following the Heartland Derby. "Bring Lancaster Lad's papers with you, please," Karen had asked. This was a first for Tilton—checking out a horse *after* a race.

Curious fans began to crowd up to the winner's circle fence. Bunny's Al had been photographed, unsaddled, and led away to the test barn, but the confrontation involving Rexroth had served to delay the presentation of the Heartland Derby trophy. Maureen, E. D., and jockey Jesse Black waited impatiently for that ceremony. They were still fizzing with the excitement of this biggest win of their lives, Doyle could see, but at the same time were as puzzled as the fans who lined the fence. When E. D. came over to Doyle, he asked quietly, "Jack, what's going down here, man?" Doyle glanced at Morley. "Keep out of this, E. D.," he answered in a low voice.

As he had only fifteen minutes earlier in the paddock prior to the race, the identifier opened up Lancaster Lad's mouth. He compared the numerals on the horse's upper lip to those on the registration papers in Karen's hand. Then Tilton moved over to the other bay horse. Rexroth attempted to sidle rearward at this point, but Damon strengthened his grip on the publisher's arm.

"I'll be damned," Tilton said after he'd examined the second horse. "This sumbitch's got the same ID as that horse right there," he said, motioning toward Lancaster Lad. "Except," he added, "this one's a helluva lot newer."

Agent Ebner elbowed his way through the crowd with Earlene Klinder in tow. The horse tattooer from Kentucky, one elbow in Ebner's large hand, held her other arm across her chest as if she was going to recite the Pledge of Allegiance. Fearfully, she glanced about her before her eyes settled on Byron Stoner.

Once Doyle had told Damon and Karen what to look for, Earlene had not been hard to track down. There were only a handful of horse tattooers in Kentucky. Earlene was the third one on the list to be questioned, and she cracked almost at once, motivated by fear of prison time and leaving her twins to fend for themselves in foster homes.

"Yessir," said Earlene, "that's the man that hired me—the short one, standing next to the fat fella. He's the one paid me to tattoo the horse over at Willowdale with the identification numbers he gave me."

Stoner sighed, then took off his gold-rimmed glasses and began to polish them. Earlene, cloaked in the armor of immunity granted her because of her cooperation, began to breathe more normally. "And that big lug held the horse while I worked on him," she said righteously, pointing at Randy Kauffman.

Doyle leaned close to Rexroth's large, sweaty face. Rexroth's eyes darted about as sweat beads multiplied on his bald head. "Isn't that an amazing coincidence?" Doyle said softly.

Rexroth gathered himself. "I don't understand you people," he barked. Pointing to Lancaster Lad, he said, "What's going on here with this horse of mine?"

"No, no, Rexy, you're too modest," Doyle answered. "We're not talking about *one* horse of yours—we're talking about *two*. Two horses that belong to you.

"This one here"—Doyle nodded toward Lancaster Lad, who was still dripping wet and blowing from his race efforts—"was shipped to Willowdale last week. I saw him come in.

"And I saw him get his butt kicked over your training track last week by this one *here*," Doyle continued, walking over to the prancing bay horse, "who has been living down at beautiful Willowdale all of his life. Who he really is, I sure as hell don't know. But that doesn't matter to me. What matters is who he *isn't*—he isn't Lancaster Lad, as you tried to pass him off to be."

Rexroth started to say something, but Stoner stepped in front of him.

"Stay out of the way, Stoner," Doyle said. "Your boss wants to ask how I know about this—how these horses got switched so that Rexroth's guaranteed winner got beat the length of a football field.

"I'll tell you how I switched these two horses in their stalls at Willowdale two nights ago. They both had halters that said Lancaster Lad, but the halter on the farm's bay horse was bright and shiny new. So, I took it off him and put it on the new arrival from the racetrack, the real Lancaster Lad. And I took that horse's halter off him and put it on your homegrown prodigy. Then I switched the horses in the stalls your man Pedro had put them in."

Doyle poked a forefinger into the middle of Rexroth's power tie. "When Pedro came to get your fast bay horse the next morning for shipping up here, for your so-called publicity and betting coup, what he got was the *real* Lancaster Lad."

Rexroth's mouth opened, but he couldn't manage to convert the garbled sounds into a statement. Damon Tirabassi said, "Interestingly enough, Mr. Rexroth, the bay horse over here"—he pointed to the frisky imposter—"was discovered in a search of your property last night. Acting on a tip from a very reliable source, we served the warrant on Mr. Doyle, your acting farm manager. He cooperated by taking us to the barn this horse was in. We transferred this horse up here today.

"Matter of fact," Damon said, almost permitting himself a grin, "his horse van had an official escort all the way from Lexington to Chicago. Very unusual for the Bureau."

Shaking his head in mock dismay, Doyle looked at Rexroth. "You know that old saying around the racetrack, 'That horse is so slow he couldn't beat a fat man'? Well, fat man, here's a slow horse that sure as hell beat you."

Rexroth said, "I'm not listening to any more of this nonsense." He began to move away when Damon commanded, "Grab him and hold him." As the astonished Rexroth was handcuffed, Karen faced him. "And that's not all," she said calmly.

At her signal, agent Kamin came through the crowd, pushing Ronald Mortvedt ahead of him. The little man had a sizable bandage on his cheek, covering the cut that Doyle's fist had inflicted. Mortvedt looked impassively at Rexroth. But when his gaze found Doyle, it carried a charge filled with hate.

"Rexy," said Doyle, grinning and putting an arm around the publisher's shoulders, "these colleagues of yours, your fellow criminals, they sold you out and sewed up the case against you. It was a beautiful thing. Dishonor among thieves gaining momentum like a tidal wave. They could hardly wait to give you up, once the picture was made clear to them.

"First, Jud Repke saw the wisdom of telling the truth to the FBI about horse killings on your property. He thought he was a little underpaid, by the way. And Jud was real good in recalling the search for the look-alike horse. That's what he called the horse he and Mortvedt found in New Mexico, the horse nearly identical to the one you tried to slip into the Heartland Derby today. Old Jud, he was off key at first, but then he got into the sing of things, so to speak," Doyle said, thoroughly enjoying himself now, as if he were rhythmically drumming the light bag in the gym.

"And that poor little woman that Stoner bribed, the horse tattooer over there? She was what you'd call extremely forthright as well.

"But the star of the linking-everything-to-Rexroth show was that little monster over there," Doyle said, pointing at Mortvedt. "When it got down to a choice between a reduced prison sentence and nailing your fat ass to the wall, Ronnie got his vocal cords and his testimony in order. Like his buddy Jud, he was kind of miffed over the level of payments you made to him—once he found out the true worth of those insurance policies you were collecting on.

"Ronnie kept a real good record of your payments to him, though—dates, names of the horses you told him to kill. Not to mention the mare you paid him to steal and *then* kill after she'd foaled the look-alike horse.

"You're going down, Rexy," Doyle said with relish, "like a cannonball tossed off the Sears Tower."

For the first time, Rexroth's armor of conceit began to melt. He looked at Doyle, then pleadingly at Stoner. As he started to speak, Stoner interjected quickly, "Let the attorneys deal with this." But Rexroth ignored him. "Why you?" Rexroth said to Doyle. "I don't understand…."

"It's a long story," Doyle said, "but the upshot of it is that Aldous Bolger, he's a friend of mine.

"There's a price to be paid for what happened to him. You're going to be one of the people paying it."

◇◇◇

Four hundred feet above the Heartland Downs infield, General Belliard's balloon continued its errant descent. The general remained unconscious. Red Marchik had now fought off Junior Kozol and was in charge of the controls. He had no clue as to how or where to land the hated contraption. The centuries-old Marchik paranoia genes boiled and burbled in Red as he fumbled about in the rapidly diminishing altitude.

Track announcer Calvin Gemmer gawked at the approaching balloon. He grabbed his microphone. With an urgency usually reserved for photo finishes, Gemmer shouted, "People, get out of the way down there at the winner's circle, get out of the way. That's a balloon coming down at you...GET OUT OF THE WAY, PEOPLE!!"

The fans bunched around the winner's circle started to scatter. As he looked skyward, Damon Tirabassi blanched, then ordered, "Get them *out* of here." With a glance over her shoulder at the oncoming balloon, which was obviously out of control and heading straight for them, Karen Engel grabbed Earlene Klinder's arm and hustled her toward shelter. The other FBI agents moved quickly to get Rexroth, Stoner, and Kauffman into the paddock tunnel, which by now was becoming crowded with fleeing fans.

As Doyle started to follow Maureen and E. D. Morley into safe range from what appeared to be a rapidly impending disaster, he realized that the only person remaining in the winner's circle was Ronald Mortvedt. His guard, agent Ebner, had moved to assist in the removal of Rexroth, leaving the ex-jockey behind him in what he thought was the custody of agent Kamin. Doyle had no idea how this mix-up had occurred, but he didn't like what he was seeing. He felt his stomach tighten as Mortvedt glared at him.

Never looking either back or upward, Mortvedt began to move purposefully toward Doyle across the twenty feet that divided them. His progress was remarkably unhurried.

"You're not gettin' away with what you done to me, mister," Mortvedt said as he advanced, fists clenched. "You got somethin' comin' from me."

Doyle pivoted to run, not from Mortvedt but from the onrushing balloon he could see dropping from the sky behind the little man. It was headed directly for the winner's circle. In a reflex action that he would later chide himself for, Doyle shouted to Mortvedt, "Look out, look out, it's coming right at you...."

So determined was he to reach the man responsible for his capture, Ronald Mortvedt did not heed Jack Doyle's warning, never looked up at the out-of-control, brightly colored vehicle that was plummeting directly toward him.

The platform of General Oscar Belliard's balloon landed on Ronald Mortvedt like an elevator car cut loose from its cables. The impact of one of the balloon's two propane tanks hitting Mortvedt's head made a horrible thunking noise. Immediately, the balloon bounced back up into the air. Beneath it Mortvedt lay face down, the back of his head crumpled. His left cheek had been nearly ripped off, and the blood from that wound spread on the ground. Nearby, grooms struggled to control the two terrified horses that were attempting to back away from the scene.

As the balloon rose, Wanda Marchik leaned out of the wicker basket, making a series of soprano whoops the content of which no one on the ground could make out. However, two of the FBI agents and a groom leaped forward to grab the line she'd dropped from the balloon. Junior Kozol unleashed another line from the other side, and that too was snatched by helpful bystanders. Tugging mightily, they combined to haul the balloon back to earth. Its wicker platform settled directly atop Ronald Mortvedt.

The only part of Mortvedt now visible was his left foot, encased in a small black boot that protruded from under the balloon wreckage. The Marchiks and Junior Kozol remained enwrapped in the ravaged envelope of the balloon as track workers rushed to extricate them.

Karen Engel ran forward from the paddock tunnel, her face pale.

"My God, Jack," she said, "it looks just like *The Wizard of Oz*...with the Wicked Witch of the West's foot sticking out from under the barn door after the tornado. There's no way Mortvedt's alive under there," Karen added with a shudder. "Did you see the way that metal tank cracked into him?"

"He had all of that coming, and more."

Chapter 37

Karen Engel's assessment of Ronald Mortvedt's prospects was accurate. The little ex-jockey was pronounced DOA at Western Community Hospital five miles from Heartland Downs, victim of massive head injuries.

Passengers in the killer balloon, the *Right to Bear Arms*, were much luckier. Examination of General Oscar Belliard established that he had, indeed, suffered a minor cardiac arrest. But the prognosis for him was good, provided he adopted some lifestyle changes.

Tough nut that she was, Wanda Marchik escaped with various minor bruises, as did Junior Kozol. Red Marchik, however, somehow managed to pull both an Achilles tendon and a groin muscle during the disastrous descent. Even as paramedics hefted him on a stretcher into the ambulance, Red was raving about lawsuits he intended to file.

"Settle down, honey," Wanda told Red as she slid into the ambulance beside him, "let's first get you fixed up and comfortable." Wanda patted her husband's hand. Then she said, "Wonder what the Sports Preacher would make out of all that happened here today?"

◇◇◇

Jack Doyle sat at the end of the long mahogany bar of O'Keefe's Ale House, watching television's ten o'clock news. All the Chicago channels had received—courtesy of the Heartland Downs television department—excellent footage of the Derby and its memorable winner's circle aftermath.

Doyle grinned as he watched himself sidestep and dodge, his old AAU footwork standing him in good stead again, as the balloon dealt its death blow to Ronald Mortvedt.

"Sheila, Bushmills Manhattan, please," Doyle called to the busy barmaid, another immigrant from County Cork. Her name was Sheila Maloney, and she was bright, friendly, and considerably better looking than her predecessor, Maureen Hoban. And Doyle was determined to keep a tremendous distance between them, having decided he'd had enough dealings with women from Cork.

An hour earlier, when he arrived at O'Keefe's, Doyle had used his government-issued cell phone to call Karen Engel at the Chicago FBI office for an update. They'd become separated in the tremendous confusion that followed the balloon crash, and Doyle had departed the track unclear about some matters, except the main one—he was off the hook with the FBI.

"You did a great job, Jack," Damon had emphasized. Both he and Karen had hurriedly thanked Doyle before they left, looking as if they meant it.

On the phone, Karen reported that Rexroth and Stoner had both been charged that evening before a federal magistrate and would be held at least until Monday morning, when bonds could be set.

"I talked to Ronald Mortvedt's aunt down in Louisiana," Karen added, "Alice Cormier. She was the only relative of his we knew how to find. Alice wasn't surprised at what had happened to Ronnie, but it hurt her anyway. I hate making those calls."

"Why doesn't Damon make them?"

Karen said, "He hates it worse than I do."

Doyle shifted his cell phone from one hand to the other as he prepared to take out his wallet and pay his bar bill.

"Who the hell were those goofs in the balloon?"

"They were carrying out some kind of protest against Harvey Rexroth," Karen replied. "People named Marchik, husband and

wife, they made these streamers attacking Rexroth. They've got
a beef against Rexroth for his firing of Mr. Marchik down in
Kentucky. At least I guess that was their motive. It's kind of
hard to figure what the Marchiks are about. But the crash was
certainly not their fault—it happened because the pilot passed
out. That's as much as we've gotten out of them.

"It wasn't their balloon," Karen continued. "The balloon's
pilot and owner is a friend of theirs. The Marchiks know him
from some off-brand, so-called militia group they all belong to
in Louisville. Apparently the pilot—he calls himself 'General'
Belliard, no less—had a slight heart attack in the course of the
flight."

Doyle said, "I'm starting to get a headache. You're saying
Merchuck or Marcik or whatever his name is gets fired from
RexCom, then winds up crashing a balloon at the racetrack on
the same day we're reeling in Harvey Rexroth? I don't think I
can listen to any more of this."

Trying to ignore Sheila Maloney, who was chattering to
him from the other side of the bar in her faux Irish colleen cos-
tume, Doyle took a swallow of his drink. Sheila leaned over the
mahogany, giving Doyle a cleavage show and a dimpled smile.
Doyle resolved to advise Sheila and whatever Cork cuties succeeded her not to try so hard.

Doyle said to Karen, "What about Mortvedt? What are they
going to do with him, bury him with a stake in his heart?"

"That's not funny, Jack," Karen said. "I know how we all feel
about Mortvedt, you especially, but still, there's a limit...." She
broke off that thought, well aware of her unreceptive audience
of one.

"Actually," Karen said, "we're shipping Mortvedt's ashes
down to Louisiana. Alice Cormier said she'd pay for him to be
cremated. Said she couldn't afford the cost of embalming, or a
coffin."

Doyle watched the ice cubes wobble around the half-finished
drink that he started to lift, then put down on the bar. He didn't
know Alice Cormier, but he could feel sorry for her. He sure as

hell had known Ronald Mortvedt, and he felt no sorrow whatsoever for him. In fact, he thought to himself, maybe they'll scatter the little bastard's ashes in one of those Cajun specialties full of other bottom feeders. They could call it Gumbo Diablo.

◇◇◇

As Doyle drove home that October Saturday night through the leaf-strewn streets north of Chicago's Loop, he couldn't help but contrast his present feelings to those he'd had four months earlier when, with $25,000 in cash in his pocket thanks to City Sarah's big win, he'd scoured his neighborhood in a fruitless quest for celebration.

This night, well, this was different. For one thing, he'd made a far larger score off the Heartland Derby than he had by helping to cause City Sarah's embarrassment, then her lucrative victory. Thirty minutes before the Heartland Derby, Doyle had taken half of what he thought of as the guilt money E. D. and Maureen had sent him—$15,000—and bet it to win on Bunny's Al.

The size of the wager, previously unthinkable in Doyle's experience, had seemed as natural as his next breath.

There had been long periods in his up and down life during which Doyle felt far from convinced that he ever *really* knew what he was doing. Yet, occasionally, moments emerged during which he felt fate's golden hand gripping him by the elbow and, for a change, not propelling him into another of life's traffic jams.

Rare moments they were. They sometimes dolphined out of the darkest, most depressing seas of Doyle's life, as when Moe Kellman, sweating in the Fit City gym, invited him to lunch for the first time at Dino's Ristorante. For Doyle they represented the "inevitability of the inevitable," a concept he had attempted to explain to both of his wives before they became ex-, to friends both former and current, sometimes even to complete strangers.

"Situations arise, and you know before they develop what's going to happen," Doyle would say. "It's like *déjà vu* in advance. You just *know*. Usually what you know is going to happen is awful—but not every time. Not *every* time. Once in a great wonderful while you just *know* that a good thing's coming, finally rolling your way. Get it?"

He had asked that question many times and rarely heard a positive reply. This night was different, he knew it just as surely as he had known his bet on Bunny's Al was going to be a winner. Doyle's fifteen grand had swelled to a profit of $75,000—the odds had drifted up to five to one just before the race—in the minute and fifty seconds it had taken Bunny's Al to run a mile and an eighth that afternoon.

He was on a roll. And it wasn't just the money that had his spirits surfing about a yard and a half over the roof of his northbound Accord.

Doyle knew that nothing could ever make up for what had happened to Aldous. But Mortvedt's getting wiped out that way—eliminating the prospect of short prison time because of his cooperating testimony—provided a large chunk of satisfaction. "We forgive but we don't forget," Doyle said aloud as he turned west off Clark Street onto Fullerton.

He smiled as he thought of the expression of gratitude he'd received as he drove away from Heartland Downs that afternoon. It had come over his cell phone from Moe Kellman, who on Doyle's advice instructed his "people" to leave Lancaster Lad out of all Heartland Derby betting they were doing and in whatever bets they were booking.

"Moe, if you don't mind my asking," Doyle had said, "how did you get this number? I never gave it to you and it's unlisted."

"Do you really care, Jack?" Moe had replied, before urging Doyle to "go out and have the celebration you deserve."

Before heading for his apartment, Doyle made two stops. The first was at the night deposit window of his bank, just off of Clark Street on Fullerton, where he dropped off the check that the Heartland Downs pari-mutuels had made out to him for his fistful of winning $100 tickets on Bunny's Al.

The second stop was at McTweedy's Travel Agency farther west on Fullerton. Doyle double-parked and dashed inside.

The office was empty except for a departing receptionist, nameplate reading *Heather*, who was in the process of locking the front door. Doyle persuaded her to gather up travel brochures and a schedule of Air New Zealand flights. After thanking Heather and wishing her a good night, he re-entered his car amid a crescendo of car horns and shouted threats from road ragers who had been forced to creep past the double-parked Accord. Doyle gave them a merry wave as he drove off.

As he steered down the ramp into the garage below his apartment building, he tried to calculate what time it was in New Zealand. If it was already tomorrow there, as he suspected, would that be too early to call Caroline Cummings? Or too late? He decided to phone her anyway.

Doyle had described the capture of Ronald Mortvedt in a phone conversation he'd had with Caroline two nights earlier. It was a lengthy call, for which he was grateful. He'd missed the sound of her voice. Caroline had updated Jack on Aldous' improved condition.

Caroline went on to thank Jack for his role in Mortvedt's capture, and then she made him promise to phone with a report on Heartland Derby Day. "I've got a feeling Saturday's going to be a corker," she said. "Be sure to call me, Jack." He promised he would. He then heard her invite him to come down for the holiday.

"What holiday?"

"It's our Labour Day. It's coming up October 27."

"I'd like that," Doyle said.

"And plan to stay with us awhile," she'd insisted. "It's a long flight to get here, and expensive as well. There'd be no sense in turning about and going right back, would there?"

There was a pause in the conversation. Then Jack said, "No, there wouldn't be any sense in that."

Doyle eased the Accord down the damp, oil-slicked ramp toward his parking place. He got out of the car and locked it. He looked around the garage and saw no one. His footsteps echoing off the concrete floor were the only sound in the dank, dimly lit structure. It was still relatively early for a Saturday night, and most of his fellow residents' vehicles were absent from their parking places.

Smiling broadly, he suddenly stopped, lifted his arms wide, and raised his eyes to the moisture-beaded ceiling only a few feet above his head.

"Where did I go right?" shouted Jack Doyle.